# LECTURES OF COL R. G. INGERSOLL
# Volume I

### By
### ROBERT GREEN INGERSOLL

# Lectures Of Col R. G. Ingersoll

*by* Robert Green Ingersoll

Copyright © 2023

All Rights reserved.
No part of this publication may be reproduced,
stored in a retrieval system, or transmitted in any
form or by any means, electronic, mechanical,
photocopying or Otherwise, without the written
permission of the publisher.

The author/editor asserts the moral right to
be identified as the author/editor of this work.

ISBN: 978-93-57278-52-2

**Published by**

# DOUBLE 9 BOOKS

2/13-B, Ansari Road, Daryaganj
New Delhi – 110002
info@double9books.com
www.double9books.com
Tel. 011-40042856

This book is under public domain

# ABOUT THE AUTHOR

Known as "the Great Agnostic," Robert G. Ingersoll was an American lawyer, author, and orator who advocated for agnosticism during the Golden Age of Free Thought. He lived from August 11, 1833, to July 21, 1899. In Dresden, New York, Robert Ingersoll was born. His father, John Ingersoll, was a radical Congregationalist preacher who supported abolition and regularly moved his family as a result of his views. While American revivalist Charles G. Finney was on a tour of Europe, Rev. John Ingersoll temporarily filled in as the preacher. After Finney's return, Rev. Ingersoll stayed as Finney's co-pastor and associate pastor. In 1853, "Bob" Ingersoll spent a time teaching in Metropolis, Illinois, where he delegated the "larger part of the instruction, while Latin and history absorbed his own attention" to one of his pupils, the future judge Angus M. L. McBane. Ingersoll had already worked as a teacher in Mount Vernon, Illinois, at some point before taking the position in Metropolis. On February 13, 1862, Ingersoll wed Eva Amelia Parker (1841–1923). Their two daughters were well-known feminists and suffragists, Eva Ingersoll-Brown, was the elder daughter.

# CONTENTS

INGERSOLL'S LECTURE ON GODS ........................................................................... 7

INGERSOLL'S LECTURE ON GHOSTS. ................................................................. 42

INGERSOLL'S LECTURE ON HELL ....................................................................... 69

INGERSOLL'S LECTURE ON INDIVIDUALITY, AN
ARRAIGNMENT OF THE CHURCH. ...................................................................... 92

INGERSOLL'S LECTURE ON HUMBOLDT ....................................................... 105

INGERSOLL'S LECTURE ON WHICH WAY? ................................................... 116

INGERSOLL'S LECTURE ON THE GREAT INFIDELS .................................. 134

INGERSOLL'S LECTURE ON TALMAGIAN THEOLOGY ............................. 144

INGERSOLL'S ORATION AT A CHILD'S GRAVE. ......................................... 163

INGERSOLL AT HIS BROTHER'S GRAVE.—A Most Exquisite,
Yet One Of The Most Sad And Mournful Sermons ................................................ 165

INGERSOLL'S LECTURE ON THE MISTAKES OF MOSES. ......................... 167

INGERSOLL'S LECTURE ON SKULLS,—And His Replies
To Prof. Swing, Dr. Collyer, And Other Critics—Reprinted from
"The Chicago Times." ................................................................................................ 189

COL. INGERSOLL'S REPLY TO DR. COLLYER. ............................................ 216

INGERSOLL'S REPLY TO PROF. SWING .......................................................... 218

INGERSOLL'S REPLY TO BROOKE HERFORD, D.D. .......................................... 220

INGERSOLL GATLING GUN TURNED ON DR. RYDER ................. 221

INGERSOLL'S REPLY TO RABBI BIEN ................................................. 223

INGERSOLL'S CATECHISM AND BIBLE-CLASS ............................................ 230

INGERSOLL'S NEW DEPARTURE—His Lecture Entitled
"What Shall We do to be Saved?"—Delivered in McVicker's Theatre,
Chicago, Sept. 19, 1880
[From the Chicago Times. Verbatim Report.] ........................................................ 235

INGERSOLL'S ANSWER TO PROF. SWING,
DR. THOMAS, AND OTHERS ............................................................................ 261

# INGERSOLL'S LECTURE ON GODS

Ladies and Gentlemen: An honest god is the noblest work of man. Each nation has created a god, and the god has always resembled his creators. He hated and loved what they hated and loved, and he was invariably found on the side of those in power. Each god was intensely patriotic, and detested all nations but his own. All these Gods demanded praise, flattery, and worship. Most of them were pleased with sacrifice, and the smell of innocent blood has ever been considered a divine perfume. All these gods have insisted upon having a vast number of priests, and the priests have always insisted upon being supported by the people, and the principal business of these priests has been to boast about their God, and to insist that he could easily vanquish all the other gods put together.

These gods have been manufactured after numberless models, and according to the most grotesque fashions. Some have a thousand arms, some a hundred heads, some are adorned with necklaces of living snakes, some are armed with clubs, some with sword and shield, some with bucklers, and some with wings as a cherub; some were invisible, some would show themselves entire, and some would only show their backs; some were jealous, some were foolish, some turned themselves into men, some into swans, some into bulls, some into doves, and some into holy ghosts, and made love to the beautiful daughters of men. Some were married—all ought to have been—and some were considered as old bachelors from all eternity. Some had children, and the children were turned into gods and worshiped as their fathers had been. Most of these gods were revengeful, savage, lustful, and ignorant; as they generally depended upon their priests for information, their ignorance can hardly excite our astonishment.

These gods did not even know the shape of the worlds they had created, but supposed them perfectly flat. Some thought the day could be lengthened by stopping the sun, that the blowing of horns could throw down the walls of a city, and all knew so little of the real nature of the people they had created, that they commanded the people to love them. Some were so ignorant as to suppose that man could believe just as he might desire, or as might command, and to be governed by observation, reason, and experience was a most foul and damning sin. None of these gods could give a true account of the creation of this little earth. All were woefully deficient in geology and astronomy. As a rule, they were most miserable legislators, and as executives, they were far inferior to the average of American presidents.

The deities have demanded the most abject and degrading obedience. In order to please them, man must lay his very face in the dust. Of course, they have always been partial to the people who created them, and they have generally shown their partiality by assisting those people to rob and destroy others, and to ravish their wives and daughters. Nothing is so pleasing to these gods as the butchery of unbelievers. Nothing so enrages them, even now as to have some one deny their existence.

Few nations have been so poor as to have but one god. Gods were made so easily, and the raw material cost so little, that generally the god market was fairly glutted, and heaven crammed with these phantoms. These gods not only attended to the skies, but were supposed to interfere in all the affairs of men. They presided over everybody and everything. They attended to every department. All was supposed to be under their immediate control. Nothing was too small—nothing too large; the falling of sparrows and the motions of planets were alike attended to by these industrious and observing deities. From their starry thrones they frequently came to the earth for the purpose of imparting information to man. It is related of one that he came amid thunderings and lightnings in order to tell the people they should not cook a kid in its mother's milk. Some left their shining abode to tell women that they should, or should not, have children, to inform a priest how to cut and wear his apron, and to give directions as to the proper manner for cleaning the intestines of a bird.

When the people failed to worship one of these gods, or failed to feed and clothe his priests, (which was much the same thing,) he generally visited them with pestilence and famine. Sometimes he allowed some other nation to drag them into slavery—to sell their wives and children; but generally he glutted his vengeance by murdering their first born. The priests always did their whole duty, not only in predicting these calamities, but in proving, when they did happen, that they were brought upon the people because they had not given quite enough to them.

These gods differed just as the nations differed; the greatest and most powerful had the most powerful gods, while the weaker ones were obliged to content themselves with the very off-scourings of the heavens. Each of these gods promised happiness here and hereafter to all his slaves, and threatened to eternally punish all who either disbelieved in his existence or suspected that some other God might be his superior; but to deny the existence of all gods was, and is, the crime of crimes. Redden your hands with human blood; blast by slander the fair fame of the innocent; strangle the smiling child upon its mother's knees; deceive, ruin and desert the beautiful girl who loves and trusts you, and your case is not hopeless. For all this, and for all these, you may be forgiven. For all this, and for all these, that bankrupt court established by the gospel, will give you a discharge; but deny the existence of these divine ghosts, of these gods, and the sweet and tearful face of Mercy becomes livid with eternal hate. Heaven's golden gates are shut, and you, with an infinite curse ringing in your ears, with the brand of infamy upon your brow, commence your endless wanderings in the lurid gloom of hell—an immortal vagrant—an eternal outcast—a deathless convict.

One of these gods, and one who demands our love, our admiration and our worship, and one who is worshiped, if mere heartless ceremony is worship, gave to his chosen people for their guidance the following laws of war: "When thou comest nigh unto a city to fight against it, then proclaim peace unto it. And it shall be if it make thee answer of peace, and open unto thee, then it shall be that all the people that is found therein shall be tributaries unto thee, and they shall serve thee. And if it will make no peace with thee, but will make war against thee, then thou shalt besiege it. And when the Lord thy God hath delivered it into thine hands, thou shalt smite every male thereof with the edge of the sword. But the women and the little ones, and the cattle, and all that is in the city, even all the spoil thereof, shalt thou take unto thyself, and thou shalt eat the spoil of thine enemies which the Lord thy God hath given thee. Thus shalt thou do unto all the cities which are very far off from thee, which are not of the cities of these nations. But of the cities of these people which the Lord thy God doth give thee for an inheritance, thou shall save alive nothing that breatheth."

Is it possible for man to conceive of anything more perfectly infamous? Can you believe that such directions were given by any except an infinite fiend? Remember that the army receiving these instructions was one of invasion. Peace was offered on condition that the people submitting should be the slaves of the invader; but if any should have the courage to defend their home, to fight for the love of wife and child, then the sword was to spare none—not even the prattling, dimpled babe.

And we are called upon to worship such a god; to get upon our knees and tell him that he is good, that he is merciful, that he is just, that he is love. We are asked to stifle every noble sentiment of the soul, and to trample under foot all the sweet charities of the heart. Because we refuse to stultify ourselves—refuse to become liars—we are denounced, hated, traduced and ostracized here, and this same god threatens to torment us in eternal fire the moment death allows him to fiercely clutch our naked helpless souls. Let the people hate, let the god threaten—we will educate them, and we will despise and defy him.

The book, called the bible, is filled with passages equally horrible, unjust and atrocious. This is the book to read in schools in order to make our children loving, kind and gentle! This is the book recognized in our Constitution as the source of authority and justice!

Strange that no one has ever been persecuted by the Church for believing God bad, while hundreds of millions have been destroyed for thinking him good. The orthodox church never will forgive the Universalist for saying "God is love." It has always been considered as one of the very highest evidence of true and undefiled religion to insist that all men, women and children deserve eternal damnation. It has always been heresy to say, "God will at last save all."

We are asked to justify these frightful passages, these infamous laws of war, because the bible is the word of God. As a matter of fact, there never was, and there never can be, an argument, even tending to prove the inspiration of any book whatever. In the absence of positive evidence, analogy and experience, argument is simply impossible, and at the very best, can amount only to a useless agitation of the air. The instant we admit that a book is too sacred to be doubted, or even reasoned about, we are mental serfs. It is infinitely absurd to suppose that a god would address a communication to intelligent beings, and yet make it a crime, to be punished in eternal flames for them to use their intelligence for the purpose of understanding his communication. If we have the right to use our reason, we certainly have the right to act in accordance with it, and no god can have the right to punish us for such action.

The doctrine that future happiness depends upon belief is monstrous. It is the infamy of infamies. The notion that faith in Christ is to be rewarded by an eternity of bliss, while a dependence upon reason, observation, and experience merits everlasting pain, is too absurd for refutation, and can be relieved only by that unhappy mixture of insanity and ignorance, called "faith." What man, who ever thinks, can believe that blood can appease God? And yet, our entire system of religion is based upon that belief. The Jews pacified Jehovah with the blood of animals, and according to the Christian system, the blood of Jesus softened the heart of God a little, and rendered possible the salvation of a fortunate few. It is hard to conceive how the human mind can give assent to such terrible ideas, or how any sane man can read the bible and still believe in the doctrine of inspiration.

Whether the bible is true or false, is of no consequence in comparison with the mental freedom of the race.

Salvation through slavery is worthless. Salvation from slavery is inestimable.

As long as man believes the bible to be infallible, that is his master. The civilization of this century is not the child of faith, but of unbelief—the result of free thought.

All that is necessary, as it seems to me, to convince any reasonable person that the bible is simply and purely of human invention—of barbarian invention—is to read it. Read it as you would any other book; think of it as you would any other; get the bandage of reverence from your eyes; drive from your heart the phantom of fear; push from the throne of your sbrain the cowled form of superstition—then read the holy bible, and you will be amazed that you ever, for one moment, supposed a being of infinite wisdom, goodness and purity to be the author of such ignorance and of such atrocity.

Our ancestors not only had their God-factories, but they made devils as well. These devils were generally disgraced and fallen gods. Some had headed unsuccessful revolts; some had been caught sweetly reclining in the shadowy folds of some fleecy clouds, kissing the wife of the God of gods. These devils generally sympathized with man. There is in regard to them a most wonderful fact: In nearly all the theologies, mythologic and religious, the devils have been much more humane and merciful than the gods. No devil ever gave one of his generals an order to kill children and to rip open the bodies of pregnant women. Such barbarities were always ordered by the good gods. The pestilences were sent by the most merciful gods. The frightful famine, during which the dying child with pallid lips sucked the withered bosom of a dead mother, was sent by the loving gods. No devil was ever charged with such fiendish brutality.

One of these gods, according to the account, drowned an entire world, with the exception of eight persons. The old, the young, the beautiful and the helpless were remorselessly devoured by the shoreless sea. This, the most fearful tragedy that the imagination of ignorant priests ever conceived, was the act not of a devil, but of God so-called, whom men ignorantly worship unto this day. What a stain such an act would leave upon the character of a devil! One of the prophets of one of these gods, having in his power a captured king, hewed him in pieces in the sight of all the people. Was ever any imp of any devil guilty of such savagery?

One of these gods is reported to have given the following directions concerning human slavery: "If thou buy a Hebrew servant six years shall he serve, and in the seventh he shall go out free for nothing. If he came in by himself, he shall go out by himself; if he were married, then his wife shall go out with him. If his master have given him a wife, and she have borne him sons or daughters, the wife and her children shall be her master's, and he shall go out by himself. And if the servant shall plainly say, I love my master, my wife and my children; I will not go out free; then his master shall bring him unto the judges: he shall also bring him unto the door, or unto the doorpost; and his Master shall bore his ear with an awl; and he shall serve him forever."

According to this, a man was given liberty upon condition that he would desert forever his wife and children. Did any devil ever force upon a husband, upon a father, so cruel and so heartless an alternative? Who can worship such a god? Who can bend the knee to such a monster? Who can pray to such a fiend?

All these gods threatened to torment forever the souls of their enemies. Did any devil ever make so infamous a threat? The basest thing recorded of the devil, is what he did concerning Job and his family, and that was done by the express permission of one of these gods and to decide a little difference of opinion between their serene highnesses as to the character of "my servant Job."

The first account we have of the devil is found in that purely scientific book called Genesis, and is as follows: "Now the serpent was more subtle than any beast of the field which the Lord God had made, and he said unto the woman, Yea, hath God said, ye shall not eat of the fruit of the trees of the garden? And the woman said unto the serpent. We may eat of the fruit of the trees of the garden; but of the fruit of the tree which is in the midst of the garden God hath said, Ye shall not eat of it, neither shall ye touch it, lest ye die. And the serpent said unto the woman, Ye shall not surely die. For God doth know that in the day ye eat thereof, then your eyes shall be opened and ye shall be as gods, knowing good and evil. And when the woman saw that the tree was good for food, and that it was pleasant to the eyes, and a tree to be desired to make one wise, she took of the fruit thereof and did eat, and gave also unto her husband with her, and he did eat...... And the Lord God said, Behold the man has become as one of us, to know good and evil; and now, lest he put forth his hand, and take also of the tree of life and eat, and live forever. Therefore the Lord God sent him forth from the garden of Eden to till the ground from which he was taken. So he drove out the man, and he placed at the east of the garden of Eden cherubims and a flaming sword, which turned every way to keep the way of the tree of life."

According to this account the promise of the devil was fulfilled to the very letter. Adam and Eve did not die, and they did become as gods, knowing good and evil. The account shows, however, that the gods dreaded education and knowledge then just as they do now. The church still faithfully guards the dangerous tree of knowledge, and has exerted in all ages her utmost power to keep mankind from eating the fruit thereof. The priests have never ceased repeating the old falsehood and the old threat: "Ye shall not eat of it, neither shall ye touch it, lest ye die." From every pulpit comes the same cry, born of the same fear "Lest they eat and become as gods, knowing good and evil." For this reason, religion hates science, faith detests reason, theology is the sworn enemy of philosophy, and the church with its flaming sword still guards the hated tree, and like its supposed founder, curses to the lowest depths the brave thinkers who eat and become as gods.

If the account given in Genesis is really true, ought we not, after all, to thank this serpent? He was the first schoolmaster, the first advocate of learning, the first enemy of ignorance, the first to whisper in human ears the sacred word liberty, the creator of ambition, the author of modesty, of inquiry, of doubt, of investigation, of progress and of civilization.

Give me the storm and tempest of thought and action, rather than the dead calm of ignorance and faith. Banish me from Eden when you will; but first let me eat of the fruit of the tree of knowledge! Some nations have borrowed their gods; of this number, we are compelled to say, is our own. The Jews having ceased to exist as a nation, and having no further use for a god, our ancestors appropriated him and adopted their devil at the same time. This borrowed god is still an object of some adoration, and this adopted devil still excites the apprehensions of our people. He is still supposed to be setting his traps and snares for the purpose of catching our unwary souls, and is still, with reasonable success, waging the old war against our god.

To me, it seems easy to account for these ideas concerning gods and devils. They are a perfectly natural production. Man has created them all, and under the same circumstances will create them again. Man has not only created all these gods, but he has created them out of the materials by which he has been surrounded. Generally he has modeled them after himself, and has given them hands, heads, feet, eyes, ears, and organs of speech. Each nation made its gods and devils speak its language not only, but put in their mouths the same mistakes in history, geography, astronomy, and in all matters of fact, generally made by the people.

No god was ever in advance of the nation that created him. The negroes represented their deities with black skins and curly hair. The Mongolian gave to his a yellow complexion and dark almond-shaped eyes. The Jews were not allowed to paint theirs, or we should have seen Jehovah with a full beard, an oval face, and an aquiline nose. Zeus was a perfect Greek and Jove looked as though a member of the Roman senate. The gods of Egypt had the patient face and placid look of the loving people who made them. The gods of northern countries were represented warmly clad in robes of fur; those of the tropics were naked. The gods of India were often mounted upon elephants, those of some islanders were great swimmers, and the deities of the Arctic zone were passionately fond of whale's blubber. Nearly all people have carved or painted representations of their gods, and these representations were, by the lower classes generally treated as the real gods, and to these images and idols they addressed prayers and offered sacrifice.

In some countries, even at this day, if the people after long praying do not obtain their desires, they turn their images off as impotent gods, or upbraid them in a most reproachful manner, loading them with blows and curses. 'How now, dog of a spirit,' they say, 'we give you lodging in a magnificent temple, we gild you with gold, feed you with the choicest food, and offer incense to you; yet, after all this care, you are so ungrateful as to refuse us what we ask.' Hereupon they will pull the god down and drag him through the filth of the street. If, in the meantime, it happens that they obtain their request, then with a great deal of ceremony, they wash him clean, carry him back and place him in his temple again, where they fall down and make excuses for what they have done. 'Of a truth,' they say, 'we were a little too hasty, and you were a little too long in your grant. Why should you bring this beating on yourself. But what is done cannot be undone.' Let us not think of it any more. If you will forget what is past, we will gild you over brighter again than before.

Man has never been at a loss for gods. He has worshiped almost everything, including the vilest and most disgusting beasts. He has worshiped fire, earth, air, water, light, stars, and for hundreds of ages, prostrated himself before enormous snakes. Savage tribes often make gods of articles they get from civilized people. The Todas worship a cow-bell. The Kotas worship two silver plates, which they regard as husband and wife, and another tribe manufactured a god out of a king of hearts.

Man, having always been the physical superior of woman, accounts for the fact that most of the high gods have been males. Had woman been the physical superior, the powers supposed to be the ruler of Nature would have been woman, and instead of being represented in the apparel of man, they would have luxuriated in trains, low necked dresses, laces and back-hair.

Nothing can be plainer than that each nation gives to its god its peculiar characteristics, and that every individual gives to his God his personal peculiarities.

Man has no ideas, and can have none, except those suggested by his surroundings. He cannot conceive of anything utterly unlike what he has seen or felt. He can exaggerate, diminish, combine, separate, deform, beautify, improve, multiply and compare what he sees, what he feels, what he hears, and all of which he takes cognizance through the medium of the senses; but he cannot create. Having seen exhibitions of power, he can say, omnipotent. Having lived, he can say, immortality. Knowing something of time, he can say, eternity. Conceiving something of intelligence, he can say God. Having seen exhibitions of malice, he can say, devil. A few gleams of happiness having fallen athwart the gloom of his life, he can say, heaven. Pain, in its numberless forms, having been experienced, he can say, hell. Yet all these ideas have a foundation in fact, and only a foundation. The superstructure has been reared by exaggerating, diminishing, combining, separating, deforming, beautifying, improving or multiplying realities, so that the edifice or fabric is but the incongruous grouping of what man has perceived through the medium of the senses. It is as though we should give to a lion the wings of an eagle, the hoofs of a bison, the tail of a horse, the pouch of a kangaroo, and the trunk of an elephant. We have in imagination created an impossible monster. And yet the various parts of this monster really exist. So it is with all the gods that man has made.

Beyond nature man cannot go even in thought—above nature he cannot rise—below nature he cannot fall.

Man, in his ignorance, supposed that all phenomena were produced by some intelligent powers, and with direct reference to him. To preserve friendly relations with these powers was, and still is, the object of all religions. Man knelt through fear and to implore assistance, or through gratitude for some favor which he supposed had been rendered. He endeavored by supplication to appease some being who, for some reason, had, as he believed become enraged. The lightning and thunder terrified him. In the presence of the volcano he sank upon his knees. The great forests filled with wild and ferocious beasts, the monstrous serpents crawling in mysterious depths, the boundless sea, the flaming comets, the sinister eclipses, the awful calmness of the stars, and more than all, the perpetual presence of death, convinced him that he was the sport and prey of unseen and malignant powers. The strange and frightful diseases to which he was subject, the freezings and burnings of fever, the contortions of epilepsy, the sudden palsies, the darkness of night, and the wild, terrible and fantastic dreams that filled his brain, satisfied him that he was haunted and pursued by countless spirits of evil. For some reason he supposed that these spirits differed in power—that they were not all alike malevolent—that the higher controlled the lower, and that his very existence depended upon gaining the assistance of the more powerful. For this purpose he resorted to prayer, to flattery, to worship and to sacrifice. These ideas appear to have been almost universal in savage man.

For ages all nations supposed that the sick and insane were possessed by evil spirits. For thousands of years the practice of medicine consisted in frightening these spirits away. Usually the priests would make the loudest and most discordant noises possible. They would blow horns, beat upon rude drums, clash cymbals, and in the meantime utter the most unearthly yells. If the noise-remedy failed, they would implore the aid of some more powerful spirit.

To pacify these spirits was considered of infinite importance. The poor barbarian, knowing that men could be softened by gifts, gave to these spirits that which to him seemed of the most value. With bursting heart he would offer the blood of his dearest child. It was impossible for him to conceive of a god utterly unlike himself, and he naturally supposed that these powers of the air would be affected a little at the sight of so great and so deep a sorrow. It was with the barbarian then as with the civilized now—one class lived upon and made merchandise of the fears of another. Certain persons took it upon themselves to appease the gods, and to instruct the people in their duties to these unseen powers. This was the origin of the priesthood. The priest pretended to stand between the wrath of the gods and the helplessness of man. He was man's attorney at the court of heaven. He carried to the invisible world a flag of truce, a protest and a request. He came back with a command, with authority and with power. Man fell upon his knees before his own servant, and the priest, taking advantage of the awe inspired by his supposed influence with the gods, made of his fellow-man a cringing hypocrite and slave. Even Christ, the supposed son of God, taught that persons were possessed of evil spirits, and frequently, according to the account, gave proof of his divine origin and mission by frightening droves of devils out of his unfortunate countrymen. Casting out devils was his principal employment, and the devils thus banished generally took occasion to acknowledge him as the true Messiah; which was not only very kind of them, but quite fortunate for him. The religious people have always regarded the testimony of these devils as perfectly conclusive, and the writers of the New Testament quote the words of these imps of darkness with great satisfaction.

The fact that Christ could withstand the temptations of the devil was considered as conclusive evidence that he was assisted by some god, or at least by some being superior to man. St. Matthew gives an account of an attempt made by the devil to tempt the supposed son of God; and it has always excited the wonder of Christians that the temptation was so nobly and heroically withstood. The account to which I refer is as follows:

"Then was Jesus led up of the spirit into the wilderness to be tempted of the devil. And when the tempter came to him, he said: 'If thou be the son of God command that these stones be made bread.' But he answered, and said 'It is written: man shall not live by bread alone, but by every word that proceedeth out of the mouth of God.' Then the devil taketh him up into the holy city and setteth him upon a pinnacle of the temple and saith unto him: 'If thou be the son of God, cast thyself down, for it is written, He shall give his angels charge concerning thee, lest at any time thou shalt dash thy foot against a stone.' Jesus said unto him 'It is written again, thou shalt not tempt the Lord thy God.' Again the devil taketh him up into an exceeding high mountain and showeth him all the kingdoms of the world and the glory of them, and saith unto him 'All these will I give thee if thou wilt fall down and worship me.'"

The Christians now claim that Jesus was God. If he was God, of course the devil knew that fact, and yet, according to this account, the devil took the omnipotent God and placed him upon a pinnacle of the temple, and endeavored to induce him to dash himself against the earth. Failing in that, he took the creator, owner and governor of the universe up into an exceeding high mountain, and offered him this world—this grain of sand—if he, the God of all the worlds, would fall down and worship him, a poor devil, without even a tax title to one foot of dirt! Is it possible the devil was such an idiot? Should any great credit be given to this deity for not being caught with such chaff? Think of it! The devil—the prince of sharpers—the king of cunning—the master of finesse, trying to bribe God with a grain of sand that belonged to God!

Is there in ail the religious literature of the world any thing more grossly absurd than this?

These devils, according to the bible, were various kinds—some could speak and hear, others were deaf and dumb. All could not be cast out in the same way. The deaf and dumb spirits were quite difficult to deal with. St. Mark tells of a gentleman who brought his son to Christ. The boy, it seems, was possessed of a dumb spirit, over which the disciples had no control. "Jesus said unto the spirit: 'Thou dumb and deaf spirit. I charge thee come out of him, and enter no more into him.'" Whereupon, the deaf spirit having heard what was said, cried out (being dumb) and immediately vacated the premises. The ease with which Christ controlled this deaf and dumb spirit excited the wonder of his disciples, and they asked him privately why they could not cast that spirit out. To whom he replied: "This kind can come forth by nothing but prayer and fasting." Is there a Christian in the whole world who would believe such a story if found in any other book? The trouble is, these pious people shut up their reason, and then open their bible.

In the olden times the existence of devils was universally admitted. The people had no doubt upon that subject, and from such belief it followed as a matter of course, that a person, in order to vanquish these devils, had either to be a god, or to be assisted by one. All founders of religions have established their claims to divine origin by controlling evil spirits—and suspending the laws of nature. Casting out devils was a certificate of divinity. A prophet, unable to cope with the powers of darkness, was regarded with contempt. The utterance of the highest and noblest sentiments, the most blameless and holy life, commanded but little respect, unless accompanied by power to work miracles and command spirits.

This belief in good and evil powers had its origin in the fact that man was surrounded by what he was pleased to call good and evil phenomena. Phenomena affecting man pleasantly were ascribed to good spirits, while those affecting him unpleasantly or injuriously, were ascribed to evil spirits. It being admitted that all phenomena were produced by spirits, the spirits were divided according to the phenomena, and the phenomena were good or bad as they affected man. Good spirits were supposed to be the authors of good phenomena, and evil spirits of the evil—so that the idea of a devil has been as universal as the idea of a god.

Many writers maintain that an idea to become universal must be true; that all universal ideas are innate, and that innate ideas cannot be false. If the fact that an idea has been universal proves that it is innate, and if the fact that an idea is innate proves that it is correct, then the believer in innate ideas must admit that the evidence of a god superior to nature, and of a devil superior to nature, is exactly the same, and that the existence of such a devil must be as self-evident as the existence of such a god. The truth is, a god was inferred from good, and a devil from bad, phenomena. And it is just as natural and logical to suppose that a devil would cause happiness as to suppose that a god would produce misery. Consequently, if an intelligence, infinite and supreme, is the immediate author of all phenomena, it is difficult to determine whether such intelligence is the friend or enemy of man. If phenomena were all good, we might say they were all produced by a perfectly beneficent being. If they were all bad, we, might say they were produced by a perfectly malevolent power; but as phenomena are, as they affect man, both good and bad, they must be produced by different and antagonistic spirits; by one who is sometimes actuated by kindness, and sometimes by malice; or all must be produced of necessity, and without reference to their consequences upon man.

The foolish doctrine that all phenomena can be traced to the interference of good and evil spirits, has been, and still is, almost universal. That most people still believe in some spirit that can change the natural order of events, is proven by the fact that nearly all resort to prayer. Thousands, at this very moment, are probably imploring some supposed power to interfere in their behalf. Some want health restored; some ask that the loved and absent be watched over and protected, some pray for riches, some for rain, some want diseases stayed, some vainly ask for food, some ask for revivals, a few ask for more wisdom, and now and then one tells the Lord to do as he thinks best. Thousands ask to be protected from the devil; some, like David, pray for revenge, and some implore, even God, not to lead them into temptation. All these prayers rest upon, and are produced by the idea that some power not only can, but probably will, change the order of the universe. This belief has been among the great majority of tribes and nations. All sacred books are filled with the accounts of such interferences, and our own bible is no exception to this rule.

If we believe in a power superior to nature, it is perfectly natural to suppose that such power can and will interfere in the affairs of this world. If there is no interference, of what practical use can such power be? The scriptures give us the most wonderful accounts of divine interference: Animals talk like men; springs gurgle from dry bones; the sun and moon stop in the heavens in order that General Joshua may have more time to murder; the shadow on a dial goes back ten degrees to convince a petty king of a barbarous people that he is not going to die of a boil; fire refused to burn; water positively declined to seek its level, but stands up like a wall; grains of sand become lice; common walking-sticks, to gratify a mere freak, twist themselves into serpents, and then swallow each other by way of exercise; murmuring streams, laughing at the attraction of gravitation, run up hill for years, following wandering tribes from a pure love of frolic; prophecy becomes altogether easier than history; the sons of God become enamored of the world's girls; women are changed into salt for the purpose of keeping a great event fresh in the minds of man; an excellent article of brimstone is imported from heaven free of duty; clothes refuse to wear out for forty years, birds keep restaurants and feed wandering prophets free of expense; bears tear children in pieces for laughing at old men without wigs; muscular development depends upon the length of one's hair; dead people come to life, simply to get a joke on their enemies and heirs; witches and wizards converse freely with the souls of the departed, and God himself becomes a stone-cutter and engraver, after having been a tailor and dressmaker.

The veil between heaven and earth was always rent or lifted. The shadows of this world, the radiance of heaven, and the glare of hell mixed and mingled until man became uncertain as to which country he really inhabited. Man dwelt in an unreal world. He mistook his ideas, his dream, for real things. His fears became terrible and malicious monsters. He lived in the midst of furies and fairies, nymphs and naiads, goblins and ghosts, witches and wizards, sprites and spooks, deities and devils. The obscure and gloomy depths were filled with claw and wing—with beak and hoof—with leering look and sneering mouths—with the malice of deformity—with the cunning of hatred, and with all the slimy forms that fear can draw and paint upon the shadowy canvas of the dark.

It is enough to make one almost insane with pity to think what man in the long night has suffered: of the tortures he has endured, surrounded, as he supposed, by malignant powers and clutched by the fierce phantoms of the air. No wonder that he fell upon his trembling knees—that he built altars and reddened them even with his own blood. No wonder that he implored ignorant priests and impudent magicians for aid. No wonder that he crawled groveling in the dust to the temple's door, and there, in the insanity of despair, besought the deaf gods to hear his bitter cry of agony and fear.

The savage as he emerges from a state of barbarism, gradually loses faith in his idols of wood and stone, and in their place puts a multitude of spirits. As he advances in knowledge, he generally discards the petty spirits, and in their stead believes in one, whom he supposes to be infinite and supreme. Supposing this great spirit to be superior to nature, he offers worship or flattery in exchange for assistance. At last, finding that he obtains no aid from this supposed deity—finding that every search after the absolute must of necessity end in failure—finding that man cannot by any possibility conceive of the conditionless—he begins to investigate the facts by which he is surrounded, and to depend upon himself.

The people are beginning to think, to reason and to investigate. Slowly, painfully, but surely, the gods are being driven from the earth. Only upon rare occasions are they, even by the most religious, supposed to interfere in the affairs of men. In most matters we are at last supposed to be free. Since the invention of steamships and railways, so that the products of all countries can be easily interchanged, the gods have quit the business of producing famine. Now and then they kill a child because it is idolized by its parents. As a rule they have given up causing accidents on railroads, exploding boilers, and bursting kerosene lamps. Cholera, yellow fever, and smallpox are still considered heavenly weapons; but measles, itch and ague are now attributed to natural causes. As a general thing, the gods have stopped drowning children, except as a punishment for violating the Sabbath. They still pay some attention to the affairs of kings, men of genius and persons of great wealth: but ordinary people are left to shift for themselves as best they may. In wars between great nations, the gods still interfere; but in prize fights, the best man with an honest referee, is almost sure to win.

The church cannot abandon the idea of special providence. To give up that doctrine is to give up all. The church must insist that prayer is answered—that some power superior to nature hears and grants the request of the sincere and humble Christian, and that this same power in some mysterious way provides for all.

A devout Clergyman sought every opportunity to impress upon the mind of his son the fact, that God takes care of all his creatures; that the falling sparrow attracts his attentions, and that his loving kindness is over all his works. Happening, one day, to see a crane wading in quest of food, the good man pointed out to his son the perfect adaptation of the crane to get his living in that manner. "See," said he, "how his legs are formed for wading! What a long slender bill he has! Observe how nicely he folds his feet when putting them in or drawing them out of the water! He does not cause the slightest ripple. He is thus enabled to approach the fish without giving them any notice of his arrival." "My son," said he, "it is impossible to look at that bird without recognizing the design, as well as the goodness of God, in thus providing the means of subsistence." "Yes" replied the boy, "I think I see the goodness of God, at least so far as the crane is concerned: but after all, father, don't you think the arrangement a little tough on the fish?"

Even the advanced religionist, although disbelieving in any great amount of interference by the gods in this age of the world, still thinks that in the beginning some god made the laws governing the universe. He believes that in consequence of these laws a man can lift a greater weight with than without a lever; that this god so made matter, and so established the order of things, that—two bodies cannot occupy the same space at the same time; so that a body once put in motion will keep moving until it is stopped; so that it is a greater distance around than across a circle; so that a perfect square has four equal sides, instead of five or seven. He insists that it took a direct interposition of providence to make the whole greater than a part, and that had it not been for this power superior to nature, twice one might have been more than twice two, and sticks and strings might have had only one end apiece. Like the old Scotch divine, he thanks God that Sunday comes at the end instead of in the middle of the week, and that death comes at the close instead of at the commencement of life, thereby giving us time to prepare for that holy day and that most solemn event. These religious people see nothing but design everywhere, and personal, intelligent interference in everything. They insist that the universe has been created, and that the adaptation of means to ends is perfectly apparent. They point us to the sunshine, to the flowers, to the April rain, and to all there is of beauty and of use in the world. Did it ever occur to them that a cancer is as beautiful in its development as is the reddest rose? That what they are pleased to call the adaptation of means to ends, is as apparent in the cancer as in the April rain? How beautiful the process of digestion! By what ingenious methods the blood is poisoned so that the cancer shall have food! By what wonderful contrivances the entire system of man is made to pay tribute to this divine and charming cancer! See by what admirable instrumentalities it feeds itself from the surrounding, quivering, dainty flesh! See how it gradually but surely expands and grows! By what marvelous mechanism it is supplied with long and slender roots that reach out to the most secret nerves of pain for sustenance and life! What beautiful colors it presents! Seen through the microscope it is a miracle of order and beauty. All the ingenuity of man cannot stop its growth. Think of the amount of thought it must have required to invent a way by which the life of one man might be given to produce one cancer? Is it possible to look upon it and doubt that there is design in the universe, and that the inventor of this wonderful cancer must be infinitely powerful, ingenious and good?

We are told that the universe was designed and created, and that it is absurd to suppose that matter has existed from eternity, but that it is perfectly self-evident that a god has.

If a god created the universe, then there must have been a time when he commenced to create. Back of that time there must have been an eternity, during which there had existed nothing—absolutely nothing—except this supposed god. According to this theory, this god spent an eternity, so to speak, in an infinite vacuum, and in perfect idleness.

Admitting that a god did create the universe, the question then arises, of what did he create it? It certainly was not made of nothing. Nothing, considered in the light of a raw material, is a most decided failure. It follows, then, that a god must have made the universe out of himself, he being the only existence. The universe is material, and if it was made of god, the god must have been material. With this very thought in his mind, Anaximander of Miletus said: "Creation is the decomposition of the infinite."

It has been demonstrated that the earth would fall to the sun, only for the fact that it is attracted by other worlds, and those worlds must be attracted by other worlds still beyond them, and so on, without end. This proves the material universe to be infinite. If an infinite universe has been made out of an infinite god, how much of the god is left?

The idea of a creative deity is gradually being abandoned, and nearly all truly scientific minds admit that matter must have existed from eternity. It is indestructible, and the indestructible cannot be created. It is the crowning glory of our century to have demonstrated the indestructibility and the eternal persistence of force. Neither matter nor force can be increased nor diminished. Force cannot exist apart from matter. Matter exists only in connection with force, and consequently a force apart from matter, and superior to nature, is a demonstrated impossibility.

Force, then, must have also existed from eternity, and could not have been created. Matter in its countless forms, from dead earth to the eyes of those we love, and force, in all its manifestations, from simple motions to the grandest thought, deny creation and defy control.

Thought is a form of force. We walk with the same force with which we think. Man is an organism that changes several forms of force into thought-force. Man is a machine into which we put what we call food, and produce what we call thought. Think of that wonderful chemistry by which bread was changed into the divine tragedy of Hamlet!

A god must not only be material, but he must be an organism, capable of changing other forms of force into thought-force. This is what we call eating. Therefore, if the god thinks he must eat, that is to say, he must of necessity have some means of supplying the force with which to think. It is impossible to conceive of a being who can eternally impart force to matter, and yet have no means of supplying the force thus imparted.

If neither matter nor force were created, what evidence have we, then, of the existence of a power superior to nature? The theologian will probably reply, "We have law and order, cause and effect, and beside all this, matter could not have put itself in motion."

Suppose, for the sake of an argument, that there is no being superior to nature, and that matter and force have existed from eternity. Now suppose that two atoms should come together, would there be an effect? Yes. Suppose they came in exactly opposite directions with equal force, they would be stopped, to say the least. This would be an effect. If this is so, then you have matter, force and effect without a being superior to nature. Now suppose that two other atoms, just like the first two, should come together under precisely the same circumstances, would not the effect be exactly the same? Yes. Like causes, producing like effects, is what we mean by law and order. Then we have matter, force, effect, law and order without a being superior to nature. Now, we know that every effect must also be a cause, and that every cause must be an effect. The atoms coming together did produce an effect, and as every effect must also be a cause, the effect produced by the collision of the atoms, must, as to something else, have been a cause. Then we have matter, force, law, order, cause and effect without a being superior to nature. Nothing is left for the supernatural but empty space. His throne is a void, and his boasted realm is without matter, without force, without law, without cause, and without effect.

But what put all this matter in motion? If matter and force have existed from eternity, then matter must have always been in motion. There can be no force without motion. Force is forever active, and there is, and there can be no cessation. If therefore, matter and force have existed from eternity, so has motion. In the whole universe there is not even one atom in a state of rest.

A deity outside of nature exists in nothing, and is nothing. Nature embraces with infinite arms all matter and all force. That which is beyond her grasp is destitute of both, and can hardly be worth the worship and adoration even of a man.

There is but one way to demonstrate the existence of a power independent of and superior to nature, and that is by breaking, if only for one moment, the continuity of cause and effect. Pluck from the endless chain of existence one little link; stop for one instant the grand procession, and you have shown beyond all contradiction that nature has a master. Change the fact, just for one second, that matter attracts matter, and a god appears.

The rudest savage has always known this fact, and for that reason always demanded the evidence of miracle. The founder of a religion must be able to turn water into wine—cure with a word the blind and lame, and raise with a simple touch the dead to life. It was necessary for him to demonstrate to the satisfaction of his barbarian disciple, that he was superior to nature. In times of ignorance this was easy to do. The credulity of the savage was almost boundless. To him the marvelous was the beautiful, the mysterious was the sublime. Consequently, every religion has for its foundation a miracle—that is to say, a violation of nature—that is to say, a falsehood.

No one, in the world's whole history, ever attempted to substantiate a truth by a miracle. Truth scorns the assistance of miracle. Nothing but falsehood ever attested itself by signs and wonders. No miracle ever was performed, and no sane man ever thought he had performed one, and until one is performed, there can be no evidence of the existence of any power superior to, and independent of nature.

The church wishes us to believe. Let the church, or one of its intellectual saints, perform a miracle, and we will believe. We are told that nature has a superior. Let this superior, for one single instant, control nature, and we will admit the truth of your assertion.

We have heard talk enough. We have listened to all the drowsy, idealess, vapid sermons that we wish to hear. We have read your bible and the works of your best minds. We have heard your prayers, your solemn groans and your reverential amens. All these amount to less than nothing. We beg at the doors of your churches for just one little fact. We pass our hats along your pews and under your pulpits and implore you for just one fact. We know all about your moldy wonders and your stale miracles. We want this year's fact. We ask only one. Give us one fact of charity. Your miracles are too ancient. The witnesses have been dead for nearly two thousand years. Their reputations for "truth and veracity" in the neighborhood where they resided is wholly unknown to us. Give us a new miracle, and substantiate it by witnesses who still have the cheerful habit of living in this world. Do not send us to Jericho to hear the winding horns, nor put us in the fire with Shadrach, Moshech, and Abednego. Do not compel us to navigate the sea with Captain Jonah, nor dine with Mr. Ezekiel. There is no sort of use in sending us fox-hunting with Samson. We have positively lost interest in that little speech so eloquently delivered by Balaam's inspired donkey. It is worse than useless to show us fishes with money in their mouths, and call our attention to vast multitudes stuffing themselves with five crackers and two sardines. We demand a new miracle and we demand it now. Let the church furnish at least one, or forever after hold her peace.

In the olden time, the church, by violating the order of nature, proved the existence of her God. At that time miracles were performed with the most astonishing ease. They became so common that the church ordered her priests to desist. And now this same church—the people having found so little sense—admits, not only, that she cannot perform a miracle, but insists—that absence of miracle—the steady, unbroken march of cause and effect, proves the existence of a power superior to nature. The fact is, however, that the indissoluble chain of cause and effect proves exactly the contrary.

Sir William Hamilton, one of the pillars of modern theology, in discussing this very subject, uses the following language: "The phenomena of matter taken by themselves, so far from warranting any inference to the existence of a god, would on the contrary ground even an argument to his negation. The phenomena of a material world are subjected to immutable laws; are produced and reproduced in the same invariable succession, and manifest only the blind force of mechanical necessity."

Nature is but an endless series of efficient causes. She cannot create, but she eternally transforms. There was no beginning; and there can be no end.

The best minds, even in the religious world, admit that in material nature there is no evidence of what they are pleased to call a god. They find their evidence in the phenomena of intelligence, and very innocently assert that intelligence is above, and in fact, opposed to nature. They insist that man, at least, is a special creation; that he had somewhere in his brain a divine spark, a little portion of the "Great First Cause." They say that matter cannot produce thought; but that thought can produce matter. They tell us that man has intelligence, and therefore there must be an intelligence greater than his. Why not say, God has intelligence, therefore there must be an intelligence greater than his? So far as we know, there is no intelligence apart from matter. We cannot conceive of thought, except as produced within a brain.

The science, by means of which they demonstrate the existence of an impossible intelligence, and an incomprehensible power, is called metaphysics or theology. The theologians admit that the phenomena of matter tend, at least, to disprove the existence of any power superior to nature, because in such phenomena we see nothing but an endless chain of efficient causes—nothing but the force of a mechanical necessity. They therefore appeal to what they denominate the phenomena of mind to establish this superior power.

The trouble is, that in the phenomena of mind we find the same endless chain of efficient causes; the same mechanical necessity. Every thought must have had an efficient cause. Every motive, every desire, every fear, hope and dream must have been necessarily produced. There is no room in the mind of a man for providence or change. The facts and forces governing thought are as absolute as those governing the motions of the planets. A poem is produced by the forces of nature, and is as necessarily and naturally produced as mountains and seas. You will seek in vain for a thought in man's brain without its efficient cause. Every mental operation is the necessary result of certain facts and conditions. Mental phenomena are considered more complicated than those of matter, and consequently more mysterious. Being more mysterious, they are considered better evidence of the existence of a god. No one infers a god from the simple, from the known, from what is understood, but from the complex, from the unknown and incomprehensible. Our ignorance is God; what we know is science.

When we abandon the doctrine that some infinite being created matter and force, and enacted a code of laws for their government, the idea of interference will be lost. The real priest will then be, not the mouth-piece of some pretended deity, but the interpreter of nature. From that moment the church ceases to exist. The tapers will die out upon the dusty altar; the moths will eat the fading velvet of pulpit and pew; the Bible will take its place with the Shastras, Puranas, Vedas, Eddas, Sagas and Korans, and the fetters of a degrading faith will fall from the minds of men.

"But," says the religionist "you cannot explain everything; you cannot understand everything; and that which you cannot explain, that which you do not comprehend, is my god."

We are explaining more every day. We are understanding more every day; consequently your God is growing smaller every day.

Nothing daunted, the religionist then insists that nothing can exist without a cause, except cause, and that this uncaused cause is God.

To this we again replied: Every cause must produce an effect, because until it does produce an effect, it is not a cause. Every effect must in its turn become a cause. Therefore, in the nature of things, there cannot be a last cause, for the reason that a so-called last cause would necessarily produce an effect, and that effect must of necessity become a cause. The converse of these propositions must be true. Every effect must have had a cause, and every cause must have been an effect. Therefore, there could have been no first cause. A first cause is just as impossible as a last effect.

Beyond the universe there is nothing, and within the universe the supernatural does not and cannot exist.

The moment these great truths are understood and admitted, a belief in general or special providence becomes impossible. From that instant men will cease their vain efforts to please an imaginary being, and will give their time and attention to the affairs of this world. They will abandon the idea of attaining any object by prayer and supplication. The element of uncertainty will, in a great measure, be removed from the domain of the future, and man, gathering courage from a succession of victories over the obstructions of nature, will attain a serene grandeur unknown to the disciples of any superstition. The plans of mankind will no longer be interfered with by the finger of a supposed omnipotence, and no one will believe that nations or individuals are protected or destroyed by any deity whatever. Science, freed from the chains of pious custom and evangelical prejudice, will, within her sphere, be supreme. The mind will investigate without reverence and publish its conclusions without fear. Agassiz will no longer hesitate to declare the Mosaic cosmogony utterly inconsistent with the demonstrated truths of geology, and will cease pretending any reverence for the Jewish scriptures. The moment science succeeds in rendering the church powerless for evil, the real thinkers will be outspoken. The little flags of truce carried by timid philosophers will disappear, and the cowardly parley will give place to victory lasting and universal.

If we admit that some infinite being has controlled the destinies of persons and people, history becomes a most cruel and bloody farce. Age after age, the strong have trampled upon the weak; the crafty and heartless have ensnared and enslaved the simple and innocent, and nowhere, in all the annals of mankind, has any god succored the oppressed.

Man should cease to expect aid from on high. By this time he should know that heaven has no ear to hear, and no hand to help. The present is the necessary child of all the past. There has been no chance, and there can be no interference.

If abuses are destroyed, man must destroy them. If slaves are freed, man must free them. If new truths are discovered, man must discover them. If the naked are clothed; if the hungry are fed; if justice is done; if labor is rewarded; if superstition is driven from the mind, if the defenseless are protected, and if the right finally triumphs, all must be the work of man. The grand victories of the future must be won by man, and by man alone.

Nature, so far as we can discern, without passion and without intention, forms, transforms, and retransforms forever. She neither weeps nor rejoices. She produces man without purpose, and obliterates him without regret. She knows no distinction between the beneficial and the hurtful. Poison and nutrition, pain and joy, life and death, smiles and tears are alike to her. She is neither merciful nor cruel. She cannot be flattered by worship nor melted by tears. She does not know even the attitude of prayer. She appreciates no difference between poison in the fangs of snakes and mercy in the hearts of men. Only through man does nature take cognizance of the good, the true, and the beautiful; and, so far as we know, man is the highest intelligence.

And yet man continues to believe that there is some power independent of and superior to nature, and still endeavors, by form, ceremony, supplication, hypocrisy, to obtain its aid. His best energies have been wasted in the service of this phantom. The horrors of witchcraft were all born of an ignorant belief in the existence of a totally depraved being superior to nature, acting in perfect independence of her laws; and all religious superstition has had for its basis a belief in at least two beings, one good and the other bad, both of whom could arbitrarily change the order of the universe. The history of religion is simply the story of man's efforts in all ages to avoid one of these powers and to pacify the other. Both powers have inspired little else than abject fear. The cold, calculating sneer of the devil, and the frown of God, were equally terrible. In any event, man's fate was to be arbitrarily fixed forever by an unknown power superior to all law, and to all fact. Until this belief is thrown aside, man must consider himself the slave of phantom masters—neither of whom promise liberty in this world nor in the next.

Man must learn to rely upon himself. Reading bibles will not protect him from the blasts of winter, but houses, fires, and clothing will. To prevent famine, one plow is worth a million sermons, and even patent medicines will cure more diseases than all the prayers uttered since the beginning of the world.

Although many eminent men have endeavored to harmonize necessity and free will, the existence of evil, and the infinite power and goodness of God, they have succeeded only in producing learned and ingenious failures. Immense efforts have been made to reconcile ideas utterly inconsistent with the facts by which we are surrounded, and all persons who have failed to perceive the pretended reconciliation, have been denounced as infidels, atheists and scoffers. The whole power of the church has been brought to bear against philosophers and scientists in order to compel a denial of the authority of demonstration,—and to induce some Judas to betray Reason, one of the saviors of mankind.

During that frightful period known as the "Dark Ages," Faith reigned, with scarcely rebellious subject. Her temples were "carpeted with knees," and the wealth of nations adorned her countless shrines. The great painters prostituted their genius to immortalize her vagaries, while the poets enshrined them in song. At her bidding, man covered the earth with blood. The scales of justice were turned with gold, and for her use were invented all the cunning instruments of pain. She built cathedrals for God, and dungeons for men. She peopled the clouds with angels and the earth with slaves. For centuries the world was retracing its steps—going steadily back toward, barbaric night! A few infidels—a few heretics cried, "Halt!" to the great rabble of ignorant devotion, and made it possible for the genius of the nineteenth century to revolutionize the cruel creeds and superstitions of mankind.

The thoughts of man, in order to be of any real worth, must be free. Under the influence of fear the brain is paralyzed, and instead of bravely solving a problem for itself, tremblingly adopts the solution of another. As long as a majority of men will cringe to the very earth before some petty prince or king, what must be the infinite abjectness of their little souls in the presence of their supposed creator and God? Under such circumstances, what can their thoughts be worth?

The originality of repetition, and the mental vigor of acquiescence, are all that we have any right to expect from the Christian world. As long as every question is answered by the word "God," scientific inquiry is simply impossible. As fast as phenomena are satisfactorily explained the domain of the power, supposed to be superior to nature must decrease, while the horizon of the known must as constantly continue to enlarge.

It is no longer satisfactory to account for the fall and rise of nations by saying, "It is the will of God." Such an explanation puts ignorance and education upon exact equality, and does away with the idea of really accounting for anything whatever.

Will the religionist pretend that the real end of science is to ascertain how and why God acts? Science, from such a standpoint, would consist in investigating the law of arbitrary action, and in a grand endeavor to ascertain the rule necessarily obeyed by infinite caprice.

From a philosophical point of view, science is knowledge of the laws of life; of the condition of happiness; of the facts by which we are surrounded, and the relations we sustain to men and things—by means of which man, so to speak, subjugates nature and bends the elemental powers to his will, making blind force the servant of his brain.

A belief in special providence does away with the spirit of investigation, and is inconsistent with personal efforts. Why should man endeavor to thwart the designs of God? "Which of you, with taking thought, can add to his stature one cubit?" Under the influence of this belief, man, basking in the sunshine of a delusion, considers the lilies of the field and refuses to take any thought for the morrow. Believing himself in the power of an infinite being, who can, at any moment, dash him to the lowest hell or raise him to the highest heaven, he necessarily abandons the idea of accomplishing anything by his own efforts. So long as this belief was general, the world was filled with ignorance, superstition and misery. The energies of man were wasted in a vain effort to obtain the aid of this power, supposed to be superior to nature. For countless ages, even men were sacrificed upon the altar of this impossible god. To please him, mothers have shed the blood of their own babies; martyrs have chanted triumphant songs in the midst of flames; priests have gorged themselves with blood; nuns have forsworn the ecstasies of love; old men have tremblingly implored; women have sobbed and entreated; every pain has been endured, and every horror has been perpetrated.

Through the dim long years that have fled, humanity has suffered more than can be conceived. Most of the misery has been endured by the weak, the loving and the innocent. Women have been treated like poisonous beasts, and little children trampled upon as though they had been vermin. Numberless altars have been reddened, even with the blood of babies; beautiful girls have been given to slimy serpents; whole races of men doomed to centuries of slavery, everywhere there has been outrage beyond the power of genius to express. During all these years the suffering have supplicated; the withered lips of famine have prayed; the pale victims have implored, and heaven has been deaf and blind.

Of what use have the gods been to man?

It is no answer to say that some god created the world, established certain laws, and then turned his attention to other matters, leaving his children, weak, ignorant and unaided, to fight the battle of life alone. It is no solution to declare that in some other world this god will render a few or even all of his subjects happy. What right have we to expect that a perfectly wise, good and powerful being will ever do better than he has done, and is doing? The world is filled with imperfections. If it was made by an infinite being, what reason have we for saying that he will render it nearer perfect than it now is? If the infinite Father allows a majority of his children to live in ignorance and wretchedness now, what evidence is there that he will ever improve their condition? Will god have more power? Will he become more merciful? Will his love for his poor creatures increase? Can the conduct of infinite wisdom, power and love ever change? Is the infinite capable of any improvement whatever.

We are informed by the clergy that this world is a kind of school; that the evils by which we are surrounded are for the purpose of developing our souls, and that only by suffering can men become pure, strong, virtuous and grand.

Supposing this to be true, what is to become of those who die in infancy? The little children, according to this philosophy, can never be developed. They were so unfortunate as to escape the ennobling influences of pain and misery, and as a consequence, are doomed to an eternity of mental inferiority. If the clergy are right on this question, none are so unfortunate as the happy, and we should envy only the suffering and distressed. If evil is necessary to the development of man, in this life, how is it possible for the soul to improve in the perfect joy of paradise?

Since Paley found his watch, the argument of "design" has been relied upon as unanswerable. The Church teaches that this world, and all that it contains, were created substantially as we now see them, that the grasses, the flowers, the trees, and all animals, including man, were special creations, and that they sustain no necessary relation to each other. The most orthodox will admit that some earth has been washed into the sea, that the sea has encroached a little upon the land, and that some mountains may be a trifle lower than in the morning of creation. The theory of gradual development was unknown to our fathers; the idea of evolution did not occur to them. Our fathers looked upon the then arrangement of things as the primal arrangement. The earth appeared to them fresh from the hands of a deity. They knew nothing of the slow evolutions of countless years, but supposed that the almost infinite variety of vegetable and animal forms had existed from the first.

Suppose that upon some island we should find a man a million years of age, and suppose that we should find him in the possession of a most beautiful carriage, constructed upon the most perfect model. And suppose further, that he should tell us that it was the result of several hundred thousand years of labor and of thought; that for fifty thousand years he used as flat a log as he could find, before it occurred to him that by splitting the log he could have the same surface with only half the weight; that it took him many thousand years to invent wheels for this log; that the wheels he first used were solid, and that fifty thousand years of thought suggested the use of spokes and tire; that for many centuries he used the wheels without linch-pins: that it took a hundred thousand years more to think of using four wheels, instead of two; that for ages he walked behind the carriage, when going down hill, in order to hold it back, and that only by a lucky chance he invented the tongue; would we conclude that this man, from the very first, had been an infinitely ingenious and perfect mechanic? Suppose we found him living in an elegant mansion, and he should inform us that he lived in that house for five hundred thousand years before he thought of putting on a roof, and that he had but recently invented windows and doors; would we say that from the beginning he had been an infinite accomplished and scientific architect.

Does not an improvement in the things created, show the corresponding improvement in the creator?

Would an infinitely wise, good and powerful God, intending to produce man, commence with the lowest possible forms of life; with the simplest organism that can be imagined, and during immeasurable periods of time, slowly and almost imperceptibly improve upon the rude beginning, until man was evolved? Would countless ages thus be wasted in the production of awkward forms, afterward abandoned? Can the intelligence of man discover the least wisdom in covering the earth with crawling, creeping horrors, that live only upon the agonies and pangs of others? Can we see the propriety of so constructing the earth, that only an insignificant portion of its surface is capable of producing an intelligent man? Who can appreciate the mercy of so making the world that all animals devour animals? so that every mouth is a slaughter-house, and every stomach a tomb? Is it possible to discover infinite intelligence and love in universal and eternal carnage?

What would we think of a father, who should give a farm to his children, and before giving them possession should plant upon it thousands of deadly shrubs and vines; should stock it with ferocious beasts; and poisonous reptiles; should take pains to put a few swamps in the neighborhood to breed malaria; should so arrange matters, that the ground would occasionally open and swallow a few of his darlings, and besides all this, should establish a few volcanoes in the immediate vicinity, that might at any moment overwhelm his children with rivers of fire? Suppose that this father neglected to tell his children which of the plants were deadly; that the reptiles were poisonous; failed to say anything about the earthquakes, and kept the volcano business a profound secret; would we pronounce him angel or fiend?

And yet this is exactly what the orthodox God has done.

According to the theologians, God prepared this globe expressly for the habitation of his loved children, and yet he filled the forests with ferocious beasts; placed serpents in every path; stuffed the world with earthquakes, and adorned its surface with mountains of flame.

Notwithstanding all this, we are told that the world is perfect; that it was created by a perfect being, and is therefore necessarily perfect. The next moment, these same persons will tell us that the world was cursed; covered with brambles, thistles and thorns, and that man was doomed to disease and death, simply because our poor, dear mother ate an apple contrary to the command of an arbitrary God.

A very pious friend of mine, having heard that I had said the world was full of imperfections, asked me if the report was true. Upon being informed that it was, he expressed great surprise that any one could be guilty of such presumption. He said that, in his judgment, it was impossible to point out an imperfection. "Be kind enough," said he, "to name even one improvement that you could make, if you had the power." "Well," said I, "I would make good health catching, instead of disease."

The truth is, it is impossible to harmonize all the ills, and pains, and agonies of this world with the idea that we were created by, and are watched over and protected by an infinitely wise, powerful and beneficent God, who is superior to and independent of nature.

The clergy, however, balance all the real ills of this life with the expected joys of the next. We are assured that all is perfection in heaven—there the skies are cloudless—there all is serenity and peace. Here empires may be overthrown; dynasties may be extinguished in blood; millions of slaves may toil 'neath the fierce rays of the sun, and the cruel strokes of the lash; yet all is happiness in heaven. Pestilence may strew the earth with corpses of the loved; the survivors may bend above them in agony—yet the placid bosom of heaven is unruffled. Children may expire vainly asking for bread; babies may be devoured by serpents, while the gods sit smiling in the clouds. The innocent may languish unto death in the obscurity of dungeons; brave men and heroic women may be changed to ashes at the bigot's stake, while heaven is filled with song and joy. Out on the wide sea, in darkness and in storm, the shipwrecked struggle with the cruel waves, while the angels play upon their golden harps. The streets of the world are filled with the diseased, the deformed and the helpless; the chambers of pain are crowded with the pale forms of the suffering, while the angels float and fly in the happy realms of day. In heaven they are too happy to have sympathy; too busy singing to aid the imploring and distressed. Their eyes are blinded; their ears are stopped and their hearts are turned to stone by the infinite selfishness of joy. The saved mariner is too happy when he touches the shore to give a moment's thought to his drowning brothers. With the indifference of happiness, with the contempt of bliss, heaven barely glances at the miseries of earth. Cities are devoured by the rushing lava; the earth opens and thousands perish; women raise their clasped hands towards heaven, but the gods are too happy to aid their children. The smiles of the deities are unacquainted with the tears of men. The shouts of heaven drown the sobs of earth.

 Having shown how man created gods, and how he became the trembling slave of his own creation, the questions naturally arise: How did he free himself even a little, from these monarchs of the sky, from these despots of the clouds, from this aristocracy of the air? How did he, even to the extent that he has, outgrow his ignorant, abject terror, and throw off, the yoke of superstition?

 Probably, the first thing that tended to disabuse his mind was the discovery of order, of regularity, of periodicity in the universe. From this he began to suspect that everything did not happen purely with reference to him. He noticed, that whatever he might do, the motions of the planets were always the same; that eclipses were periodical, and that even comets came at certain intervals. This convinced him that eclipses and comets had nothing to do with him, and that his conduct had nothing to do with them. He perceived that they were not caused for his benefit or injury. He thus learned to regard them with admiration instead of fear. He began to suspect that famine was not sent by some enraged and revengeful deity but resulted often from the neglect and ignorance of man. He learned that diseases were not produced by evil spirits. He found that sickness was occasioned by natural causes, and would be cured by natural means. He demonstrated, to his own satisfaction at least, that prayer is not a medicine. He found by sad experience that his gods were of no practical use, as they never assisted him, except when he was perfectly able to help himself. At last, he began to discover that his individual action had nothing whatever to do with strange appearances in the heavens; that it was impossible for him to be bad enough to cause a whirlwind, or good enough to stop one. After many centuries of thought, he about half concluded that making mouths at a priest would not necessarily cause an earthquake. He noticed, and no doubt with considerable astonishment, that very good men were occasionally struck by lightning, while very bad ones escaped. He was frequently forced to the painful conclusion (and it is the most painful to which any human being ever was forced) that the right did not always prevail. He noticed that the gods did not interfere in behalf of the weak and innocent. He was now and then astonished by seeing an unbeliever in the enjoyment of most excellent health. He finally ascertained that there could be no possible connection between an unusually severe winter and his failure to give sheep to a priest. He began to suspect that the order of the universe was not constantly being changed to assist him because he repeated a creed. He observed that some children would steal after having been regularly baptized. He noticed a vast difference between religions and justice, and that the worshipers of the same God took delight in cutting each other's throats. He saw that these religious disputes filled the world with hatred and slavery. At last he had the courage to suspect, that no God at any time interferes with the order of events. He learned a few facts, and these facts positively refused to harmonize with the ignorant superstitions of his fathers. Finding his sacred books incorrect and false in some particulars, his faith in their authenticity began to be shaken; finding his priests ignorant on some points, he began to lose respect for the cloth. This was the commencement of intellectual freedom.

The civilization of man has increased just to the same extent that religious power has decreased. The intellectual advancement of man depends upon how often he can exchange an old superstition for a new truth. The Church never enabled a human being to make even one of these exchanges; on the contrary, all her power has been used to prevent them. In spite, however, of the Church, man found that some of his religious conceptions were wrong. By reading his bible, he found that the ideas of his God were more cruel and brutal than those of the most depraved savage. He also discovered that this holy book was filled with ignorance, and that it must have been written by persons wholly unacquainted with the nature of the phenomena by which we are surrounded; and now and then, some man had the goodness and courage to speak his honest thoughts. In every age some thinker, some doubter, some investigator, some hater of hypocrisy, some despiser of sham, some brave lover of the right, has gladly, proudly and heroically braved the ignorant fury of superstition for the sake of man and truth. These divine men were generally torn in pieces by the worshipers of the gods. Socrates was poisoned because he lacked reverence for some of the deities. Christ was crucified by the religious rabble for the crime of blasphemy. Nothing is more gratifying to a religionist than to destroy his enemies at the command of God. Religious persecution springs from a due admixture of love towards God and hatred towards man.

The terrible religious wars that inundated the world with blood tended at least to bring all religion into disgrace and hatred. Thoughtful people began to question the divine origin of a religion that made its believers hold the rights of others in absolute contempt. A few began to compare Christianity with the religions of heathen people, and were forced to admit that the difference was hardly worth dying for. They also found that other nations were even happier and more prosperous than their own. They began to suspect, that their religion, after all, was not of much real value.

For three hundred years the Christian world endeavored to rescue from the "Infidel" the empty sepulchre of Christ. For three hundred years the armies of the cross were baffled and beaten by the victorious hosts of an impudent impostor. This immense fact sowed the seeds of distrust throughout all Christendom, and millions began to lose confidence in a God who had been vanquished by Mohammed. The people also found that commerce made friends where religion made enemies, and that religious zeal was utterly incompatible with peace between nations or individuals. The discovered that those who loved the gods most were apt to love men least; that the arrogance of universal forgiveness was amazing; that the most malicious had the effrontery to pray for their enemies, and that humility and tyranny were the fruit of the same tree.

For ages, a deadly conflict has been waged between a few brave men and women of thought and genius upon the one side, and the great ignorant religious mass on the other. This is the war between Science and Faith. The few have appealed to reason, to honor, to law, to freedom, to the known, and to happiness here in this world. The many have appealed to prejudice, to fear, to miracle, to slavery, to the unknown, and to misery hereafter. The few have said, "Think!" The many have said, "Believe!"

The first doubt was the womb and cradle of progress, and from the first doubt, man has continued to advance. Men began to investigate, and the church began to oppose. The astronomer scanned the heavens, while the church branded his grand forehead with the word, "Infidel"; and now, not a glittering star in all the vast expanse bears a Christian name. In spite of all religion, the geologist penetrated the earth, read her history in books of stone, and found hidden within her bosom, souvenirs of all the ages. Old ideas perished in the retort of the chemist, useful truths took their places. One by one religious conceptions have been placed in the crucible of science, and thus far, nothing but dross has been found. A new world has been discovered by the microscope; everywhere has been found the infinite; in every direction man has investigated and explored, and nowhere, in earth or stars, has been found the footstep of any being superior to or independent of nature. Nowhere has been discovered the slightest evidence of any interference from without. These are the sublime truths that enable man to throw off the yoke of superstition. These are the splendid facts that snatched the sceptre of authority from the hands of priests.

In the vast cemetery called the past are most of the religions of men, and there, too, are nearly all their gods. The sacred temples of India were ruins long ago. Over column and cornice; over the painted and pictured walls, cling and creep the trailing vines. Brahma, the golden, with four heads and four arms; Vishnu, the sombre, the punisher of the wicked, with his three eyes, his crescent, and his necklace of skulls; Siva, the destroyer, red with seas of blood; Kali, the goddess; Draupadi, the white-armed, and Chrishna, the Christ, all passed away and left the thrones of heaven desolate. Along the banks of the sacred Nile, Isis no longer wandering weeps, searching for the dead Osiris. The shadow of Typhon's scowl falls no more upon the waves. The sun rises as of yore, and his golden beams still smite the lips of Memnon, but Memnon is as voiceless as the Sphinx. The sacred fanes are lost in desert sands; the dusty mummies are still waiting for the resurrection promised by their priests, and the old beliefs, wrought in curiously sculptured stone, sleep in the mystery of a language lost and dead. Odin, the author of life and soul, Vili and Ve, and the mighty giant Ymir, strode long ago from the icy halls of the North; and Thor, with iron glove and glittering hammer, dashes mountains to the earth no more. Broken are the circles and cromlechs of the ancient Druids; fallen upon the summits of the hills, and covered with the centuries' moss, are the sacred cairns. The divine fires of Persia and of the Aztecs, have died out in the ashes of the past, and there is none to rekindle, and none to feed the holy flames. The harp of Orpheus is still; the drained cup of Bacchus has been thrown aside; Venus lies dead in stone, and her white bosom heaves no more with love. The streams still murmur, but no naiads bathe; the trees still wave, but in the forest aisles no dryads dance. The gods have flown from high Olympus. Not even the beautiful women can lure them back, and Danee lies unnoticed, naked to the stars. Hushed forever are the thunders of Sinai; lost are the voices of the prophets, and the land once flowing with milk and honey is but a desert and waste.

One by one, the myths have faded from the clouds; one by one, the phantom host has disappeared, and one by one facts, truths and realities have taken their places. The supernatural has almost gone, but the natural remains. The gods have fled, but man is here.

Nations, like individuals, have their periods of youth, of manhood and decay. Religions are the same. The same inexorable destiny awaits them all. The gods created by the nations must perish with their creators. They were created by men, and like men, they must pass away. The deities of one age are the by-words of the next. The religion of one day and country, is no more exempt from the sneer of the future than others have been. When India was supreme, Brahma sat upon the world's throne. When the scepter passed to Egypt, Isis and Osiris received the homage of mankind. Greece, with her fierce valor, swept to empire, and Zeus put on the purple of authority. The earth trembled with the tread of Rome's intrepid sons, and Jove grasped with mailed hand the thunderbolts of heaven. Rome fell, and Christians from her territory, with the red sword of war, carved out the ruling nations of the world, and now Christ sits upon the old throne. Who will be his successor?

Day by day, religious conceptions grow less and less intense. Day by day, the old spirit dies out of book and creed. The burning enthusiasm, the quenchless zeal of the early church have gone, never, never to return. The ceremonies remain, but the ancient faith is fading out of the human heart. The worn out arguments fail to convince, and denunciations that once blanched the faces of a race, excite in us only derision and disgust. As time rolls on, the miracles grow mean and small, and the evidences our fathers thought conclusive utterly fail to satisfy us. There is an "irrepressible conflict" between religion and science, and they cannot peaceably occupy the same brain nor the same world.

While utterly discarding all creeds, and denying the truth of all religions, there is neither in my heart nor upon my lips a sneer for the hopeful, loving and tender souls who believe that from all this discord will result a perfect harmony; that every evil will in some mysterious way become a good, and that above and over all there is a being who, in some way, will reclaim and glorify everyone of the children of men; but for those who heartlessly try to prove that salvation is almost impossible; that damnation is almost certain; that the highway of the universe leads to hell; who fill life with fear and death with horror; who curse the cradle and mock the tomb, it is impossible to entertain other than feelings of pity, contempt and scorn.

Reason, Observation and Experience—the Holy Trinity of Science—have taught us that happiness is the only good; that the time to be happy is now, and the way to be happy is to make others so. This is enough for us. In this belief we are content to live and die. If by any possibility the existence of a power superior to, and independent of, nature shall be demonstrated, there will then be time enough to kneel. Until then, let us stand erect.

Notwithstanding the fact that infidels in all ages have battled for the rights of man, and have at all times been the fearless advocates of liberty and justice, we are constantly charged by the Church with tearing down without building again. The Church should by this time know that it is utterly impossible to rob men of their opinions. The history of religious persecutions fully establishes the fact that the mind necessarily resists and defies every attempt to control it by violence. The mind necessarily clings to old ideas until prepared for the new. The moment we comprehend the truth, all erroneous ideas are of necessity cast aside.

A surgeon once called upon a poor cripple and kindly offered to render him any assistance in his power. The surgeon began to discourse very learnedly upon the nature and origin of disease; of the curative properties of certain medicines; of the advantages of exercise, air and light, and of the various ways in which health and strength could be restored. These remarks were so full of good sense, and discovered so much profound thought and accurate knowledge, that the cripple, becoming thoroughly alarmed, cried out, "Do not, I pray you, take away my crutches. They are my only support, and without them, I should be miserable, indeed." "I am not going," said the surgeon, "to take away your crutches. I am going to cure you, and then you will throw the crutches away yourself."

For the vagaries of the clouds, the infidels propose to substitute the realities of the earth; for superstition, the splendid demonstrations and achievements of science; and for the theological tyranny, the chainless liberty of thought.

We do not say we have discovered all; that our doctrines are the all in all in truth. We know of no end to the development of man. We cannot unravel the infinite complications of matter and force. The history of one monad is as unknown as that of the universe; one drop of water is as wonderful as all the seas; one leaf, as all the forests; and one grain of sand, as all the stars.

We are not endeavoring to chain the future, but to free the present. We are not forgoing fetters for our children, but we are breaking those our fathers made for us. We are the advocates of inquiry, of investigation and thought. This of itself, is an admission that we are not perfectly satisfied with all our conclusions. Philosophy has not the egotism of faith. While superstition builds walls and creates obstructions, science opens all the highways of thought. We do not pretend to have circumnavigated everything, and to have solved all difficulties, but we do believe that it is better to love men than to fear gods, that it is grander and nobler to think and investigate for yourself than to repeat a creed. We are satisfied that there can be but little liberty on earth while men worship a tyrant in heaven. We do not expect to accomplish everything in our day; but we want to do what good we can, and to render all the service possible in the holy cause of human progress. We know that doing away with gods and supernatural persons and powers is not an end. It is a means to an end; the real end being the happiness of man.

Felling forests is not the end of agriculture. Driving pirates from the sea is not all there is of commerce.

We are laying the foundations of a grand temple of the future—not the temple of all the gods, but of all the people—wherein, with appropriate rites, will be celebrated the religion of Humanity. We are doing what little we can to hasten the coming of the day when society shall cease producing millionaires and mendicants—gorged indolence and famished industry—truth in rags, and superstition robed and crowned. We are looking for the time when the useful shall be the honorable; and when REASON, throned upon the world's brain, shall be the King of Kings, and God of Gods.

# INGERSOLL'S LECTURE ON GHOSTS.

Ladies and Gentlemen: In the first place, allow me to tender my sincere thanks to the clergy of this city. I feel that I am greatly indebted to them for this magnificent audience. It has been said, and I believe it myself, that there is a vast amount of intolerance in the church of today, but when twenty-four clergymen, three of whom, I believe, are bishops, act as my advance agents, without expecting any remuneration, or reward in this world, I must admit that perhaps I was mistaken on the question of intolerance. And I will say, further, that against those men I have not the slightest feeling in the world; every man is the product of his own surroundings; he is the product of every circumstance that has ever touched him; he is the product to a certain degree of the religion and creed of his day, and when men show the slightest intolerance I blame the creed, I blame the religion, I blame the superstition that forced them to do so. I do not blame those men.

Allow me to say, further, that this world is not, in my judgment, yet perfect. I am doing, in a very feeble way, to be sure, but I am still endeavoring, according to my Idea, to make this world just a little better; to give a little more liberty to men, a little more liberty to women. I believe in the government of kindness; I believe in truth, in investigation, in free thought. I do not believe that the hand of want will be eternally extended in the world; I do not believe that the prison will forever scar the ground; I do not believe that the shadow of the gallows will forever curse the earth; I do not believe that it will always be true that the men who do the most work will have the least to wear and the least to eat. I do believe that the time will come when liberty and morality and justice, like the rings of Saturn, will surround the world; that the world will be better, and every true man and every free man will do what he can to hasten the coming of the religion of human advancement.

I understand that for the thousands and thousands of years that have gone by, all questions have been settled by religion. I understand that during all this time the people have gotten their information from the sacerdotal class—

from priests. I know that when India was supreme they worshipped Brahma and Vishnu, and that when Rome held in its hand the red sword of war they worshipped Jove, and I know now that our religion has swept to the top. Any man living in India a few hundred or thousand years ago would have said, this is the only true religion. Why? Because here is the only true civilization. A man afterward living in Egypt would have said, this is the only true religion, because we have the best civilization; a Greek in Athens would have said this is the only true religion, and a Roman would have said we have the true religion, and now those religions all having died, although they were all true religions, we say ours is the only religion, because we are the greatest commercial nation in the world.

There will come other nations; there will come other religions. Man has made every religion in this world, in my judgment, and the religion, has been good or bad according as the men who made it were good or bad. If they were savages and barbarians, they made a God like the Jehovah of the Jews; if they were civilized, if they were kind and tender, they filled the heavens with kindness and love. Every man makes his own God. Show me the God a man worships, and I will tell you what kind of a man he is. Every one makes his own God, every one worships his own God; and if you are a civilized man you will have a civilized God, and we have been civilizing ours for hundreds and hundreds of years. He is getting better every day.

I am going to tell you tonight just exactly what I think. The other lecture I delivered here was my conservative lecture; this is my radical one! We even hear it suggested that our religion, our Bible, has given us all we have of prosperity and greatness and grandeur. I deny it! We have become civilized in spite of it, and I will show you tonight that the obstruction that every science has had is what we have been pleased to call our religion—or superstition. I had a conversation with a gentleman once—and these gentlemen are always mistaking something that goes along with a thing for the cause of the thing—and he stated to me that his particular religion was the cause of all advancement. I said to him: "No, Sir; the causes of all advancement, in my judgment, are plug hats and suspenders." And I said to him: "You go to Turkey, where they are semi-barbarians, and you won't find a pair of suspenders or a plug hat in all that country; you go to Russia, and you will find now and then a pair of suspenders at Moscow or St. Petersburg; you go on down till you strike Austria, and black hats begin; then you go on to Paris, Berlin and New York, and you will find everybody wears suspenders and everybody wears black hats. Wherever you find education and music there you will find black hats and suspenders." He said that any man who said to him that plug hats and suspenders had done more for mankind than the Bible and religion he would not talk to.

As a matter of fact, we are controlled today by men who do not exist. We are controlled today by phenomena that never did exist. We are controlled by ghosts and dead men, and in the grasp of death is a scepter that controls the living present. I propose that we shall govern ourselves! I propose that we shall let the past go, and let the dead past bury the dead past. I believe the American people have brains enough, and nerve enough, and courage enough, to control and govern themselves, without any assistance from dust or ghosts. That is my doctrine, and I am going to do what I can while I live to increase that feeling of independence and manhood in the American people.—We can control ourselves. I believe in the gospel of this world; I believe in happiness right here; I do not believe in drinking skim milk all my life with the expectation of butter beyond the clouds. I believe in the gospel, I say, in this world. This is a mighty good world. There are plenty of good people in this world. There is lots of happiness in this world and, I say, let us, in every way we can, increase it. I envy every man who is content with his lot, whether he is poor or whether he is rich. I tell you, the man that tries to make somebody else happy, and who owns his own soul, nobody having a mortgage or deed of trust upon his manhood or liberty—this world is a pretty good world for such a man. I do not care: I am going to say my say, whether I make money or grow poor; no matter whether I get high office or walk along the dusty highway of the common. I am going to say my say, and I had rather be a farmer and live on forty acres of land—live in a log cabin that I built myself, and have a little grassy path going down to the spring, so that I can go there and hear the waters gurgling, and know that it is coming out from the lips of the earth, like a poem, whispering to the white pebbles—I would rather live there, and have some hollyhocks at the corner of the house, and the larks singing and swinging in the trees, and some lattice over the window, so that the sunlight can fall checkered on the babe in the cradle. I had rather live there, and have the freedom of my own brain; I had rather do that than live in a palace of gold, and crawl, a slimy hypocrite, through this world. Superstition has done enough harm already; every religion, nearly, suspects everything that is pleasant, everything that is joyous, and they always have a notion that God feels best when we feel worst. They have chained the Andromeda of joy to the cold rock of ignorance and fear, there to be devoured by the dragon of superstition. Church and State are two vultures that have fed upon the heart of chained Prometheus. I say, let the human race have a chance let every man think for himself and express that thought. There is no wrath in the serene heavens; there is no scowl in the blue of the sky. Upon the throne of the universe tyranny does not sit as a king.

The speaker here took from his pocket a pair of spectacles, and adjusted them, saying: I am sorry to admit it; I have got to come to it. I hate to put on a pair of spectacles, but the other day, as I was putting them on, a thought struck me. I see progress in this. To progress is to overcome the obstacles of nature, and in order to overcome this obstacle of the loss of sight man invented spectacles. Spectacles led men to the telescope, with which he read all the starry heavens; and had it not been for the failure of sight we wouldn't have seen a millionth part that we have. In the first place, we owe nothing but truth to the dead. I am going to tell the truth about them. There are three theories by which men account for all phenomena—for everything that happens: First, the supernatural. In the olden time, everything that happened some deity produced, some spirit, some devil, some hobgoblin, some dryad, some fairy, some spook, something except nature. First, then, the supernatural; and a barbarian, looking at the wide, mysterious sea, wandering through the depths of the forest, encountering the wild beasts, troubled by strange dreams, accounted for everything by the action of spirits, good and bad. Second, the supernatural and natural. There is where the religious world is today—a mingling of the supernatural and natural, the idea being that God created the world and imposed upon men certain laws, and then let them run, and if they ever got into any trouble then he would do a miracle, and accomplish any good that he desired to do. Third—and that is the grand theory—the natural. Between these theories there has been from the dawn of civilization a conflict. In this great war nearly all the soldiers have been in the ranks of the supernatural. The believers in the supernatural insist that matter is controlled and directed entirely by powers from without. The naturalists maintain that nature acts from within; that nature is not acted upon; that the universe is all there is; that nature, with infinite arms, embraces everything that exists, and that the supposed powers beyond the limits of the materially real are simply ghosts.

You say, ah! this is materialism! this is the doctrine of matter! What is matter? I take a handful of earth in my hands, and into that dust I put seeds, and arrows from the eternal quiver of the sun smite it, and the seeds grow and bud and blossom, and fill the air with perfume in my sight. Do you understand that? Do you understand how this dust and these seeds and that light and this moisture produced that bud and that flower and that perfume?

Do you understand that any better than you do the production of thought? Do you understand that any better than you do a dream? Do you understand that any better than you do the thoughts of love that you see in the eyes of the one you adore? Can you explain it? Can you tell what matter is? Have you the slightest conception? Yet you talk about matter as though you were acquainted with its origin; as though you had compelled, with clenched hands, the very rocks to give up the secret of existence? Do you know what force is? Can you account for molecular action? Are you familiar with chemistry? Can you account for the loves and the hatreds of the atoms? Is there not something in matter that forever excludes you? Can you tell what matter really is? Before you cry materialism, you had better find what matter is. Can you tell of anything without a material basis? Is it possible to imagine the annihilation of a single atom? Is it possible for you to conceive of the creation of a single atom? Can you have a thought that is not suggested to you by what you call matter? Did any man or woman or child ever have a solitary thought, dream or conception, that was not suggested to them by something they had seen in nature? Can you conceive of anything the different parts of which have been suggested to you by nature? You can conceive of an animal with the hoofs of a bison, with the pouch of a kangaroo, with the head of a buffalo, with the tail of a lion, with the scales of a fish, with the wings of a bird, and yet every part of this impossible monster has been suggested to you by nature. You say time, therefore you can think eternity. You say pain, therefore you can think hell. You say strength, therefore you can think omnipotence. You say wisdom, therefore you can think infinite wisdom. Everything you see, everything you can dream of or think of, has been suggested to you by your surroundings, by nature. Man cannot rise above nature; below nature man cannot fall. Imagine, if you please, the creation of a single atom. Can any one here imagine the creation out of nothing of one atom? Can any one here imagine the destruction of one atom? Can you imagine an atom being changed to nothing? Can you imagine nothing being changed to an atom? There is not a solitary person here with an imagination strong enough to think either of the creation of an atom or of the annihilation of an atom.

Matter and the universe are the same yesterday, today and forever. There is just as much matter in the universe today as there ever was, and as there ever will be; there is just as much force and just as much energy as there ever was or ever will be; but it is continually taking different shapes and forms; one day it is a man, another day it is animal, another day it is earth, another day it is metal, another day it is gas, it gains nothing and it loses nothing. Our fathers denounced materialism and accounted for all phenomena how? By the caprice of gods and devils. For thousands of years it was believed that ghosts, good ghosts, bad ghosts, benevolent and malevolent, in some mysterious way produced all phenomena; that disease and health, happiness and misery, fortune and misfortune, peace and war, life and death, success and failure, were but arrows shot by those ghosts or shadowy phantoms, to reward or punish mankind; that they were displeased or pleased by our actions, that they blessed the earth with harvest or cursed it with famine; that they fed or starved the children of men; that they crowned or uncrowned kings; that they controlled war; that they gave prosperous voyages, allowing the brave mariner to meet his wife and children inside the harbor bar, or strewed the sad shore with wrecks of ships and the bodies of men. Formerly these ghosts were believed to be almost innumerable. Earth, air and water were filled with these phantoms, but in modern times they have greatly decreased in number, because the second proposition that I stated, the supernatural and the natural, has generally been adopted, but the remaining ghosts are supposed to perform the same functions as of yore.

Let me say right here that the object of every religion ever made by man has been to get on the good side of supposed powers; has been to petition the gods to stop the earthquakes, to stop famine, to stop pestilence. It has always been something that man should do to prevent being punished by the powers of the air or to get from them some favors. It has always been believed that these ghosts could in some way be appeased; that they could be bettered by sacrifices, by prayer, by fasting, by the building of temples and cathedrals, by shedding the blood of men and beasts, by forms, by ceremonies, by kneelings, by prostrations and flagellations, by living alone in the wild desert, by the practice of celibacy, by inventing instruments of torture, by destroying men, women and children, by covering the earth with dungeons, by burning unbelievers and by putting chains upon the thoughts and manacles upon the lips of men, by believing things without evidence, by believing things against evidence, by disbelieving and denying demonstrations, by despising facts, by hating reason, by discouraging investigation, by making an idiot of yourself—all these have been done to appease the winged monsters of the air.

In the history of our poor world no horror has been omitted, no infamy has been left undone by believers in ghosts, and all the shadows were born of cowardice and malignity; they were painted by the pencil of fear upon the canvas of ignorance by that artist called Superstition. From these ghosts our fathers received their information. These ghosts were the schoolmasters of our ancestors. They were the scientists, the philosophers, the geologists, the legislators, the astronomers, the physicians, the metaphysicians and historians of the past.

Let me give you my definition of metaphysics, that is to say, the science of the unknown, the science of guessing. Metaphysics is where two fools get together, and each one admits that neither can prove, and both say, "Hence we infer." That is the science of metaphysics. For this these ghosts were supposed to have the only experience and real knowledge; they inspired men to write books, and the books were sacred. If facts were found to be inconsistent with these books, so much the worse for the facts, and especially for the discoverers of these facts. It was then and still is believed that these sacred books are the basis of the idea of immortality, to give up the idea that these books were inspired is and to renounce the idea of immortal life. I deny it! Men existed before books; and all the books that were ever written were written, in my judgment, by men, and the idea of immortality was not born of a book, but was born of the man who wrote the book. The idea of immortality, like the great sea, has ebbed and flowed in the human heart, beating its countless waves of hope and joy against the shores of time, and was not born of any book, nor of any religion, nor of any creed; it was born of human affection, and it will continue to ebb and flow beneath the clouds and mists of doubt and darkness as long as love kisses the lips of death. It is the rainbow of hope shining upon the tears of grief. We love, therefore we wish to live, and the foundation of the idea of immortality is human affection and human love, and I have a thousand times more confidence in the affections of the human heart, in the deep and splendid feelings of the human soul than I have in any book that ever was or ever can be written by mortal man.

From the books written by those ghosts we have at least ascertained that they knew nothing whatever of the world in which we live. Did they know anything about any other? Upon every point where contradiction is possible, the ghosts have been contradicted. By these ghosts, by these citizens of the air, by this aristocracy of the clouds the affairs of government were administered all authority to govern came from them. The emperors, kings and potentates, every one of them, had the divine petroleum poured upon his head, the kerosene of authority.

The emperors, king and potentates had communications from the phantoms. Man was not considered as the source of power; to rebel against the king was to rebel against the ghosts, and nothing less than the blood of the offenders could appease the invisible phantoms and by the authority of the ghosts man was crushed and slayed and plundered. Many toiled wearily in the sun and storm that a few favorites of the ghosts might live in idleness, and many lived in huts and caves and dens that the few might dwell in palaces, and many clothed themselves with rags that a few might robe themselves in purple and gold, and many crept and cringed and crawled that a few might tread upon their necks with feet of iron. From the ghosts men received not only authority but information. They told us the form of the earth; they informed us that eclipses were caused by the sins of man, especially the failure to pay tithes that the universe was made in six days; that gazing at the sky with a telescope was dangerous; that trying to be wise beyond what they had written was born of a rebellious and irreverent spirit; they told us there was no virtue like belief; no crime like doubt, that investigation was simply impudence, and the punishment therefore violent torment; they not only told us all about this world but about two others, and if their statements about the other two are as true as they were about this, no one can estimate the value of their information.

For countless ages the world was governed by ghosts, and they spared no pains to change the eagle of the human intellect into a bat of darkness. To accomplish this infamous purpose, to drive the love of truth from the human heart; to prevent the advancement of mankind to shut out from the world every ray of intellectual light to pollute every mind with superstition, the power of kings, the cunning and cruelty of priests, and the wealth of nations were used.

In order to show you the information we got from the ghosts, and the condition of the world when the ghosts were the kings, let me call your attention to this: During these years of persecution, ignorance, superstition and slavery, nearly all the people, the kings, lawyers and doctors, learned and unlearned, believed in that frightful production of ignorance, of fear and faith, called witchcraft. Witchcraft today is religion carried out. They believed that man was the sport and prey of devils; that the very air was thick with these enemies of man, and, with few exceptions, this hideous belief was universal. Under these conditions progress was almost impossible. Fear paralyzed the brain.

Progress is born of courage. Fear believes, courage doubts. Fear falls upon the earth and prays; courage stands erect and thinks. Fear retreats; courage advances. Fear is barbarism, courage is civilization. Fear believes in witchcraft; courage in science and in eternal law. The facts upon which this terrible belief rested were proved over and over again in nearly every court in Europe. Thousands confessed themselves guilty, admitted they had sold themselves to the devil. They gave the particulars of the sale; told what they said and what the devil replied. They confessed themselves guilty when they knew that confession was death; knew that their property would be confiscated and their children left to beg their bread. This is one of the miracles of history, one of the strangest contradictions of the human mind. Without doubt they really believed themselves guilty.

In the first place, they believed in witchcraft as a fact, and when charged with it, they became insane. They had read the account of the witch of Endor calling up the dead body of Samuel. He is an old man; he has his mantle on. They had read the account of Saul stooping to the earth and conversing with the spirit that had been called from the region of space by a witch. They had read a command from the Almighty, "Thou shalt not suffer a witch to live," and they believed the world was full of witches, or else the Almighty Would not have made a law against them. They believed in witchcraft, and when they were charged with it, they probably became insane, and in their insanity they confessed their guilt. They found themselves abhorred and deserted, charged with a crime they could not disprove. Like a man in quicksand, every effort only sunk them deeper. Caught in this frightful web, at the mercy of the devotees of superstition, hope fled and nothing remained but the insanity of confession.

The whole world appeared insane. In the time of James I, a man was burned for causing a storm at sea, with the intention of drowning one of the royal family, but I do not think it would have been much of a crime if he had been really guilty. How could he disprove it? How could he show that he did not cause a storm at sea? All storms were at that time supposed to be inspired by the devil; the people believed that all storms were caused by him, or by persons whom he assisted. I implore you to remember that the men who believed these things wrote our creeds and our confessions of faith, and it is by their dust that I am asked to kneel and pay implicit homage, instead of investigating; and I implore you to recollect that they wrote our creeds.

A woman was tried and convicted before Sir Matthew Hale, one of the greatest judges and lawyers of England, for having caused children to vomit crooked pins. Think of that! The learned judge charged the intelligent jury that there was no doubt as to the existence of witches, that it was established by all history and expressly taught by the Bible. The woman was hung and her body was burned. Sir Thomas Moore declared that to give up witchcraft was to throw away the sacred scriptures. John Wesley, too, was a firm believer in ghosts, and insisted upon their existence after all laws upon the subject had been repealed in England, and I beg of you to remember that John Wesley was the founder of the Methodist Church. In New England a woman was charged with being a witch and with having changed herself into a fox; while in that condition she was attacked and bitten by some dogs, and a committee of three men was ordered by the Court to examine this woman. They removed her clothing, and searched for what they were pleased to call witch-spots—that is to say, spots into which a needle could be thrust without giving pain; they reported to the Court that such spots were found. She denied that she had ever changed herself into a fox. On the report of the committee she was found guilty, and she was actually executed by our Puritan fathers, the gentlemen who braved the danger of the deep for the sake of worshiping God and persecuting their fellow men. I belong to their blood, and the best thing I can say about them, and that which rises like a white shaft to their eternal honor, is that they were in favor of education.

A man was attacked by a wolf; he defended himself and succeeded in cutting off one of the animal's paws, and the wolf ran away; he put it in his pocket and carried it home; there he found his wife with one of her hands gone, and he took that paw from his pocket and put it upon her arm, and it assumed the appearance of a human hand, and he charged his wife with being a witch. She was tried, she confessed her guilt, and she was hung and her body was burned! My! is it possible? Did not somebody say something against such an infamous proceeding? Yes, they did! There was a Young Men's Association who invited a man to come and give his ideas upon the subject.

He denounced it. He said it was outrageous, that it was nonsensical, that it was infamous and the moment he went away the young men met and passed a resolution that he had deceived them; and the clergy at that time protested and said, of course, let the man think, if you call that kind of stuff thinking.

But there was one man belonging to this Association who had the courage to stand by the truth.

Whether he believed in what the speaker said or not, he had that manliness; and I take this opportunity to thank from the bottom of my heart a man. I have no idea he agrees with me except in this: Whatever you do, do it like a man and be honest about it.

People were burned for causing frost in summer; for destroying crops with hail; for causing storms—for making cows go dry; for souring beer; for putting the devil in emptyings so that they would not rise. The life of no one was secure. To be charged was to be convicted. Every man was at the mercy of every other. This infamous belief was so firmly seated in the minds of the people, that, to express a doubt as to its existence was to be suspected yourself. They believed that animals were often taken possession of by devils, and they believed that the killing of the animal would destroy the devil. They absolutely tried, convicted and executed dumb beasts.

At Vail, in 1470, a rooster was tried upon the charge of having laid an egg, and the clergy said they had no doubt of it. Rooster eggs were used only in making witch-ointment. This everybody knew. The rooster was convicted, and with all due solemnity, he was burned in the public square.

So a hog and six pig died for having killed and partially eaten a child. The hog was convicted, but the pigs, on account of their extreme youth, were acquitted.

As late as 1740, a cow, charged with being possessed of a devil, was tried and was convicted. They used to exorcise rats, snakes and vermin; they used to go through the alleys and streets and fields and warn them to leave within a certain number of days, and if they did not leave, they threatened them with certain pains and penalties which they proceeded to recount.

But let us be careful how we laugh about those things; let us not pride ourselves too much on the progress of our age. We must not forget that some of our people are yet in the same intelligent business. Only a little while ago the Governor of Minnesota appointed a day of fasting and prayer to see if the Lord could not be induced to kill the grasshoppers—or send them into some other State.

About the close of the fifteenth century was the excitement in regard to witchcraft, and Pope Innocent the Eighth issued a bull directing the inquisitors to be vigilant in searching out and punishing all guilty of this crime. Forms for the crime were regularly issued. For two hundred and fifty years the church was busy in punishing the impossible crime of witchcraft by burning, hanging and torturing men, women and little children.

Protestants were as active as Catholics; and in Geneva five hundred witches were burned at the stake in three months, and one thousand were executed in one year in the diocese of Couro; at least one hundred thousand victims suffered in Germany, the last execution being in Galesburgh, and taking place in 1794, and the last in Switzerland, 1780. In England statutes were passed from Henry VI to James I, defining the crime and punishment, and the last act passed in the British Parliament was when Lord Bacon was a member of the house.

In 1716 Mrs. Hicks and daughter, nine years of age, were hung for selling their souls to the devil; and raising a storm at sea by pulling off their stockings and making a lather of soap. In England it has been estimated that at least 30,000 were hung or burned. The last victim executed in Scotland was 1722. She was an innocent old woman who had so little idea of her condition, that she rejoiced at the sight of the fire destined to consume her to ashes. She had a daughter, lame in her hands, a circumstance accounted for from the fact that the witch had been used to transfer her daughter into a pony and get her shod by the devil! Intelligent ancestors!

In 1692 nineteen persons were executed in Salem, Massachusetts, for the crime of witchcraft. It was thought in those days that men and women made contracts with the devil, and those contracts were confirmed at a meeting of witches and ghosts, over which the devil presided; these contracts in some cases were for a few years, others for life. General assemblages of witches were held once a year. To these they rode from great distances on brooms and dogs, and there they did homage to the prince of hell and offered him sacrifices.

In 1836 the populace of Holland plunged into the sea a woman reputed to be a sorceress, and as the miserable woman persisted in rising to the surface, she was pronounced guilty, and was beaten to death. It was believed that the devil could transform people into any shape he pleased, and whoever denounced this idea was denounced as an Infidel; that the believers in witchcraft appealed to the devil; that with the devil were associated innumerable spirits, who ranged over the world endeavoring to torment mankind; that these spirits possessed a power and wisdom transcending the limits of human faculties. They believed the devil could carry persons hundreds of miles in a few seconds; they believed this because they knew that Christ had been carried by the devil, in the same manner, into a high mountain, and placed upon a pinnacle. According to their account, the prince of the air had absolutely taken the God of this infinite Universe, the Creator of all its shining, wheeling stars—he had been absolutely taken by the devil to a pinnacle of the temple, and there had been tempted by the devil to cast himself to the earth.

Take from the church itself the threat and fear of hell and it becomes an extinct volcano. With the doctrine of hell taken from the Church, that is the end of the fall of man, that is the end of the scheme of atonement. Take from them the idea of an eternal place of torment, and the Church is thrown back simply upon facts.

And Dean Stanley, the leading ecclesiastic of Great Britain, only the other day in Winchester Abbey, said science will be the only theology of the future. Morality is the only religion of the years to come. Not withstanding all the infamous things laid to the charge of the Church, we are told that the civilization of today is the child of what we are pleased to call superstition. Let me call your attention to what they received from their fears of these ghosts. Let me give you an outline of the sciences as taught by those philosophers. There is one thing that a man is interested in, if he is in anything, and that is in the science of medicine. A doctor is, so to speak, in partnership with Nature. He is a preserver if he is worthy of the name. And now I want to show what they have gotten from these ghosts upon the science of medicine.

According to them, all of the diseases were produced as a punishment by the good ghosts, or out of pure malignity by the bad ones. There were, properly speaking, no diseases; the sick were simply possessed by ghosts. The science of medicine consisted in knowing how to persuade these ghosts to vacate the premises and for thousands of years all diseases were treated with incantations, hideous noises, with the beating of drums and gongs; everything was done to make the position of a ghost as unpleasant as possible; and they generally succeeded in making things so disagreeable that if the ghost did not leave, the patient died. These ghosts were supposed to be different in rank, power and dignity. Now, then, a man pretended to have won the favor of some powerful ghost who gave him power over the little ones. Such a man became a very great physician. It was found that a certain kind of smoke was exceedingly offensive to the nostrils of your ordinary ghost. With this smoke the sick room would be filled until the ghost vanished or the patient died. It was also believed that certain words, when properly pronounced, were the most effective weapons, for it was for a long time supposed that Latin words were the best, I suppose because Latin was a dead language. For thousands of years medicine consisted in driving the devils out of men. In some instances bargains and promises were made with the ghosts. One case is given where a multitude of devils traded a man off for a herd of swine. In this transaction the devils were the losers, the swine having immediately drowned themselves in the sea. This idea of disease appears to have been almost universal and is not yet extinct. The contortions of the epileptic, the strange twitching of those afflicted with cholera, were all seized as proof that the bodies of men were filled with vile and malignant spirits. Whoever endeavored to account for these things by natural causes; whoever endeavored to cure disease by natural means was denounced as an Infidel. To explain anything was a crime. It was to the interest of the sacerdotal class that all things should be accounted for by the will and power of God and the devil. The moment it is admitted that all phenomena are within the domain of the natural, and that all the prayers in the world cannot change one solitary fact, the necessity for the priest disappears. Religion breathes the idea of miracles. Take from the minds of men the idea of the supernatural, and superstition ceases to exist; for this reason the Church has always despised the man who explains the wonderful. The moment that it began to be apparent that prayer could do nothing for the body, the priest shifted his ground and began praying for the soul.

After the devil was substantially abandoned in the practice of medicine, and when it was admitted that God had nothing to do with ordinary coughs and colds, it was still believed that all the diseases were sent by Him as punishment for the people; it was thought to be a kind of blasphemy to even stay the ravages of pestilence. Formerly, when a pestilence fell upon a people, the arguments of the priest were boundless. He told the people that they had refused to pay their tithes, and they had doubted some of the doctrines of the church, that in their hearts they had contempt for some of the priests of the Lord, and God was now taking his revenge, and the people, for the most part, believed this issue of falsehood, and hastened to fall upon their knees and to pour out their wealth upon the altars of hypocrisy.

The Church never wanted disease to be absolutely under the control of man. Timothy Dwight, president of Yale College, preached a sermon against vaccination. His idea was that if God had decreed that through all eternity certain men should die of small pox, it was a frightful sin to endeavor to prevent it; that plagues and pestilence were instruments in the hands of God with which to gain the love and worship of mankind; to find the cure for the disease was to take the punishment from the Church. No one tries to cure the ague with prayer because quinine has been found to be altogether more reliable. Just as soon as a specific is found for a disease, that disease is left out of the list of prayer. The number of diseases with which God from time to time afflicts mankind is continually decreasing, because the number of diseases that man can cure is continually increasing. In a few years all diseases will be under the control of man. The science of medicine has but one enemy—superstition. Man was afraid to save his body for fear he would lose his soul. Is it any wonder that the people in those days believed in and taught the infamous doctrine of eternal punishment, that makes God a heartless monster and man a slimy hypocrite and slave?

The ghosts were also historians, and wrote the grossest absurdities. They wrote as though they had been eye witnesses of every occurrence. They told all the past, they predicted all the future, with an impudence that amounted to sublimity. They said that the Tartars originally came from hell, and that they were called Tartars because that was one of the names of hell. These gentlemen accounted for the red on the breasts of robins from the fact that those birds used to carry water to the unhappy infants in hell. Other eminent historians say that Nero was in the habit of vomiting frogs. When I read that, I said some of the croakers of the present day would be better for such a vomit. Others say that the walls of a city fell down in answer to prayer. They tell us that King Arthur was not born like other mortals; that he had great luck in killing giants; that one of the giants that he killed wore clothes woven from the beards of kings that he had slain, and, to cap the climax, the authors of this history were rewarded for having written the only reliable history of their country. These are the men from whom we get our creeds and our confessions of faith.

In all the histories of those days there is hardly a truth. Facts were not considered of any importance. They wrote, and the people believed that the tracks of Pharaoh's chariot were still visible upon the sands of the Red Sea, and that they had been miraculously preserved as perpetual witnesses of the miracles that had been performed, and they said to any man who denied it, "Go there and you will find the tracks still upon the sand." They accounted for everything as the work of good and evil spirits; with cause and effect they had nothing to do. Facts were in no way related to each other. God, governed by infinite caprice, filled the world with miracles and disconnected events, and from his quiver came the arrows of pestilence and death. The moment the idea is abandoned that everything in this universe is natural—that all phenomena are the necessary links in the endless chain of being—the conception of history becomes impossible that the ghost of the present is not the child of the past; the present is not the mother of the future. In the domain of superstition all is accident and caprice; and do not, I pray you, forget that the writers of our creeds and confessions of faith believed this to be a world of chance. Nothing happens by accident; nothing happens by chance. In the wide universe everything is necessarily produced, every effect has behind it a cause, every effect is in its turn a cause, and there is in the wide domain of the infinite not room enough for a miracle.

When I say this, I mean this is my idea. I may be wrong, but that is my idea. It was believed by our intelligent ancestors that all law derived its greatness and force from the fact that it had been communicated to man by ghosts. Of course, it is not pretended that the ghosts told everybody the law, but they told it to a few, and the few told it to the people, and the people, as a rule, paid them exceedingly well for the trouble. It was a long time before the people commenced making laws for themselves, and, strange as it may appear, most of their laws are vastly superior to the ghost article. Through the web and woof of human legislation gradually began to run and shine and glitter the golden thread of justice.

During these years of darkness it was believed that, rather than see an act of injustice done, rather than see the guilty triumph, some ghost would interfere and I do wish, from the bottom of my heart, that that was the truth. There never was forced upon my heart a more frightful conviction than this—the right does not always prevail; there never was forced upon my mind a more cruel conclusion than this—innocence is not always a sufficient shield. I wish it was. I wish, too, that man suffered nothing but that which he brings upon himself and yet I find that in nine districts in India, between the 1st day of last January and the 1st day of June, 2,800,000 people starved to death, and that little children, with their lips upon the breasts of famine, died, wasted away. And why, simply because a little while before the wind did not veer the one hundredth part of a degree, and send clouds over the country, freighted with rain, freighted with love and joy. But if that wind had just turned that way there would have been happy men, women and children, all clad in the garments of health. I wish that I could know in my heart that there was some power that would see to it that men and women got exact justice somewhere. I do wish that I knew—the right would prevail—that innocence was an infinite shield.

During these years it was believed that rather than see an act of injustice done some ghost would interfere. This belief, as a rule, gave great satisfaction to the victorious party, and, as the other man was dead, no complaint was ever made by him. This doctrine was a sanctification of brute force and chance. Prisoners were made to grasp hot irons, and if it burned them their guilt was established. Others were tied hands and feet and cast into the sea, and if they sank, the verdict of guilt was unanimous; if they did not sink then they said water is such a pure element that it refuses to take a guilty person, and consequently he is a witch or wizard. Why, in England, persons accused of crime could appeal to the cross, and to a piece of sacramental bread. If he could swallow this without choking he was acquitted. And this practice was continued until the time of King Edward, who was choked to death; after which it was discontinued.

Ghosts and their followers always took delight in torturing with unusual pain any infraction of their laws, and generally death was the penalty. Sometimes, when a man committed only murder, he was permitted to flee to a place of refuge—murder being only a crime against man—but for saying certain words, or denying certain doctrines, or for worshiping wrong ghosts, or for failing to pray to the right one, or for laughing at a priest, or for saying that wine was not blood, or bread was not flesh, or for failing to regard rams' horns as artillery, or for saying that a raven as a rule, was a poor landlord, death, produced by all the ways that ingenuity or hatred could devise, was the penalty suffered by these men. I tell you tonight law is a growth; law is a science. Right and wrong exist in the nature of things. Things are not right because they are commanded; they are not wrong because they are prohibited. They are prohibited because we believe them wrong; they are commended because we believe them right. There are real crimes enough without creating artificial ones. All progress in legislation for a thousand years has consisted in repealing the laws of the ghosts. The idea of right and wrong is born of man's capacity to enjoy and suffer. If man could not suffer, if he could not inflict injury upon his brother, if he could neither feel nor inflict punishment, the idea of law, the idea of right, the idea of wrong, never could have entered into his brain. If man could not suffer, if he could not inflict suffering, the word conscience never would have passed the lips of man. There is one good—happiness. There is one sin—selfishness. All laws should be for the preservation of the one and the destruction of the other. Under the regime of the ghosts the laws were not understood to exist in the nature of things; they were supposed to be irresponsible commands, and these commands were not supposed to rest upon reason; they were simply the product of arbitrary will. These penalties for the violations of those laws were as cruel as the penalties were absurd. There were over two hundred offenses for which man was punished with death. Think of it! And these laws are said to have come from a most merciful God. And yet we have become civilized to that degree in this country that in the State of New York there is only one crime punishable with death. Think of it! Did I not tell you that we were now civilizing our gods? The tendency of those horrible laws, the tendency of those frightful penalties, was to blot the idea of justice from the human soul. Now, I want to show you how perfectly every department of human knowledge, or rather of ignorance, was saturated with superstition. I will for a moment refer to the science of language.

It was thought by our fathers that Hebrew was the original language; that it was taught to Adam and Eve in the Garden of Eden by the Almighty himself. Every fact inconsistent with that idea was thrown away. According to the ghosts, the trouble at the Tower of Babel accounted for the fact that all the people did not speak the Hebrew language. The Babel question settled all questions in the science of language. After a time so many facts were found to be so inconsistent with the Hebrew idea that it began to fall into disrepute, and other languages began to be used. Andrew Kent published a work on the science of language, in which he stated that God spoke to Adam, and Adam answered, in Hebrew, and that the serpent probably spoke to Eve in French. In 1580 another celebrated work was published at Antwerp, in which the whole matter was put at rest, showing beyond a doubt that the language spoken in Paradise was neither more nor less than plain Holland Dutch. Another celebrated writer, a contemporary of Sir Isaac Newton, discouraged the idea that all languages could be traced to one; he maintained that language was of natural growth; that we speak as naturally as we grow; we talk as naturally as sings a bird, or as blooms and blossoms a flower. Experience teaches us that this be so; words are continually dying and continually may being born—words are the garments of thought. Through the lapse of time some were as rude as the skins of wild beasts, and others pleasing and cultured like silk and gold. Words have been born of hatred and revenge, of love and self sacrifice and fear, of agony and joy the stars have fashioned them, and in them mingled the darkness and the dawn.

Every word that we get from the past is, so to speak, a mummy robed in the linen of the grave. They are the crystallizations of human history, of all that man enjoyed, of all that man has suffered, his victories and defeats, all that he has lost and won. Words are the shadows of all that has been; they are the mirrors of all that is. The ghosts also enlightened our fathers in astronomy and geology. According to them the world was made out of nothing, and a little more nothing having been taken than was used in the construction of the world, the stars were made out of the scraps that were left over. Cosmos, in the sixth century, taught that the stars were impelled by angels, who carried them upon their shoulders, rolled them in front of them, or drew them after. He also taught that each angel who pushed a star took great pains to observe what the other angels were doing, so that the relative distances between the stars might always remain the same.

He stated that this world was a vast body of water, with a strip of land on the outside; that Adam and Eve lived on the outer strip; that their descendants were drowned on the outer strip, all except Noah and his family; he accounted for night and day by saying that on the outer strip of land was a mountain, around which the sun revolved, producing darkness when it was hidden from sight, and daylight when it emerged; he also declared the earth to be flat. This he proved by many passages from the Bible; among other reasons for believing the earth to be flat he referred to a passage in the New Testament, which says that Christ shall come again in glory and power, and every eye shall see him, and said, now, if the world is round how are the people on the other side going to see Christ when he comes? That settled the question, and the church not only indorsed this book but declared that whoever believed either less or more was a heretic and would be dealt with as such.

In those blessed days ignorance was a king and science was an outcast. The church knew that the moment the earth ceased to be the center of the universe, and became a mere speck in the starry sphere of existence, every religion would become a thing of the past. In the name and by the authority of the ghosts, men enslaved their fellowmen; they trampled upon the rights of women and children. In the name and by the authority of ghosts, they bought and sold each other. They filled heaven with tyrants and the earth with slaves. They filled the present with intolerance and the future with horror. In the name and by the authority of the ghosts, they declared superstition to be the real religion. In the name and by the authority of the ghosts, they imprisoned the human mind; they polluted the conscience, they subverted justice, and they sainted hypocrisy. I have endeavored in some degree to show you what has been and always will be when men are governed by superstition.

When they destroy the sublime standard of reason; when they take the words of others and do not investigate them themselves, even the great men of those days appear nearly as weak as the most ignorant. One of the greatest men of the world, an astronomer second to none, discoverer of the three great laws that explain the solar system, was an astrologer and believed that he could predict the career of a man by finding what star was in the ascendant at his birth. He believed in what is called the music of the spheres, and he ascribed the qualities of the music—alto, bass, tenor and treble—to certain of the planets. Another man kept an idiot, whose words he put down and then put them together in such a manner as to make promises, and waited patiently to see that they were fulfilled. Luther believed he had actually seen the devil and discussed points of theology with him. The human mind was enchained. Every idea, almost, was a mystery. Facts were looked upon as worthless; only the wonderful was worth preserving. Devils were thought to be the most industrious beings in the universe, and with these imps every occurrence of an unusual character was connected. There was no order, certainty; everything depended upon ghosts and phantoms, and man, for the most part, considered himself at the mercy of malevolent spirits. He protected himself as best he could with holy water, and with tapers, and wafers, and cathedrals. He made noises to frighten the ghosts and music to charm them; he fasted when he was hungry and he feasted when he was not; he believed everything unreasonable; he humbled himself; he crawled in the dust; he shut the doors and windows; and excluded every ray of light from his soul; and he delayed not a day to repair the walls of his own prison; and from the garden of the human heart they plucked and trampled into the bloody dust the flowers and blossoms; they denounced man as totally depraved; they made reason blasphemy; they made pity a crime; nothing so delighted them as painting the torments and tortures of the damned. Over the worm that never dies they grew poetic. According to them, the cries ascending from hell were the perfume of heaven.

They divided the world into saints and sinners, and all the saints were going to heaven, and all the sinners yonder. Now, then, you stand in the presence of a great disaster. A house is on fire, and there is seen at a window the frightened face of a woman with a babe in her arms, appealing for help; humanity cries out: "Will someone go to the rescue?" They do not ask for a Methodist, a Baptist, or a Catholic; they ask for a man; all at once there starts from the crowd one that nobody ever suspected of being a saint; one may be, with a bad reputation; but he goes up the ladder and is lost in the smoke and flame; and a moment after he emerges, and the great circles of flame hiss around him; in a moment more he has reached the window; in another moment, with the woman and child in his arms, he reaches the ground and gives his fainting burden to the bystanders and the people all stand hushed for a moment, as they always do at such times, and then the air is rent with acclamations. Tell me that that man is going to be sent to hell, to eternal flames, who is willing to risk his life rather than a woman and child should suffer from the fire one moment! I despise that doctrine of hell! Any man that believes in eternal hell is afflicted with at least two diseases—petrifaction of the heart and petrifaction of the brain.

I have seen upon the field of battle a boy sixteen years of age struck by a fragment of a shell; I have seen him fall; I have seen him die with a curse upon his lips and the face of his mother in his heart. Tell me that his soul will be hurled from the field of battle where he lost his life that his country might live—where he lost his life for the liberties of man—tell me that he will be hurled from that field to eternal torment! I pronounce it an infamous lie. And yet, according to these gentlemen, that is to be the fate of nearly all the splendid fellows in this world.

I had in my possession a little while ago a piece of fresco that used to adorn a church at Stratford-on-Avon, the place where Shakespeare lived, and there was a picture representing the morning of the resurrection and people were getting out of their graves and devils were grabbing them by their heels. And there was an immense monster, with jaws open so wide that a man could walk down its throat, and the flames were issuing therefrom, and there were devils driving people in droves down the throat of this monster; and there was an immense kettle in which they had put these men, and the fire was being stirred under it, and hot pitch was being poured on top, and little devils were setting it on fire and then on the walls there were hundreds hung up by their tongues to hooks and nails; and then the saved—there were some five or six saved—upon the horizon, and they had a most self-satisfied grin of "I told you so."

At the risk of being tiresome, I have said that I have to show the direction of the human mind in slavery, the effects of widespread ignorance, and the result of fear. I want to convince you that every form of slavery, physical or mental, is a viper that will finally fill with poison the breast of any man alive. I want to show you that there should be republicanism in the domain of thought as well as in civil government. The first step toward progress is for man to cease to be the slave of the creatures of his creation. Men found at last that the event is more valuable than the prophecy, especially if it never comes to pass. They found that diseases were not produced by spirits; that they could not be cured by frightening them away. They found that death was as natural as life. They began to study the anatomy and chemistry of the human body, and they found that all was natural, and the conjurer and the sorcerer were dismissed, and the physician and surgeon were employed. They learned that being born under a star or planet had nothing to do with their luck; the astrologer was discharged and the astronomer took his place. They found that the world had swept through the constellation for millions of ages. They found that diseases were produced as easily as grass, and were not sent as punishment on men for failing to believe a creed. They found that man, through intelligence, could take advantage of the affairs of nature; that he could make the waves, the winds, the flames, and the lightnings slaves at his bidding to administer to his wants; they found the ghosts knew nothing of benefit to man; that they were entirely ignorant of history; that they were bad doctors and worse surgeons; that they knew nothing of the law and less of justice that they were poor politicians; that they were tyrants, and that they were without brains and utterly destitute of hearts.

The condition of this world during the dark ages shows exactly the result of enslaving the souls of men. In those days there was no liberty. Liberty was despised, and the laborer was considered but little above the beast. Ignorance, like a vast cowl, covered the brain of the world; superstition ran riot, and credulity sat upon the throne of the soul. Murder and hypocrisy were the companions of man, and industry was a slave. Every country maintained that it was no robbery to take the property of Mohammedans by force, and no murder to kill the owner. Lord Bacon was the first man who maintained that a Christian country was bound to keep its plighted faith with a Mohammedan nation. Every man who could read or write was suspected of being a heretic in those days. Only one person in 40,000 could read or write. All thought was discouraged. The whole earth was ruled by the mitre and sceptre, by the altar and throne, by fear and force, by ignorance and faith, by ghouls and ghosts. In the 15th century the following law was in force in England: "Whosoever reads the Scripture in the mother tongue shall forfeit land, cattle, life and goods, for themselves and their heirs forever, and should be condemned for heretics to God, enemies to the crown, and traitors to the land."

During the period this law was in force, thirty-nine were hanged and their bodies burned. In the 16th century men were burned because they failed to kneel to a procession of monks. Even the Reformers, so called, had no idea of liberty only when in the minority; the moment they were clothed with power, they began to exterminate with fire and sword. Castillo—and I want you to recollect it—was the first minister in the world that declared in favor of universal toleration. Castillo was pursued by John Calvin like a wild beast. Calvin said that such a monstrous doctrine he crucified Christ afresh, and they pursued that man until he died; recollect it! They can't do that now-a-days! You don't know how splendid I feel about the liberty I have. The horizon is filled with glory and the air is filled with wings. If there are any in this world who think they had better not tell what they really think because it will take bread from their little children, because it will take clothing from their families—don't do it! don't make martyrs of yourselves! I don't believe in martyrdom! Go right along with them; go to church and say amen as near the right place as you can. I will do your talking for you. They can't take the bread away from me. I will talk. Bodemus, a lawyer of France, wrote a few words in favor of freedom of conscience. Montaigne was the first to raise his voice against torture in France; but what was the voice of one man against the terrible cry of ignorant, infatuated, malevolent millions! I intend to do what little I can, and I am going to do it kindly. I am going to appeal to reason and to charity, to justice, to science, and to the future. For my part, I glory in the fact that in the New World, in the United States, liberty of conscience was first granted to man, and that the Constitution of the United States was the first great decree entered in the high court of human equity forever divorcing Church and State. It is the grandest step ever taken by the human race and the Declaration of Independence was the first document that retired ghosts from politics. It is the first document that said authority does not come from the phantoms of the air; authority is not from that direction; it comes from the people themselves. The Declaration of Independence enthroned man and dethroned the phantoms. You will ask what has caused this change in three hundred years. I answer, the inventions and discoveries of the few; the brave thoughts and heroic utterances of the few; the acquisition of a few facts; getting acquainted with our mother, Nature. Besides this, you must remember that every wrong in some way, tends to abolish itself. It is hard to make a lie last always. A lie will not fit the truth; it will only fit another lie told on purpose to fit it. Nothing but truth lives.

The nobles and the kings quarreled; the priests began to dispute, and the millions began to get their rights. In 1441 printing was discovered. At that time the past was a vast cemetery, without an epitaph. The ideas of men had mostly perished in the brains that had produced them. Printing gives an opening for thought; it preserves ideas; it made it possible for a man to bequeath to the world the wealth of his thoughts. About the same time, or a little before, the Moors had gone into Europe, and it can be truthfully said that science was thrust into the brain of Europe upon the point of a Moorish lance. They gave us paper, and what is printing without paper?

A bird without wings. I tell you paper has been a splendid thing.

The discovery of America, whose shores were trod by the restless feet of adventure and the people of every nation—out of this strange mingling of facts and fancies came the great Republic. Every fact has pushed a superstition from the brain and a ghost from the cloud. Every mechanical art is an educator; every loom, every reaper, every mower, every steamboat, every locomotive, every engine, every press, every telegraph is a missionary of science and an apostle of progress; every mill, every furnace with its wheels and levers, in which something is made for the convenience, for the use and the comfort and the well-being of man, is my kind of church, and every schoolhouse is a temple. Education is the most radical thing in this world. To teach the alphabet is to inaugurate a revolution; to build a schoolhouse is to construct a fort; every library is an arsenal filled with the weapons and ammunition of progress; every fact is a monitor with sides of iron and a turret of steel. I thank the inventors and discoverers. I thank Columbus and Magellan. I thank

Locke and Hume, Bacon and Shakespeare. I thank Fulton and Watt, Franklin and Morse, who made lightning the messenger of man. I thank Luther for protesting against the abuses of the Church, but denounce him because he was an enemy of liberty. I thank Calvin for writing a book in favor of religious freedom, but I abhor him because he burned Servetus. I thank the Puritans for saying that resistance to tyrants is obedience to God, and yet I am compelled to admit that they were tyrants themselves. I thank Thomas Paine because he was a believer in liberty. I thank Voltaire, that great man who for half a century was the intellectual monarch of Europe, and who, from his throne at the foot of the Alps, pointed the finger of scorn at every hypocrite in Christendom. I thank the inventors, I thank the discoverers, the thinkers and the scientists, and I thank the honest millions who have toiled. I thank the brave men with brave thoughts. They are the Atlases upon whose broad and mighty shoulders rests the grand fabric of civilization; they are the men who have broken, and are still breaking, the chains of superstition.

We are beginning to learn that to swap off a superstition for a fact, to ascertain the real, is to progress. All that gives us better bodies and minds and clothes and food and pictures, grander music, better heads, better hearts, and that makes us better husbands and wives and better citizens, all these things combined produce what we call the progress of the human race. Man advances only as he overcomes the obstacles of nature. It is done by labor and thought. Labor is the foundation. Without great labor it is impossible to progress. Without labor on the part of those who conduct all great industries of life, of those who battle with the obstacles of the sea, on the part of the inventors, the discoverers, and the brave, heroic thinkers, no surplus is produced; and from the surplus produced by labor, spring the schools and universities, the painters, the sculptors, the poets, the hopes, the loves and the aspirations of the world.

The surplus has given us the books. It has given us all there is of beauty and eloquence. I am aware there is a vast difference of opinion as to what progress is, and that many denounce my ideas. I know there are many worshipers of the past. They see no beauty in anything from which they do not blow the dust of ages with the breath of praise. They see nothing like the ancients; no orators, poets or statesmen like those who have been dust for thousands of years.

In a sermon on a certain evening, some time ago, the Rev. Dr. Magee of Albany, N. Y., stated that Colonel Ingersoll, referring to Jesus Christ, called him a "dirty little Jew." I denounce that as a dirty little lie.

I have as much reverence for any man who ever did what he believed was right, and died in order to benefit mankind, as any man in this world. Do they treat an opponent with fairness? Are they investigating? Do they pull forward or do they hold back? Is science indebted to the Church for a single fact? Let us know what it is. What church has been the asylum for a persecuted truth? What reform has been inaugurated by the Church? Did the Church abolish slavery? No. Who commenced it? Such men as Garrison and Pillsbury and Wendel Phillips. They were the titans that attacked the monster, and not a solitary one of them ever belonged to a church. Has the Church raised its voice against war? No. Are men restrained by superstition? Are men restrained by what you call religion? I used to think they were not; now I admit they are. No man has ever been restrained from the commission of a real crime, but from an artificial one he has. There was a man who committed murder. They got the evidence, but he confessed that he did it. "What did you do it for?" "Money." "Did you get any money?" "Yes." "How much?" "Fifteen cents." "What kind of a man was he?" "A laboring man I killed." "What did you do with the money?" "I bought liquor with it." "Did he have anything else?" "I think he had some meat and bread." "What did you do with that?" "I ate the bread and threw away the meat; it was Friday." So you see it will restrain in some things.

Just to the extent that man has freed himself from the dominion of ghosts he has advanced; to that extent he has freed himself from the tyrant's poison. Man has found that he must give liberty to others in order to have it himself. He has found that a master is a slave; that a tyrant is also a slave. He has found that governments should be administered by men for men; that the rights of all are to be protected; that woman is at least the equal for man; that men existed before books; that all creeds were made by men; that the few have a right to contradict what the pulpit asserts; that man is responsible to himself and to others. True religion must be free; without liberty the brain is a dungeon and the mind the convict. The slave may bow and cringe and crawl, but he cannot worship, he cannot adore. True religion is the perfume of the free and grateful air. True religion is the subordination of the passions to the intellect. It is not a creed; it is a life. The theory that is afraid of investigation is not deserving of a place in the human mind.

I do not pretend to tell what all the truth is. I do not pretend to have fathomed the abyss, nor to have floated on outstretched wings level with the heights of thought. I simply plead for freedom. I denounce the cruelties and horrors of slavery. I ask for light and air for the souls of men. I say, take off those chains—break those manacles—free those limbs—release that brain. I plead for the right to think—to reason—to investigate. I ask that the future may be enriched with the honest thoughts of men. I implore every human being to be a soldier in the army of progress. I will not invade the rights of others. You have no right to erect your toll-gates upon the highways of thought. You have no right to leap from the hedges of superstition and strike down the pioneers of the human race. You have no right to sacrifice the liberties of man upon the altars of ghosts. Believe what you may; preach what you desire; have all the forms and ceremonies you please; exercise your liberties in your own way, and extend to all others the same right.

I attack the monsters, the phantoms of imagination that have ruled the world. I attack slavery. I ask for room—room for the human mind.

Why should we sacrifice a real world that we have for one we know not of? Why should we enslave ourselves? Why should we forge fetters for our own hands? Why should we be the slaves of phantoms—phantoms that we create ourselves? The darkness of barbarism was the womb of these shadows. In the light of science they cannot cloud the sky forever. They have reddened the hands of man with innocent blood. They made the cradle a curse, and the grave a place of torment.

They blinded the eyes and stopped the ears of the human race. They subverted all the ideas of justice by promising infinite rewards for finite virtues, and threatening infinite punishment for finite offenses.

I plead for light, for air, for opportunity. I plead for individual independence. I plead for the rights of labor and of thought. I plead for a chainless future. Let the ghosts go—justice remains. Let them disappear—men, women and children are left. Let the monster fade away—the world remains, with its hills and seas and plains, with its seasons of smiles and frowns, its Springs of leaf and bud, its Summer of shade and flower, its Autumn with the laden boughs, when

> The withered banners of the corn are still,
> And gathered fields are growing strangely wan,
> While Death, poetic Death, with hands that color
> Whate'er they touch, weaves in the Autumn wood
> Her tapestries of gold and brown.

The world remains, with its Winters and homes and firesides, where grow and bloom the virtues of our race. All these are left; and music, with its sad and thrilling voice, and all there is of art and song and hope, and love and aspiration high. All these remain. Let the ghosts go—we will worship them no more.

Man is greater than these phantoms. Humanity is grander than all the creeds, than all the books. Humanity is the great sea, and these creeds and books and religions are but the waves of a day. Humanity is the sky, and these religions and dogmas and theories are but the mists and clouds, changing continually, destined finally to melt away.

Let the ghosts go. We will worship them no more. Let them cover their eyeless sockets with their fleshless hands, and fade forever from the imaginations of men.

# INGERSOLL'S LECTURE ON HELL

Ladies and Gentlemen: The idea of a hell was born of revenge and brutality on the one side, and cowardice on the other. In my judgment the American people are too brave, too charitable, too generous, too magnanimous to believe in the infamous dogma of an eternal hell. I have no respect for any human being who believes in it. I have no respect for the man who will pollute the imagination of childhood with that infamous lie. I have no respect for the man who will add to the sorrows of this world with the frightful dogma. I have no respect for any man who endeavors to put that infinite cloud, that infinite shadow, over the heart of humanity. I want to be frank with you. I dislike this doctrine, I hate it, I despise it; I defy this doctrine. For a good many years the learned intellects of christendom have been examining into the religions of other countries in the world, the religions of the thousands that have passed away. They examined into the religions of Egypt, the religion of Greece, the religion of Rome and of the Scandinavian countries. In the presence of the ruins of those religions the learned men of christendom insisted that those religions were baseless, that they are fraudulent. But they have all passed away. While this was being done the christianity of our day applauded, and when the learned men got through with the religions of other countries they turned their attention to our religion. By the same mode of reasoning, by the same methods, by the same arguments that they used with the old religions, they were overturning the religion of our day. Why? Every religion in this world is the work of man. Every one! Every book has been written by man. Men existed before the books. If books had existed before man, I might admit there was such a thing as a sacred volume.

In my judgment man has made every religion and made every book. There is another thing to which I wish to call your attention. Man never had an idea; man will never have an idea, except those supplied to him by his surroundings. Every idea in the world that man has, came to him by nature. Man cannot conceive of anything the hint of which you have not received from your surroundings. You can imagine an animal with the hoof of a bison, with the pouch of the kangaroo, with the wings of an eagle, with the beak of a bird, and with the tail of the lion; and yet every point of this monster you borrowed from nature. Every thing you can think of—every thing you can dream of, is borrowed from your surroundings—everything. And there is nothing on this earth coming from any other sphere whatever. Man has produced every religion in the world. And why? Because each generation bodes forth the knowledge and the belief of the people at the time it was made, and in no book is there any knowledge found, except that of the people who wrote it. In no book is there found any knowledge, except that of the time in which it was written. Barbarians have produced, and always will produce barbarian religions. Barbarians have produced, and always will produce ideas in harmony with their surroundings, and all the religions of the past were produced by barbarians—every one of them. We are making religions today. We are making religions to-night. That is to say, we are changing them, and the religion of to-day is not the religion of one year ago. What changed it? Science has done it; education and the growing heart of man has done it. We are making these religions every day, and just to the extent that we become civilized ourselves will we improve the religion of our fathers. If the religion of one hundred years ago, compared with the religion of to-day is so low, what will it be in one thousand years?

If we continue making the inroads upon orthodoxy which we have been making during the last twenty-five years, what will it be fifty years from to-night? It will have to be remonetized by that time, or else it will not be legal tender. In my judgment, every religion that stands by appealing to miracles is dishonor. [sic] Every religion in the world has denounced every other religion as a fraud. That proves to me that they all tell the truth—about others. Why? Suppose Mr. Smith should tell Mr. Brown that he—Smith—saw a corpse get out of the grave, and that when he first saw it, it was covered with the worm's of death, and that in his presence it was reclothed in healthy, beautiful flesh. And then suppose Mr. Brown should tell Mr. Smith, "I saw the same thing myself. I was in a graveyard once, and I saw a dead man rise." Suppose then that Smith should say to Brown, "You're a liar," and Brown should reply to Smith, "And you're a liar," what would you think? It would simply be because Smith, never having seen it himself, didn't believe Brown; and Brown, never having seen it, didn't believe Smith had. Now, if Smith had really seen it, and Brown told him he had seen it too, then Smith would regard it as a corroboration of his story, and he would regard Brown as one of his principal witnesses. But, on the contrary, he says, "You never saw it." So, when man says, "I was upon

Mount Sinai, and there I met God, and he told me, 'Stand aside and let me drown these people';" and another man says to him, "I was upon a mountain, and there I met the Supreme Brahma," and Moses says, "That's not true," and contends that the other man never did see Brahma, and he contends that Moses never did see God, that is in my judgment proof that they both speak truly.

Every religion, then, has charged every other religion with having been an unmitigated fraud; and yet, if any man had ever seen the miracle himself, his mind would be prepared to believe that another man had seen the same thing. Whenever a man appeals to a miracle he tells what is not true. Truth relies upon reason, and the undeviating course of all the laws of nature.

Now, we have a religion—that is, some people have. I do not pretend to have religion myself. I believe in living for this world—that's my doctrine—in living here, now, to-day, to-night—that's my doctrine, to make everybody happy that you can. Now, let the future take care of itself and if I ever touch the shores of another world I will be just as ready and anxious to get into some remunerative employment as anybody else. Now, we have got in this country a religion which men have preached for about eighteen hundred years, and just in proportion as their belief in that religion has grown great, men have grown mean and wicked; just in proportion as they have ceased to believe it, men have become just and charitable. And if they believe it to-night as they once believed it, I wouldn't be allowed to speak in the city of New York. It is from the coldness and infidelity of the churches that I get my right to preach; and I say it to their credit. Now we have a religion. What is it? They say in the first place that all this vast universe was created by a deity. I don't know whether it was or not. They say, too, that had it not been for the first sin of Adam there would never have been any devil in this world, and if there had been no devil there would have been no sin, and if there had been no sin there never would have been any death. For my part I am glad there was Somebody had to die to give me room, and when my turn comes I'll be willing to let somebody else take my place. But whether there is another life or not, if there is any being who gave me this, I shall thank him from the bottom of my heart, because, upon the whole, my life has been a joy. Now they say, because of this first sin all men were consigned to eternal hell. And this because Adam was our representative. Well, I always had an idea that my representative ought to live somewhere about the same time I do. I always had an idea that I should have some voice in choosing my representative. And if I had a voice I never should have voted for the old gentleman called Adam. Now in order to regain man from the frightful hell of eternity, Christ himself came to this world and took upon himself flesh, and in order that we might know the road to eternal salvation he gave us a book, and that book is called the Bible, and whenever that Bible has been read men have immediately commenced cutting each others' throats. Wherever that Bible has been circulated, they have invented inquisitions and instruments of torture, and they commenced hating each other with all their hearts. But I am told now, we are all told that this Bible is the foundation of civilization, but I say that this Bible is the foundation of Hell, and we never shall get rid of the dogma of hell until we get rid of the idea that it is an inspired book. Now, what does the Bible teach? I am not going to talk about what this minister or that minister says it teaches; the question is "ought a man to be sent to eternal hell for not believing this Bible to be the work of a Merciful Father?" and the only way to find out is to read it; and a very few people do read it now. I will read a few passages. This is the book to be read in the schools, in order to make our children charitable and good; this is the book that we must read in order that our children may have ideas of mercy, charity and justice. Does the Bible teach mercy? Now be honest, I read: "I will make mine arrows drunk with blood; and the sword shall devour flesh." (Deut. xxxii, 42.) Pretty good start for a merciful God! "That thy foot may be dipped in the blood of thine enemies and the tongue of thy dogs in the same." (Ps. lxviii, 23.) Again: "And the Lord thy God will put out those nations before thee by little and little; thou mayest not consume them at once, lest the beasts of the field increase upon thee." (Deut. vii, 22.)

"But the Lord thy God shall deliver them unto thee, and shall destroy them with a mighty destruction, until they be destroyed.

"And he shall deliver their kings into thine hand, and thou shalt destroy their name from under heaven; there shall no man be able to stand before thee, until thou have destroyed them." (Deut. vii, 23, 24.)

"So Joshua came, and all the people of war with him, against them by waters of Merom suddenly; and they fell upon them.

"And the lord delivered them into the hand of Israel, who smote them, and chased them unto great Zidon, and unto Misrephothimaim, and unto the valley of Mizpeh eastward; and they smote them, until they left them none remaining.

"And Joshua did unto them as the Lord bade him; he houghed their horses, and burnt their chariots with fire.

"And Joshua at that time turned back, and took Hazor, and smote the king thereof with the sword; for Hazor beforetime was the head of all those kingdoms.

"And they smote all the souls that were therein with the edge of the sword, utterly destroying them: there was not any left to breathe; and he burnt Hazor with fire.

"And all the cities of those kings, and all the kings of them, did Joshua take, and smote them with the edge of the sword, and he utterly destroyed them, as Moses the servant of the Lord commanded.

"But as for the cities that stood still in their strength, Israel burnt none of them, save Hazor only; that did Joshua burn.

"And all the spoil of these cities and the cattle, the children of Israel took for a prey unto themselves, but every man they smote with the edge of the sword [Brave!] until they had destroyed them, neither left they any to breathe. [As the moral god had commanded them.]

"As the Lord commanded Moses, his servant, so did Moses command Joshua, and so did Joshua; he left nothing undone of all that the Lord commanded Moses.

"So Joshua took all that land, the hills, and all the south country, and all the land of Goshen, and the valley of the same.

"Even from the mount Halak, that goeth up to Seir; even unto Baalgad in the valley of Lebanon under mount Hermon; and all their kings he took, and smote them, and slew them.

"Joshua made war a long time with all those kings.

"There was not a city that made peace with the children of Israel, save the Hivites, the inhabitants of Gideon; all other they took in battle.

"For it was of the Lord to harden their hearts, that they should come against Israel in battle, that he might destroy them utterly, and that they might have no favor, but that he might destroy them, as the Lord commanded Moses.

"And at that time came Joshua, and cut off the Anakims from the mountains, from Hebron, for Debit, from Anab, and from all the mountains of Judah, and from all the mountains of Israel; Joshua destroyed them utterly with their cities.

"There was none of the Anakims left in the land of the children of Israel, only in Gaza, in Gath, and in Ashdod there remained.

"So Joshua took the whole land, according to all that the Lord said unto Moses; and Joshua gave it for an inheritance unto Israel according to their divisions by their tribes. And the land rested from war." (Josh. xi, 7 to 23.)

"When thou comest nigh unto a city to fight against it, then proclaim peace unto it.

"And it shall be, if it make thee answer of peace, and open unto thee, then it shall be that all the people that is found therein shall be tributaries unto thee, and they shall serve thee.

"And if it will make no peace with thee, but will make war against thee, then thou shalt besiege it.

"And when the Lord thy God hath delivered it into thine hands, thou shalt smite every male thereof with the edge of the sword.

"But the women, and the little ones, and the cattle, and all that is in the city, even all the spoil thereof, shalt thou take unto thyself; and thou shalt eat the spoil of thine enemies, which the Lord thy God hath given thee.

"Thus shalt thou do unto all the cities which are very far off from thee, which are not of the cities of these nations.

"But of the cities of these people, which the Lord thy God doth give thee for an inheritance, thou shalt save alive nothing that breatheth:

"But thou shalt utterly destroy them." (Deut. xx, 10-17.)

Neither the old men nor the women, nor the maidens, nor the sweet-dimpled babe, smiling upon the lap of his mother, were to be spared.

"And he said unto them, Thus saith the Lord God of Israel [a merciful god indeed]. Put every man his sword by his side, and go in and out from gate to gate through-out the camp, and slay every man his brother, and every man his companion, and every man his neighbor." (Exod. xxxii, 27.)

Now recollect, these instructions were given to an army of invasion, and the people who were slayed were guilty of the crime of fighting for their homes. Oh, most merciful God! The old testament is full of curses, vengeance, jealousy and hatred, and of barbarity and brutality. Now do you not for one moment believe that these words were written by the most merciful God. Don't pluck from the heart the sweet flowers of piety and crush them by superstition. Do not believe that God ever ordered the murder of innocent women and helpless babes. Do not let this supposition turn your hearts into stone. When anything is said to have been written by the most merciful God, and the thing is not merciful, then I deny it, and say he never wrote it. I will live by the standard of reason, and if thinking in accordance with reason takes me to perdition, then I will go to hell with my reason rather that to heaven without it.

Now does this bible teach political freedom, or does it teach political tyranny? Does it teach a man to resist oppression? Does it teach a man to tear from the throne of tyranny the crowned thing and robber called a king? Let us see [Reading:]

"Let every soul be subject to the higher powers: For there is no power but of God, the powers that are ordained of God." (Rom. xii, 1.)

All the kings, and princes, and governors, and thieves and robbers that happened to be in authority were placed there by the infinite father of all!

"Whosoever therefore resisteth the power, resisteth the ordinance of God."

And when George Washington resisted the power of George the Third he resisted the power of God. And when our fathers said, "Resistance to tyrants is obedience to God," they falsified the bible itself.

"For he is the minister of God to thee for good. But if thou do that which is evil, be afraid; for he beareth not the sword in vain; for he is the minister of God, revenger to execute wrath upon him that doeth evil.

"Wherefore ye must needs be subject not only for wrath, but also for conscience sake." (Rom. xiii, 4, 5.)

I deny this wretched doctrine. Wherever the sword of rebellion is drawn to protect the rights of man, I am a rebel. Wherever the sword of rebellion is drawn to give man liberty, to clothe him in all his just rights, I am on the side of that rebellion. I deny that the rulers are crowned by the Most High; the rulers are the people, and the presidents and others are but the servants of the people. All authority comes from the people, and not from the aristocracy of the air. Upon these texts of scripture which I have just read rest the thrones of Europe, and these are the voices that are repeated from age to age by brainless kings and heartless kings.

Does the bible give woman her rights? Is this bible humane? Does it treat woman as she ought to be treated, or is it barbarian? Let us see.

"Let the woman learn in silence with all subjection." (1 Timothy ii, 11.)

If a woman would know anything let her ask her husband. Imagine the ignorance of a lady who had only that source of information!

"But I suffer not a woman to teach, not to usurp authority over the man, but to be in silence. For Adam was first formed, then Eve. [What magnificent reason!]"

"And Adam was not deceived, but the woman being deceived, was in the transgression." [Splendid!]

"But I would have you know that the head of every man is Christ; and the head of the woman is the man; and the head of Christ is God." That is to say, there is as much difference between the woman and man as there is between Christ and man. This is the liberty of woman.

"For the man is not of the woman, but the woman is of the man." It was the man's cut till that was taken, not the woman's. "Neither was the man created for the woman." Well, what was he created for? "But the woman was created for the man. Wives, submit yourselves unto your husbands, as unto the Lord." There's Liberty!

"For the husband is the head of the wife, even as Christ is the head of the church; and he is the savior of the body.

"Therefore, as the church is subject unto Christ so let the wives be to their own husbands in everything."

Good again! Even the savior didn't put man and woman upon an equality. The man could divorce the wife, but the wife could not divorce the husband, and according to the old testament, the mother had to ask for forgiveness for being the mother of babes. Splendid!

Here is something from the old testament: "When thou goest forth to war against thine enemies, and the Lord thy God hath delivered them into thine hands, and thou has taken them captive.

"And seest among the captives a beautiful woman, and has a desire unto her, that thou wouldst have her to thy wife.

"Then thou shalt bring her home to thine house; and she shall shave her head, and pare her nails." (Deut. xxi, 10-12.)

That is in self-defense, I suppose!

This sacred book, this foundation of human liberty, of morality, does it teach concubinage and polygamy? Read the thirty-first chapter of Numbers, read the twenty-first chapter of Deuteronomy, read the blessed lives of Abraham, of David or of Solomon, and then tell me that the sacred scripture does not teach polygamy and concubinage! All the language of the world is not sufficient to express the infamy of polygamy; it makes man a beast and woman a stone. It destroys the fireside and makes virtue an outcast. And yet it is the doctrine of the bible—the doctrine defended by Luther and Melanchthon! It takes from our language those sweetest words, father, husband, wife, and mother, and takes us back to barbarism, and fills our hearts with the crawling, slimy serpents of loathsome lust.

Does the bible teach the existence of devils? Of course it does. Yes, it teaches not only the existence of a good being, but a bad being. This good being had to have a home; that home was heaven. This bad being had to have a home; and that home was hell. This hell is supposed to be nearer to earth than I would care to have it, and to be peopled with spirits, spooks, hobgoblins, and all the fiery shapes with which the imagination of ignorance and fear could people that horrible place; and the bible teaches the existence of hell and this big devil and all these little devils. The bible teaches the doctrine of witchcraft and makes us believe that there are sorcerers and witches, and that the dead could be raised by the power of sorcery. Does anybody believe it now?

"Then said Saul unto his servants, Seek me a woman that hath a familiar spirit, that I may go to her, and inquire of her. And his servants said to him, Behold, there is a woman that hath a familiar spirit at Endor.

"And Saul disguised himself and put on other raiment, and he went, and two men with him, and they came to the woman by night; and he said, I pray thee, divine unto me by the familiar spirit, and bring me him up whom I shall name unto thee. [That was a pretty good spiritual seance.]

"And the woman said unto him, Behold, thou knowest what Saul hath done, how he hath cut off those that have familiar spirits, and the wizards, out of the land; wherefore then layest thou a snare for my life to cause me to die?

"And Saul sware to her by the Lord, saying, As the Lord liveth there shall no punishment happen to thee for this thing.

"Then said the woman, Whom shall I bring up unto thee? And he said, Bring me up Samuel.

"And when the woman saw Samuel, she cried with a loud voice; and the woman spake to Saul, saying, Why hast thou deceived me? for thou art Saul.

"And the king said unto her, Be not afraid; for what sawest thou? And the woman said unto Saul, I saw gods ascending out of the earth.

"And he said unto her, What form is he of? And she said, An old man cometh up; and he is covered with a mantle. And Saul perceived that it was Samuel, and he stooped with his face to the ground, and bowed himself." (1 Saml. xxviii, 7-14.)

In another place he declares that witchcraft is an abomination unto the Lord. He wanted no rivals in this business. Now what does the new testament teach?

"Then was Jesus led up of the Spirit into the wilderness to be tempted of the devil.

"And when he had fasted forty days and forty nights, he was afterward an hungered. [sic]

"And when the tempter came to him, he said, If thou be the Son of God, command that these stones be made bread.

"But he answered and said, It is written, Man shall not live by bread alone, but by every word that proceedeth out of the mouth of God.

"Then the devil taketh him up into the holy city, and setteth him on a pinnacle of the temple,

"And saith unto him, If thou be the Son of God, Hell cast thyself down, for it is written, He shall give his angels charge concerning thee; and in their hands they shall bear thee up, lest at any time thou dash thy foot against a stone.

"Jesus said unto him, It is written again, Thou shalt not tempt the Lord thy God." (Matt. iv, 1 7.)

Is it possible that anyone can believe that the devil absolutely took God almighty, and put him on the pinnacle of the temple, and endeavored to persuade him to jump down? Is it possible?

"Again the devil taketh him up into an exceeding high mountain and showeth him all the kingdoms of the world, and the glory of them;

"And Saith unto him, All these things will I give thee, if thou will fall down and worship me.

"Then saith Jesus unto him, Get thee hence, Satan, for it is written, Thou shalt worship the Lord thy God, and him only shalt thou serve." (Matt. iv, 8-10.)

Now, the devil must have known at that time that he was God, and God at that time must have known that the other was the devil. How could the latter be conceived to have the impudence to promise God a world in which he did not have a tax-title to an inch of land?

"Then the devil leaveth him; and, behold, angels came and ministered unto him." (Matt. iv, 11.)

"And they came over unto the other side of the sea, into the country of the Gadarines.

"And when he was come out of the ship, immediately there met him out of the tombs a man with an unclean spirit,

"Who had his dwelling among the tombs; and no man could bind him, no, not with chains,

"Because that he had been often bound with fetters and chains, and the chains had been plucked asunder by him, and the fetters broken in pieces; neither could any man tame him,

"And always, night and day, he was in the mountains and tombs, crying and cutting himself with stones.

"But when he saw Jesus afar off, he came and worshiped him.

"And cried with a loud voice and said, What have I to do with thee, Jesus, thou Son of the Most High God? I adjure thee by God, that thou torment me not.

"(For he said unto him, Come out of the man, thou unclean spirit.)

"And he asked him, What is thy name? And he answered saying, My name is Legion: for we are many.

"And he besought him much that he would not send them away out of the country.

"Now there was there nigh unto the mountains a great herd of swine feeding.

"And all the devils besought him, saying, Send us into the swine that we may enter into them.

"And forthwith Jesus gave them leave. And the unclean spirits went out, and entered into the swine; and the herd ran violently down a steep place into the sea (they were about two thousand), and were choked in the sea." (Mark v, 1-13.)

Now I will ask a question: Should reasonable men, in the nineteenth century in the United States of America, believe that that was an actual occurrence? If my salvation depends upon believing that, I am lost. I have never experienced the signs by which it is said a believer may be known. I deny all the witch stories in this world. These fables of devils have covered the world with blood; they have filled the world with fear, and I am going to do what I can to free the world of these insatiate monsters, small and great; they have filled the world with monsters, they have made the world a synonym of liar and ferocity. And it is this book that ought to be read in all the schools—this book that teaches man to enslave his brother! If it is larceny to steal the result of labor, how much more is it larceny to steal the laborer himself?

"Moreover, of the children of the strangers that do sojourn among you, of them shall ye buy, and of their families that are with you, which they begat in your land; and they shall be your possession.

"And ye shall take them as an inheritance for your children after you, to inherit them for a possession; they shall be your bondmen forever; but over your brethren the children of Israel, ye shall not rule one over another with rigor." (Lev. xxv, 45, 46.)

Why? Because they are not as good as you will buy of the heathen roundabout.

Now these are the judgments which thou shalt set before them.

"If thou buy an Hebrew servant, six years he shall serve; and in the seventh he shall go out free for nothing.

"If he came in by himself, he shall go out by himself; if he were married, then his wife shall go out with him.

"If his master have given him a wife, and she have borne him sons or daughters; the wife and her children shall be her master's, and he shall go out by himself.

"And if the servant shall plainly say, I love my master, my wife, and my children; I will not go out free.

"Then his master shall bring him unto the judges; he shall also bring him to the door, or unto the door-post; and his master shall bore his ear through with an awl; and he shall serve him forever." (Exod. xxi, 1-6.)

This is the doctrine which has ever lent itself to the chains of slavery, and makes a man imprison himself rather than desert his wife and children. I hate it.

Now, listen to the new testament, the tidings of great joy for all people!

"Servants, be obedient to them that are your masters according to the flesh, with fear and trembling, in singleness of your heart, as unto Christ.

"Not with eye-service, as men pleasers; but as the servants of Christ, doing the will of God from the heart." (Eph. vi, 5, 6.) trembling, in singleness of your heart, as unto Christ.

"Not with eye-service, as men pleasers; but as the servants of Christ, doing the will of God from the heart." (Eph. vi, 5,6.) Splendid doctrine.

"Servants, be subject to your masters with all fear; not only to the good and gentle, but also to the froward.

"For this is thankworthy, if a man for conscience toward God endure grief, suffering wrongfully." (1 Peter ii, 18, 19.)

"Servants, obey in all things your masters according to the flesh."

He was afraid they might not work all the time, so he adds:

"Not with the eye-service, as men pleasers, but in the singleness of heart fearing God."

Read the twenty-first chapter of Exodus, 7 to 11.

"And if a man sell his daughter to be a maid servant, she shall not go out as the men-servants do.

"If she please not her master, who hath betrothed her to himself, then shall he let her be redeemed; to sell her unto a strange nation he shall have no power, seeing he hath dealt deceitfully with her. And if he have betrothed her unto his son, he shall deal with her after the manner of daughters.

"If he take him another wife, her food, her raiment and her duty of marriage shall he not diminish.

"And if he do not these three unto her, then shall she go out free without money."

"Servants, be obedient to your masters," is the salutation of the most merciful God to one who works for nothing and who receives upon his naked back the lash, as legal tender for service performed.

"Servants, be obedient to your masters," is the salutation of the most merciful God to the slave-mother bending over her infant's grave.

"Servants, be obedient to your masters," is the salutation to a man endeavoring to escape pursuit, followed by savage blood-hounds, and with his eye fixed upon the northern star. This book ought to be read in the schools, so that our children will love liberty.

What does this same book say of the rights of little children? Let us see how they are treated by the "most merciful God."

"If a man have a stubborn and rebellious son, which will not obey the voice of his father, or the voice of his mother, and that when they have chastened him, will not hearken unto them.

"Then shall his father and his mother lay hold of him, and bring him out unto the elders of his city, and unto the gate of his place.

"And they shall say unto the elders of his city, this our son is stubborn and rebellious, he will not obey our voice, he is a glutton, and a drunkard.

"And all the men of his city shall stone him with stones, that he die; so shalt thou put evil away from among you; and all Israel shall hear and fear." (Deut. xxi, 18-21.)

Abraham was commanded to offer his son Isaac as a sacrifice, and he intended to obey. The boy was not consulted.

Did you ever hear the story of Jephthah's daughter? Returning him Jephthah said:

"And Jephthah vowed a vow unto the Lord, and said, if thou shalt without fail deliver the children of Ammon into mine hands,

"Then it shall be, that whatsoever cometh forth of the doors of my house to meet me, when I return in peace from the children of Ammon shall surely be the Lord's, and I will offer it up for a burnt offering.

"So Jephthah passed over unto the children of Ammon to fight against them; and the Lord delivered them into his hands.

"And he smote them from Aroer, even till thou come to Minnith, even twenty cities, and unto the plain of the vineyards with a very great slaughter. Thus the children of Ammon were subdued before the children of Israel.

"And Jephthah came to Mizpeh unto his house, and, behold, his daughter came out to meet him with timbrels and with dances; and she was his only child: besides her he had neither son nor daughter.

"And it came to pass when he saw her, that he rent his clothes, and said, Alas, my daughter! thou has brought me very low, and thou art one of them that trouble me; for I have opened my mouth unto the Lord, and I cannot go back.

"And she said unto him, My father, if thou has opened thy mouth unto the Lord, do to me according to that which hath proceeded out of thy mouth; forasmuch as the Lord hath taken vengeance for thee of thine enemies, even to the children of Ammon.

"And she said unto her father, Let this thing be done for me: let me alone two months, that I may go up and down upon the mountains, and bewail my virginity, I and my fellows.

"And he said, Go. And he sent her away for two months, and she went with her companions, and bewailed her virginity upon the mountains.

"And it came to pass at the end of two months that she returned unto her father, who did with her according to his vow which he had vowed."

Is there in the history of the world a sadder story than this? Can a god who would accept such a sacrifice be worthy of the worship of civilized men? I believe in the rights of children. I plead for the republic of home, for the democracy of the fireside, and for this I am called a heathen and a devil by those who believe in the cheerful and comforting doctrine of eternal damnation.

Read the book of Job; read that God met the devil and asked him where he had been, and he said, "Walking up and down the country;" and the Lord said to him, "Have you noticed my man Job over here, how good he is?" And the devil said, "Of course he's good, you give him everything he wants. Just take away his property and he'll curse you. You just try it." And he did try it, and took away his goods, but Job still remained good. The devil laughed and said that he had not been tried enough. Then the Lord touched his flesh, but he was still true. Then he took away his children, but he remained faithful, and in the end, to show how much Job made by his fidelity, his property was all doubled, and he had more children than ever. If you have a child, and you love it, would you be satisfied with a god who would destroy it, and endeavor to make it up by giving you another that was better looking? No, you want that one; you want no other, and yet this is the idea of the love of children taught in the bible.

Does the bible teach you freedom of religion? To day we say that every man has a right to worship God or not, to worship him as he pleases. Is it the doctrine of the bible? Let us see.

"If thy brother, the son of thy mother, or thy son, or thy daughter, or the wife of thy bosom, or thy friend, which is as thine own soul, entice thee secretly, saying. Let us go and serve other gods, which thou has not known, thou, nor thy fathers;

"Namely, of the gods of the people which are round about you, nigh unto thee, or far off from thee, from the one end of the earth even unto the other end of the earth;

"Thou shalt not consent unto him, nor hearken unto him; neither shall thine eye pity him, neither shalt thou spare, neither shalt thou conceal him;

"But thou shalt surely kill him; thine hand shall be first upon him to put him to death, and afterwards the hand of all the people.

"And thou shalt stone him with stones, that he die; because he has sought to thrust thee away from the Lord thy God, which brought thee out of the land of Egypt, from the house of bondage." (Deut. xiii, 6-10.)

And do you know, according to that, if your wife—your wife that you love as your own soul—if you had lived in Palestine, and your wife had said to you, "Let us worship a sun whose golden beams clothe the world in glory; let us worship the sun, let us bow to that great luminary; I love the sun because it gave me your face; because it gave me the features of my babe; let us worship the sun," it was then your duty to lay your hands upon her, your eye must not pity her, but it was your duty to cast the first stone against that tender and loving breast! I hate such doctrine! I hate such books! I hate gods that will write such books! I tell you that it is infamous!

"If there be found among you, within any of thy gates which the Lord thy God giveth thee, man or woman that hath wrought wickedness in the sight of the Lord thy God, in transgressing his covenant,

"And hath gone and served other gods, and worshiped them, either the sun, or moon, or any of the host of heaven, which I have not commanded;

"And it be told thee, and thou hast heard of it, and inquired diligently, and behold, it be true, and the thing certain, that such abomination is wrought in Israel;

"Then shalt thou bring forth that man or that woman, which have committed that wicked thing, unto thy gates even that man or that woman, and shalt stone them with stones till they die." (Deut. xvii, 2-5.)

That is the religious liberty of the bible—that's it. And this god taught that doctrine to the Jews, and said to them, "Any one that teaches a different religion, kill him!" Now, let me ask, and I want to do it reverently, if, as is contended, God gave these frightful laws to the flesh, and come among the Jews, and taught a different religion, and these Jews, in accordance with the laws which this same God gave them, crucified him, did he not reap what he had sown? The mercy of all this comes in what is called "the plan of salvation." What is that plan? According to this great plan, the innocent suffer for the guilty to satisfy a law.

What sort of a law must it be that would be satisfied with the suffering of innocence? According to this plan, the salvation of the whole world depends upon the bigotry of the Jews and the treachery of Judas. According to the same plan, we all would have gone to eternal hell. According to the same plan, there would have been no death in the world if there had been no sin, and if there had been no death you and I would not have been called into existence, and if we did not exist we could not have been saved, so we owe our salvation to the bigotry of the Jews and the treachery of Judas, and we are indebted to the devil for our existence. I speak this reverently. It strikes me that what they call the atonement is a kind of moral bankruptcy. Under its merciful provisions man is allowed the privilege of sinning credit, and whenever he is guilty of a mean action he says, "Charge it." In my judgment, this kind of bookkeeping breeds extravagance in sin. Suppose we had a law in New York that every merchant should give credit to every man who asked it, under pain and penitentiary, and that every man should take the benefit of the bankruptcy statute any Saturday night? Doesn't the credit system in morals breed extravagance in sin? That's the question. Who's afraid of punishment which is so far away? Whom does the doctrine of hell stop? The great, the rich, the powerful? No; the poor, the weak, the despised, the mean. Did you ever hear of a man going to hell who died in New York worth a million of dollars, or with an income of twenty-five thousand a year? Did you? Did you ever hear of a man going to hell who rode in a carriage? Never. They are the gentlemen who talk about their assets, and who say: "Hell is not for me; it is for the poor. I have all the luxuries I want, give that to the poor." Who goes to hell? Tramps!

Let me tell you a story. There was once a frightful rain, and all the animals held a convention, to see whose fault it was, and the fox nominated the lion for chairman. The wolf seconded the motion, and the hyena said "that suits." When the convention was called to order the fox was called upon to confess his sins. He stated, however, that it would be much more appropriate for the lion to commence first. Thereupon the lion said: "I am not conscious of having committed evil. It is true I have devoured a few men, but for what other purpose were men made?" And they all cheered, and were satisfied. The fox gave his views upon the goose question, and the wolf admitted that he had devoured sheep, and occasionally had killed a shepherd, "but all acquainted with the history of my family will bear me out when I say that shepherds have been the enemies of my family from the beginning of the world." Then way in the rear there arose a simple donkey, with a kind of Abrahamic countenance. He said: "I expect it's me. I had eaten nothing for three days except three thistles. I was passing a monastery, the monks were at mass. The gates were open leading to a yard full of sweet clover. I knew it was wrong but I did slip in and I took a mouthful, but my conscience smote me and I went out;" and all the animals shouted, "He's the fellow!" and in two minutes they had his hide on the fence. That's the kind of people that go to hell.

Now this doctrine of hell, that has been such a comfort to my race, which so many ministers are pleading for, has been defended for ages by the fathers of the church. Your preacher says that the sovereignty of God implies that He has an absolute, unlimited and independent right to dispose of His creatures as He will, because He made them. Has He? Suppose I take this book and change it immediately into a servient human being. Would I have a right to torture it because I made it? No; on the contrary, I would say, having brought you into existence, it is my duty to do the best for you I can. They say God has a right to damn me because He made me. I deny it. Another one says God is not obliged to save even those who believe in Christ, and that he can either bestow salvation upon his children or retain it without any diminution of his glory. Another one says God may save any sinner whatsoever, consistently with his justice. Let a natural person—and I claim to be one—moral or immoral, wise or unwise; let him be as just as he can, no matter what his prayers may be, what pains he may have taken to be saved, or whatever circumstances he may be in. God, according to this writer, can deny him salvation, without the least disparagement of His glory. His glories will not be in the least obscured—there is no natural man, be his character what it may, but God may cast down to hell without being charged with unfair dealing in any respect with regard to that man. Theologians tell us that God's design in the creation was simply to glorify himself. Magnificent object!

"The same shall drink of the wine of the wrath of God, which is poured out without mixture into the cup of his indignation; and he shall be tormented with fire and brimstone in the presence of the holy angels, and in the presence of the Lamb." (Rev. xiv, 1-10.)

Do you know nobody would have had an idea of hell in this world if it hadn't been for volcanoes? They were looked upon as the chimneys of hell. The idea of eternal fire never would have polluted the imagination of man but for them. An eminent theologian, describing hell, says: "There is no recounting the millions of ages the damned shall suffer. All arithmetic ends here"—and all sense, too! "They shall have nothing to do in passing away this eternity but to conflict with torments. God shall have no other use or employment for them." These words were said by gentlemen who died Christians, and who are now in the harp business in the world to come. Another declares there is nothing to keep any man or Christian out of hell except the mere pleasure of God, and their pains never grow any easier by their becoming accustomed to them. It is also declared that the devil goes about like a lion, ready to doom the wicked. Did it never occur to you what a contradiction it is to say that the devil will persecute his own friends? He wants all the recruits he can get; why then should he persecute his friends? In my judgment he should give them the best hell affords.

It is in the very nature of things that torments inflicted have no tendency to bring a wicked man to repentance. Then why torment him if it will not do him good? It is simply unadulterated revenge. All the punishment in the world will not reform a man, unless he knows that he who inflicts it upon him does it for the sake of reformation, and really and truly loves him, and has his good at heart. Punishment inflicted for gratifying the appetite makes man afraid, but debases him.

Various reasons are given for punishing the wicked; first, that God will vindicate his injured majesty. Well, I am glad of that! Second, He will glorify his justice—think of that. Third, He will show and glorify his grace. Every time the saved shall look upon the damned in hell it will cause in them a lively and admiring sense of the grace of God. Every look upon the damned will double the ardor and the joy of the saints in heaven. Can the believing husband in heaven look down upon the torments of the unbelieving wife in hell and then feel a thrill of joy? That's the old doctrine—not of our days; we are too civilized for that. O, but it is the doctrine that if you saw your wife in hell—the wife you love, who, in your last sickness, nursed you, that, perhaps supported you by her needle when you were ill; the wife who watched by your couch night and day, and held your corpse in her loving arms when you were dead—the sight would give you great joy. That doctrine is not preached to-day. They do not preach that the sight would give you joy; but they do preach that it will not diminish your happiness. That is the doctrine of every orthodox minister in New York, and I repeat that I have no respect for men who preach such doctrines. The sight of the torments of the damned in hell will increase the ecstasy of the saints forever! On this principle man never enjoys a good dinner so much as when a fellow-creature is dying of famine before his eyes, or he never enjoys the cheerful warmth of his own fireside so greatly as when a poor and abandoned wretch is dying on his doorstep. The saints enjoy the ecstasy and the groans of the tormented are music to them. I say here to-night that you cannot commit a sin against an infinite being. I can sin against my brother or my neighbor, because I can injure them. There can be no sin where there is no injury. Neither can a finite being commit infinite sin.

An old saint believed that hell was in the interior of the earth, and that the rotation of the earth was caused by the souls trying to get away from the fire. The old church at Stratford-on-Avon, Shakespeare's home, in adorned with pictures of hell and the like. One of the pictures represents resurrection morning. People are getting out of their graves, and devils are catching hold of their heels. In one place there is a huge brass monster, and devils are driving scores of lost souls into his mouth. Over hot fires hang caldrons with fifty or sixty people in each, and devils are poking the fires. People are hung up on hooks by their tongues, and devils are lashing them. Up in the right hand corner are some of the saved, with grins on their faces stretching from ear to ear. They seem to say: "Aha, what did I tell you?"

Some of the old saints—gentlemen who died in the odor of sanctity, and are now in the harp business—insisted that heaven and hell would be plainly in view of each other. Only a few years ago, Rev. J. Furness (an appropriate name) published a little pamphlet called "A Sight in Hell." I remember when I first read that. My little child, seven years old, was ill and in bed. I thought she would not hear me, and I read some of it aloud. She arose and asked, "Who says that?" I answered, "That's what they preach in some of the churches." "I never will enter a church as long as I live!" she said, and she never has.

The doctrine of orthodox Christianity is that the damned shall suffer torment forever and forever. And if you were a wanderer, footsore, weary, with parched tongue, dying for a drop of water, and you met one who divided his poor portion with you, and died as he saw you reviving—if he was an unbeliever and you a believer, and you died and went to heaven, and he called to you from hell for a draught of water, it would be your duty to laugh at him.

Rev. Mr. Spurgeon says that everywhere in hell will be written the words "for ever." They will be branded on every wave of flame, they will be forged in every link of every chain, they will be seen in every lurid flash of brimstone—everywhere will be those words "for ever." Everybody will be yelling and screaming them. Just think of that picture of the mercy and justice of the eternal Father of us all. If these words are necessary why are they not written now everywhere in the world, on every tree, and every field, and on every blade of grass? I say I am entitled to have it so. I say that it is God's duty to furnish me with the evidence. Here is another good book read in every Sunday-school—a splendid book—Pollok's "Course of Time." Every copy in the world of such books as that ought to be burned. Well, the author pretends to have gone to hell, and I think that he ought to have stopped there.

[The lecturer read the passage from the work descriptive of the torments of the damned, and proceeded:] And that book is put into the hands of children in order that they may love and worship the most merciful God. In old time they had to find a place for hell and they found a hundred places for it. One says that it was under Lake Avernus, but the Christians thought differently. One divine tells us that it must be below the earth because Christ descended into hell. Another gives it as his opinion that hell is in the sun, and he tells us that nobody, without an express revelation from God, can prove that it is not there. Most likely. Well, he had the idea at all events of utilizing the damned as fuel to warm the earth. But I will quote from another poet—if it is lawful to call him a poet. I mean Tupper.

[Colonel Ingersoll quoted from that orthodox author, and continued:] Another divine preached a sermon no further back than 1876, in which he said that the damned will grow worse; and the same divine says that the devil was the first Universalist. Then I am on the side of the devil.

The fact is, that you have got not merely to believe the bible; but you must also believe in a certain interpretation of it, and, mind you, you must also believe in the doctrine of the trinity. I want to explain what that is, so that you may never have an excuse for not knowing it.

I quote from the best theologian that ever wrote. [Then he went on to give in substance the Athanasian definition of the trinity, winding up with a long string of adjectives, culminating in the description "entirely incomprehensible."] If you don't understand it after that, it is you own fault. Now, you must believe in that doctrine. If you do not, all the orthodox churches agree in condemning you to everlasting flames. We have got to burn through all our lives simply with the view of making them happy. We are taught to love our enemies, to pray for those that persecute us, to forgive. Should not the merciful God practice what he preaches? I say that reverently. Why should he say, "Forgive your enemies," if he will not himself forgive? Why should he say "Pray for those that despise and persecute you," but if they refuse to believe his doctrine he will burn them forever? I cannot believe it. Here is a little child, residing in the purlieus of the city—some boy who is taught that it is his duty to steal by his mother, who applauds his success and pats him on the head and calls him a good boy—would it be just to condemn him to an eternity of torture? Suppose there is a God; let us bring to this question some common sense.

I care nothing about the doctrines of religions or creeds of the past. Let us come to the bar of the nineteenth century and judge matter by what we know, by what we think, by what we love. But they say to us, "If you throw away the Bible what are we to depend on then?" But no two persons in the world agree as to what the Bible is, what they are to believe, or what they are not to believe. It is like a guidepost that has been thrown down in some time of disaster, and has been put up the wrong way. Nobody can accept its guidance, for nobody knows where it would direct him. I say, "Tear down the useless guidepost," but they answer, "Oh, do not do that or we will have nothing to go by." I would say, "Old Church, you take that road and I will take this." Another minister has said that the Bible is the great town-clock, at which we all may set our watches. But I have said to a friend of that minister: "Suppose we all should set our watches by that town-clock, there would be many persons to tell you that in old times the long hand was the hour hand, and besides, the clock hasn't been wound up for a long time." I say let us wait till the sun rises and set our watches by nature. For my part, I am willing to give up heaven to get rid of hell. I had rather there should be no heaven than that any solitary soul should be condemned to suffer forever and ever. But they tell me that the Bible is the good book. Now, in the Old Testament there is not in my judgment a single reference to another life. Is there a burial service mentioned in it in which a word of hope is spoken at the grave of the dead? The idea of eternal life was not born of any book. That wave of hope and joy ebbs and flows, and will continue to ebb and flow as long as love kisses the lips of death.

Let me tell you a tale of the Persian religion of a man who, having done good for long years of his life, presented himself at the gates of Paradise, but the gates remained closed against him. He went back and followed up his good works for seven years longer, and the gates of Paradise still remaining shut against him, he toiled in works of charity until at last they were opened unto him. Think of that, pursued the lecturer, and send out your missionaries among those people. There is no religion but goodness, but justice, but charity. Religion is not theory; it is life. It is not intellectual conviction; it is divine humanity, and nothing else. Colonel Ingersoll here told another tale from the Hindoo, of a man who refused to enter Paradise without a faithful dog, urging that ingratitude was the blackest of all sins. "And the God," he said, "admitted him, dog and all." Compare that religion with the orthodox tenets of the city of New York.

There is a prayer which every Brahmin prays, in which he declares that he will never enter into a final state of bliss alone, but that everywhere he will strive for universal redemption; that never will he leave the world of sin and sorrow, but remain suffering and striving and sorrowing after universal salvation. Compare that with the orthodox idea, and send out your missionaries to the benighted Hindoos.

The doctrine of hell is infamous beyond all power to express. I wish there were words mean enough to express my feelings of loathing on this subject. What harm has it not done? What waste places has it not made? It has planted misery and wretchedness in this world; it peoples the future with selfish joys and lurid abysses of eternal flame. But we are getting more sense every day. We begin to despise those monstrous doctrines. If you want to better men and women, change their conditions here. Don't promise them something somewhere else. One biscuit will do more good than all the tracts that were ever peddled in the world. Give them more whitewash, more light, more air. You have to change men physically before you change them intellectually. I believe the time will come when every criminal will be treated as we now treat the diseased and sick, when every penitentiary will become a reformatory, and that if criminals go to them with hatred in their bosoms, they will leave them without feelings of revenge. Let me tell you the story of Orpheus and Eurydice. Eurydice had been carried away by the god of hell, and Orpheus, her lover, went in quest of her. He took with him his lyre, and played such exquisite music that all hell was amazed. Ixion forgot his labors at the wheel, the daughters of Danaus ceased from their hopeless task, Tantalus forgot his thirst, even Pluto smiled, and, for the first time in the history of hell, the eyes of the Furies were wet with tears. As it was with the lyre of Orpheus, so it is today with the great harmonies of Science, which are rescuing from the prisons of superstition the torn and bleeding heart of man.

# INGERSOLL'S LECTURE ON INDIVIDUALITY, AN ARRAIGNMENT OF THE CHURCH.

"His soul was like a star and dwelt apart."

On every hand are the enemies of individuality, and mental freedom. Custom meets us at the cradle,—and leaves us only at the tomb. Our first questions are answered by ignorance, and our last by superstition. We are pushed and dragged by countless hands along the beaten track, and our entire training can be summed up in the word "suppression." Our desire to have a thing or to do a thing is considered as conclusive evidence that we ought to do it. At every turn we run not to have it, and ought not against a cherubim and a flaming sword, guarding some entrance to the Eden of our desire. We are allowed to investigate all subjects in which we feel no particular interest, and to express the opinions of the majority with the utmost freedom. We are taught that liberty of speech should never be carried to the extent of contradicting the dead witnesses of a popular superstition. Society offers continual rewards for self-betrayal, and they are nearly all earned and claimed, and some are paid.

We have all read accounts of Christian gentlemen remarking when about to be hanged, how much better it would have been for them if they had only followed a mother's advice! But, after all, how fortunate it is for the world that the maternal advice has not been followed! How lucky it is for us all that it is somewhat unnatural for a human being to obey! Universal obedience is universal stagnation; disobedience is one of the conditions of progress. Select any age of the world and tell me what would have been the effect of implicit obedience. Suppose the church had had absolute control of the human mind at any time, would not the word liberty and progress have been blotted from the human speech? In defiance of advice, the world has advanced.

Suppose the astronomers had controlled the science of astronomy; suppose the doctors had controlled the science of medicine; suppose kings had been left to fix the form of government! Suppose our fathers had taken the advice of Paul, who was subject to the powers that be, "because they are ordained of God;" suppose the church could control the world today, we would go back to chaos and old night. Philosophy would be branded as infamous; science would again press its pale and thoughtful face against the prison bars; and round the limbs of liberty would climb the bigot's flame.

It is a blessed thing that in every age some one has had individuality enough and courage enough to stand by his own convictions; some one who had the grit to say his say. I believe it was Magellan who said, "the church says the earth is flat; but I have seen its shadow on the moon, and I have more confidence even in a shadow than in the church." On the prow of his ship were disobedience, defiance, scorn and success.

The trouble with most people is that they bow to what is called authority; they have a certain reverence for the old because it is old. They think a man is better for being dead, especially if he has been dead a long time, and that the forefathers of their nation were the greatest and best of all mankind. All these things they implicitly believe because it is popular and patriotic, and because they were told so when very small, and remember distinctly of hearing mother read it out of a book, and they are all willing to swear that mother was a good woman. It is hard to overestimate the influence of early training—in the direction of superstition. You first teach children that a certain book is true—that it was written by God himself—that to question its truth is sin, that to deny it is a crime, and that should they die without believing that book they will be forever damned without benefit of clergy; the consequence is that before they read that book they believe it to be true. When they do read, their minds are wholly unfitted to investigate its claim. They accept it as a matter of course.

In this way the reason is overcome, the sweet instincts of humanity are blotted from the heart, and while reading its infamous pages even justice throws aside her scales, shrieking for revenge; and charity, with bloody hands, applauds a deed of murder. In this way we are taught that the revenge of man is the justice of God, that mercy is not the same everywhere. In this way the ideas of our race have been subverted. In this way we have made tyrants, bigots, and inquisitors. In this way the brain of man has become a kind of palimpsest upon which, and over the writings of Nature, superstition has scribbled her countless lies. Our great trouble is that most teachers are dishonest. They teach as certainties those things concerning which they entertain doubts. They do not say, "We think this is so." but "We know this is so." They do not appeal to the reason of the pupil, but they command his faith. They keep all doubts to themselves; they do not explain, they assert. All this is infamous. In this way you make Christians, but you cannot make men; you cannot make women. You can make followers but no leaders; disciples, but no Christs. You may promise power, honor, and happiness to all those who will blindly follow, but you cannot keep your promise.

An eastern monarch said to a hermit, "Come with me and I will give you power." "I have all the power that I know how to use," replied the hermit. "Come," said the king, "I will give you wealth." "I have no wants that money can supply." "I will give you honor." "Ah! honor cannot be given; it must be earned." "Come," said the king, making a last appeal, "and I will give you happiness." "No," said the man of solitude; "there is no happiness without liberty, and he who follows cannot be free." "You shall have liberty too." "Then I will stay." And all the king's courtiers thought the hermit a fool.

Now and then somebody examines, and, in spite of all, keeps up his manhood and has courage to follow where his reason leads. Then the pious get together and repeat wise saws and exchange knowing nods and most prophetic winks. The stupidly wise sit owl-like on the dead limbs of the tree of knowledge, and solemnly, hoot. Wealth sneers, and fashion laughs, and respectability passes on the other side, and scorn points with all her skinny fingers, and, like the snakes of superstition, writhe and hiss, and slander lends her tongue, and infamy her brand, perjury her oath, and the law its power; and bigotry tortures and the church kills.

The church hates a thinker precisely for the same reason that a robber dislikes a sheriff, or that a thief despises the prosecuting witness. Tyranny likes courtiers, flatterers, followers, fawners, and superstition wants believers, disciples, zealots, hypocrites, and subscribers. The church demands worship, the very thing that man should give to no being, human or divine. To worship another is to degrade yourself. Worship is awe, and dread, and vague fear, and blind hope. It is the spirit of worship that elevates the one and degrades the many; and manacles even its own hands. The spirit of worship is the spirit of tyranny. The worshiper always regrets that he is not the worshiped. We should all remember that the intellect has no knees, and that whatever the attitude of the body may be, the brave soul is always found erect. Whoever worships, abdicates. Whoever believes, at the commands of power, tramples his own individuality beneath his feet, and voluntarily robs himself of all that renders man superior to brute.

The despotism of faith is justified upon the ground that Christian countries are the grandest and most prosperous of the world. At one time the same thing could have been truly said in India, in Egypt, in Greece, in Rome, and in every country that has in the history of the world, swept to empire. This argument proves too much not only, but the assumption upon which it is based is utterly false. Numberless circumstances and countless conditions have produced the prosperity of the Christian world. The truth is that we have advanced in spite of religious zeal, ignorance, and opposition. The church has won no victories for the rights of man. Over every fortress of tyranny has waved, and still waves, the banner of the church. Wherever brave blood has been shed the sword of the church has been wet. On every chain has been the sign of the cross. The alter and the throne have leaned against and supported each other. Who can appreciate the infinite impudence of one man assuming to think for others? Who can imagine the impudence of a church that threatens to inflict eternal punishment upon those who honestly reject its claims and scorn its pretensions? In the presence of the unknown we have all an equal right to guess.

Over the vast plain called life we are all travelers, and not one traveler is perfectly certain that he is going in the right direction. True it is that no other plain is so well supplied with guideboards. At every turn and crossing you find them, and upon each one is written the exact direction and distance. One great trouble is, however, that these boards are all different, and the result is that most travelers are confused in proportion to the number they read. Thousands of people are around each of these signs, and each one is doing his best to convince the traveler that his particular board is the only one upon which the least reliance can be placed, and that if his road is taken the reward for so doing will be infinite and eternal, while all the other roads are said to lead to hell, and all the makers of the other guideboards are declared to be heretics, hypocrites, and liars. "Well," says a traveler "you may be right in what you say, but allow me at least to read some of the other directions and examine a little into their claims. I wish to rely a little upon my own judgment in a matter of such great importance." "No sir!" shouts the zealot; "that is the very thing you are not allowed to do. You must go my way, without investigation or you are as good as damned already." "Well," says the traveler, "if that is so, I believe I had better go your way." And so most of them go along, taking the word of those who know as little as themselves. Now and then comes one who, in spite of all threats, calmly examines the claims of all, and as calmly rejects them all.

These travelers take roads of their own, and are denounced by all the others as infidels and atheists.

In my judgment every human being should take a road of his own. Every mind should be true to itself; should think, investigate and conclude for itself. This is a duty alike incumbent upon pauper and prince. Every soul should repel dictation and tyranny, no matter from what source they come—from earth or heaven, from men or gods. Besides, every traveler upon this vast plain should give to every other traveler his best idea as to the road that should be taken. Each is entitled to the honest opinion of all. And there is but one way to get an honest opinion upon any subject whatever. The person giving the opinion must be free from fear. The merchant must not fear to lose his custom, the doctor his practice, nor the preacher his pulpit. There can be no advance without liberty. Suppression of honest inquiry is retrogression, and must end in intellectual night. The tendency of orthodox religion today is towards mental slavery and barbarism. Not one of the orthodox ministers dare preach what he thinks if he knows that a majority of his congregation think otherwise. He knows that every member of his church stands guard over his brain with a creed, like a club, in his hand. He knows that he is not expected to search after the truth, but that he is employed to defend the creed. Every pulpit is a pillory in which stands a hired culprit, defending the justice of his own imprisonment.

Is it desirable that all should be exactly alike in their religious convictions? Is any such thing possible? Do we not know that there are no two persons alike in the whole world? No two trees, no two leaves, no two anythings that are alike? Infinite diversity is the law. Religion tries to force all minds into one mold. Knowing that all cannot believe, the church endeavors to make all say that they believe. She longs for the unity of hypocrisy, and detests the splendid diversity of individuality and freedom.

Nearly all people stand in great horror of annihilation, and yet to give up your individuality is to annihilate yourself. Mental slavery is mental death, and every man who has given up his intellectual freedom is the living coffin of his dead soul. In this sense every church is a cemetery and every creed an epitaph. We should all remember that to be like other folks is to be unlike ourselves, and that nothing can be more detestable in character than servile imitation. The great trouble with imitation is that we are apt to ape those who are in reality far below us. After all, the poorest bargain that a human being can make is to trade off his individuality for what is called respectability.

There is no saying more degrading than this: "It is better to be the tail of a lion than the head of a dog." It is a responsibility to think and act for yourself. Most people hate responsibility; therefore they join something and become the tail of some lion. They say, "My party can act for me—my church can do my thinking. It is enough for me to pay taxes and obey the lion to which I belong without troubling myself about the right, the wrong, or the why or the wherefore of anything whatever." These people are respectable. They hate reformers, and dislike exceedingly to have their minds disturbed. They regard convictions as very disagreeable things to have. They love forms, and enjoy, beyond everything else, telling what a splendid tail their lion has, and what a troublesome dog their neighbor is. Besides this natural inclination to avoid personal responsibility is and always has been the fact that every religionist has warned men against the presumption and wickedness of thinking for themselves. The reason has been denounced by all Christendom as the only unsafe guide. The church has left nothing undone to prevent, man following the logic of his brain. The plainest facts have been covered with the mantle of mystery. The grossest absurdities have been declared to be self-evident facts. The order of nature has been, as it were, reversed, in order that the hypocritical few might govern the honest many. The man who stood by the conclusion of his reason was denounced as a scorner and hater of God and his holy church. From the organization of the first church until this moment every member has borne the marks of collar and chain, and whip. No man ever seriously attempted to reform a church without being cast out and hunted down by the hounds of hypocrisy. The highest crime against a creed is to change it. Reformation is treason.

Thousands of young men are being educated at this moment by the various churches. What for? In order that they may be prepared to investigate the phenomena by which we are surrounded? No! The object, and the only object, is that they may be prepared to defend a creed. That they may learn the arguments of their respective churches and repeat them in the dull ears of a thoughtless congregation. If one after being thus trained at the expense of the Methodists turns Presbyterian or Baptist, he is denounced as an ungrateful wretch. Honest investigation is utterly impossible within the pale of any church, for the reason that if you think the church is right you will not investigate, and if you think it wrong, the church will investigate you. The consequence of this is that most of the theological literature is the result of suppression, of fear, of tyranny, and hypocrisy.

Every orthodox writer necessarily said to himself, "If I write that, my wife and children may want for bread, I will be covered with shame and branded with infamy, but if I write this, I will gain position, power and honor. My church rewards defenders and burns reformers." Under these conditions, all your Scotts, Henrys and McKnights have written; and weighed in these scales what are their commentaries worth? They are not the ideas and decisions of honest judges, but the sophisms of the paid attorneys of superstition. Who can tell what the world has lost by this infamous system of suppression? How many grand thinkers died with the mailed hand of superstition on their lips? How many splendid ideas have perished in the cradle of the brain, strangled in the poisonous coils of that python, the church!

For thousands of years a thinker was hunted down like an escaped convict. To him, who had braved the church, every door was shut, every knife was open. To shelter him from the wild storm, to give him a crust of bread when dying, to put a cup of water to his cracked and bleeding lips; these were all crimes, not one of which the church ever did forgive; and with the justice taught of God his helpless children were exterminated as scorpions and vipers.

Who at the present day can imagine the courage, the devotion to principle, the intellectual and moral grandeur it once required to be an infidel, to brave the church, her racks, her fagots, her dungeons, her tongues of fire—to defy and scorn her heaven and her devil and her God? They were the noblest sons of earth. They were the real saviors of our race, the destroyers of superstition and the creators of science. They were the real Titans who bared their grand foreheads to all the thunderbolts of all the gods. The church has been, and still is, the great robber. She has rifled not only the pockets but the brains of the world. She is the stone at the sepulcher of liberty; the upas tree in whose shade the intellect of man has withered; the gorgon beneath whose gaze the human heart has turned to stone.

Under her influence even the Protestant mother expects to be in heaven, while her brave boy, who is fighting for the rights of man, shall writhe in hell. It is said that some of the Indian tribes place the heads of their children between pieces of bark until the form of the skull is permanently changed. To us this seems a most shocking custom, and yet, after all, is it as bad as to put the souls of our children in the straight-jacket of a creed, to so utterly deform their minds that they regard the God of the bible as a being of infinite mercy, and really consider it a virtue to believe a thing just because it seems unreasonable? Every child in the Christian world has uttered its wondering protest against this outrage. All the machinery of the church is constantly employed in thus corrupting the reason of children. In every possible way they are robbed of their own thoughts and forced to accept the statements of others. Every Sunday-school has for its object the crushing out of every germ of individuality. The poor children are taught that nothing can be more acceptable to God than unreasoning obedience and eyeless faith, and that to believe that God did an impossible act is far better than to do a good one yourself. They are told that all the religions have been simply the John the Baptist of ours; that all the gods of antiquity have withered and sunken into the Jehovah of the Jews; that all the longings and aspirations of the race are realized in the motto of the Evangelical Alliance, "Liberty in non-essentials;" that all there is, or ever was of religion can be found in the apostle's creed; that there is nothing left to be discovered; that all the thinkers are dead, and all the living should simply be believers; that we have only to repeat the epitaph found on the grave of wisdom; that graveyards are the best possible universities, and that the children must be forever beaten with the bones of the fathers.

It has always seemed absurd to suppose that a God would choose for his companions during all eternity the dear souls whose highest and only ambition is to obey. He certainly would now and then be tempted to make the same remark made by an English gentleman to his poor guest. This gentleman had invited a man in humble circumstances to dine with him. The man was so overcome with honor that to everything the gentleman said he replied, "Yes." Tired at last with the monotony of acquiescence, the gentleman cried out, "For God's sake, my good man, say 'No' just once, so there will be two of us."

Is it possible that an infinite God created this world simply to be the dwelling-place of slaves and serfs? Simply for the purpose of raising orthodox Christians; that he did a few miracles to astonish them; that all the evils of life are simply his punishments, and that he is finally going to turn heaven into a kind of religious museum, filled with Baptist barnacles, petrified Presbyterians, and Methodist mummies? I want no heaven for which I must give my reason; no happiness in exchange for my liberty, and no immortality that demands the surrender of my individuality. Better rot in the windowless tomb to which there is no door but the red mouth of the pallid worm, than wear the jeweled collar even of a God.

Religion does not and cannot contemplate man as free. She accepts only the homage of the prostrate, and scorns the offerings of those who stand erect. She cannot tolerate the liberty of thought. The wide and sunny fields belong not to her domain. The star-lit heights of genius and individuality are above and beyond her appreciation and power. Her subjects cringe at her feet covered with the dust of obedience. They are not athletes standing posed by rich life and brave endeavor like the antique statues, but shriveled deformities studying with furtive glance the cruel face of power.

No religionist seems capable of comprehending this plain truth. There is this difference between thought and action: For our actions we are responsible to ourselves and to those injuriously affected; for thoughts there can, in the nature of things, be no responsibility to gods or men, here or hereafter. And yet the Protestant has vied with the Catholic in denouncing freedom of thought, and while I was taught to hate Catholicism with every drop of my blood, it is only justice to say that in all essential particulars it is precisely the same as every other religion. Luther denounced mental liberty with all the coarse and brutal vigor of his nature; Calvin despised from the very bottom of his petrified heart anything that even looked like religious toleration, and solemnly declared to advocate it was to crucify Christ afresh. All the founders of all the orthodox churches have advocated the same infamous tenet. The truth is that what is called religion is necessarily inconsistent with free thought.

A believer is a songless bird in a cage, a freethinker is an eagle parting the clouds with tireless wings.

At present, owing to the inroads that have been made by liberals and infidels, most of the churches pretend to be in favor of religious liberty. Of these churches we will ask this question: "How can a man who conscientiously believes in religious liberty worship a God who does not?" They say to us: "We will not imprison you on account of your belief, but our God will. We will not burn you because you throw away the sacred scriptures; but their Author will," "We think it an infamous crime to persecute our brethren for opinion's sake; but the God whom we ignorantly worship will on that account damn his own children forever." Why is it that these Christians do not only detest the infidels, but so cordially despise each other? Why do they refuse to worship in the temples of each other? Why do they care so little for the damnation of men, and so much for the baptism of children? Why will they adorn their churches with the money of thieves, and flatter vice for the sake of subscription? Why will they attempt to bribe science to certify to the writings of God? Why do they torture the words of the great into an acknowledgment of the truth of Christianity? Why do they stand with hat in hand before presidents, kings, emperors and scientists, begging like Lazarus for a few crumbs of religious comfort? Why are they so delighted to find an allusion to providence in the message of Lincoln? Why are they so afraid that some one will find out that Paley wrote an essay in favor of the Epicurean philosophy, and that Sir Isaac

Newton was once an infidel? Why are they so anxious to show that Voltaire recanted, that Paine died palsied with fear; that the Emperor Julian cried out, "Galilean, thou hast conquered;" that Gibbon died a Catholic; that Agassiz had a little confidence in Moses; that the old Napoleon was once complimentary enough to say that he thought Christ greater than himself or Caesar; that Washington was caught on his knees at Valley Forge; that blunt old Ethan Allen told his child to believe the religion of her mother; that Franklin said, "Don't unchain the tiger;" that Volney got frightened in a storm at sea, and that Oakes Ames was a wholesale liar?

Is it because the foundation of their temple is crumbling, because the walls are cracked, the pillars leaning, the great dome swaying to its fall, and because science has written over the high altar its mene, mene, tekel, upharsin, the old words destined to be the epitaph of all religions?

Every assertion of individual independence has been a step towards infidelity. Luther started toward Humboldt, Wesley toward Bradlaugh. To really reform the church is to destroy it. Every new religion has a little less superstition than the old, so that the religion of science is but a question of time. I will not say the church has been an unmitigated evil in all respects. Its history is infamous and glorious. It has delighted in the production of extremes. It has furnished murderers for its own martyrs. It has sometimes fed the body, but has always starved the soul. It has been a charitable highwayman, a generous pirate. It has produced some angels and a multitude of devils. It has built more prisons than asylums. It made a hundred orphans while it cared for one. In one hand it carried the alms-dish, and in the other a sword. It has founded schools and endowed universities for the purpose of destroying true learning. It filled the world with hypocrites and zealots, and upon the cross of its own Christ it crucified the individuality of man. It has sought to destroy the independence of the soul, and put the world upon its knees. This is its crime. The commission of this crime was necessary to its existence. In order to compel obedience it declared that it had the truth and all the truth; that God had made it the keeper of all his secrets; his agent and his vice-agent. It declared that all other religions were false and infamous. It rendered all compromises impossible, and all thought superfluous. Thought was an enemy, obedience was its friend. Investigation was fraught with danger; therefore investigation was suppressed. The holy of holies was behind the curtain. All this was upon the principle that forgers hate to have the signature examined by an expert, and that imposture detests curiosity.

"He that hath ears to hear let him hear," has always been one of the favorite texts of the church.

In short, Christianity has always opposed every forward movement of the human race. Across the highway of progress it has always been building breastworks of bibles, tracts, commentaries, prayerbooks, creeds, dogmas and platforms, and at every advance the Christians have gathered behind these heaps of rubbish and shot the poisoned arrows of malice at the soldiers of freedom.

And even the liberal Christian of today has his holy of holies, and in the niche of the temple of his heart has his idol. He still clings to a part of the old superstition, and all the pleasant memories of the old belief linger in the horizon of his thoughts like a sunset. We associate the memory of those we love with the religion of our childhood. It seems almost a sacrilege to rudely destroy the idols that our fathers worshiped, and turn their sacred and beautiful truths into the silly fables of barbarism. Some throw away the old testament and cling to the new, while others give up everything except the idea that there is a personal God, and that in some wonderful way we are the objects of His care.

Even this, in my opinion, as science, the great iconoclast, marches onward, will have to be abandoned with the rest. The great ghost will surely share the fate of the little ones. They fled at the first appearance of the dawn, and the other will vanish with the perfect day. Until then, the independence of man is little more than a dream. Overshadowed by an immense personality—in the presence of the irresponsible and the infinite, the individuality of man is lost, and he falls prostrate in the very dust of fear. Beneath the frown of the absolute, man stands a wretched, trembling slave—beneath his smile be is at best only a fortunate serf. Governed by a being whose arbitrary will is law, chained to the chariot of power, his destiny rests in the pleasure of the unknown. Under these circumstances what wretched object can he have in lengthening out his aimless life?

And yet, in most minds, there is a vague fear of what the gods may do, and the safe side is considered the best side.

A gentleman walking among the ruins of Athens came upon a fallen statue of Jupiter. Making an exceedingly low bow, he said: "Jupiter, I salute thee." He then added: "Should you ever get up in the world again, do not forget, I pray you, that I treated you politely while you were prostrate."

We have all been taught by the church that nothing is so well calculated to excite the ire of Deity as to express a doubt as to His existence, and that to deny it is an unpardonable sin. Numerous well-attested instances were referred to, of atheists being struck dead for denying the existence of God. According to these religious people, God is infinitely above us in every respect, infinitely merciful, and yet He cannot bear to hear a poor finite man honestly question His existence. Knowing as He does that His children are groping in darkness and struggling with doubt and fear; knowing that He could enlighten them if He would, He still holds the expression of a sincere doubt as to His existence the most infamous of crimes.

According to the orthodox logic, God having furnished us with imperfect minds has a right to demand a perfect result. Suppose Mr. Smith should overhear a couple of small bugs holding a discussion as to the existence of Mr. Smith, and suppose one should have the temerity to declare upon the honor of a bug that he had examined the whole question to the best of his ability, including the argument based upon design, and had come to the conclusion that no man by the name of Smith had ever lived. Think then of Mr. Smith flying into an ecstasy of rage, crushing the atheist bug beneath his iron heel, while he exclaimed, "I will teach you, blasphemous wretch, that Smith is a diabolical fact!" What then can we think of God who would open the artillery of heaven upon one of his own children for simply expressing his honest thought? And what man, who really thinks, can help repeating the words of Aeneas, "If there are gods they certainly pay no attention to the affairs of man."

In religious ideas and conceptions there has been for ages a slow and steady development. At the bottom of the ladder (speaking of modern times) is Catholicism, and at the top are atheism and science. The intermediate rounds of this ladder are occupied by the various sects, whose name is legion.

But whatever may be the truth on any subject has nothing to do with our right to investigate that subject, and express any opinion we may form. All that I ask is the right I freely accord to all others.

A few years ago a Methodist clergyman took it upon himself to give me a piece of friendly advice. "Although you may disbelieve the bible," said he, "you ought not to say so. That you should keep to yourself." "Do you believe the bible?" said I. He replied, "Most assuredly." To which I retorted, "Your answer conveys no information to me. You may be following your own advice. You told me to suppress my opinions. Of course a man who will advise others to dissimulate will not always be particular about telling the truth himself."

It is the duty of each and every one to maintain his individuality. "This above all, to thine own self be true, and it must follow as the night the day, thou canst not then be false to any man." It is a magnificent thing to be the sole proprietor of yourself. It is a terrible thing to wake up at night and say: "There is nobody in this bed!" It is humiliating to know that your ideas are all borrowed, and that you are indebted to your memory for your principles, that your religion is simply one of your habits, and that you would have convictions if they were only contagious. It is mortifying to feel that you belong to a mental mob and cry "crucify him" because the others do. That you reap what the great and brave have sown, and that you can benefit the world only by leaving it.

Surely every human being ought to attain to the dignity of the unit. Surely it is worth something to be one and to feel that the census of the universe would not be complete without counting you.

Surely there is grandeur in knowing that in the realm of thought, at least, you are without a chain; that you have the right to explore all heights and all depths; that there are no walls, fences, prohibited places, nor sacred corners in all the vast expanse of thought; that your intellect owes no allegiance to any being, human or divine; that you hold all in fee and upon no condition and by no tenure whatever; that in the world of mind you are relieved from all personal dictation, and from the ignorant tyranny of majorities.

Surely it is worth something to feel that there are no priests, no popes, no parties, no governments, no kings, no gods to whom your intellect can be compelled to pay a reluctant homage.

Surely it is a joy to know that all the cruel ingenuity of bigotry can devise no prison, no lock, no cell, in which for one instant to confine a thought; that ideas cannot be dislocated by racks, nor crushed in iron boots, nor burned with fire.

Surely it is sublime to think that the brain is a castle, and that within its curious bastions and winding halls the soul, in spite of all worlds and all beings, is the supreme sovereign of itself.

# INGERSOLL'S LECTURE ON HUMBOLDT

Ladies and Gentlemen: Great minds seem to be a part of the infinite. Those possessing them seem to be brothers of the mountains and the seas.

Humboldt was one of these. He was one of the few great enough to rise above the superstition and prejudice of his time, and to know that experience, observation and reason are the only basis of knowledge.

He became one of the greatest of men in spite of having been born rich and noble—in spite of position. I say in spite of these things, because wealth and position are generally the enemies of genius, and the destroyers of talent.

It is often said of this or that man that he is a self-made man—that he was born of the poorest and humblest parents, and that with every obstacle to overcome he became great. This is a mistake. Poverty is generally an advantage. Most of the intellectual giants of the world have been nursed at the sad but loving breast of poverty. Most of those who have climbed highest on the shining ladder of fame commenced at the lowest round. They were reared in the straw-thatched cottages of Europe, in the log-houses of America, in the factories of the great cities, in the midst of toil, in the smoke and din of labor, and on the verge of want. They were rocked by the feet of mothers whose hands, at the same time, were busy with the needle or the wheel.

It is hard for the rich to resist the thousand allurements of pleasure, and so I say that Humboldt, in spite of having been born to wealth and high social position, became truly and grandly great.

In the antiquated and romantic castle of Tegel, by the side of the pine forest, on the shore of the charming lake, near the beautiful city of Berlin, the great Humboldt, one hundred years ago to-day, was born, and there he was educated after the method suggested by Rousseau—Campe, the philologist and critic, and the intellectual Kunth being his tutors. There he received the impressions that determined his career; there the great idea that the universe is governed by law took possession of his mind, and there he dedicated his life to the demonstration of this sublime truth.

He came to the conclusion that the source of man's unhappiness is his ignorance of nature.

He longed to give a physical description of the universe—a grand picture of nature; to account for all phenomena; to discover the laws governing the world; to do away with that splendid delusion called special-providence, and to establish the fact that the universe is governed by law.

To establish this truth was, and is, of infinite importance to mankind. That fact is the death-knell of superstition; it gives liberty to every soul, annihilates fear, and ushers in the Age of Reason.

The object of this illustrious man was to comprehend the phenomena of physical objects in their general connection, and to represent nature as one great whole, moved and animated by internal forces.

For this purpose he turned his attention to descriptive botany, traversing distant lands and mountain ranges to ascertain with certainty the geographical distribution of plants. He investigated the laws regulating the differences of temperature and climate, and the changes of the atmosphere. He studied the formation of the earth's crust, explored the deepest mines, ascended the highest mountains, and wandered through the craters of extinct volcanoes.

He became thoroughly acquainted with chemistry, with astronomy, with terrestrial magnetism; and as the investigation of one subject leads to all others, for the reason that there is a mutual dependence and a necessary connection between all facts, so Humboldt became acquainted with all the known sciences.

His fame does not depend so much upon his discoveries (although he discovered enough to make hundreds of reputations) as upon his vast and splendid generalizations.

He was to science what Shakespeare was to the drama.

He found, so to speak, the world full of unconnected facts, all portions of a vast system—parts of a great machine; he discovered the connection that each bears to all, put them together, and demonstrated beyond all contradiction that the earth is governed by law.

He knew that to discover the connection of phenomena is the primary aim of all natural investigation. He was infinitely practical.

Origin and destiny were questions with which he had nothing to do.

His surroundings made him what he was.

In accordance with a law not fully comprehended, he was a production of his time.

Great men do not live alone; they are surrounded by the great; they are the instruments used to accomplish the tendencies of their generation; they fulfill the prophecies of their age.

Nearly all of the scientific men of the eighteenth century had the same idea entertained by Humboldt, but most of them in a dim and confused way. There was, however, a general belief among the intelligent that the world is governed by law, and that there really exists a connection between all facts, or that all facts are simply the different aspects of a general fact, and that the task of science is to discover this connection; to comprehend this general fact or to announce the laws of things.

Germany was full of thought, and her universities swarmed with philosophers and grand thinkers in every department of knowledge.

Humboldt was the friend and companion of the greatest poets, historians, philologists, artists, statesmen, critics and logicians of his time.

He was the companion of Schiller, who believed that man would be regenerated through the influence of the beautiful; of Goethe, the grand patriarch of German literature; of Wieland, who has been called the Voltaire of Germany; of Herder, who wrote the outlines of a philosophical history of man; of Kotzebue, who lived in the world of romance; of Schleiermacher, the pantheist; of Schlegel, who gave to his country the enchanted realm of Shakespeare—of the sublime Kant, author of the first work published in Germany on Pure Reason; of Fichte, the infinite idealist; of Schopenhauer, the European Buddhist who followed the great Gautama to the painless and dreamless Nirvana, and of hundreds of others whose names are familiar to and honored by the scientific world.

The German mind had been grandly roused from the long lethargy of the dark ages of ignorance, fear and faith. Guided by the holy light of reason, every department of knowledge was investigated, enriched and illustrated.

Humboldt breathed the atmosphere of investigation; old ideas were abandoned; old creeds, hallowed by centuries, were thrown aside; thought became courageous; the athlete, Reason, challenged to mortal combat the monsters of superstition.

No wonder that under these influences Humboldt formed the great purpose of presenting to the world a picture of nature, in order that men might, for the first time, behold the face of their Mother.

Europe becoming too small for his genius, he visited the tropics in the new world, where, in the most circumscribed limits, he could find the greatest number of plants, of animals, and the greatest diversity of climate, that he might ascertain the laws governing the production and distribution of plants, animals and men, and the effects of climate upon them all. He sailed along the gigantic Amazon—the mysterious Orinoco—traversed the Pampas—climbed the Andes until he stood upon the crags of Chimborazo, more than eighteen thousand feet above the level of the sea, and climbed on until blood flowed from his eyes and lips. For nearly five years he pursued his investigations in the new world, accompanied by the intrepid Bonpland. Nothing escaped his attention. He was the best intellectual organ of these new revelations of science. He was calm, reflective and eloquent; filled with a sense of the beautiful, and the love of truth. His collections were immense, and valuable beyond calculation to every science. He endured innumerable hardships, braved countless dangers in unknown and savage lands, and exhausted his fortune for the advancement of true learning.

Upon his return to Europe he was hailed as the second Columbus; as the scientific discoverer of America; as the revealer of a new world; as the great demonstrator of the sublime truth that universe is governed by law.

I have seen a picture of the old man, sitting upon a mountain side—above him the eternal snow; below, smiling valley of the tropics, filled with vine and palm. His chin upon his breast, his eyes deep, thoughtful and calm, his forehead majestic—grander than the mountain upon which he sat. "Crowned with the snow of his whitened hair," he looked the intellectual autocrat of this world.

Not satisfied with his discoveries in America, he crossed the steppes of Asia, the wastes of Siberia, the great Ural range, adding to the knowledge of mankind at every step. His energy acknowledged no obstacle, his life knew no leisure; every day was filled with labor and with thought. He was one of the apostles of science, and he served his divine master with a self-sacrificing zeal that knew no abatement—with an ardor that constantly increased, and with a devotion unwavering and constant as the polar star.

In order that the people at large might have the benefit of his numerous discoveries, and his vast knowledge, he delivered at Berlin a course of lectures, consisting of sixty-one free addresses, upon the following subjects:

Five upon the nature and limits of physical geography.

Three were devoted to a history of science.

Two to inducements to a study of natural science.

Sixteen on the heavens.

Five on the form, density, latent heat, and magnetic power of the earth, and to the polar light.

Four were on the nature of the crust of the earth, on hot springs, earthquakes and volcanoes.

Two on mountains, and the type of their formation.

Two on the form of the earth's surface, on the connection of continents, and the elevation of soil over ravines.

Three on the sea as a globular fluid surrounding the earth.

Ten on the atmosphere—as an elastic fluid surrounding the earth, and on the distribution of heat.

One on the geographic distribution of organized matter in general,

Three on the geography of plants.

Three on the geography of animals; and

Two on the races of men.

These lectures are what is known as the Cosmos, and present a scientific picture of the world—of infinite diversity in unity; of ceaseless motion in the eternal grasp of law.

These lectures contain the result of his investigation, observation and experience; they furnish the connection between phenomena; they disclose some of the changes through which the earth has passed in the countless ages; the history of vegetation, animals and men; the effects of climate upon individuals and nations; the relation we sustain to other worlds, and demonstrate that all phenomena, whether insignificant or grand, exist in accordance with inexorable law.

There are some truths, however, that we never should forget: Superstition has always been the relentless enemy of science; faith has been a hater of demonstration; hypocrisy has been sincere only in its dread of truth, and all religions are inconsistent with mental freedom.

Since the murder of Hypatia in the fifth century, when the polished blade of Greek philosophy was broken by the club of ignorant Catholicism, until today, superstition has detested every effort of reason.

It is almost impossible to conceive of the completeness of the victory that the church achieved over philosophy. For ages science was utterly ignored;

thought was a poor slave; an ignorant priest was master of the world; faith put out the eyes of the soul; the reason was a trembling coward; the imagination was set on fire of hell; every human feeling was sought to be suppressed; love was considered infinitely sinful; pleasure was the road to eternal fire, and God was supposed to be happy only when his children were miserable. The world was governed by an Almighty's whim; prayers could change the order of things, halt the grand procession of nature; could produce rain, avert pestilence, famine, and death in all its forms. There was no idea of the certain; all depended upon divine pleasure—or displeasure, rather; heaven was full of inconsistent malevolence, and earth of ignorance. Everything was done to appease the divine wrath; every public calamity was caused by the sins of the people; by a failure to pay tithes, or for having, even in secret, felt a disrespect for a priest. To the poor multitude the earth was a kind of enchanted forest, full of demons ready to devour, and theological serpents lurking, with infinite power, to fascinate and torture the unhappy and impotent soul. Life to them was a dim and mysterious labyrinth, in which they wandered weary, and lost, guided by priests as bewildered as themselves, without knowing that at every step the Ariadne of reason offered them the long lost clue.

The very heavens were full of death; the lightning was regarded as the glittering vengeance of God, and the earth was thick with snares for the unwary feet of man. The soul was supposed to be crowded with the wild beasts of desire; the heart to be totally corrupt, prompting only to crime; virtues were regarded as deadly sins in disguise; there was a continual warfare being waged between the Deity and the devil for the possession of every soul, the latter generally being considered victorious. The flood, the tornado, the volcano, were all evidences of the displeasure of heaven and the sinfulness of man. The blight that withered, the frost that blackened, the earthquake that devoured, were the messengers of the creator.

The world was governed by fear.

Against all the evils of nature there was known only the defense of prayer, of fasting, of credulity, and devotion. Man, in his helplessness, endeavored to soften the heart of God. The faces of the multitude were blanched with fear, and wet with tears; they were the prey of hypocrites, kings and priests.

My heart bleeds when I contemplate the sufferings endured by the millions now dead; of those who lived when the world appeared to be insane; when the heavens were filled with an infinite HORROR, who snatched babes, with dimpled hands and rosy cheeks, from the white breasts of mothers and dashed them into an abyss of eternal flame.

Slowly, beautifully, like the coming of the dawn, came the grand truth that the universe is governed by law—that disease fastens itself upon the good and upon the bad; that the tornado cannot be stopped by counting beads; that the rushing lava pauses not for bended knees, the lightning for clasped and uplifted hands, nor the cruel waves of the sea for prayer; that paying tithes causes rather than prevents famine; that pleasure is not sin; that happiness is the only good; that demons and gods exist only in the imagination; that faith is a lullaby, sung to put the soul to sleep; that devotion is a bribe that fear offers to supposed power; that offering rewards in another world for obedience in this, is simply buying a soul on credit; that knowledge consists in ascertaining the laws of nature, and that wisdom is the science of happiness. Slowly, grandly, beautifully, these truths are dawning upon mankind.

From Copernicus we learned that this earth is only a grain of sand on the infinite shore of the universe; that everywhere we are surrounded by shining worlds vastly greater than our own, all moving and existing in accordance with law. True, the earth began to grow small, but man began to grow great.

The moment the fact was established that other worlds are governed by law, it was only natural to conclude that our little world was also under its dominion. The old theological method of accounting for physical phenomena by the pleasure and displeasure of the Deity was, by the intellectual, abandoned. They found: that disease, death, life, thought, heat, cold, the seasons, the winds, the dreams of man, the instinct of animals—in short, that all physical and mental phenomena are governed by law, absolute, eternal and inexorable.

Let it be understood by the term Law is meant the same invariable relations of succession and resemblance predicated of all facts springing from like conditions. Law is a fact—not a cause. It is a fact that like conditions produce like results; this fact is LAW. When we say that the universe is governed by law, we mean that this fact, called law, is incapable of change; that it is, has been, and forever will be, the same inexorable, immutable FACT, inseparable from all phenomena. Law, in this sense, was not enacted or made. It could not have been otherwise than as it is. That which necessarily exists has no creator.

Only a few years ago this earth was considered the real center of the universe; all the stars were supposed to revolve around this insignificant atom. The German mind, more than any other, has done away with this piece of egotism. Purbach and Mullerus, in the fifteenth century, contributed most to the advancement of astronomy in their day. To the latter the world is indebted for the introduction of decimal fractions, which completed our arithmetical notation, and formed the second of the three steps by which, in modern times, the science of numbers has been so greatly improved; and yet both of these men believed in the most childish absurdities—at least in enough of them to die without their orthodoxy having ever been questioned.

Next came the great Copernicus, and he stands at the head of the heroic thinkers of his time, who had the courage and the mental strength to break the chains of prejudice, custom and authority, and to establish truth on the basis of experience, observation and reason. He removed the earth, so to speak, from the center of the universe, and ascribed to it a twofold motion, and demonstrated the true position which it occupies in the solar system.

At his bidding the earth began to revolve. At the command of his genius it commenced its grand flight amid the eternal constellations around the sun. For fifty years his discoveries were disregarded. All at once, by the exertions of Galileo, they were kindled into so grand a conflagration as to consume the philosophy of Aristotle, to alarm the hierarchy of Rome, and to threaten the existence of every opinion not founded upon experience, observation and reason.

The earth was no longer considered a universe governed by the caprices of some revengeful Deity, who had made the stars out of what he had left after completing the world, and had stuck them in the sky simply to adorn the night.

I have said this much concerning astronomy because it was the first splendid step forward! The first sublime blow that shattered the lance and shivered the shield of superstition; the first real help that man received from heaven. Because it was the first great lever placed beneath the altar of a false religion; the first revelation of the infinite to man, the first authoritative declaration that the universe is governed by law; the first science that gave the lie direct to the cosmogony of barbarism; and because it is the sublimest victory that reason has achieved.

In speaking of astronomy I have confined myself to the discoveries made since the revival of learning. Long ago, on the banks of the Ganges, ages before Copernicus lived, Aryabhatta taught that the earth is a sphere and revolves on its own axis. This, however, does not detract from the glory of the great German. The discovery of the Hindoo had been lost in the midnight of Europe—in the age of faith—and Copernicus was as much a discoverer as though Aryabhatta had never lived.

In this short address there is no time to speak of other sciences, and to point out the particular evidence furnished by each to establish the dominion of law, nor to more than mention the name of Descartes, the first who undertook to give an explanation of the celestial motions, or who formed the vast and philosophic conception of reducing all the phenomena of the universe to the same law; of Montaigne, one of the heroes of common sense; of Galvani, whose experiments gave the telegraph to the world; of Voltaire, who contributed more than any other of the sons of men to the destruction of religious intolerance; of August Comte, whose genius erected to itself a monument that still touches the stars; of Guttenberg, Watt, Stephenson, Arkwright, all soldiers of science in the grand army of the dead kings.

The glory of science is that it is freeing the soul-breaking the mental manacles—getting the brain out of bondage—giving courage to thought—filling the world with mercy, justice and joy.

Science found agriculture plowing with a stick—reaping with a sickle—commerce at the mercy of the treacherous waves and the inconstant winds—a world without books—without schools—man denying the authority of reason, employing his ingenuity in the manufacture of instruments of torture—in building inquisitions and cathedrals. It found the land filled with malicious monks—with persecuting Protestants, and the burners of men. It found a world full of fear, ignorance upon its knees; credulity the greatest virtue; women treated like beasts, of burden; cruelty the only means of reformation. It found the world at the mercy of disease and famine; men trying to read their fates in the stars, and to tell their fortunes by signs and wonders; generals thinking to conquer their enemies by making the sign of the cross, or by telling a rosary. It found all history full of petty and ridiculous falsehood, and the Almighty was supposed to spend most of his time turning sticks into snakes, drowning boys for swimming on Sunday, and killing little children for the purpose of converting their parents. It found the earth filled with slaves and tyrants, the people in all countries downtrodden, half naked, half starved, without hope, and without reason in the world.

Such was the condition of man when the morning of science dawned upon his brain, and before he had heard the sublime declaration that the universe is governed by law.

For the change that has taken place we are indebted solely to science—the only lever capable of raising mankind. Abject faith is barbarism; reason is civilization. To obey is slavish; to act from a sense of obligation perceived by the reason is noble. Ignorance worships mystery; reason explains it—the one grovels, the other soars.

No wonder that fable is the enemy of knowledge. A man with a false diamond shuns the society of lapidaries, and it is upon this principle that superstition abhors science.

In all ages the people have honored those who dishonored them. The have worshiped their destroyers—they have canonized the most gigantic liars, and buried the great thieves in marble and gold. Under the loftiest monuments sleeps the dust of murder.

Imposture has always worn a crown.

The world is beginning to change because the people are beginning to think. To think is to advance. Everywhere the great minds are investigating the creeds and the superstitions of men—the phenomena of nature, and the laws of things. At the head of this great army of investigators stood Humboldt—the serene leader of an intellectual host—a king by the suffrage of science, and the divine right of genius.

And today we are not honoring some butcher called a soldier—some wily politician called a statesman—some robber called a king—nor some malicious metaphysician called a saint. We are honoring the grand Humboldt, whose victories were all achieved in the arena of thought; who destroyed prejudice, ignorance and error—not men: who shed light—not blood, and who contributed to the knowledge, the wealth and the happiness of all mankind.

His life was pure, his aims lofty, his learning varied and profound, and his achievements vast.

We honor him because he has ennobled our race, because he has contributed as much as any man living or dead to the real prosperity of the world. We honor him because he honored us—because he labored for others—because he was the most learned man of the most learned nation—because he left a legacy of glory to every human being. For these reasons he is honored throughout the world. Millions are doing homage to his genius at this moment, and millions are pronouncing his name with reverence, and recounting what he accomplished.

We associate the name of Humboldt with oceans, continents mountains and volcanoes—with the great plains—the wide deserts—the snow-lipped craters of the Andes—with primeval forests and European capitals—with wildernesses and universities—with savages and savants—with the lonely rivers of unpeopled wastes—with peaks and pampas, and steppes, and cliffs and crags—with the progress of the world—with every science known to man, and with every star glittering in the immensity of space.

Humboldt adopted none of the soul-shrinking creeds of his day; wasted none of his time in the stupidities, inanities and contradictions of theological metaphysics; he did not endeavor to harmonize the astronomy and geology of a barbarous people with the science of the nineteenth century. Never, for one moment, did he abandon the sublime standard of truth; he investigated, he studied, he thought, he separated the gold from the dross in the crucible of his grand brain. He was never found on his knees before the altar of superstition. He stood erect by the grand, tranquil column of reason. He was an admirer, a lover, an adorer of nature, and at the age of ninety, bowed by the weight of nearly a century, covered with the insignia of honor, loved by a nation, respected by a world, with kings for his servants, he laid his weary head upon her bosom—upon the bosom of the universal mother—and with her loving arms around him, sank into that slumber called death.

History added another name to the starry scroll of the immortals.

The world is his monument; upon the eternal granite of her hills he inscribed his name, and there, upon everlasting stone, his genius wrote this, the sublimest of truths:

"THE UNIVERSE IS GOVERNED BY LAW!"

# INGERSOLL'S LECTURE ON WHICH WAY?

Ladies and Gentlemen: For thousands of years men have been asking the questions: "How shall we civilize the world? How shall we protect life, liberty, property and reputations? How shall we do away with crime and poverty? How clothe, and feed, and educate, and civilize mankind?" These are the questions that are asked by thoughtful men and thoughtful women. The question with them is not, "What will we do in some other world?" Time enough to ask that when we get there. The business we will attend to now is, how are, we to civilize the world? What priest shall I ask? What sacred volume shall I search? What oracle can I consult? At what shrine must I bow to find out what is to be done? Each church has a different answer; each has a different recipe for the salvation of the people, but not while they are in this world. All that is to be done in this world is to get ready for the next.

In the first place I am met by the theological world. Have I the right to inquire? They say, "Certainly; it is your duty to inquire." Each church has a recipe for the salvation of this world, but not while you are in this world—afterward. They treat time as a kind of pier—a kind of wharf running out into the great ocean of eternity; and they treat us all as though we were waiting there, sitting on our trunks, for the gospel ship.

I want to know what to do here. Have I the right to inquire? Yes. If I have the right to inquire, then I have the right to investigate. If I have the right to investigate, I have the right to accept. If I have the right to accept, I have the right to reject. And what religion have I the right to reject? That which does not conform with my reason, with my standard of truth, with my standard of common sense. Millions of men have been endeavoring to govern this world by means of the supernatural. Thousands and thousands of churches exist, thousands of cathedrals and temples have been built, millions of men have been engaged to preach this gospel; and what has been the result in this world? Will one church have any sympathy with another? Does the religion of one country have any respect for that of another? Or does not each religion claim to be the only one? And does not the priest of every religion, with infinite impudence, consign the disciples of all others to eternal fire?

Why is it the churches have failed to civilize this world? Why is it that the Christian countries are no better than any other countries? Why is it that Christian men are no better than any other men? Why is it that ministers as a class are no better than doctors, or lawyers, or merchants, or mechanics, or locomotive engineers? And a locomotive engineer is a thousand times more useful. Give me a good engineer and a bad preacher to go through this world with rather than a bad engineer and a good preacher; and there is this curious fact about the believers in the supernatural: The priests of one church have no confidence in the miracles and wonders told by the priests of the other churches. Maybe they know each other. A Christian missionary will tell the Hindoo of the miracles of the bible; the Hindoo smiles. The Hindoo tells the Christian missionary of the miracles of his sacred books; and the missionary looks upon him with pity and contempt. No priest takes the word of another.

I heard once a little story that illustrates this point: A gentleman in a little party was telling of a most wonderful occurrence, and when he had finished everybody said: "Is it possible? Why, did you ever hear anything like that?" All united in a kind of wondering chorus except one man. He said nothing. He was perfectly still and unmoved; and one who had been greatly astonished by the story said to him: "Did you hear that story?" "Yes." "Well, you don't appear to be excited." "Well no," he said; "I am a liar myself."

There is another trouble with the supernatural. It has no honesty; it is consumed by egotism; it does not think—it knows; consequently it has no patience with the honest doubter. And how has the church treated the honest doubter? He has been answered by force, by authority, by popes, by cardinals and bishops, and councils, and, above all, by mobs. In that way the honest doubter has been answered. There is this difference between the minister, the church, the clergy, and the men who believe in this world. I might as well state the question—I may go further than you. The real question is this: Are we to be governed by a supernatural being, or are we to govern ourselves? That is the question. Is God the source of power, or does all authority spring, in governing, from the consent of the governed? That is the question. In other words, is the universe a monarchy, a despotism, or a democracy? I take the democratic side, not in a political sense. The question is, whether this world should be governed by God or by man; and when I say "God" I mean the being that these gentlemen have treated and enthroned upon the ignorance of mankind.

Now let us admit, for the sake of argument, that the bible is true. Let us admit, for the sake of argument, that God once governed this world—not that He did, but let us admit it, and I intend to speak of no god but our God, because we all insist that of all the gods ours is the best, and if He is not good we need not trouble ourselves about the others. Let them take care of themselves.

Now, the first question is, whether this world shall be governed by God or man. Admitting that the being spoken of in the bible is God, He governed this world once. There was a theocracy at the start. That was the first government of the world. Now, how do you judge of a man? The best test of a man is, how does he use power? That is the supreme test of manhood. How does he treat those within his control? The greater the man, the grander the man, the more careful he is in the use of power—the tenderer he is, the nearer just, the greater, the more merciful, the grander, the more charitable. Tell me how a man treats his wife or his children, his poor debtors, his servants, and I will tell you what manner of a man he be. That, I say, is the supreme test, and we know tonight how a good and great man treats his inferiors. We know that. And a man endeavoring to raise his fellow-men higher in the scale of civilization—what will that man appeal to? Will he appeal to the lowest or to the highest that is in man? Let us be honest. Will he appeal to prejudice—the fortress, the armor, the sword and shield of ignorance? Will he appeal to credulity—the ring in the nose by which priests lead stupidity? Will he appeal to the cowardly man? Will he play upon his fears—fear, the capital stock of imposture, the lever and fulcrum of hypocrisy? Will he appeal to the selfishness and all the slimy serpents that crawl in the den of savagery? Or will he appeal to reason, the torch of the mind? Will he appeal to justice? Will he appeal to charity, which is justice in blossom? Will he appeal to liberty and love? These are the questions. What will he do? What did our God do? Let us see. The first thing we know of Him is in the Garden of Eden. How did He endeavor to make His children great, and strong, and good, and free? Did He say anything to Adam and Eve about the sacred relation of marriage? Did He say anything to them about loving children? Did He say anything to them about learning anything under heaven? Did He say one word about intellectual liberty? Did he say one word about reason or about justice? Did He make the slightest effort to improve them? All that He did in the world was to give them one poor little miserable, barren command, "Thou shalt not eat of a certain fruit." That's all that amounted to anything; and, when they sinned, did this great God take them in the arms of His love and endeavor to reform them? No; He simply put upon them a curse. When they were expelled He said to the woman: "I will greatly multiply thy sorrow. In sorrow shalt thou bring forth children. Thy husband shall rule over thee." God made every mother a criminal, and placed a perpetual penalty of pain upon human love. Our God made wives slaves—slaves of their husbands. Our God corrupted the marriage relation and paralyzed the firesides of this world. That is what our God did. And what did He say to poor Adam? "Cursed be the ground for thy sake; in sorrow shalt thou eat of it all the days of thy life; thorns and thistles shall it bring forth to thee; and thou shalt eat the herb of the field, and in the sweat of thy face shalt thou eat bread." Did He say one word calculated to make him a better man? Did He put in the horizon of the future one star of hope? Let us be honest, and see what this God did, and we will judge of Him simply by ordinary common sense.

After a while Cain murdered his brother, and he was detected by this God. And what did this God say to him? Did He say one word of the crime of shedding human blood? Not a word. Did He say one word calculated to excite in the breast of Cain the slightest real sorrow for his deed? Not the slightest. Did He tell him anything about where Abel was? Nothing. Did He endeavor to make him a better man? Not a bit. What had He ever taught him before on that subject? Nothing. And so Cain went out to the other sons and daughters of Adam, according to the bible, and they multiplied and increased until they covered the earth. God gave them no code of laws. God never built them a schoolhouse. God never sent a teacher. God never said a word to them about a future state. God never held up before their gaze that dazzling reward of heaven; never spoke about the lurid gulfs of hell; kept divine punishment a perfect secret, and without having given them the slightest opportunity, simply drowned the world. Splendid administration! Cleveland will do better than that. And, after the waters had gone away, then He gave them some commandments. I suppose that He saw by that time that they needed guidance.

And here are the commandments:

1. You may eat all kinds of birds, beasts and fishes.

2. You must not eat blood; if you do, I will kill you.

3. Whosoever sheddeth man's blood, by man shall his blood be shed.

Nothing more. No good advice; not a word about government; not a word about the rights of man or woman, or children; not a word about any law of nature; not a word about any science—nothing, not even arithmetic.

Nothing. And so He let them go on, and in a little while they came to the same old state; and began building the Tower of Babel; and he went there and confounded, as they said, their languages. Never said a word to them; never told them how foolish it was to try and reach heaven that way. And the next we find Him talking to Abraham, and with Abraham He makes a contract. And how did He do it? "I will bless them that bless thee, and curse them that curse thee." Fine contract for a God. And thereupon He made certain promises to Abraham—promised to give him the whole world, all the nations round about, and that his seed should be as the sands of the sea. Never kept one of His promises—not one. He made the same promises to Isaac, and broke every one. Then He made them all over to Jacob, and broke every one; made them again to Moses, and broke them all. Never said a word about anybody behaving themselves—not a word. Finally, these people whom He had taken under His special care became slaves in the land of Egypt. How ashamed God must have been! Finally He made up His mind to rescue them from that servitude, and He sent Moses and Aaron. He never said a word to Moses or Aaron that Pharaoh was wrong. He never said a word to them about how the women felt when their male children were taken and destroyed. He simply sent Moses before Pharaoh with a cane in his hand that he could turn into a serpent; and, when Pharaoh called in magicians and they did the same, Pharaoh laughed. And then they made frogs; and Pharaoh sent for his magicians, and they did the same, and Pharaoh still laughed. And this God had infinite power, but Pharaoh defeated Him at every point!

It puts me in mind of the story that great Fenian told when the great excitement was about Ireland. An Irishman was telling about the condition of Ireland. He said: "We have got in Ireland now over 300,000 soldiers, all equipped. Every man of them has got a musket and ammunition. They are ready to march at a minute's notice." "But," said the other man, "why don't they march?" "Why," said the other man, "the police won't let them." How admirable! Imagine the infinite God endeavoring to liberate the Hebrews, and prevented by a king, who would not let the children of Israel go until he had done some little miracles with sticks! Think of it! But, said Christians, "you must wait a little while if you wish to find the foundation of law."

Christians now assert that from Sinai came to this world all knowledge of right and wrong, and that from its flaming top we received the first ideas of law and justice. Let us look at those ten commandments. Which of those ten commandments were new, and which of those ten commandments were old? "Thou shalt not kill." That was as old as life. Murder has been a crime; also, because men object to being murdered. If you read the same bible you will find that Moses, seeing an Israelite and an Egyptian contending together, smote the Egyptian and hid his body in the sand. After he had committed that crime Moses fled from the land. Why? Simply because there was a law against murder. That is all. "Honor thy father and thy mother." That is as old as birth. "Thou shalt not commit adultery." That is as old as sex. "Thou shalt not steal." That is as old as work, and as old as property. "Thou shalt not bear false witness against thy neighbor." That is as old as the earth. Never was there a nation, never was there a tribe on the earth that did not have substantially, those commandments. What, then, were new? First, "Thou shalt worship no other God; thou shalt have no other God." Why? "Because I am a jealous God." Second, "Thou shalt not make any graven image." Third, "Thou shalt not take My name in vain." Fourth, "Thou shalt not work on the Sabbath day." What use were these commandments? None—not the slightest. How much better it would have been if God from Sinai, instead of the commandments, had said: "Thou shalt not enslave thy fellow-man; no human being is entitled to the results of another's labor." Suppose He had said: "Thou shalt not persecute for opinion's sake; thought and speech must be forever free." Suppose He had said, instead of "Thou shalt not work on the Sabbath day," "A man shall have but one wife; a woman shall have but one husband; husbands shall love their wives; wives shall love their husbands and their children with all their hearts and as themselves"—how much better it would have been for this world.

Long before Moses was born the Egyptians taught one God; but afterwards, I believe, in their weakness, they degenerated into a belief in the Trinity. They taught the divine origin of the soul, and taught judgment after death. They taught as a reward for belief in their doctrine eternal joy, and as a punishment for non-belief eternal pain. Egypt, as a matter of fact, was far better governed than Palestine. The laws of Egypt were better than the laws of God. In Egypt woman was equal with man. Long before Moses was born there were queens upon the Egyptian throne. Long before Moses was born they had a written code of laws, and their laws were administered by courts and judges. They had rules of evidence. They understood the philosophy of damages. Long before Moses was born they had asylums for the insane and hospitals for the sick. Long before God appeared on Sinai there were schools in Egypt, and the highest office next to the throne was opened to the successful scholar. The Egyptian married but one wife. His wife was called the lady of the house. Women were not secluded; and, above all and over all, the people of Egypt were not divided into castes, and were infinitely better governed than God ever thought of. I am speaking of the God of this bible. If Moses had remembered more of what he saw in Egypt his government would have been far better than it was. Long before these commandments were given, Zoroaster taught the Hindoos that there was one infinite and supreme God. They had a code of laws, and their laws were administered by judges in their courts. By those laws, at the death of a father, the unmarried daughter received twice as much of his property as his son. Compare those laws with the laws of Moses.

So, too, the Romans had their code of laws. The Romans were the greatest lawyers the world produced. The Romans had a code of civil laws, and that code today is the foundation of all law in the civilized world. The Romans built temples to Truth, to Faith, to Valor, to Concord, to Modesty, to Charity and to Chastity. And so with the Grecians. And yet you will find Christian ministers today contending that all ideas of law, of justice and of right came from Sinai, from the ten commandments, from the Mosaic laws. No lawyer who understands his profession will claim that is so. No lawyer who has studied the history of law will claim it. No man who knows history itself will claim it. No man will claim it but an ignorant zealot.

Let us go another step—let us compare the ideas of this God with the ideas of uninspired men. I am making this long preface because I want to get it out of your minds that the bible is inspired.

Now let us go along a little and see what is God's opinion of liberty. Nothing is of more value in this world today than liberty—liberty of body and liberty of mind. Without liberty, the universe would be as a dungeon into which human beings are flung like poor and miserable convicts. Intellectual liberty is the air of the soul, the sunshine of the mind. Without it we should be in darkness. Now, Jehovah commanded the Jewish people to take captives the strangers and sojourners amongst them, and ordered that they and their children should be bondsmen and bondswomen for ever.

Now let us compare Jehovah to Epictetus—a man to whom no revelation was ever made—a man to whom this God did not appear. Let us listen to him: "Remember your servants are to be treated as your own brothers—children of the same God." On the subject of liberty is not Epictetus a better authority than Jehovah, who told the Jews to make bondsmen and bondswomen of the heathen round about? And He said they were to make them their bondsmen and bondswomen forever. Why? Because they were heathen. Why? Because they were not children of the Jews. He was the God of the Jews and not of the rest of mankind. So He said to His chosen people: "Pillage upon the enemy and destroy the people of other gods. Buy the heathen round about." Yet Cicero, a poor pagan lawyer, said this—and he had not even read the old testament—had not even had the advantage of being enlightened by the prophets: "They who say that we should love our fellow-citizens, and not foreigners, destroy the universal brotherhood of mankind, and with it benevolence and justice would perish forever." Is not Cicero greater than Jehovah? The bible, inspired by Jehovah, says: "If a man smite his servant with a rod and he die under his hand he shall be punished. It he continue a day or two and then die, he shall not be punished." Zeno, the founder of the stoics, who had never heard of Jehovah, and never read a word of Moses, said this: "No man can be the owner of another, and the title is bad. Whether the slave became a slave by conquest or by purchase, the title is bad." Let us come and see whether Jehovah has any humanity in Him. Jehovah ordered the Jewish general to make war, and this was the order: "And when the Lord thy God shall deliver them before thee, thou shalt smite them and utterly destroy them; thou shalt make no covenant with them, nor show mercy unto them." And yet Epictetus, whom I have already quoted, said: "Treat those in thy power as thou wouldst have thy superiors treat thee."

I am on the side of the pagan. Is it possible that a being of infinite goodness said: "I will heap mischief upon them; I will send My arrows upon them. They shall be burned with hunger; they shall be devoured with burning heat and with bitter destruction. I will also send the teeth of locusts upon them, with the poisonous serpent of the desert. The sound without and the terror within, shall destroy both the young men and the virgins, the sucklings also, and the men with gray hairs." While Seneca, a poor uninspired Roman, said: "A wise man will not pardon any crime that ought to be punished, but will accomplish in other way all that is sought. He will spare some; he will pardon and watch over some because of their youth; he will pardon these on account of their ignorance. His clemency will not fail what is sought by justice, but his clemency will fulfill justice." That was said by Seneca. Can we believe that this Jehovah said: "Let his children be fatherless and his wife a widow. Let his children be continually vagabonds, and beg. Let them seek their bread out of desolate places. Let the extortioner catch all that he hath, and let the stranger spoil his labor. Let no one extend mercy unto them, neither let any favor his fatherless children." Did Jehovah say this? Surely He had never heard this line—this plaintive music from the Hindoo: "Sweet is the lute to those who have not heard the voices of their own children." Let us see the generosity of Jehovah out of the cloud of darkness on Mount Sinai. He said to the Jews: "Thou shalt have no other God before Me. Thou shalt not bow down to any other gods, for the Lord thy God is a jealous God, visiting the iniquities of the fathers upon the children to the third an fourth generation of them that hate Me." Just think of God saying to people: "If you do not love Me I will damn you." Contrast this with the words put by the Hindoo poet into the mouth of Brahma: "I am the same to all mankind. The who honestly worship other gods involuntarily worship me. I am he that partaketh of all worship. I am the reward of worship." How perfectly sublime! Let me read it to you again: "I am the same to all mankind. They who honestly worship other gods involuntarily worship me. I am he that partaketh of all worship. I am the reward of worship." Compare these passages. The first is a dungeon, which crude hands have digged with jealous slime. The other is like the dome of the firmament, inlaid with constellations. Is it possible God ever said: "If a prophet deceive when he hath spoken a thing, I, the Lord, hath deceived that prophet?" Compare that passage with the poet, a pagan: "Better remain silent the remainder of life than speak falsely."

Can we believe a being of infinite mercy gave this command: "Put every man his sword by his side; go from the gate throughout the camp, and slay every man his brother, every man his companion, and every man his neighbor. Consecrate it, yourselves this day. Let every man lay his sword even upon his son, upon his brother, that he bestow blessing upon Me this day." Surely that was not the outcome of a great, magnanimous spirit, like that of the Roman emperor, who declared: "I had rather keep a single Roman citizen alive than slay a thousand enemies." Compare the last command given to the children of Israel with the words of Marcus Aurelius: "I have formed an ideal of the State, in which there is the same law for all, and equal rights and equal liberty of speech established for all—an Empire where nothing is honored so much as the freedom of the citizens." I am on the side of the Roman emperor.

What is more beautiful than the old story from Sufi? There was a man who for seven years did every act of good, every kind of charity, and at the end of the seven years he mounted the steps to the gate of heaven and knocked. A voice cried, "Who is there?" He cried, "Thy servant, O Lord;" and the gates were shut. Seven other years he did every good work, and again mounted the steps to heaven and knocked. The voice cried, "Who is there?" He answered, "Thy slave, O God;" and the gates were shut. Seven other years he did every good deed, and again mounted the steps to heaven, and the voice said: "Who is there?" He replied "Thyself, O God;" and the gates wide open flew. Is there anything in our religion so warm or so beautiful as that? Compare that story from a pagan with the Presbyterian religion.

Take this story of Endesthora, who was a king of Egypt, and started for the place where the horizon touched the earth, where he was to meet God. With him followed Argune and Bemis and Traubation. They were taught that, when any man started after God in that way, if he had been guilty of any crime he would fall by the way. Endesthora walked at the head and suddenly he missed Argune. He said, "He was not always merciful in the hour of victory." A little while after he missed Bemis, and said, "He fought not so much for the rights of man as for his own glory." A little farther on he missed Traubation. He said, "My God, I know no reason for his failing to reach the place where the horizon touches the earth;" and the god Ram appeared to him, and opening the curtains of the sky, said to him: "Enter." And Endesthora said: "But where are my brethren? Where are Argune and Beinis and Traubation?" And the god said: "They sinned in their time, and they are condemned to suffer below." Then said Endestbora: "I do not wish to enter into your heaven without my friends. If they are below, then I will join them." But the god said: "They are here before you; I simply said this to try your soul." Endesthora simply turned and said: "But what of my dog?" The god said, "Thou knowest that if the shadow of a dog fall upon the sacrifice, it is unclean. How, then, can a dog enter heaven?" And Endesthora replies: "I know that, and I know another thing; that ingratitude is the blackest of crimes, whether it be to man or beast. That dog has been my faithful friend. He has followed me and I will not desert even him." And the god said: "Let the dog follow." Compare that with the bible stories.

Long before the advent of Christ, Aristotle said: "We should conduct ourselves toward others as we would have them conduct themselves toward us." Seneca said: "Do not to your neighbor what you would not have your neighbor do to you." Socrates said: "Act toward others as you would have others act toward you. Forgive your enemies, render good for evil, and kiss even the hand that is upraised to smite." Krishna said: "Cease to do evil; aim to do well; love your enemies. It is the law of love that virtue is the only thing that has strength." Poor, miserable pagans! Did you ever hear anything like this? Is it possible that one of the authors of the new testament was inspired when he said that man was not created for woman, but woman for man? Epictetus said: "What is more delightful than to be so dear to your wife as to be on her account dearer even to yourself?" Compare that with St. Paul: "But I would have you know that the head of every man is Christ, and the head of the woman is the man, and the head of Christ is God. Wives, submit yourselves unto your husbands as unto the Lord." That was inspiration. This was written by a poor, despised heathen: "In whatever house the husband is contented with the wife and the wife with the husband, in that house will fortune dwell. In the house where the woman is not honored, let the curse be pronounced. Where the wife is honored, there God is truly worshiped." I wish Jehovah had said something like that from Sinai. Is there anything as beautiful as this in the new testament: "Shall I tell you where nature is more blest and fair? It is where those we love abide. Though the space be small, it is ample as earth; though it be a desert, through it run the rivers of Paradise."

Compare these things with the curses pronounced in the old testament, where you read of the heathen being given over to butchery and death, and the women and babes to destruction; and, after you have read them, read the chapters of horrors in the new testament, threatening eternal fire and flame; and then read this, the greatest thought uttered by the greatest of human beings:

The quality of mercy is not strained. It droppeth as the gentle rain from heaven Upon the place beneath. It is twice blessed: It blesseth him that gives and him that takes; 'Tis mightiest in the mighty; It becomes the throned monarch better this his crown.

Compare that with your doctrine of the new testament! If Jehovah was an infinite God and knew things from the beginning, He knew that His bible would be a breast-work behind which tyranny and hypocrisy would crouch, and knew His bible would be the auction-block on which the mother would stand while her babe was sold from her, because He knew His bible would be quoted by tyrants; that it would be quoted in defense of robbers called kings, and by hypocrites called priests. He knew that He had taught the Jewish people; He knew that He had found them free and left them slaves; He knew that He had broken every single promise made to them; He knew that, while other nations advanced in knowledge, in art, in science, His chosen people were subjects still. He promised them the world; He gave them a desert. He promised them liberty, and made them slaves. He promised them power; He gave them exile, and any one who reads the old testament is compelled to say that nothing could add to their misery.

Let us be honest. How do you account for this religion? This world; where did it come from? You hear every minister say that man is a religious animal—that religion is natural. While man is an ignorant animal man will be a theological animal, and no longer. Where did we get this religion? The savage knew but little of nature, but thought that everything happened in reference to him. He thought his sins caused earthquakes, and that his virtues made the sunshine.

Nothing is so egotistical as ignorance. You know, and so do I, that if no human being existed, the sun would shine, and that tempests would now and then devastate the earth; violets would spread their velvet bosoms to the sun, daisies would grow, roses would fill the air with perfume, and now and then volcanoes would illuminate the horizon with their lurid glare; the grass would grow, the waters would run, and so far as nature is concerned, everything would be as joyous as though the earth were filled with happy homes. We know the barbarian savage thinks that all this was on his account. He thinks that there dwelt two very powerful deities; that there was a good one, because he knows good things happen to him; and that there was a bad one, because he knows bad things happen to him. Behind the evil influence he puts a devil, and behind the good, an intention of God; and then he imagines both these beings are in opposition, and that, between them, they struggle for the possession of his ignorant soul. He also thinks that the place where the good deity lives is heaven, and that the place where the other deity keeps himself is a place of torture and punishment. And about that time other barbarians have chosen too keep the ignorant ones in subjection by means of the doctrine of fear and punishment.

There is no reforming power in fear. You can scare a man, maybe, so bad that he won't do a thing, but you can't scare him so bad he won't want to do it. There is no reforming power in punishment or brute force; but our barbarians rather imagined that every being would punish in accordance with his power, and his dignity, and that God would subject them to torture in the same way as those who made Him angry. They knew the king would inflict torments upon one in his power, and they supposed that God would inflict torture according to His power. They knew the worst torture was a slow, burning fire; added to it the idea of eternity, and hell was produced. That was their idea. All meanness, revenge, selfishness, cruelty, and hatred of which men here are capable burst into blossom and bore fruit in that one word, "Hell."

In this way a God of infinite wisdom experimented with man, keeping him between an outstretched abyss beneath and a heaven above; and in time the man came to believe that he could please God by having read a few sacred books, could count beads, could sprinkle water, eat little square pieces of bread, and that he could shut his eyes and say words to the clouds; but the moment he left this world nothing remained except to damn him. He was to be kept miserable one day in seven, and he could slander and persecute other men all the other days in the week. That was the chance that God gave a man here, but the moment he left this world that settled it. He would go to eternal pain or else to eternal joy. That was the way that the supernatural governed this world—through fear, through terror, through eternity of punishment; and that government, I say tonight, has failed. How has it been kept alive so long? It was born in ignorance. Let me tell you, whoever attacks a creed will be confronted with a list of great men who have believed in it. Probably their belief in that creed was the only weakness they had. But he will be asked, "So you know more than all the great men who have taught and all the respectable men who have believed in that faith?" For the church is always going about to get a certificate from some governor, or even perhaps members of the Legislature, and you are told, because so-and-so believed all these things, and you have no more talents than they, that you should believe the same thing. But I contend, as against this argument, that you should not take the testimony of these men unless you are willing to take at the same time all their beliefs on other subjects. Then, again, they tell you that the rich people are all on their side, and I say so, too. The churches today seek the rich, and poverty unwillingly seeks them. Light thrown from diamonds adorns the repentant here. We are told that the rich, the fortunate, and the holders of place are Christians now; and yet ministers grow eloquent over the poverty of Christ, who was born in a manger, and say that the Holy Ghost passed the titled ladies of the world and selected the wife of a poor mechanic for the mother of God. Such is the difference between theory and practice. The church condemns the men of Jerusalem who held positions and who held the pretensions of the Savior in contempt. They admit that He was so little known that they had to bribe a man to point Him out to the soldiers. They assert that He performed miracles; yet He remained absolutely unknown, hidden in the depth of obscurity. No one knew Him, and one of His disciples had to be bribed to point Him out. Surely He and His disciples could have met the arguments which were urged against their religion at that time.

So long as the church honored philosophers she kept her great men in the majority. How is it now? I say tonight that no man of genius in the world is in the orthodox pulpit, so far as I know. Where are they? Where are the orthodox great men? I challenge the Christian church to produce a man like Alexander Humboldt. I challenge the world to produce a naturalist like Haeckel. I challenge the Christian world to produce a man like Darwin. Where in the ranks of orthodoxy are historians like Draper and Buckle? Where are the naturalists like Tyndall, philosophers like Mills and Spencer, and women like George Eliot and Harriet Martineau? You may get tired of the great-men argument; but the names of the great thinkers, and naturalists and scientists of our time cannot be matched by the supernatural world.

What is the next argument they will bring forward? The father and mother argument. You must not disgrace your parents. How did Christ come to leave the religion of His mother? That argument proves too much. There is one way every man can honor his mother—that is by finding out more than she knew. There is one way a man can honor his father—by correcting the old man's errors.

Most people imagine that the creed we have came from the brain and heart of Christ. They have no idea how it was made. They think it was all made at one time. They don't understand that it was a slow growth. They don't understand that theology is a science made up of mistakes, prejudices and falsehoods. Let me tell you a few facts: The Emperor Constantine, who lifted the Christian religion into power, murdered his wife and his eldest son the very year that he convened the Council of Nice to decide whether Jesus Christ was man or God; and that was not decided until the year of grace 325. Then Theodosius called a council at Constantinople in 381, and this council decided that the Holy Ghost proceeded from the Father. You see, there was a little doubt on that question before this was done. Then another council was called later to determine who the Virgin Mary really was, and it was solemnly decided that she was the mother of Christ. In 431, and then in 451, a council was held in Chalcedon, by the Emperor Marcian, and that decided that Christ had two natures—a human and a divine. In 680 another council was held at Constantinople; and in 1274 at Lyons, it was decided that the Holy Ghost proceeded not only from the Father but from the Son; and when you take into consideration the fact that a belief in the Trinity is absolutely essential to salvation, you see how important it was that these doctrines should have been established in 1274, when millions of people had dropped into hell in the interim solely because they had forgotten that question. At last we know how religions are made. We know how miracles are manufactured. We know the history of relics, and bones, and pieces of the true cross. And at last we understand apostolic succession. At last we have examined other religions, and we find them all the same, and we are beginning to suspect that ours is like the rest. I think we understand it.

I read a little story, a short time ago, from the Japanese, that throws light upon the question. There was an old priest at a monastery. This monastery was built over the bones of what he called a saint, and people came there and were cured of many diseases. This priest had an assistant. After the assistant grew up and got quite to understand his business, the old priest gave him a little donkey, and told him that henceforth he was to take care of himself. The young priest started out with his little donkey, and asked alms of those he met. Few gave to him. Finally he got very poor. He could not raise money enough to feed the donkey. Finally the donkey died; he was about to bury it when a thought occurred to him. He buried the donkey and sat down on the grave, and to the next stranger that passed he said: "Will you not give a little money to erect a shrine over the bones of a sinless one?" Thereupon a man gave money. Others followed his example, a shrine was raised, and in a little while a monastery was built over the bones of the sinless one. Down in the grave the young priest made an orifice, so that persons afflicted with any disease could reach down and touch the bones of the sinless one. Hundreds were thus cured, and persons left their crutches as testimonials to the miraculous power of the bones of the sinless one. Finally the priest became so rich that he thought he would visit his old master. He went to the old monastery with a fine retinue. His old master asked him how he became so rich and prosperous. He replied: "Old age is stupid, but youth has thought." Later on he explained to the old priest how the donkey had died, and how he had raised a monastery over the bones of the sinless one; and again reminded him that old age is stupid, but youth has thought. The old priest exclaimed: "Not quite so fast, young man; not quite so fast. Don't imagine you worked out anything new. This shrine of mine is built over the bones of the mother of your little donkey."

We have now reached a point in the history of the world when we know that theocracy as a form of government is a failure, and we see that theology as a foundation of government is an absolute failure. We can see that theocracy and theology created, not liberty, but despotism. We know enough of the history of the churches in this world to know that they never can civilize mankind; that they are not imbued with the spirit of progress; that they are not imbued with the spirit of justice and mercy. What I ask you tonight is: What has the church done to civilize mankind? What has the church done for us? How has it added to the prosperity of this world? Has it ever produced anything? Nothing. Why, they say, it has been charitable. How can a beggar be charitable? A beggar produces nothing. The church has been an eternal and everlasting pauper. It is not charitable. It is an object of charity, and yet it claims to be charitable. The giver is the charitable one. Somebody who has made something, somebody who has by his labor produced something, he alone can be charitable.

And let me say another thing: The church is always on the wrong side. Let us take, first, the Episcopal church—if you call that a church. Let me tell you one thing about that church. You know what is called the rebellion in England in 1688? Do you know what caused it? I will tell you. King James was a Catholic, and notwithstanding that fact, he issued an edict of toleration for the Dissenters and Catholics. And what next did he do? He ordered all the bishops to have this edict of toleration read in the Episcopal churches. They refused to do it—most of them. You recollect that trial of the seven bishops? That is what it was all about; they would not read the edict of toleration. Then what happened? A strange thing to say, and it is one of the miracles of this world: The Dissenters, in whose favor that edict was issued, joined hands with the Episcopalians, and raised the rebellion against the king, because he wanted to give the Dissenters liberty, and these Dissenters and these Episcopalians, on account of toleration, drove King James into exile. This is the history of the first rebellion the Church of England ever raised against the king, simply because he issued an edict of toleration and the poor, miserable wretches in whose favor the edict was issued joined hands with their oppressors. I want to show you how much the Church of England has done for England. I get it from good authority. Let me read it to you to show how little influence the Christian church, the Church of England, had with the government of that country. Let me tell you that up to the reign of George I. there were in that country sixty-seven offenses punishable with death. There is not a lawyer in this city who can think of those offenses and write them down in one day. Think of it! Sixty-seven offenses punishable with death! Now, between the accession of George I. and the termination of the reign of George III. there were added 156 new crimes punishable with death, making in all 223 crimes in England punishable with death. There is no lawyer in this State who can think of that many crimes in a week. Now, during all those years the government was becoming more and more cruel; more and more barbarous; and we do not find, and we have not found, that the Church of England, with its 15,000 or 20,000 Ministers, with its more than a score of bishops in the House of Lords, has ever raised its voice or perfected any organization in favor of a more merciful code, or in condemnation of the enormous cruelty which the laws were continually inflicting. And was not Voltaire justified in saying that "The English were a people who murdered by law?" Now, that is an extract from a speech made by John Bright in May, 1883. That shows what the Church of England did. Two hundred and twenty-three offenses in England punishable with death, and no minister, no bishop, no church organization raising his or its voice, against the monstrous cruelty. And why? Even then it was better than the law of Jehovah.

And the Protestants were as bad as the Catholics. You remember the time of Henry IV. in France, when the edict of Nantes was issued simply to give the Protestants the right to worship God according to the dictates of their conscience. Just as soon as that edict was issued the Protestants themselves, in the cities where they had the power, prevented the Catholics from worshiping their God according to the dictates of their conscience, and it was on account of the refusal of those Protestants to allow the Catholics to worship God as they desired that there was a civil war lasting for seven years in France. Richelieu came into authority about the second or third year of that war. He made no difference between Protestants and Catholics; and it was owing to Richelieu that the Thirty Years' War terminated. It was owing to Richelieu that the peace of Westphalia was made in 1643, although I believe he had been dead a year before that time; but it was owing to him, and it was the first peace ever made between nations on a secular basis, with everything religious left out, and it was the last great religious war.

You may ask me what I want. Well, in the first place I want to get theology out of government. It has no business there. Man gets his authority from man, and is responsible only to man. I want to get theology out of politics. Our ancestors in 1776 retired God from politics, because of the jealousies among the churches, and the result has been splendid for mankind. I want to get theology out of education. Teach the children what somebody knows, not what somebody guesses. I want to get theology out of morality, and out of charity. Don't give for God's sake, but for man's sake.

I want you to know another thing; that neither Protestants nor Catholics are fit to govern this world. They are not fit to govern themselves. How could you elect a minister of any religion president of the United States. Could you elect a bishop of the Catholic church, or a Methodist bishop, or Episcopal minister, or one of the elders? No. And why? We are afraid of the ecclesiastic spirit. We are afraid to trust the liberties of men in the hands of people who acknowledge that they are bound by a standard different from that of the welfare of mankind.

The history of Italy, France, Spain, Portugal, Cuba, and Brazil all show that slavery existed where Catholicism was a power. I would suggest an education that would rule theology out of the government, and teach people to rely more on themselves and less on providence. There are two ways of living—the broad way of life lived for others, and the narrow theological way. It is wise to so live that death can be serenely faced, and then, if there is another world, the best way to prepare for it is to make the best of this; and if there be no other world, the best way to live here is to so live as to be happy and make everybody else happy.

# INGERSOLL'S LECTURE ON THE GREAT INFIDELS

Ladies and Gentlemen: There is nothing grander in this world than to rescue from the leprosy of slander a great and splendid name. There is nothing nobler than to benefit our benefactors. The infidels of one age have been the aureole saints of the next. The destroyers of the old have always been the creators of the new. The old passes away and the new becomes old. There is in the intellectual world, as in the material, decay and growth; and even by the sunken grave of age stand youth and joy. The history of progress is written in the lives of infidels. Political rights have been preserved by traitors; intellectual rights by infidels.

To attack the kings was treason; to dispute the priests blasphemy. The sword and cross have always been allies; they defended each other. The throne and altar are twins—vultures born of the same egg. It was James I. who said: "No king, no bishop; no church, no crown; no tyrant in heaven, no tyrant on earth." Every monarchy that has disgraced the world, every despotism that has covered the cheeks of men with fear has been copied after the supposed despotism of hell. The king owned the bodies and the priest owned the souls; one lived on taxes and the other on alms; one was a robber and the other a beggar.

The history of the world will not show you one charitable beggar. He who lives on charity never has anything to give away. The robbers and beggars controlled not only this world, but the next. The king made laws, the priest made creeds; with bowed backs the people received and bore the burdens of the one, and with the open mouth of wonder the creed of the other. If any aspired to be free they were crushed by the king, and every priest was a hero who slaughtered the children of the brave. The king ruled by force, the priest by fear and by the bible. The king said to the people: "God made you peasants and me a king; He clothed you in rags and housed you in hovels; upon me He put robes and gave me a palace." Such is the justice of God. The priest said to the people: "God made you ignorant and vile, me holy and wise; obey me, or God will punish you here and hereafter." Such is the mercy of God.

Infidels are the intellectual discoverers. Infidels have sailed the unknown sea and have discovered the isles and continents in the vast realms of thought. What would the world have been had infidels never existed? What the infidel is in religion the inventor is in mechanics. What the infidel is in religion the man willing to fight the hosts of tyranny is in the political world. An infidel is a gentleman who has discovered a fact and is not afraid to tell about it. There has been for many thousands of years an idea prevalent that in some way you can prove whether the theories defended or advanced by a man are right or wrong by showing what kind of a man he was, what kind of a life he lived, and what manner of death he died. There is nothing to this. It makes no difference what the character of the man was who made the first multiplication table. It is absolutely true, and whenever you find an absolute fact, it makes no difference who discovered it. The golden rule would have been just as good if it had first been whispered by the devil.

It is good for what it contains, not because a certain man said it. Gold is just as good in the hands of crime as in the hands of virtue. Whatever it may be, it is gold. A statement made by a great man is not necessarily true. A man entertains certain opinions, and then he is proscribed because he refuses to change his mind. He is burned to ashes, and in the midst of the flames he cries out that he is of the same opinion still. Hundreds then say that he has sealed his testimony with his blood, and that his doctrines must be true. All the martyrs in the history of the world are not sufficient to establish the correctness of any one opinion. Martyrdom as a rule establishes the sincerity of the martyr, not the correctness of his thought. Things are true or false independently of the man who entertains them. Truth cannot be affected by opinion; an error cannot be believed sincerely enough to make it the truth. No Christian will admit that any amount of heroism displayed by a Mormon is sufficient to show that Joseph Smith was an inspired prophet. All the courage and culture, all the poetry and art of ancient Greece do not even tend to establish the truth of any myth.

The testimony of the dying concerning some other world, or in regard to the supernatural, cannot be any better than that of the living. In the early days of Christian experience an intrepid faith was regarded as a testimony in favor of the church. No doubt, in the arms of death, many a one went back and died in the lay of the old faith. After awhile Christians got to dying and clinging to their faith; and then it was that Christians began to say: "No man can die serenely without clinging to the cross." According to the theologians, God has always punished the dying who did not happen to believe in Him. As long as men did nothing except to render their fellowmen wretched, God maintained the strictest neutrality, but when some honest man expressed a doubt as to the Jewish scriptures, or prayed to the wrong god, or to the right God by the wrong man, then the real God leaped like a wounded tiger upon this dying man, and from his body tore his wretched soul.

There is no recorded instance where the uplifted hand of murder has been paralyzed, or the innocent have been shielded by God. Thousands of crimes are committed every day, and God has no time to prevent them. He is too busy numbering hairs and matching sparrows; He is listening for blasphemy; He is looking for persons who laugh at priests; He is examining baptismal registers; He is watching professors in colleges who begin to doubt the geology of Moses or the astronomy of Joshua. All kinds of criminals, except infidels, meet death with reasonable serenity. As a rule, there is nothing in the death of a pirate to cast discredit upon his profession. The murderer upon the scaffold smilingly exhorts the multitude to meet him in heaven. The Emperor Constantine, who lifted Christianity into power, murdered his wife and oldest son.

Now and then, in the history of the world, there has been a man of genius, a man of intellectual honesty. These men have denounced the superstition of their day. They were honest enough to tell their thoughts. Some of them died naturally in their beds, but it would not do for the church to admit that they died peaceably; that would show that religion was not necessary in the last moments. The first grave, the first cathedral; the first corpse was the first priest. If there was no death in the world there would be no superstition. The church has taken great pains to show that the last moments of all infidels have been infinitely wretched. Upon this point, Catholics and Protestants have always stood together. They are no longer men; they become hyenas, they dig open graves. They devour the dead. It is an auto da fe presided over by God and his angels. These men believed in the accountability of men in the practice of virtue and justice. They believed in liberty, but they did not believe in the inspiration of the bible. That was their crime. In order to show that infidels died overwhelmed with remorse and fear they have generally selected from all the infidels since the days of Christ until now five men—the Emperor Julian, Bruno, Diderot, David Hume and Thomas Paine.

They forget that Christ himself was not a Christian, that He did what He could to tear down the religion of His day; that He held the temple in contempt. I like Him because He held the old Jewish religion in contempt;

because He had sense enough to say that doctrine was not true. In vain have their calumniators been called upon to prove their statements. They simply charge it, they simply relate it, but that is no evidence. The Emperor Julian did what he could to prevent Christians destroying each other. He held pomp and pride in contempt. In battle with the Persians he was mortally wounded. Feeling that he had but a short time to live, he spent his last hours in discussing with his friends the immortality of the soul. He declared that he was satisfied with his conduct, and that he had no remorse to express for any act he had ever done.

The first great infidel was Giordano Bruno. He was born in the year of grace 1550. He was a Dominican friar—Catholic—and afterwards he changed his mind.

The reason he changed was because he had a mind. He was a lover of nature, and said to the poor hermits in their caves, to the poor monks in their monasteries, to the poor nuns in their cells: "Come out in the glad fields; come and breathe the fresh, free air; come and enjoy all the beauty there is in the world. There is no God who can be made happier by you being miserable; there is no God who delights to see upon the human face the tears of pain, of grief, of agony. Come out and enjoy all there is of human life; enjoy progress, enjoy thought, enjoy being somebody and belonging to yourself."

He revolted at the idea of transubstantiation; he revolted at the idea that the eternal God could be in a wafer. He revolted at the idea that you could make the Trinity out of dough—bake God in an oven as you would a biscuit. I should think he would have revolted. The idea of a man devouring the creator of the universe by swallowing a piece of bread. And yet that is just as sensible as any of it. Those who, when smitten on one cheek turn the other, threatened to kill this man. He fled from his native land and was a vagabond in nearly every nation of Europe. He declared that he fought not what men really believed, but what they pretended to believe. And, do you know, that is the business I am in? I am simply saying what other people think; I am furnishing clothes for their children, I am putting on exhibition their offspring, and they like to hear it, they like to see it. We have passed midnight in the history of the world. Bruno was driven from his native country because he taught the rotation of the earth; you can see what a dangerous man he must have been in a well regulated monarchy. You see he had found a fact, and a fact has the same effect upon religion that dynamite has upon a Russian czar. A fellow with a new fact was suspected and arrested, and they always thought they could destroy it by burning him, but they never did. All the fires of martyrdom never destroyed one truth; all the churches of the world have never made one lie true. Germany and France would not tolerate Bruno. According to the Christian system, this world was the center of everything. The stars were made out of what little God happened to have left when He got the world done. God lived up in the sky, and they said this earth must rest upon something, and finally science passed its hand clear under, and there was nothing. It was self-existent in infinite space. Then the church began to say they didn't say it was flat—not so awful flat—it was kind of rounding. According to the ancient Christians God lived from all eternity, and never worked but six days in His whole life, and then had the impudence to tell us to be industrious. I heard of a man going to California over the plains, and, there was a clergyman on board, and he had a great deal to say, and finally he fell in conversation with the '49-er, and the latter said to the clergyman: "Do you believe that God made this world in six days?" "Yes, I do." They were then going along the Humboldt. Says he: "Don't you think He could put in another day to advantage right around here?"

Bruno went to England and delivered lectures at Oxford. He found that there was nothing taught there but superstition, and so called Oxford the "wisdom of learning." Then they told him they didn't want him any more. He went back to Italy, where there was a kind of fascination that threw him back to the very doors of the Inquisition. He was arrested for teaching that there were other worlds, and that stars are suns around which revolve other planets. He was in prison for six years. (During those six years Galileo was teaching mathematics.) Six years in a dungeon; and then he was tried, denounced by the Inquisition, excommunicated, condemned by brute force, pushed upon his knees while he received the benediction of the church, and on the 16th of February, in the year of our Lord 1600, he was burned at the stake.

He believed that the world is animated by an intelligent soul, the cause of force but not of matter; that matter and force have existed from eternity; that this force lives in all things, even in such as appear not to live—in the rock as much as in the man; that matter is the mother of forms and the grace of forms; that the matter and force together constitute God. He was a pantheist—that is to say, he was an atheist. He had the courage to die for what he believed to be right. The murder of Bruno will never, in my judgment, be completely and perfectly revenged until from the city of Rome shall be swept every vestige of priests and pope—until from the shapeless ruins of St. Peter's, the crumbled Vatican and the fallen cross of Rome, rises a monument sacred to the philosopher, the benefactor and the martyr—Bruno.

Voltaire was born in 1694. When he was born, the natural was about the only thing that the church did not believe in. Monks sold amulets, and the priests cured in the name of the church. The worship of the devil was actually established, which today is the religion of China. They say: "God is good; He won't bother you; Joss is the one." They offer him gifts, and try and soften his heart;—so, in the middle ages, the poor people tried to see if they could not get a short cut, and trade directly with the devil, instead of going roundabout through the church. In these days witnesses were cross-examined with instruments of torture. Voltaire did more for human liberty than any other man who ever lived or died. He appealed to the common sense of mankind— he held up the great contradictions of the sacred scriptures in a way that no man, once having read him, could forget. For one, I thank Voltaire for the liberty I am enjoying this moment. How small a man a priest looked when he pointed his finger at him; how contemptible a king.

Toward the last of May, 1778, it was whispered in Paris that Voltaire was dying. He expired with the most perfect tranquility. There have been constructed most shameless lies about the death of this great and wonderful man, compared with whom all his calumniators, living or dead, were but dust and vermin. From his throne at the foot of the Alps he pointed the finger of scorn at every hypocrite in Europe. He was the pioneer of his century.

In 1771, in Scotland, David Hume was born. Scotch Presbyterianism is the worst form of religion that has ever been produced. The Scotch Kirk had all the faults of the Church of Rome, without a redeeming feature. The church hated music, despised painting, abhorred statuary, and held architecture in contempt. Anything touched with humanity, with the weakness of love, with the dimple of joy, was detested by the Scotch Kirk. God was to be feared; God was infinitely practical; no nonsense about God. They used to preach four times a day. They preached on Friday before the Sunday upon which they partook of the sacrament, and then on Saturday; four sermons on Sunday, and two or three on Monday to sober up on. They were bigoted and heartless. One case will illustrate. In the beginning of this nineteenth century a boy seventeen years of age was indicted at Edinburgh for blasphemy. He had given it as his opinion that Moses had learned magic in Egypt, and had fooled the Jews. They proved that on two or three occasions, when he was real cold, he jocularly remarked that he wished he was in hell, so that he could warm up. He was tried, convicted, and sentenced to be hanged. He recanted; he even wrote that he believed the whole business; and that he just said it for pure devilment. It made no difference. They hung him, and his bruised and bleeding corpse was denied to his own mother, who came and besought them to let her take her boy home. That was Scotch Presbyterianism. If the devil had been let loose in Scotland he would have improved that country at that time.

David Hume was one of the few Scotchmen who was not owned by the church. He had the courage to examine things for himself, and to give his conclusion to the world. His life was unstained by an unjust act. He did not, like Abraham, turn a woman from his door with his child in her arms. He did not, like King David, murder a man that he might steal his wife. He didn't believe in Scotch Presbyterianism. I don't see how any good man ever did. Just think of going to the day of judgment, if there is one, and standing up before God and admitting, without a blush, that you have lived and died a Scotch Presbyterian. I would expect the next sentence would be, "Depart ye cursed in everlasting fire." Hume took the ground that a miracle could not be used as evidence until you had proved the miracle. Of course that excited the church. Why? Because they could not prove one of them. How are you going to prove a miracle? Who saw it, and who would know a devil if he did see him? Hume insisted that at the bottom of all good is something useful; that after all, human happiness was the great object, end, and aim of life; that virtue was not a termagant, with sunken cheeks and frightful eyes, but was the most beautiful thing in the world, and would strew your path with flowers from the cradle to the grave. When he died they gave an account of how he had suffered. They knew that the horrors of death would fall upon him, and that God would get his revenge. But his attending physician said that his death was the most serene and most perfectly tranquil of any he had ever seen. Adam Smith said he was as near perfect as the frailty incident to humanity would allow human being to be.

The next is Benedict Spinoza, a Jew, born at Amsterdam in 1768. He studied theology, and asked the rabbis too many questions, and talked too much about what he called reason, and finally he was excommunicated from the synagogue, and became an outcast at the age of twenty-four, without friends. Cursed, anathematized, bearing upon his forehead the mark of Cain, he undertook to solve the problem of the universe. To him the universe was one. The infinite embraced the all. That all was God. He was right; the universe is all there is, and if God does not exist in the universe He exists nowhere. The idea of putting some little Jewish jehovah outside the universe, as if to say that from an eternity of idleness he woke up one morning and thought he would make something.

The propositions of Spinoza are as luminous as the stars, and his demonstrations, each one of them, is a Gibraltar, behind which logic sits laughing at all the sophistries of theological thought. In every relation of life he was just, true, gentle, patient, loving, affectionate. He died in 1812. In his life of forty-four years he had climbed to the very highest alpine of human thought. He was a great and splendid man, an intellectual hero, one of the benefactors, one of the Titans of our race.

And now I will say a few words about our infidels. We had three, to say the least of them—Paine, Franklin and Jefferson. In their day the colonies were filled with superstition, and the Puritans with the spirit of persecution. Law, savage, ignorant and malignant, had been passed in every colony for the purpose of destroying intellectual liberty. Manly freedom was unknown. The toleration act of Maryland tolerated only chickens, not thinkers, not investigators. It tolerated faith, not brains. The charity of Roger Williams was not extended to one who denied the bible. Let me show you how we have advanced. Suppose you took every man and woman out of the Penitentiary in New England and shipped them to a new country where man before had never trod, and told them to make a government, and constitution, and a code of laws for themselves. I say tonight that they would make a better constitution and a better code of laws than any that were made in any of the original thirteen colonies of the United States.

Not that they are better men, not that they are more honest, but that they have got more sense. They have been touched with the dawn of the eternal day of liberty that will finally come to this world. They would have more respect for others' rights than they had at that time. But the churches were jealous of each other, and we got a constitution without religion in it from the mutual jealousies of the church, and from the genius of men like Paine, Franklin and Jefferson. We are indebted to them for a constitution without a God in it. They knew that if you put God in there, an infinite God, there wouldn't be any room for the people. Our fathers retired Jehovah from politics. Our fathers, under the directions and leadership of those infidels, said, "All power comes from the consent of the governed." George Washington wanted to establish a church by law in Virginia. Thomas Jefferson prevented it. Under the guaranty of liberty of conscience which was given, our legislation has improved, and it will not be many years before all laws touching liberty of conscience, excepting it may be in the State of Delaware, will be blotted out, and when that time comes we or our children may thank the infidels of 1776. The church never pretended that Franklin died in fear. Franklin wrote no books against the bible. He thought it useless to cast the pearls of thought before the swine of his generation.

Jefferson was a statesman. He was the author of the Declaration of Independence, founder of a university, father of a political body, president of the United States, a statesman, and a philosopher. He was too powerful for the churches of his day. Paine attacked the Trinity and the bible both. He had done these things openly—His arguments were so good that his reputation got bad. I want you to recollect tonight that he was the first man who wrote these words: "The United States of America." I want you to know tonight that he was the first man who suggested the Federal Constitution. I want you to know that he did more for the actual separation from Great Britain than any man that ever lived. I want you to know that he did as much for liberty with his pen as any soldier did with his sword. I want you to know that during the Revolution his "Crisis" was the pillar of fire by night and a cloud by day. I want you to know that his "Common Sense" was the one star in the horizon of despotism. I want you to know that he did as much as any living man to give our free flag to the free air. He was not content to waste all his energies here. When the volcano covered Europe with the shreds of robes and the broken fragments of thrones, Paine went to France. He was elected by four constituencies. He had the courage to vote against the death of Louis, and was imprisoned. He wrote to Washington, the president, and asked him to interfere. Washington threw the letter in the wastebasket of forgetfulness. When Paine was finally released he gave his opinion of George Washington, and, under such circumstances, I say a man can be pardoned for having said even unjust things. The eighteenth century was crowning its gray hairs with the wreaths of progress, and Thomas Paine said: "I will do something to liberate mankind from superstition." He wrote the "Age of Reason." For his good, he wrote it too soon; for ours, not a day too quick. From that moment he was a despised and calumniated man. When he came back to this country he could not safely walk the streets for fear of being mobbed. Under the Constitution he had suggested, his rights were not safe; under the flag that he had helped give to heaven, with which he had enriched the air, his liberty was not safe. Is it not a disgrace to us that all the lies that have been told about him, and will be told about him, are a perpetual disgrace? I tell you that upon the grave of Thomas Paine the churches of America have sacrificed their reputation for veracity. Who can hate a man with a creed:

"I believe in one God and no more, and I hope for immortality; I believe in the equality of man, and that religious duty consists in doing justice, in doing mercy, and in endeavoring to make our fellow-creatures happy. It is necessary to the happiness of man that he be faithful to himself. One good schoolmaster is worth a thousand priests. Man has no property in man, and the key of heaven is in the keeping of no saint."

Grand, splendid, brave man!—with some faults, with many virtues; the world is better because he lived; and if Thomas Paine had not lived I could not have delivered this lecture here tonight.

Did all the priests of Rome increase the mental wealth of man as much as Bruno? Did all the priests of France do as great a work for the civilization of this world as Diderot and Voltaire? Did all the ministers of Scotland add as much to the sum of human knowledge as David Hume? Have all the clergymen, monks, friars, ministers, priests, bishops, cardinals and popes from the day of Pentecost to the last election done as much for human liberty as Thomas Paine? What would the world be now if infidels had never been? Infidels have been the flower of all this world. Recollect, by infidels I mean every man who has made an intellectual advance. By orthodox I mean a gentleman who is petrified in his mind, whopping around intellectually, simply to save the funeral expenses of his soul. Infidels are the creditors of all the years to come. They have made this world fit to live in, and without them the human brain would be as empty as the Chronicles soon will be. Unless they preach something that the people want to hear, it is not a crime to benefit our fellow-man intellectually. The churches point to their decayed saints and their crumbled popes and say, "Do you know more than all the ministers that ever lived?" And, without the slightest egotism or blush, I say, "Yes; and the name of Humboldt outweighs them all." The men who stand in the front rank, the men who know most of the secrets of nature, the men who know most are today the advanced infidels of this world. I have lived long enough to see the brand of intellectual inferiority on every orthodox brain.

# INGERSOLL'S LECTURE ON TALMAGIAN THEOLOGY.

Ladies and Gentlemen: Nothing can be more certain than that no human being can by any possibility control his thought. We are in this world—we see, we hear, we feel, we taste; and everything in nature makes an impression upon the brain, and that wonderful something, enthroned there with these materials, weaves what we call thought, and the brain can no more help thinking than the heart can help beating. The blood pursues its old accustomed round without our will. The heart beats without asking leave of us, and the brain thinks in spite of all that we can do. This being true, no human being can justly be held responsible for his thought any more than for the beating of his heart, any more than for the course pursued by the blood, any more than for breathing air. And yet for thousands of years thought has been thought to be a crime, and thousands and millions have threatened us with eternal fire if we give the product of that brain. Each brain, in my judgment, is a field where nature sows the seeds of thought, and thought is the crop that man reaps, and it certainly cannot be a crime to gather; it certainly cannot be a crime to tell it, which simply amounts to the right to sell your crop or to exchange your product for the product of some other man's brain. That is all it is. Most brains—at least some—are rather poor fields, and the orthodox worst of all. That field produces mostly sorrel and mullin, while there are fields which, like the tropic world, are filled with growth, and where you find the vine and palm, royal children of the sun and brain. I then stand simply for absolute freedom of thought—absolute; and I don't believe, if there be a God, that it will be or can be pleasing to Him to see one of His children afraid to express what he thinks. And, if I were God, I never would cease making men until I succeeded in making one grand enough to tell his honest opinion.

Now there has been a struggle, you know, a long time between the believers in the natural and the supernatural—between gentlemen who are going to reward us in another world and those who propose to make life worth living here and now. In all ages the priest, the medicine man, the magician, the astrologer, in other words, gentlemen who have traded upon the fear and ignorance of their fellow-man in all countries—they have sought to, make their living out of others. There was a time when a God presided over every department of human interest, when a man about to take a voyage bribed the priest of Neptune so that he might have a safe journey, and when he came back, he paid more, telling the priest that he was infinitely obliged to him; that he had kept waves from the sea and storms in their caves. And so, when one was sick he went to a priest; when one was about to take a journey he visited the priest of Mercury; if he were going to war he consulted the representative of Mars. We have gone along. When the poor agriculturist plowed his ground and put in the seed he went to the priest of some god and paid him to keep off the frost. And the priest said he would do it; "but," added the priest, "you must have faith." If the frost came early he said, "You didn't have faith." And besides all that he says to him: "Anything that has happened badly, after all, was for your good." Well, we found out, day by day, that a good boat for the purpose of navigating the sea was better than prayers, better than the influence of priests; and you had better have a good captain attending to business than thousands of priests ashore praying.

We also found that we could cure some diseases, and just as soon as we found that we could cure diseases we dismissed the priest. We have left him out now of all of them, except it may be cholera and smallpox. When visited by a plague some people get frightened enough to go back to the old idea—go back to the priest, and the priest says: "It has been sent as a punishment." Well, sensible people began to look about; they saw that the good died as readily as the bad; they saw that this disease would attack the dimpled child in the cradle and allow the murderer to go unpunished; and so they began to think in time that it was not sent as a punishment; that it was a natural result; and so the priest stepped out of medicine.

In agriculture we need him no longer; he has nothing to do with the crops. All the clergymen in this world can never get one drop of rain out of the sky; and all the clergymen in the civilized world could not save one human life if they tried it.

Oh, but they say, "We do not expect a direct answer to prayer; it is the reflex action we are after." It is like a man endeavoring to lift himself up by the straps of his boots; he will never do it, but he will get a great deal of useful exercise.

The missionary goes to some pagan land, and there he finds a man praying to a god of stone, and it excites the wrath of the missionary. I ask you tonight, does not that stone god answer prayer just as well as ours? Does he not cause rain? Does he not delay frost? Does he not snatch the ones that we love from the grasp of death precisely the same as ours? Yet we have ministers that are still engaged in that business. They tell us that they have been "called;" that they do not go at their profession as other people do, but they are "called;" that God, looking over the world, carefully selects His priests, His ministers, and His exhorters.

I don't know. They say their calling is sacred. I say to you tonight that every kind of business that is honest that a man engages in for the purpose of feeding his wife and children, for the purpose of building up his home, for the purpose of feeding and clothing the ones he loves—that business is sacred. They tell us that statesmen and poets, philosophers, heroes, and scientists and inventors come by chance; that all other departments depend entirely upon luck; but when God wants exhorters He selects.

They also tell us that it is infinitely wicked to attack the Christian religion, and when I speak of the Christian religion I do not refer especially to the Christianity of the new testament; I refer to the Christianity of the orthodox church, and when I refer to the clergy I refer to the clergy of the orthodox church. There was a time when men of genius were in the pulpits of the orthodox church; that time is past. When you find a man with brains now occupying an orthodox pulpit you will find him touched with heresy—every one of them.

How do they get most of these ministers? There will be a man in the neighborhood not very well—not having constitution enough to be wicked, and it instantly suggests itself to everybody who sees him that he would make an excellent minister. There are so many other professions, so many cities to be built, so many railways to be constructed, so many poems to be sung, so much music to be composed, so many papers to edit, so many books to read, so many splendid things, so many avenues to distinction and glory, so many things beckoning from the horizon of the future to every great and splendid man that the pulpit has to put up with the leavings—ravelings, selvage.

These preachers say, "How can any man be wicked and infamous enough to attack our religion and take from the world the solace of orthodox Christianity?" What is that solace? Let us be honest. What is it? If the Christian religion be true, the grandest, greatest, noblest of the world are now in hell, and the narrowest and meanest are now in heaven. Humboldt, the Shakespeare of science, the most learned man of the most learned nation, with a mind grand enough to grasp not simply this globe, but this constellation—a man who shed light upon the whole earth—a man who honored human nature, and who won all his victories on the field of thought—that man, pure and upright, noble beyond description, if Christianity be true, is in hell this moment. That is what they call "solace"—"tidings of great joy." LaPlace, who read the heavens like an open book, who enlarged the horizon of human thought, is there too. Beethoven, Master of melody and harmony, who added to the joy of human life, and who has borne upon the wings of harmony and melody millions of spirits to the height of joy, with his heart still filled with melody—he is in hell today. Robert Burns, poet of love and liberty, and from his heart, like a spring gurgling and running down the highways, his poems have filled the world with music. They have added luster to human love. That man who, in four lines, gave all the philosophy of life—

> To make a happy fireside clime
> For weans and wife
> Is the true pathos and
> Sublime Of human life

—he is there with the rest.

Charles Dickens, whose genius will be a perpetual shield, saving thousands and millions of children from blows, who did more to make us tender with children than any other writer that ever touched a pen—he is there with the rest, according to our Christian religion. A little while ago there died in this country a philosopher—Ralph Waldo Emerson—a man of the loftiest ideal, a perfect model of integrity, whose mind was like a placid lake and reflected truths like stars. If the Christian religion be true, he is in perdition today. And yet he sowed the seeds of thought, and raised the whole world intellectually. And Longfellow, whose poems, tender as the dawn, have gone into millions of homes, not an impure, not a stained word in them all; but he was not a Christian. He did not believe in the "tidings of great joy." He didn't believe that God so loved the world that He intended to damn most everybody. And now he has gone to his reward. And Charles Darwin—a child of nature—one who knew more about his mother than any other child she ever had. What is philosophy? It is to account for phenomena by which we are surrounded—that is, to find the hidden cord that unites everything. Charles Darwin threw more light upon the problem of human existence than all the priests who ever lived from Melchisedec to the last exhorter. He would have traversed this globe on foot had it been possible to have found one new fact or to have corrected one error that he had made. No nobler man has lived—no man who has studied with more reverence (and by reverence I mean simply one who lives and studies for the truth)—no man who studied with more reverence than he. And yet, according to orthodox religion, Charles Darwin is in hell. Consolation!

So, if Christianity be true, Shakespeare, the greatest man who ever touched this planet, within whose brain were the fruits of all thought past, the seeds of all to be—Shakespeare, who was an intellectual ocean toward which all rivers ran, and from which now the isles and continents of thought received their dew and rain—that man who has added more to the intelligence of the world than any other who ever lived—that man, whose creations will live as long as man has imagination, and who has given more happiness upon the stage and more instruction than has flown from all the pulpits of this earth—that man is in hell, too. And Harriet Martineau, who did as much for English liberty as any man, brave and free—she is there. "George Eliot," the greatest woman the English-speaking people ever produced—she is with the rest. And this is called "Tidings of great joy."

Who are in heaven? How could there be much of a heaven without the men I have mentioned—the great men that have endeavored to make the world grander—such men as Voltaire, such men as Diderot, such men as the encyclopedists, such men as Hume, such men as Bruno, such men as Thomas Paine? If Christianity is true, that man who spent his life in breaking chains is now wearing the chains of God; that man who wished to break down the prison walls of tyranny is now in the prison of the most merciful Christ. It will not do. I can hardly express to you today my contempt for such a doctrine; and if it be true, I make my choice today, and I prefer hell.

Who is in heaven? John Calvin! John Knox! Jonathan Edwards! Torquemada—the builders of dungeons, the men who have obstructed the march of the human race. These are the men who are in heaven; and who else? Those who never had brain enough to harbor a doubt. And they ask me: How can you be wicked enough to attack the Christian religion?

"Oh," but they say, "God will never forgive you if you attack the orthodox religion." Now, when I read the history of this world, and when I think of the experience of my fellow-men, when I think of the millions living in poverty, and when I know that in the very air we breathe and in the sunlight that visits our homes there lurks an assassin ready to take our lives, and even when we believe we are in the fullness health and joy, they are undermining us with their contagion—when I know that we are surrounded by all these evils, and when I think of what man has suffered, I do not wonder if God can forgive man, but I often ask myself, "Can man forgive God?"

There is another thing. Some of these ministers have talked about me, and have made it their business to say unpleasant things. Among others the Rev. Mr. Talmage, of Brooklyn—a man of not much imagination, but of most excellent judgment—charges that I am a "blasphemer." A frightful charge! Terrible, if true! What is blasphemy? It is a sin, as I understand, against God. Is God infinite? He is, so they say; He is infinite; absolutely conditionless? Can I injure the conditionless? No. Can I sin against anything that I cannot injure? No. That is a perfectly plain proposition. I can injure my fellow-man, because he is a conditioned being, and I can help to change those conditions. He must have air; he must have food, he must have clothing; he must have shelter; but God is conditionless, and I cannot by any possibility affect Him. Consequently I cannot sin against Him. But I can sin against my fellow-man, so that I ought to be a thousand times more careful of doing injustice than of uttering blasphemy. There is no blasphemy but injustice, and there is no worship except the practice of justice. It is a thousand times more important that we should love our fellow-men than that we should love God. It is better to love wife and children than to love Jesus Christ, He is dead; they are alive. I can make their lives happy and fill all their hours with the fullness of joy. That is my religion; and the holiest temple ever erected beneath the stars is the home; the holiest altar is the fireside.

What is this blasphemy? First, it is a geographical question. There was a time when it was blasphemy in Jerusalem to say that Christ was God. In this country it is now blasphemy to say that He was not. It is blasphemy in Constantinople to deny that Mahomet was the Prophet of God; it is blasphemy here to say that he was. It is a geographical question; you cannot tell whether it is blasphemy or not without looking at the map. What is blasphemy? It is what the mistake says about the fact. It is what the last year's leaf says about this year's bud. It is the last cry of the defeated priest. Blasphemy is the little breastwork behind which hypocrisy hides; behind which mental impotency feels safe. There is no blasphemy but the avowal of thought, and he who speaks what he thinks blasphemes.

That I have had the hardihood—it doesn't take much—to attack the sacred scriptures. I have simply given my opinion; and yet they tell me that that book is holy—that you can take rags, make pulp, put ink on it, bind it in leather, and make something holy. The Catholics have a man for a pope; the Protestants have a book. The Catholics have the best of it. If they elect an idiot he will not live forever, and it is impossible for us to get rid of the barbarisms in our book. The Catholics said, "We will not let the common people read the bible." That was right. If it is necessary to believe it in order to get to heaven no man should run the risk of reading it. To allow a man to read the bible on such conditions is to set a trap for his soul. The right way is never to open it, and when you get to the day of judgment, and they ask you if you believe it say "Yes, I have never read it." The Protestant gives the book to a poor man and says: "Read it. You are at liberty to read it." "Well, suppose I don't believe it, when I get through?" "Then you will be damned." No man should be allowed to read it on those conditions. And yet Protestants have done that infinitely cruel thing. If I thought it was necessary to believe it I would say never read another line in it but just believe it and stick to it. And yet these people really think that there is something miraculous about the book. They regard it as a fetish—a kind of amulet—a something charmed, that will keep off evil spirits, or bad luck, stop bullets, and do a thousand handy-things for the preservation of life.

I heard a story upon that subject. You know that thousands of them are printed in the Sunday-school books. Here is one they don't print. There was a poor man who had belonged to the church, but he got cold, and he rather neglected it, and he had bad luck in his business, and he went down and down and down until he hadn't a dollar—not a thing to eat; and his wife said to him, "John, this comes of you having abandoned the church, this comes of your having done away with family worship. Now, I beg of you, let's go back." Well, John said it wouldn't do any harm to try. So he took down the bible, blew the dust off it, read a little from a chapter, and had family worship. As he was putting it up he opened it again, and there was a $10 bill between the leaves. He rushed out to the butcher's and bought meat, to the grocer's and bought tea and bread, and butter and eggs, and rushed back home and got them cooked, and the house was filled with the perfume of food; and he sat down at the table, tears in every eye and a smile on every face. She said, "What did I tell you?" Just then there was a knock on the door, and in came a constable, who arrested him for passing a $10 counterfeit bill.

They tell me that I ought not to attack the bible—that I have misrepresented it, and among other things that I have said that, according to the bible, the world was made of nothing. Well, what was it made of? They say God created everything. Consequently, there must have been nothing when He commenced. If he didn't make it of nothing, what did he make it of? Where there was, nothing, He made something. Yes; out of what? I don't know. This doctor of divinity, and I should think such a divinity would need a doctor, says that God made the universe out of His omnipotence. Why not out of His omniscience, or His omnipresence? Omnipotence is not a raw material. It is the something to work raw material with. Omnipotence is simply all powerful, and what good would strength do with nothing? The weakest man ever born could lift as much nothing as God. And he could do as much with it after he got it lifted. And yet a doctor of divinity tells me that this world was made of omnipotence. And right here let me say I find even in the mind of the clergymen the seeds of infidelity. He is trying to explain things. That is a bad symptom. The greater the miracle the greater the reward for believing it. God cannot afford to reward a man for believing anything reasonable. Why, even the scribes and Pharisees would believe a reasonable thing. Do you suppose God is to crown you with eternal joy and give you a musical instrument for believing something where the evidence is clear? No, sir. The larger the miracle the more grace. And let me advise the ministers of Chicago and of this country, never to explain a miracle; it cannot be explained. If you succeed in explaining it, the miracle is gone. If you fail you are gone. My advice to the clergy is, use assertion; just say "it is so," and the larger the miracle the greater the glory reaped by the eternal. And yet this man is trying to explain, pretending that He had some raw material of some kind on hand. And then I objected to the fact that He didn't make the sun until the fourth day, and that, consequently, the grass could not have grown—could not have thrown its mantle of green over the shoulders of the hill—and that the trees would not blossom and cast their shade upon the sod without some sunshine; and what does this man say? Why, that the rocks, when they crystallized, emitted light, even enough to raise a crop by. And he says "vegetation might have depended on the glare of volcanoes in the moon." What do you think would be the fate of agriculture depending on the "glare of volcanoes in the moon?" Then he says "the aurora borealis." Why, you couldn't raise cucumbers by the aurora borealis. And he says "liquid rivers of molten granite." I would like to have a farm on that stream. He guesses everything of the kind except lightning-bugs and foxfire. Now, think of that explanation in the last half of the nineteenth century by a minister. The truth is, the gentleman who wrote the account knew nothing of astronomy—knew as little as the modern preacher does—just about the same; and if they don't know more about the next world than they do about this, it is hardly worth while talking with them on the subject. There was a time, you know, when the minister was the educated man in the country, and when, if you wanted to know anything, you asked him. Now you do if you don't. So I find this man expounding the flood, and he says it was not very wet. He begins to doubt whether God had water enough to cover the whole earth. Why not stand by his book? He says that some of the animals got into the ark to keep out of the wet. I believe that is the way the Democrats got to the polls last Tuesday.

Another divine says that God would have drowned them all, but it was purely for the sake of economy that He saved any of them. Just think of that! According to this Christian religion all the people in the world were totally depraved through the fall, and God found he could not do anything with them, so he drowned them. Now, if God wanted to get up a flood big enough to drown sin, why did He not get up a flood big enough to drown the snake? That was His mistake. Now, these people say that if Jonah had walked rapidly up and down the whale's belly he would have avoided the action of its gastric-juice. Imagine Jonah sitting in the whale's mouth, on the back of a molar-tooth; and yet this doctor of divinity would have us believe that the infinite God of the universe was sitting under his gourd and made the worm that was at the root of Jonah's vine. Great business.

David is said to have been a man after God's own heart, and if you will read the twenty-eighth chapter of Chronicles you will find that David died full of years and honors. So I find in the great book of prophecy, concerning Solomon: "He shall reign in peace and quietness, he shall be my son, and I shall be his father, and I will preserve his Kingdom." Was that true?

It won't do. But they say God couldn't do away with slavery suddenly, nor with polygamy all at once—that He had to do it gradually—that if He had told this man you mustn't have slaves, and one man that he must have one wife, and one wife that she must have one husband, He would have lost the control over them notwithstanding all the miraculous power. Is it not wonderful that when they did all these miracles nobody paid any attention to them? Isn't it wonderful that, in Egypt, when they performed these wonders—when the waters were turned into blood, when the people were smitten with disease and covered with the horrible animals—isn't it wonderful that it had no influence on them? Do you know why all these miracles didn't affect the Egyptians? They were there at the time. Isn't it wonderful, too, that the Jews who had been brought from bondage—had followed a cloud by day and a pillar of fire by night—who had been miraculously fed, and for whose benefit water had leaked from the rocks and followed them up and down hill through all their journeying—isn't it wonderful, when they had seen the earth open and their companions swallowed, when they had seen God Himself write in robes of flames from Sinai's crags, when they had seen Him talking face to face with Moses—isn't it a little wonderful that He had no more influence over them? They were there at the time. And that is the reason they didn't mind it—they were there. And yet, with all these miracles, this God could not prevent polygamy and slavery. Was there no room on the two tables of stone to put two more commandments? Better have written them on the back, then. Better have left the others all off and put these two on. Man shall not enslave his brother, (you shall not live on unpaid labor), and the one man shall have the one wife. If these two had been written and the other ten left off, it would have been a thousand times better for this world.

But, they say, God works gradually. No hurry about it. He is not gradual about keeping Sunday, because, if He met a man picking up sticks, He killed Him; but in other things He is gradual. Suppose we wanted now to break certain cannibals of eating missionaries—wanted to stop them from eating them raw? Of course we would not tell them, in the first place, it was wrong. That would not do. We would induce them to cook them. That would be the first step toward civilization. We would have them stew them. We would not say it is wrong to eat missionary, but it is wrong to eat missionary raw. Then, after they began stewing them, we would put in a little mutton—not enough to excite suspicion but just a little, and so, day by day, we would put in a little more mutton and a little less missionary until, in about what the bible calls "the fullness of time," we would have clear mutton and no missionary. That is God's way. The next great charge against me is that I have disgraced my parents by expressing my honest thoughts. No man can disgrace his parents that way. I want my children to express their real opinions, whether they agree with mine or not. I want my children to find out more than I have found, and I would be gratified to have them discover the errors I have made. And if my father and mother were still alive I feel and know that I am pursuing a course of which they would approve. I am true to my manhood. But think of it! Suppose the father of Dr. Talmage had been a Methodist and his mother an infidel. Then what. Would he have to disgrace them both to be a Presbyterian. The disciples of Christ, according to this doctrine, disgraced their parents. The founder of every new religion, according to this doctrine, was a disgrace to his father and mother. Now there must have been a time when a Talmage was not a Presbyterian, and the one that left something else to join that church disgraced his father and mother. Why, if this doctrine be true why do you send missionaries to other lands and ask those people to disgrace their parents? If this doctrine be true nobody has religious liberty except foundlings, and it should be written over every Foundling Hospital: "Home for Religious Liberty." It won't do.

What is the next thing I have said? I have taken the ground, and I take it again today, that the bible has only words of humiliation for woman. The bible treats woman as the slave, the serf of man, and wherever that book is believed in thoroughly woman is a slave. It is the infidelity in the church that gives her what liberty she has today. Oh! but, says the gentleman, think of the heroines in the bible. How could a book be opposed to woman which has pictured such heroines? Well, that is a good argument. Let's answer it. Who are the heroines? He tells us. The first is Esther. Who was she? Esther is a very peculiar book, and the story is about this: Ahasaerus was a king. His wife's name was Vashti. She didn't please him. He divorced her, and advertised for another. A gentleman by the name of Mordecai had a good looking niece, and he took her to market. Her name was Esther. I don't feel like reading the whole of the second chapter. It is sufficient to say she was selected. After a time there was a gentleman by the name of Haman who, I should think, was in the cabinet, according to the story. And this man Mordecai began to put on considerable style because his niece was the king's wife, and he would not bow, or he would not rise, or he would not meet this gentleman with marks of distinguished consideration, so he made up his mind to have him hung. Then they got out an order to kill the Jews, and this Esther went to see the king. In those days they believed in the Bismarkian style of government—all power came from the king, not from the people; if anybody went to see this king without an invitation, and he failed to hold out his sceptre to him, the person was killed just to preserve the dignity of the monarch. When Esther arrived he held out the sceptre, and there-upon she induced him to send out another order for the fellows who were to kill the Jews, and they killed 75,000 or 80,000 of them. And they came back and said, "Kill Haman and his ten sons," and they hung the family up. That is all there is to the story. And yet this Esther is held up as a model of womanly grace and tenderness, and there is not a more infamous story in the literature of the world.

The next heroine is Ruth. I admit, that is a very pretty story. But Ruth was guilty of more things that would be deemed indiscreet than any girl in Brooklyn. That is all there is about Ruth. The next heroine is Hannah. And what do you suppose was the matter with her? She made a coat for her boy; that's all. I have known a woman make a whole suit! The next heroine was Abigail. She was the wife of Natal. King David had a few soldiers with him, and he called at the house of Natal, and asked if he could not get food for his men. Abigail went down to give him something to eat, and she was very much struck with David, David evidently fancied her. Natal died within a week. I think he was poisoned. David and Abigail were married. If that had happened in Chicago there would have been a coroner's jury, and an inquest; but that is all there was to that.

The next is Dorcas. She was in the new testament. She was real good to the ministers. Those ladies have always stood well with the church. She was real good to the poor. She died one day, and you never hear of her again.

Then there was that person that was raised from the dead. I would like to know from a person that had recently been raised from the dead, where he was when he was wanted, what he was traveling about, and what he was engaged in. I cannot imagine a more interesting person than one that has just been raised from the dead. Lazarus comes from the tomb, and I think sometimes that there must be a mistake about it, because when they come to die again thousands of people would say, "Why, he knows all about it!" Would it not be noted if a man had two funerals?

Now, then, these are all the heroines, to show you how little they thought of woman in that day. In the days of the old testament they did not even tell us when the mother of us all (Eve) died, nor where she is buried, nor anything about it. They do not even tell us where the mother of Christ sleeps, nor when she died. Never is she spoken of after the morning of the resurrection. He who descended from the cross went not to see her; and the son had no word for the broken-hearted mother.

The story is not true. I believe Christ was a great and good man, but He had nothing about Him miraculous except the courage to tell what he thought about the religion of His day. The new testament, in relating what occurred between Christ and his mother, mentions three instances; once, when they thought He had been lost in Jerusalem, when He said to them, "Wist ye not that I must be about my Father's business?" Next, at the marriage of Cana, when He said to the woman, "What have I to do with thee?"—words which He never said; and again from the cross, "Mother, behold Thy Son;" and to the disciple, "Behold thy Mother!" So of Mary Magdalene. In some respects there is no character in the new testament that so appeals to us as loving Christ—first at the sepulchre—and yet when He meets her after the resurrection He had for her the comfort only of the chilling words, "Touch me not!" I don't believe it. There were thousands of heroic women then. There are heroic women now. Think of the women who cling to fallen and disgraced husbands day by day, until they reach the gutter, and who stoop down to lift them from that position, and raise them up to be men once more! Every country is civilized in proportion as it honors woman. There are women in England working in mines, deformed by labor, that would become wild beasts were it not for the love they bear for home. Can you find among the women of the new testament any women that can equal the women born of Shakespeare's brain? You can find no woman like Isabella, where reason and purity blend into perfect truth; no woman like Juliet, where passion and purity meet like red and white within the bosom of a flower; no woman like Imogen, who said, "What is it to be false?" No woman like Cordelia, that would not show her wealth of love in hope of gain; nor like Hermione, who bore the cross of shame for years; nor like Miranda, who told her love as the flower exposes its bosom to the sun; nor like Desdemona, who was so pure that she could not suspect that another could suspect her of a crime.

And we are told that woman sinned first and man second; that man was made first and woman not till afterwards. The idea is that we could have gotten along without the woman well enough, but they never could have gotten along without us. I tell you that love is better than piety, love is better than all the ceremonial worship of the world, and it is better to love something than to believe anything on this globe. So this minister, seeking a mark to throw an arrow somewhere—trying to find some little place in the armor—charges me with having disparaged Queen Victoria. That you know is next to blasphemy. Well, I never did anything of the kind—never said a word against her in in life, neither as wife, or mother, or Queen—never doubted but that she is a good woman enough, and I have always admitted that her reputation was good in the neighborhood where she resides. I never had any other opinion. All I said in the world was—I was endeavoring to show that we are now to have an aristocracy of brain and heart—that is all—and I said, 'speaking of Louis Napoleon, he was not satisfied with simply being an emperor and having a little crown on his head, but wanted to prove that he had something in his head, so he wrote the life of Julius Caesar, and that made him a member of the French Academy; and speaking of King William, upon whose head is the divine petroleum of authority, I asked how he would like to exchange brains with Haeckel, the philosopher. Then I went over to England, and said "Queen Victoria wears the garment of power given her by blind fortune, by eyeless chance; 'George Eliot' is arrayed in robes of glory, woven in the loom of her own genius." Thereupon I am charged with disparaging a woman. And this priest, in order to get even with me, digs open the grave of "George Eliot" and endeavors to stain her unresisting dust. He calls her an adulteress—the vilest word in the languages of men—and he does it because she hated the Presbyterian creed, because she, according to his definition, was an atheist, because she lived without faith and died without fear, because she grandly bore the taunts and slanders of the Christian world. "George Eliot" carried tenderly in her heart the faults and frailties of her race. She saw the highway of eternal right through all the winding paths, where folly vainly stalks with thorn-pierced hands, the fading flowers of selfish joy; and whatever you may think or I may think of the one mistake in all her sad and loving life, I know and feel that in the court where her conscience sat as judge she stood acquitted, pure as light and stainless as a star. "George Eliot" has joined the choir invisible whose music is the gladness of this world, and her wondrous lines, her touching poems, will be read hundreds of years after every sermon in which a priest has sought to stain her name shall have vanished utterly from human speech. How appropriate here, with some slight change, the words of Laertes at Ophelia's grave:

Lay her in the earth; And from her fair and unpolluted flesh May violets spring; I tell thee, priest and minister, A ministering angel shall this woman be When thou liest howling.

I have no words with which to express my loathing hatred and condemnation of the man who will stain a noble woman's grave.

The next argument in favor of the "sacred scriptures" is the argument of numbers; and this minister congratulates himself that the infidels could not carry a precinct, or a county, or a state in the United States. Well, I tell you, they can come proportionately near it—just in proportion that that part of the country is educated. The whole world doesn't move together in one life. There has to be some man to take a step forward and the people follow; and when they get where that man was, some other Titan has taken another step, and you can see him there on the great mountain of progress. That is why the world moves. There must be pioneers, and if nobody is right except he who is with the majority, then we must turn and walk toward the setting sun. He says "We will settle this by suffrage." The Christian religion was submitted to a popular vote in Jerusalem, and what was the result? "Crucify Him "—an infamous result, showing that you can't depend on the vote of barbarians. But I am told that there are 300,000,000 Christians in the world. Well, what of it? There are more Buddhists. And they say, what a number of bibles are printed!—more bibles than any other book. Does this prove anything? True, because more of them. Suppose you should find published in the New York Herald something about you, and you should go to the editor and tell him: "That is a lie;" and he should say: "That can't be; the Herald has the largest circulation of any paper in the world." Three hundred millions of Christians, and here are the nations that prove the truth of Christianity: Russia 80,000,000 Christians. I am willing to admit it; a country without freedom of speech, without freedom of press—a country in which every mouth is a Bastille and every tongue a prisoner for life—a country in which assassins are the best men in it. They call that Christian. Girls sixteen years of age, for having spoken in favor of human liberty, are now working in Siberian mines. That is a Christian country. Only a little while ago a man shot at the emperor twice. The emperor was protected by his armor. The man was convicted, and they asked him if he wished religious consolation. "No." "Do you believe in a God?" "No;" if there was a God there would be no Russia. Sixteen millions of Christians in Spain—Spain that never touched a shore except as a robber—Spain that took the gold and silver of the new world and used it as an engine of oppression in the old—a country in which cruelty was worship, in which murder was prayer—a country where flourished the Inquisition—I admit Spain is a Christian country. If you don't believe it I do. Read the history of Holland, read the history of South America, read the history of Mexico—a chapter of cruelty beyond the power of language to express. I admit that Spain is orthodox. If you will go there you will find the man who robs you and asks God to forgive you—a country where infidelity hasn't made much headway, but, thank God, where there is even yet a dawn, where there are such men as Castelar and others, who begin to see that one schoolhouse is equal to three cathedrals and one teacher worth all the priests.

Italy is another Christian nation, with 28,000,000 Christians. In Italy lives the only authorized agent of God, the pope. For hundreds of years Italy was the beggar of the earth, and held out both hands. Gold and silver flowed from every land into her palms, and she became covered with nunneries, monasteries, and the pilgrims of the world. Italy was sacred dust. Her soil was a perpetual blessing, her sky was an eternal smile. Italy was guilty not simply of the death of the Catholic church, but Italy was dead and buried and would have been in her grave still had it not been for Mazzini, Garibaldi, and Cavour. When the prophecy of Garibaldi shall be fulfilled, when the priests, with spades in their hands, shall dig ditches to drain the Pontine marshes, when the monasteries shall be factories, when the whirling wheels of industry shall drown the drowsy and hypocritical prayers, then and not till then, will Italy be great and free. Italy is the only instance in our history and in the history of the world, so far as we know, of the resurrection of a nation. She is the first fruits of them that sleep.

Portugal is another Christian country. She made her living in the slave trade for centuries. I admit that all the blessings that that country enjoyed flowed naturally from Catholicism, and we believe in the same scriptures. If you don't believe it, read the history of the persecution of the Jewish people. I admit that Germany is a Christian nation; that is, Christians are in power. When the bill was introduced for the purpose of ameliorating the condition of the Jews, Bismark spoke against it, and said "Germany is a Christian nation, and therefore, we cannot pass the bill." Austria is another Christian nation. If you don't believe it, read the history of Hungary, and, if you still have doubts, read the history of the partition of Poland. But there is one good thing in that country. They believe in education, and education is the enemy of ecclesiasticism. Every thoroughly educated man is his own church, and his own pope, and his own priest.

They tell me that the United States—our country—is Christian. I deny it. It is neither Christian nor pagan; it is human. Our fathers retired all the gods from politics. Our fathers laid down the doctrine that the right to govern comes from the consent of the governed, and not from the clouds. Our fathers knew that if they put an infinite God in the Constitution there would be no room left for the people. Our fathers used the language of Lincoln, and they made a government for the people by the people. This is not a Christian country. Some gentleman said, "How about Delaware?" I told him there was a man in Washington some twenty or thirty years ago who came there and said he was a Revolutionary soldier and wanted a pension. He was so bent and bowed over that the wind blew his shoestrings into his eyes. They asked him how old he was, and he said fifty years. "Why, good man, you can't get a pension, because the war was over before you were born. You mustn't fool us." "Well," said he, "I'll tell you the truth: I lived sixty years in Delaware, but I never count it, and hope God won't." And these Christian nations which have been brought forward as the witnesses of the truth of the scriptures owe $25,000,000,000, which represents Christian war, Christian cannon, Christian shot, and Christian shell. The sum is so great that the imagination is dazed in its contemplation. That is the result of loving your neighbor as yourself.

The next great argument brought forward by these gentlemen is the persecution of the Jews. We are told in the nineteenth century that God has the Jews persecuted simply for the purpose of establishing the authenticity of the scriptures, and every Jewish home burned in Russia throws light on the gospel, and every violated Jewish maiden is another evidence that God still takes an interest in the holy scriptures. That is their doctrine. They are "fulfilling prophecy." The Christian grasps the Jew, strips him, robs him, makes him an outcast, and then points to him as a fulfillment of prophecy;

and we are today laying the foundation of future persecution—we are teaching our children the monstrous falsehood that Jews crucified God, and the nation consented. They crucified a good man. What nation has not? What race has not? Think of the number killed by the Presbyterians; by the Catholics. Every sect, with maybe two or three exceptions, have crucified their fellows, and every race has burned its greatest and its best. And yet we are filling the minds of children with hatred of the Jewish people. It is a poor business. "Ah?" but they say, "these people are cursed by God." I say they never had any good fortune until the Jehovah of the bible deserted them. Whenever they have had a reasonable chance they have been the most prosperous people in the world. I never saw one begging. I never saw one in the criminal dock. For hundreds of years they were not allowed to own any land, for hundreds of years they were not allowed to work at any trade; they were driven simply to dealing in money, and in precious stones, and things of that character, and, by a kind of poetic justice, they have today the control of the money of the world. I am glad to see that kings and emperors go to the offices of the Jews, with their hats in their hands, to have their notes discounted. And yet I am told by clergymen that all this infamy has been kept up simply to establish the truth of the gospel. I despise such doctrine. As long as the liberty of one Jew is unsafe, my liberty is not secure. Liberty for all, and not until then will the liberty of any be assured. "Ah"; but says this man, "nobody ever died cheerfully for a lie. The Jewish people have suffered persecution for 1,600 years, and they have suffered it cheerfully." If this doctrine is true, then Judaism must be true and Christianity must be false. But martyrdom doesn't prove the truth if the martyr knows it. It simply proves the barbarity of his persecutors, and has no sincerity. That is all it proves.

But you must remember that this gentleman who believes in this doctrine is a Presbyterian, and why should a Presbyterian object? After a few hundred years of burning he expects to enjoy the eternal auto da fe of hell—an auto da fe that will be presided over by God and His angels, and they will be expected to applaud. He is a Presbyterian; and what is that? It is the worst religion of this earth. I admit that thousands and millions of Presbyterians are good people, no man ever being half so bad as his creed. I am not attacking them. I am attacking their creed. I am attacking what this religion calls "Tidings of great joy." And, according to that, hundreds of billions and billions of years ago our fate was irrevocably and forever fixed, and God in the secret counsels of His own inscrutable will, made up His mind whom He would save and whom He would damn. When thinking of that God I always think of the mistake of a

Methodist preacher during the war. He commenced the prayer—and never did one more appropriate for the Presbyterian God or the Methodist go up—"O, Thou great and unscrupulous God." This Presbyterian believes that billions of years before that baby in the cradle—that little dimpled child, basking in the light of a mother's smile—was born, God had made up His mind to damn it; and when Talmage looks at one of those children who will probably be damned he is cheerful about it; he enjoys it. That is Presbyterianism—that God made man and damned him for His own glory. If there is such a God, I hate Him with every drop of my blood; and if there is a heaven it must be where He is not. Now think of that doctrine! Only a little while ago there was a ship from Liverpool out eighty days with its rudder washed away; for ten days nothing to eat—nothing but the bare decks and hunger; and the captain took a revolver in his hand and put it to his brain and said: "Some of us must die for the others. And it might as well be I." One of his companions grasped the pistol and said: "Captain, wait; wait one day more. We can live another day." And the next morning the horizon was rich with a sail, and they were saved. And yet if Presbyterianism is true; if that man had put the bullet through his infinitely generous brain so that his comrades could have eaten of his flesh and reached their homes and felt about their necks the dimpled arms of children and the kisses of wives upon their lips—if Presbyterianism be true, God had a constable ready there to clutch that soul and thrust it down to eternal hell. Tidings of great joy. And yet this is religion. Why, if that doctrine be true, every soldier in the Revolutionary War who died not a Christian has been damned; every one in the War of 1812, who kept our flag upon the sea, if he died not a Christian has been damned; and every one in the Civil War who fought to keep our flag in heaven, not a Christian, and the ones who died in Andersonville and Libby, not Christians, are now in the prison of God, where the famine of Andersonville and Libby would be regarded as a joy. Orthodox Christianity! Why, we have an account in the bible—it comes from the other world—from both countries—from heaven and from hell—let us see what it is. Here is a rich man who dies. The only fault about him was, he was rich; no other crime was charged against him. We are told that the rich man died, and when he lifted up his eyes he found no sympathy, yet even in hell he remembered his five brethren, and prayed that some one should be sent to them so that they should not come there. I tell you I had rather be in hell with human sympathy than in heaven without it.

The bible is not inspired, and ministers know nothing about another world. They don't know. I am satisfied there is no world of eternal pain. If there is a world of joy, so much the better. I have never put out the faintest star of human hope that ever trembled in the night of life. There was a time when I was not; after that I was; now I am. And it is just as probable that I will live again as it was that I could have lived before I did. Let it go. Ah! but what will life be? The world will be here. Men and women will be here. The page of history will be open. The walls of the world will be adorned with art, the niches with sculpture; music will be here, and all there is of life and joy. And there will be homes here, and the fireside, and there will be a common hope without a common fear. Love will be here, and love is the only bow on life's dark cloud. Love was the first to dream of immortality. Love is the morning and evening star. It shines upon the child; it sheds its radiance upon the peaceful tomb. Love is the mother of beauty—the mother of melody, for music is its voice. Love is the builder of every hope, the kindler of every fire on every hearth. Love is the enchanter, the magician that changes worthless things to joy, and makes right royal kings and queens out of common clay. Love is the perfume of that wondrous flower the heart. Without that divine passion, without that divine sway, we are less than beasts, and with it earth is heaven and we are gods.

# INGERSOLL'S ORATION AT A CHILD'S GRAVE.

In a remote corner of the Congressional Cemetery at Washington, a small group of people with uncovered heads were ranged around a newly-opened grave. They included Detective and Mrs. George O. Miller and family and friends, who had gathered to witness the burial of the former's bright little son Harry. As the casket rested upon the trestles there was a painful pause, broken only by the mother's sobs, until the undertaker advanced toward a stout, florid-complexioned gentleman in the party and whispered to him, the words being inaudible to the lookers-on. This gentleman was Col. Robert G. Ingersoll, a friend of the Millers, who had attended the funeral—at their request. He shook his head when the undertaker first addressed him, and then said suddenly, "Does Mrs. Miller desire it?" The undertaker gave an affirmative nod. Mr. Miller looked appealingly toward the distinguished orator, and then Colonel Ingersoll advanced to the side of the grave, made a motion denoting a desire for silence, and, in a voice of exquisite cadence, delivered one of his characteristic eulogies for the dead.

The scene was intensely dramatic. A fine drizzling rain was falling, and every head was bent, and every ear turned to catch the impassioned words of eloquence and hope that fell from the lips of the famed orator. Colonel Ingersoll was unprotected by either hat or umbrella. His invocation thrilled his hearers with awe, each eye that had previously been bedimmed with tears brightening, and sobs becoming hushed. The colonel said:

My Friends: I know how vain it is to gild a grief with words, and yet I wish to take from every grave its fear. Here in this world, where life and death are equal kings, all should be brave enough to meet what all have met. The future has been filled with fear, stained and polluted by the heartless past. From the wondrous tree of life the buds and blossoms fall with ripened fruit, and in the common bed of earth patriarchs and babes sleep side by side. Why should we fear that which will come to all that is? We cannot tell. We do not know which is the greatest blessing, life or death. We cannot say that death is not good. We do not know whether the grave is the end of this life or the door of another, or whether the night here is not somewhere else a dawn. Neither can we tell which is the more fortunate, the child dying in its mother's arms before its lips have learned to form a word, or he who journeys all the length of life's uneven road, painfully taking the last slow steps with staff and crutch. Every cradle asks us "Whence?" and every coffin "Whither?" The poor barbarian weeping above his dead can answer the question as intelligently and satisfactorily as the robed priest of the most authentic creed. The tearful ignorance of the one is just as consoling as the learned and unmeaning words of the other. No man standing where the horizon of a life has touched a grave has any right to prophesy a future filled with pain and tears. It may be that death gives all there is of worth to life. If those who press and strain against our hearts could never die, perhaps that love would wither from the earth. Maybe a common faith treads from out the paths between our hearts the weeds of selfishness, and I should rather live and love where death is king than have eternal life where love is not. Another life is naught, unless we know and love again the ones who love us here.

They who stand with breaking hearts around this little grave need have no fear. The largest and the nobler faith in all that is, and is to be, tells us that death, even at its worst, is only perfect rest. We know that through the common wants of life, the needs and duties of each hour, their grief will lessen day by day until at last these graves will be to them a place of rest and peace—almost of joy. There is for them this consolation: The dead do not suffer. If they live again their lives will surely be as good as ours. We have no fear; we are all children of the same mother and the same fate awaits us all. We, too, have our religion, and it is this: "Help for the living, hope for the dead."

# INGERSOLL AT HIS BROTHER'S GRAVE.—A Most Exquisite, Yet One Of The Most Sad And Mournful Sermons

The funeral of Hon. Ebon C. Ingersoll, brother of Col. Robert G. Ingersoll, of Illinois, took place at his residence in Washington, D.C., June 2, 1879. The ceremonies were extremely simple, consisting merely of viewing the remains by relatives and friends, and a funeral oration by Col. Robert G. Ingersoll, brother of the deceased. A large number of distinguished gentlemen were present, including Secretary Sherman, Assistant Secretary Hawley, Senators Blaine, Vorhees, Paddock, Allison, Logan, Hon. Thomas Henderson, Gov. Pound, Hon. Wm. M. Morrison, Gen. Jeffreys, Gen. Williams, Col. James Fishback, and others. The pall-bearers were Senators Blaine, Vorhees, David Davis, Paddock and Allison, Col. Ward, H. Lamon, Hon. Jeremiah Wilson of Indiana, and Hon. Thomas A. Boyd of Illinois.

Soon after Mr. Ingersoll began to read his eloquent characterization of the dead, his eyes filled with tears. He tried to hide them behind his eye-glasses, but he could not do it, and finally he bowed his head upon the dead man's coffin in uncontrollable grief. It was after some delay and the greatest efforts of self-mastery, that Col. Ingersoll was able to finish reading his address, which was as follows:

My Friends: I am going to do that which the dead often promised he would do for me. The loved and loving brother, husband, father, friend, died where manhood's morning almost touches noon, and while the shadows still were falling toward the west. He had not passed on life's highway the stone that marks the highest point, but being weary for a moment he lay down by the wayside, and, using his burden for a pillow, fell into that dreamless sleep that kisses down his eyelids still. While yet in love with life and raptured with the world, he passed to silence and pathetic dust. Yet, after all, it may be best, just in the happiest, sunniest hour of all the voyage, while eager winds are kissing every sail, to dash against the unseen rock, and in an instant hear the billows roar over a sunken ship. For, whether in mid-sea or among the breakers of the farther shore, a wreck must mark at last the end of each and all. And every life, no matter if its every hour is rich with love, and every moment jeweled with a joy, will, at its close, become a tragedy, as sad, and deep, and dark as can be woven of the warp and woof of mystery and death. This brave and tender man in every storm of life was oak and rock, but in the sunshine he was vine and flower. He was the friend of all heroic souls. He climbed the heights and left all superstitions far below, while on his forehead fell the golden dawning of a grander day. He loved the beautiful and was with color, form and music touched to tears. He sided with the weak, and with a willing hand gave alms; with loyal heart and with the purest hand he faithful discharged all public trusts. He was a worshiper of liberty and a friend of the oppressed. A thousand times I have heard him quote the words: "For justice all place a temple and all season summer." He believed that happiness was the only good, reason the only torch, justice the only worshiper, humanity the only religion, and love the priest.

He added to the sum of human joy, and were every one for whom he did some loving service to bring a blossom to his grave he would sleep tonight beneath a wilderness of flowers. Life is a narrow vale between the cold and barren peaks of two eternities. We strive in vain to look beyond the heights. We cry aloud, and the only answer is the echo of our wailing cry. From the voiceless lips of the unreplying dead there comes no word; but in the night of death hope sees a star and listening love can hear the rustle of a wing. He who sleeps here, when dying, mistaking the approach of death for the return of health, whispered with his latest breath, "I am better now." Let us believe, in spite of doubts and dogmas and tears and fears that these dear words are true of all the countless dead. And now, to you who have been chosen from among the many men he loved to do the last sad office, for the dead, we give his sacred dust. Speech can not contain our love. There was—there is—no gentler, stronger, manlier man.

# INGERSOLL'S LECTURE ON THE MISTAKES OF MOSES.

Now and then some one asks me why I am endeavoring to interfere with the religious faith of others, and why I try to take from the world the consolation naturally arising from a belief in eternal fire. And I answer, I want to do what little I can to make my country truly free. I want to broaden the intellectual horizon of our people. I want it so that we can differ upon all those questions, and yet grasp each other's hands in genuine friendship. I want in the first place to free the clergy. I am a great friend of theirs, but they don't seem to have found it out generally. I want it so that every minister will be not a parrot, not an owl sitting upon the limb of the tree of knowledge and hooting the hoots that have been hooted for eighteen hundred years. But I want it so that each one can be an investigator, a thinker; and I want to make his congregation grand enough so that they will not only allow him to think, but will demand that he shall think, and give to them the honest truth of his thought. As it is now, ministers are employed like attorneys—for the plaintiff or the defendant. If a few people know of a young man in the neighborhood maybe who has not a good constitution,—he may not be healthy enough to be wicked—a young man who has shown no decided talent—it occurs to them to make him a minister. They contribute and send him to some school. If it turns out that that young man has more of the man in him than they thought, and he changes his opinion, everyone who contributed will feel himself individually swindled—and they will follow that young man to the grave with the poisoned shafts of malice and slander. I want it so that every one will be free—so that a pulpit will not be a pillory. They have in Massachusetts, at a place called Andover, a kind of minister factory; and every professor in that factory takes an oath once in every five years—that is as long as an oath will last—that not only has he not during the last five years, but so help him God, he will not during the next five years intellectually advance; and probably there is no oath he could easier keep. Since the foundation of that institution there has not been one case of perjury. They believe the same creed they first taught when the foundation stone was laid, and now when they send out a minister they brand him as hardware from Sheffield and Birmingham. And every man who knows where he was educated knows his creed, knows every argument of his creed, every book that he reads, and just what he amounts to intellectually, and knows he will shrink and shrivel, and become solemnly stupid day after day until he meets with death. It is all wrong; it is cruel. Those men should be allowed to grow. They should have the air of liberty and the sunshine of thought.

I want to free the schools of our country. I want it so that when a professor in a college finds some fact inconsistent with Moses, he will not hide the fact. I wish to see an eternal divorce and separation between church and schools. The common school is the bread of life, but there should be nothing taught except what somebody knows; and anything else should not be maintained by a system of general taxation. I want its professors so that they will tell everything they find; that they will be free to investigate in every direction, and will not be trammeled by the superstitions of our day. What has religion to do with facts? Nothing. Is there any such thing as Methodist mathematics, Presbyterian botany, Catholic astronomy or Baptist biology? What has any form of superstition or religion to do with a fact or with any science? Nothing but to hinder, delay or embarrass. I want, then, to free the schools; and I want to free the politicians, so that a man will not have to pretend he is a Methodist, or his wife a Baptist, or his grandmother a Catholic; so that he can go through a campaign, and when he gets through will find none of the dust of hypocrisy on his knees.

I want the people splendid enough that when they desire men to make laws for them, they will take one who knows something, who has brains enough to prophesy the destiny of the American Republic, no matter what his opinions may be upon any religious subject. Suppose we are in a storm out at sea, and the billows are washing over our ship, and it is necessary that some one should reef the topsail, and a man presents himself. Would you stop him at the foot of the mast to find out his opinion on the five points of Calvinism? What has that to do with it? Congress has nothing to do with baptism or any particular creed, and from what little experience I have had in Washington, very little to do with any kind of religion whatever. Now I hope, this afternoon, this magnificent and splendid audience will forget that they are Baptists or Methodists, and remember that they are men and women. These are the highest titles humanity can bear—and every title you add, belittles them. Man is the highest; woman is the highest. Let us remember that our views depend largely upon the country in which we happen to live. Suppose we were born in Turkey most of us would have been Mohammedans; and when we read in the book that when Mohammed visited heaven he became acquainted with an angel named Gabriel, who was so broad between his eyes that it would take a smart camel three hundred days to make the journey, we probably would have believed it. If we did not, people would say: "That young man is dangerous; he is trying to tear down the fabric of our religion. What do you propose to give us instead of that angel? We cannot afford to trade off an angel of that size for nothing." Or if we had been born in India, we would have believed in a god with three heads. Now we believe in three gods with one head. And so we might make a tour of the world and see that every superstition that could be imagined by the brain of man has been in some place held to be sacred.

Now some one says, "The religion of my father and mother is good enough for me." Suppose we all said that, where would be the progress of the world? We would have the rudest and most barbaric religion—religion which no one could believe. I do not believe that it is showing real respect to our parents to believe something simply because they did. Every good father and every good mother wish their children to find out more than they knew every good father wants his son to overcome some obstacle that he could not grapple with and if you wish to reflect credit on your father and mother, do it by accomplishing more than they did, because you live in a better time. Every nation has had what you call a sacred record, and the older the more sacred, the more contradictory and the more inspired is the record. We, of course, are not an exception, and I propose to talk a little about what is called the Pentateuch, a book, or a collection of books, said to have been written by Moses. And right here in the commencement let me say that Moses never wrote one word of the Pentateuch—not one word was written until he had been dust and ashes for hundreds of years. But as the general opinion is that Moses wrote these books, I have entitled this lecture "The Mistakes of Moses." For the sake of this lecture, we will admit that he wrote it. Nearly every maker of religion has commenced by making the world; and it is one of the safest things to do, because no one can contradict as having been present, and it gives free scope to the imagination. These books, in times when there was a vast difference between the educated and the ignorant, became inspired and people bowed down and worshiped them.

I saw a little while ago a Bible with immense oaken covers, with hasps and clasps large enough almost for a penitentiary, and I can imagine how that book would be regarded by barbarians in Europe when not more than one person in a dozen could read and write. In imagination I saw it carried into the cathedral, heard the chant of the priest, saw the swinging of the censer and the smoke rising; and when that Bible was put on the altar I can imagine the barbarians looking at it and wondering what influence that book could have on their lives and future. I do not wonder that they imagined it was inspired. None of them could write a book, and consequently when they saw it they adored it; they were stricken with awe; and rascals took advantage of that awe.

Now they say that the book is inspired. I do not care whether it is or not; the question is: Is it true? If it is true it doesn't need to be inspired. Nothing needs inspiration except a falsehood or a mistake. A fact never went into partnership with a miracle. Truth scorns the assistance of wonders. A fact will fit every other fact in the universe, and that is how you can tell—whether it is or not a fact. A lie will not fit anything except a lie made for the express purpose; and, finally, some one gets tired of lying, and the last lie will not fit the next fact, and then there is a chance for inspiration. Right then and there a miracle is needed. The real question is, in the light of science, in the light of the brain and heart of the nineteenth century, is this book true? The gentleman who wrote it begins by telling us that God made the universe out of nothing. That I cannot conceive; it may be so, but I cannot conceive it. Nothing in the light of raw material, is, to my mind, a decided and disastrous failure. I cannot imagine of nothing being made into something, any more than I can of something being changed back into nothing. I cannot conceive of force aside from matter, because force to be force must be active, and unless there is matter there is nothing for force to act upon, and consequently it cannot be active. So I simply say I cannot comprehend it. I cannot believe it. I may roast for this, but it is my honest opinion. The next thing he proceeds to tell us is that God divided the darkness from the light, and right here let me say when I speak about God I simply mean the being described by the Jews. There may be in immensity a being beneath whose wing the universe exists, whose every thought is a glittering star, but I know nothing about Him,—not the slightest,—and this afternoon I am simply talking about the being described by the Jewish people. When I say God, I mean Him. Moses describes God dividing the light from the darkness. I suppose that at that time they must have been mixed. You can readily see how light and darkness can get mixed. They must have been entities. The reason I think so is because in that same book I find that darkness overspread Egypt so thick that it could be felt, and they used to have on exhibition in Rome a bottle of the darkness that once overspread Egypt. The gentleman who wrote this in imagination saw God dividing light from the darkness. I am sure the man who wrote it, believed darkness to be an entity, a something, a tangible thing that can be mixed with light.

The next thing that he informs us is that God divided the waters above the firmament from those below the firmament. The man who wrote that believed the firmament to be a solid affair. And that is what the gods did. You recollect the gods came down and made love to the daughters of men—and I never blamed them for it. I have never read a description of any heaven I would not leave on the same errand. That is where the gods lived. There is where they kept the water. It was solid. That is the reason the people prayed for rain. They believed that an angel could take a lever, raise a window and let out the desired quantity. I find in the Psalms that "He bowed the heavens and came down;" and we read that the children of men built a tower to reach the heavens and climb into the abode of the gods. The man who wrote that believed the firmament to be solid. He knew nothing about the laws of evaporation. He did not know that the sun wooed with amorous kiss the waves of the sea, and that, disappointed, their vaporous sighs changed to tears and fell again as rain. The next thing he tells us is that the grass began to grow; and the branches of the trees laughed into blossom, and the grass ran up the shoulder of the hills, and yet not a solitary ray of light had left the eternal quiver of the sun. Not a blade of grass had ever been touched by a gleam of light. And I do not think that grass will grow to hurt without a gleam of sunshine. I think the man who wrote that simply made a mistake, and is excusable to a certain degree. The next day he made the sun and moon—the sun to rule the day and the moon to rule the night. Do you think the man who wrote that knew anything about the size of the sun? I think he thought it was about three feet in diameter, because I find in some book that the sun was stopped a whole day, to give a general named Joshua time to kill a few more Amalekites; and the moon was stopped also. Now it seems to me that the sun would give light enough without stopping the moon; but as they were in the stopping business they did it just for devilment. At another time, we read, the sun was turned ten degrees backward to convince Hezekiah that he was not going to die of a boil. How much easier it would have been to cure the boil. The man who wrote that thought the sun was two or three feet in diameter, and could be stopped and pulled around like the sun and moon in a theatre. Do you know that the sun throws out every second of time as much heat as could be generated by burning eleven thousand millions tons of coal? I don't believe he knew that, or that he knew the motion of the earth. I don't believe he knew that it was turning on its axis at the rate of a thousand miles an hour, because if he did, he would have understood the immensity of heat that would have been generated by stopping the world. It has been calculated by one of the best mathematicians and astronomers that to stop the world would cause as much heat as it would take to burn a lump of solid coal three times as big as the globe. And yet we find in that book that the sun was not only stopped, but turned back ten degrees, simply to convince a gentleman that he was not going to die of a boil. They will say I will be damned if I do not believe that, and I tell them I will if I do.

Then he gives us the history of astronomy, and he gives it to us in five words: "He made the stars also." He came very near forgetting the stars. Do you believe that the man who wrote that knew that there are stars as much larger than this earth as this earth is larger than the apple which Adam and Eve are said to have eaten. Do you believe that he knew that this world is but a speck in the shining, glittering universe of existence? I would gather from that that he made the stars after he got the world done. The telescope, in reading the infinite leaves of the heavens, has ascertained that light travels at the rate of 192,000 miles per second, and it would require millions of years to come from some of the stars to this earth. Yet the beams of those stars mingle in our atmosphere, so that if those distant orbs were fashioned when this world began, we must have been whirling in space not six thousand, but many millions of years. Do you believe the man who wrote that as a history of astronomy really knew that this world was but a speck compared with millions of sparkling orbs? I do not. He then proceeds to tell us that God made fish and cattle, and that man and woman were created male and female. The first account stops at the second verse of the second chapter. You see, the Bible originally was not divided into chapters; the first Bible that was ever divided into chapters in our language was made in the year of grace 1550. The Bible was originally written in the Hebrew language, and the Hebrew language at that time had no vowels in writing. It was written with consonants, and without being divided into chapters or into verses, and there was no system of punctuation whatever. After you go home tonight write an English sentence or two with only consonants close together, and you will find that it will take twice as much inspiration to read it as it did to write it. When the Bible was divided into verses and chapters, the divisions were not always correct, and so the division between the first and second chapter of Genesis is not in the right place. The second account of the creation commences at the third verse and it differs from the first in two essential points. In the first account man is the last made; in the second man is made before the beasts. In the first account, man is made "male and female"; in the second only a male is made, and there is no intention of making a woman whatever.

You will find by reading that second chapter that God tried to palm off on Adam a beast as his helpmeet. Everybody talks about the Bible and nobody reads it; that is the reason it is so generally believed. I am probably the only man in the United States who has read the Bible through this year. I have wasted that time, but I had a purpose in view. Just read it, and you will find, about the twenty-third verse, that God caused all the animals to walk before Adam in order that he might name them. And the animals came like a menagerie into town, and as Adam looked at all the crawlers, jumpers and creepers, this God stood by to see what he would call them. After this procession passed, it was pathetically remarked, "Yet was there not found any helpmeet for Adam." Adam didn't see anything that he could fancy. And I am glad he didn't. If he had, there would not have been a free-thinker in this world; we should have all died orthodox. And finding Adam was so particular, God had to make him a helpmeet, and having used up the nothing, he was compelled to take part of the man to make the woman with, and he took from the man a rib. How did he get it? And then imagine a God with a bone in his hand, and about to start a woman, trying to make up his mind whether to make a blonde or a brunette.

Right here it is only proper that I should warn you of the consequences of laughing at any story in the Bible. When you come to die, your laughing at this story will be a thorn in your pillow. As you look back upon the record of your life, no matter how many men you have wrecked and ruined, and no matter how many women you have deceived and deserted—all that may be forgiven you but if you recollect that you have laughed at God's book you will see through the shadows of death, the leering looks of fiends and the forked tongues of devils. Let me show you how it will be. For instance it is the day of judgment. When the man is called up by the recording secretary, or whoever does the cross-examining, he says to his soul "Where are you from?" "I am from the world." "Yes sir. What kind of a man were you?" "Well, I don't like to talk about myself." "But you have to. What kind of a man were you?" "Well, I was a good fellow; I loved my wife, I loved my children. My home was my heaven; my fire-side was my paradise, and to sit there and see the lights and shadows falling on the faces of those I love, that to me was a perpetual joy. I never gave one of them a solitary moment of pain. I don't owe a dollar in the world and I left enough to pay my funeral expenses and keep the wolf of want from the door of the house I loved. That is the kind of a man I am." "Did you belong to any church?" "I did not. They were too narrow for me. They were always expecting to be happy simply because somebody else was to be damned."

"Well, did you believe that rib story?" "What rib story—Do you mean that Adam and Eve business? No, I did not. To tell you the God's truth, that was a little more than I could swallow." "To hell with him. Next. Where are you from?" "I'm from the world, too. Do you belong to any church?" "Yes, sir, and to the Young Men's Christian Association." "What is your business?" "Cashier in a bank." "Did you ever run off with any money? I don't like to tell, Sir." "Well, you have to." "Yes, Sir I did." "What kind of a bank did you have?" "A savings bank." "How much did you run off with?" "One hundred thousand dollars." "Did you take anything else along with you?" "Yes Sir." "What?" "I took my neighbor's wife." "Did you have a wife and children of your own?" "Yes, Sir." "And you deserted them?" "Oh, yes; but such was my confidence in God that I believed he would take care of them." "Have you heard of them since?" "No, Sir. Did you believe that rib story?" "Ah, bless your soul, yes! I believe all of it, Sir; I often used to be sorry that there were not harder stories yet in the Bible, so that I could show what my faith could do." "You believed it, did you?" "Yes, with all my heart." "Give him a harp."

I simply wanted to show you how important it is to believe these stories. Of all the authors in the world God hates a critic the worst. Having got this woman done he brought her to the man, and they started house-keeping, and a few minutes afterward a snake came through a crack in the fence and commenced to talk with her on the subject of fruit. She was not acquainted in the neighborhood, and she did not know whether snakes talked or not, or whether they knew anything about the apples or not. Well, she was misled, and the husband ate some of those apples and laid it all on his wife; and there is where the mistake was made. God ought to have rubbed him out at once. He might have known that no good could come of starting the world with a man like that. They were turned out. Then the trouble commenced, and people got worse and worse. God, you must recollect, was holding the reins of government, but He did nothing for them. He allowed them to live six hundred and sixty-nine years without knowing their A. B. C. He never started a school, not even a Sunday school. He didn't even keep His own boys at home. And the world got worse every day, and finally he concluded to drown them. Yet that same God has the impudence to tell me how to raise my own children. What would you think of a neighbor, who had just killed his babes giving you his views on domestic economy? God found that he could do nothing with them and He said: "I will drown them all except a few." And he picked out a fellow by the name of Noah, that had been a bachelor for five hundred years. If I had to drown anybody, I would have drowned him. I believe that Noah had then been married something like one hundred years. God told him to build a boat, and he built one five hundred feet long, eighty or ninety feet broad and fifty-five feet high, with one door shutting on the outside, and one window twenty-two inches square. If Noah had any hobby in the world it was ventilation. Then into this ark he put a certain number of all the animals in the world. Naturalists have ascertained that at that time there were at least eleven hundred thousand insects necessary to go into the ark, about forty thousand mammalia, sixteen hundred reptiles, to say nothing of the mastodon, the elephant and the animalcule, of which thousands live upon a single leaf and which cannot be seen by the naked eye. Noah had no microscope, and yet he had pick them out by pairs. You have no idea the trouble that man had. Some say that the flood was not universal, that it was partial. Why then did God say "I will destroy every living thing beneath the heavens." If it was partial why did Noah save the birds? An ordinary bird, tending strictly to business, can beat a partial flood. Why did he put the birds in there—the eagles, the vultures, the condors—if it was only a partial flood? And how did he get them in there? Were they inspired to go there, or did he drive them up? Did the polar bear leave his home of ice and start for the tropic inquiring for Noah; or could the kangaroo come from Australia unless he was inspired, or somebody was behind him? Then there are animals on this hemisphere not on that. How did he get them across? And there are some animals which would be very unpleasant in an ark unless the ventilation was very perfect.

When he got the animals in the ark, God shut the door and Noah pulled down the window. And then it began to rain, and it kept on raining until the water went twenty nine feet over the highest mountain. Chimborazo, then as now, lifted its head above the clouds, and then as now, there sat the condor. And yet the waters rose and rose over every mountain in the world—twenty-nine feet above the highest peaks, covered with snow and ice. How deep were these waters? About five and a half miles. How long did it rain? Forty days. How much did it have to rain a day? About eight hundred feet. How is that for dampness? No wonder they said the windows of the heavens were open. If I had been there I would have said the whole side of the house was out. How long were they in this ark? A year and ten days, floating around with no rudder, no sail, nobody on the outside at all. The window was shut, and there was no door, except the one that shut on the outside. Who ran this ark—who took care of it? Finally it came down on Mount Ararat, a peak seventeen thousand feet above the level of the sea, with about three thousand feet of snow, and it stopped there simply to give the animals from the tropics a chance. Then Noah opened the window and got a breath of fresh air, and let out all the animals; and then Noah took a drink, and God made a bargain with him that He would not drown us any more, and He put a rainbow in the clouds and said: "When I see that I will recollect that I have promised not to drown you." Because if it was not for that He is apt to drown us at any moment. Now can anybody believe that that is the origin of the rainbow? Are you not all familiar with the natural causes which bring those beautiful arches before our eyes? Then the people started out again, and they were as bad as before. Here let me ask why God did not make Noah in the first place? He knew He would have to drown Adam and Eve and all his family. Then another thing, why did He want to drown the animals? What had they done? What crime had they committed? It is very hard to answer these questions—that is, for a man who has only been born once. After a while they tried to build a tower to get into heaven, and the gods heard about it and said "Let's go down and see what man is up to." They came, and found things a great deal worse than they thought, and thereupon He confounded the language to prevent them succeeding, so that the fellow up above could not shout down "mortar" or "brick" to the one below, and they had to give it up. Is it possible that any one believes that that is the reason why we have the variety of languages in the world? Do you know that language is born of human experience, and is a physical science? Do you know that every word has been suggested in some way by the feelings or observations of man—that there are words as tender as the dawn, as serene as the stars, and others as wild as the beasts? Do you know that language is dying and being born continually—that every language has its cemetery and its cradle, its bud and blossom, and withered leaf? Man has loved, enjoyed and suffered, and language is simply the expression he gives those experiences.

Then the world began to divide, and the Jewish nation was started. Now I want to say that at one time your ancestors, like mine, were barbarians. If the Jewish people had to write these books now they would be civilized books, and I do not hold them responsible for what their ancestors did. We find the Jewish people first in Canaan, and there were seventy of them, counting Joseph and his children already in Egypt. They lived two hundred and fifteen years, and they then went down into Egypt and stayed there two hundred and fifteen years they were four hundred and thirty years in Canaan and Egypt. How many did they have when they went to Egypt? Seventy. How many were they at the end of two hundred and fifteen years? Three millions. That is a good many. We had at the time of the Revolution in this country three millions of people. Since that time there have been four doubles, until we have forty-eight millions today. How many would the Jews number at the same ratio in two hundred and fifteen years? Call it eight doubles and we have forty thousand. But instead of forty thousand they had three millions. How do I know they had three millions? Because they had six hundred thousand men of war. For every honest voter in the State of Illinois there will be five other people, and there are always more voters than men of war. They must have had at the lowest possible estimate three millions of people. Is that true? Is there a minister in the city of Chicago that will testify to his own idiocy by claiming that they could have increased to three millions by that time? If there is, let him say so. Do not let him talk about the civilizing influence of a lie.

When they got into the desert they took a census to see how man first-born children there were. They found they had twenty-thousand two hundred and seventy-three first-born males. It is reasonable to suppose there was about the same number of first-born girls, or forty-five thousand first-born children. There must have been about as many mothers as first-born children. Dividing three millions by forty-five thousand mothers, and you will find that the women in Israel had to have on the average sixty-eight children apiece. Some stories are too thin. This is too thick. Now, we know that among three million people there will be about three hundred births a day; and according to the Old Testament, whenever a child was born the mother had to make a sacrifice—a sin-offering for the crime of having been a mother. If there is in this universe anything that is infinitely pure, it is a mother with her child in her arms. Every woman had to have a sacrifice of a couple of pigeons, and the priests had to eat those pigeons in the most holy place. At that time there were at least three hundred births a day, and the priests had to cook and eat these pigeons in the most holy place; and at that time there were only three priests. Two hundred birds apiece per day! I look upon them as the champion bird-eaters of the world.

Then where were these Jews? They were upon the desert of Sinai; and Sahara compared to that is a garden. Imagine an ocean of lava, torn by storm and vexed by tempest, suddenly gazed at by a Gorgon and changed to stone. Such was the desert of Sinai. The whole supplies of the world could not maintain three millions of people on the desert of Sinai for forty years. It would cost one hundred thousand millions of dollars, and would bankrupt

Christendom. And yet there they were with flocks and herds—so many that they sacrificed over one hundred and fifty thousand first-born lambs at one time.

It would require millions of acres to support these flocks, and yet there was no blade of grass, and there is no account of it raining baled hay. They sacrificed one hundred and fifty thousand lambs, and the blood had all to be sprinkled on the altar within two hours, and there, were only three priests. They would have to sprinkle the blood of twelve hundred and fifty lambs per minute. Then all the people gathered in front of the tabernacle eighteen feet deep. Three millions of people would make a column six miles long. Some reverend gentlemen say they were ninety feet deep. Well, that would make a column of over a mile.

Where were these people going? They were going to the Holy Land. How large was it? Twelve thousand square miles—one-fifth the size of Illinois—a frightful country, covered with rocks and desolation. There never was a land agent in the city of Chicago that would not have blushed with shame to have described that land as flowing with milk and honey. Do you believe that God Almighty ever went into partnership with hornets? Is it necessary unto salvation? God said to the Jews "I will send hornets before you, to drive out the Canaanites." How would a hornet know a Canaanite? Is it possible that God inspired the hornets—that he granted letters of marque and reprisal to hornets? I am willing to admit that nothing in the world would be better calculated to make a man leave his native country than a few hornets attending strictly to business. God said "Kill the Canaanites slowly." Why? "Lest the beasts of the field increase upon you." How many Jews were there? Three millions. Going to a country, how large? Twelve thousand square miles. But were there nations already in this Holy Land? Yes, there were seven nations "mightier than the Jews." Say there would be twenty-one millions when they got there, or twenty-four millions with themselves. Yet they were told to kill them slowly, lest the beasts of the field increase upon them. Is there a man in Chicago that believes that! Then what does he teach it to little children for? Let him tell the truth.

So the same God went into partnership with snakes. The children of Israel lived on manna—one account says all the time, and another only a little while. That is the reason there is a chance for commentaries, and you can exercise faith. If the book was reasonable everybody could get to heaven in a moment. But whenever it looks as if it could not be that way and you believe, you are almost a saint, and when you know it is not that way and believe, you are a saint. He fed them on manna. Now manna is very peculiar stuff. It would melt in the sun, and yet they used to cook it by seething and baking. I would as soon think of frying snow and boiling icicles. But this manna had other peculiar qualities. It shrank to an omer, no matter how much they gathered, and swelled up to an omer, no matter how little they gathered. What a magnificent thing manna would be for the currency, shrinking and swelling according to the volume of business! There was not a change in the bill of fare for forty years, and they knew that God could just as well give them three square meals a day. They remembered about the cucumbers, and the melons, and the leeks and the onions of Egypt, and they said: "Our souls abhorreth this light bread." Then this God got mad—you know cooks are always touchy—and thereupon He sent snakes to bite the men, women and children. He also sent them quails in wrath and anger, and while they had the flesh between their teeth, he struck thousands of them dead. He always acted in that way, all of a sudden. People had no chance to explain—no chance to move for a new trial—nothing. I want to know if it is reasonable He should kill people for asking for one change of diet in forty years. Suppose you had been boarding with an old lady for forty years, and she never had a solitary thing on her table but hash, and one morning you said: "My soul abhorreth hash!" What would you say if she let a basketful of rattlesnakes upon you? Now is it possible for people to believe this? The Bible says their clothes did not wax old, they did not get shiny at the knees or elbows; and their shoes did not wear out. They grew right along with them. The little boy starting out with his first pants grew up and his pants grew with him. Some commentators have insisted that angels attended to their wardrobes. I never could believe it. Just think of one angel hunting another and saying: "There goes another button." I cannot believe it.

There must be a mistake somewhere or somehow. Do you believe the real God—if there is one—ever killed a man for making hair-oil? And yet you find in the Pentateuch that God gave Moses a recipe for making hair-oil to grease Aaron's beard; and said if anybody made the same hair-oil he should be killed. And He gave him a formula for making ointment, and He said if anybody made ointment like that he should be killed. I think that is carrying patent-laws to excess. There must be some mistake about it. I cannot imagine the infinite Creator of all the shining worlds giving a recipe for hair-oil. Do you believe that the real God came down to Mount Sinai with a lot of patterns for making a tabernacle-patterns for tongs, for snuffers, and such things? Do you believe that God came down on that mountain and told Moses how to cut a coat, and how it should be trimmed? What would an infinite God care on which side he cut the breast, what color the fringe was, or how the buttons were placed? Do you believe God told Moses to make curtains of fine linen? Where did they get their flax in the desert? How did they weave it? Did He tell him to make things of gold, silver and precious stones, when they hadn't them? Is it possible that God told them not to eat any fruit until after the fourth year of planting the trees? You see all these things were written hundreds of years afterwards, and the priests, in order to collect the tithes, dated the laws back. They did not say, "This is our law," but, "Thus said God to Moses in the wilderness." Now, can you believe that? Imagine a scene: The eternal God tells Moses "Here is the way I want you to consecrate my priests. Catch a sheep and cut his throat." I never could understand why God wanted a sheep killed just because a man had done a mean trick; perhaps it was because his priests were fond of mutton. He tells Moses further to take some of the blood and put it on his right thumb, a little on his right ear, and a little on his right big toe? Do you believe God ever gave such instructions for the consecration of His priests? If you should see the South Sea Islanders going through such a performance you could not keep your face straight. And will you tell me that it had to be done in order to consecrate a man to the service of the infinite God? Supposing the blood got on the left toe?

Then we find in this book how God went to work to make the Egyptians let the Israelites go. Suppose we wish to make a treaty with the mikado of Japan, and Mr. Hayes sent a commissioner there; and suppose he should employ Hermann, the wonderful German, to go along with him; and when they came in the presence of the mikado Herman threw down an umbrella, which changed into a turtle, and the commissioner said: "This is my certificate." You would say the country is disgraced. You would say the president of a republic like this disgraces himself with jugglery. Yet we are told God sent Moses and Aaron before Pharaoh, and when they got there Moses threw down a stick which turned into a snake. That God is a juggler—he is the infinite prestidigitator. Is that possible? Was that really a snake, or was it the appearance of a snake? If it was the appearance of a snake, it was a fraud. Then the necromancers of Egypt were sent for, and they threw down sticks, which turned into snakes, but those were not so large as Moses' snakes, which swallowed them. I maintain that it is just as hard to make small snakes as it is to make large ones; the only difference is that to make large snakes either larger sticks or more practice is required.

Do you believe that God rained hail on innocent cattle, killing them in the highways and in the field? Why should he inflict punishment on cattle for something their owners had done? I could never have any respect for a God that would so inflict pain upon a brute beast simply on account of the crime of its owner. Is it possible that God worked miracles to convince Pharaoh that slavery was wrong? Why did he not tell Pharaoh that any nation founded on slavery could not stand? Why did he not tell him, "Your government is founded on slavery, and it will go down, and the sands of the desert will hide from the view of man your temples, your altars, and your fanes?" Why did he not speak about the infamy of slavery? Because he believed in the infamy of slavery himself. Can we believe that God will allow a man to give his wife the right of divorcement and make the mother of his children a wanderer and a vagrant. There is not one word about woman in the Old Testament except the word of shame and humiliation. The God of the Bible does not think woman is as good as man. She never was worth mentioning. It did not take the pains to recount the death of the mother of us all. I have no respect for any book that does not treat woman as the equal of man. And if there is any God in this universe who thinks more of me than he thinks of my wife, he is not well acquainted with both of us. And yet they say that that was done on account of the hardness of their hearts; and that was done in a community where the law was so fierce that it stoned a man to death for picking up sticks on Sunday. Would it not have been better to stone to death every man who abused his wife and allowed them to pick up sticks on account of the hardness of their hearts? If God wanted to take those Jews from Egypt to the land of Canaan, why didn't He do it instantly? If He was going to do a miracle why didn't He do one worth talking about?

After God had killed all the first-born in Egypt, after He had killed all the cattle, still Egypt could raise an army that could put to flight six hundred thousand men. And because this God overwhelmed the Egyptian army, he bragged about it for a thousand years, repeatedly calling the attention of the Jews to the fact that he overthrew Pharaoh and his hosts. Did he help much with their six-hundred thousand men? We find by the records of the day that the Egyptian standing army at that time was never more than one hundred thousand men. Must we believe all these stories in order to get to Heaven when we die? Must we judge of a man's character by the number of stories he believes? Are we to get to Heaven by creed or by deed? That is the question. Shall we reason, or shall we simply believe? Ah, but they say the Bible is not inspired about those little things. The Bible says the rabbit and the hare chew the cud. But they do not. They have a tremulous motion of the lip. But the Being that made them says they chew the cud. The Bible, therefore, is not inspired in natural history. Is it inspired in its astrology? No. Well, what is it inspired in? In its law? Thousands of people say that if it had not been for the ten commandments we would not have known any better than to rob and steal. Suppose a man planted an acre of potatoes, hoed them all summer, and dug them in the fall; and suppose a man had sat upon the fence all the time and watched him? Do you believe it would be necessary for that man to read the ten commandments to find out who, in his judgment had a right to take those potatoes? All laws against larceny have been made by industry to protect the fruits of its labor. Why is there a law against murder? Simply because a large majority of people object to being murdered. That is all. And all these laws were in force thousands of years before that time.

One of the commandments said they should not make any graven images, and that was the death of art in Palestine. No sculptor has ever enriched stone with the divine forms of beauty in that country; and any commandment that is the death of art is not a good commandment. But they say the Bible is morally inspired; and they tell me there is no civilization without this Bible. Then God knows that just as well as you do. God always knew it, and if you can't civilize a nation without a Bible, why didn't God give every nation just one Bible to start with? Why did God allow hundreds of thousands and billions of billions to go down to hell just for the lack of a Bible? They say that it is morally inspired. Well, let us examine it. I want to be fair about this thing, because I am willing to stake my salvation or damnation upon this question—whether the Bible is true or not. I say it is not and upon that I am willing to wager my soul. Is there a woman here who believes in the institution of polygamy? Is there a man here who believes in that infamy? You say: "No, we do not." Then you are better than your God was four thousand years ago. Four thousand years ago he believed in it, taught it and upheld it. I pronounce it and denounce it the infamy of infamies. It robs our language of every sweet and tender word in it. It takes the fire-side away forever. It takes the meaning out of the words father, mother, sister, brother, and turns the temple of love into a vile den where crawl the slimy snakes of lust and hatred. I was in Utah a little while ago, and was on the mountain where God used to talk to Brigham Young. He never said anything to me. I said that it was just as reasonable that God in the nineteenth century should talk to a polygamist in Utah as it was that four thousand years ago, on Mount Sinai, he talked to Moses upon that hellish and damnable question.

I have no love for any God who believes in polygamy. There is no heaven on this earth save where the one woman loves the one man and the one man loves the one woman. I guess it is not inspired on the polygamy question. May be it is inspired about religious liberty. God says if anybody differs with you about religion, "kill him." He told His peculiar people, "If any one teaches a different religion, kill him!" He did not say, "Try and convince him that he is wrong," but "kill him." He did not say, "I am in the miracle business, and I will convince him," but "kill him." He said to every husband, "If your wife, that you love as you love your own soul, says, 'let us go and worship other gods,' then 'Thy hand shall be first upon her and she shall be stoned with stones until she dies.'" Well, now, I hate a God of that kind, and I cannot think of being nearer heaven than to be away from Him. A God tells a man to kill his wife simply because she differs with him on religion! If the real God were to tell me to kill my wife, I would not do it. If you had lived in Palestine at that time, and your wife—the mother of your children—had woke up at night and said "I am tired of Jehovah. He is always turning up that board-bill. He is always telling about whipping the Egyptians. He is always killing somebody. I am tired of Him. Let us worship the sun. The sun has clothed the world in beauty; it has covered the earth with green and flowers; by its divine light I first saw your face; its light has enabled me to look into the eyes of my beautiful babe. Let us worship the sun, father and mother of light and love and joy." Then what would it be your duty to do—kill her? Do you believe a real God ever did that? Your hand should be first upon her, and when you took up some ragged rock and hurled it against the white bosom filled with love for you, and saw running away the red current of her sweet life, then you would look up to heaven and receive the congratulations of the infinite fiend whose commandments you had to obey. I guess the Bible was not inspired about religious liberty. Let me ask you right here: Suppose, as a matter of fact, God gave those laws to the Jews and told them "whenever a man preaches a different religion, kill him," and suppose that afterwards the same God took upon Himself flesh, and came to the world and taught and preached a different religion, and the Jews crucified Him—did He not reap exactly what He sowed?

May be this book is inspired about war. God told the Israelites to overrun that country, and kill every man, woman and child for defending their native land. Kill the old men? Yes. Kill the women? Certainly. And the little dimpled babes in the cradle, that smile and coo in the face of murder—dash out their brains; that is the will of God. Will you tell me that any God ever commanded such infamy? Kill the men and the women, and the young men and the babes! "What shall we do with the maidens?" "Give them to the rabble murderers!" Do you believe that God ever allowed the roses of love and the violets of modesty that shed their perfume in the heart of a maiden to be trampled beneath the brutal feet of lust? If there is any God, I pray Him to write in the book of eternal remembrance opposite to my name, that I denied that lie.

Whenever a woman reads a Bible and comes to that passage, she ought to throw the book from her in contempt and scorn. Do you tell me that any decent god would do that? What would the devil have done under the same circumstances? Just think of it, and yet that is the God that we want to get into the Constitution. That is the God we teach our children about so that they will be sweet and tender, amiable and kind! That monster—that fiend—I guess the Bible is not inspired about religious liberty, nor about war.

Then, if it is not inspired about these things, may be it is inspired about slavery. God tells the Jews to buy up the children of the heathen round about and they should be servants for them. What is a "servant?" If they struck a "servant" and he died immediately, punishment was to follow; but if the injured man should linger a while, there was no punishment, because the servant represented their money! Do you believe that it is right—that God made one man to work for another and to receive pay in rations? Do you believe God said that a whip on the naked back was the legal tender for labor performed? Is it possible that the real God ever gave such infamous, bloodthirsty laws? What more does He say? When the time of a married slave expired, he could not take his wife and children with him. Then if the slave did not wish to desert his family, he had his ears pierced with an awl, and became his master's property forever. Do you believe that God ever turned the dimpled cheeks of little children into iron chains to hold a man in slavery? Do you know that a God like that would not make a respectable devil? I want none of his mercy. I want no part and no lot in the heaven of such a God. I will go to perdition, where there is human sympathy. The only voice we have ever had from either of those other worlds came from hell. There was a rich man who prayed his brothers to attend to Lazarus so that they might "not come to this place." That is the only instance, so far as we know, of souls across the river having any sympathy. And I would rather be in hell, asking for water, than in heaven denying that petition. Well, what is this book inspired about? Where does the inspiration come from? Why was it that so many animals were killed? It was simply to make atonement for man—that is all. They killed something that had not committed a crime, in order that the one who had committed the crime might be acquitted. Based upon that idea is the atonement of the Christian religion. That is the reason I attack this book—because it is the basis of another infamy, viz: that one man can be good for another, or that one man can sin for another. I deny it. You have got to be good for yourself; you have got to sin for yourself. The trouble about the atonement is, that it saves the wrong man. For instance, I kill some one. He is a good man. He loves his wife and children and tries to make them happy; but he is not a Christian, and he goes to hell. Just as soon as I am convicted and cannot get a pardon I get religion, and I go to heaven. The hand of mercy cannot reach down through the shadows of hell to my victim.

There is no atonement for the saint—only for the sinner and the criminal. The atonement saves the wrong man. I have said that I would never make a lecture at all without attacking this doctrine. I did not care what I started out on. I was always going to attack this doctrine. And in my conclusion I want to draw you a few pictures of the Christian heaven. But before I do that I want to say the rest I have to say about Moses. I want you to understand that the Bible was never printed until 1488. I want you to know that up to that time it was in manuscript, in possession of those who could change it if they wished; and they did change it, because no two ever agreed. Much of it was in the waste basket of credulity, in the open mouth of tradition, and in the dull ear of memory. I want you also to know that the Jews themselves never agreed as to what books were inspired, and that there were a lot of books written that were not incorporated in the Old Testament. I want you to know that two or three years before Christ, the Hebrew manuscript was translated into Greek, and that the original from which the translation was made, has never been seen since. Some Latin Bibles were found in Africa but no two agreed; and then they translated the Septuagint into the languages of Europe, and no two agreed. Henry VIII. took a little time between murdering his wives to see that the Word of God was translated correctly. You must recollect that we are indebted to murderers for our Bibles and our creeds. Constantine, who helped on the good work in its early stage, murdered his wife and child, mingling their blood with the blood of the Savior.

The Bible that Henry VIII. got up did not suit, and then his daughter, the murderess of Mary, Queen of Scots, got up another edition, which also did not suit; and finally, that philosophical idiot, King James, prepared the edition which we now have. There are at least one hundred thousand errors in the Old Testament, but everybody sees that it is not enough to invalidate its claim to infallibility. But these errors are gradually being fixed, and hereafter the prophet will be fed by Arabs instead of "ravens," and Samson's three hundred foxes will be three hundred "sheaves" already bound, which were fired and thrown into the standing wheat. I want you all to know that there was no contemporaneous literature at the time the Bible was composed, and that the Jews were infinitely ignorant in their day and generation—that they were isolated by bigotry and wickedness from the rest of the world. I want you to know that there are fourteen hundred millions of people in the world; and that with all the talk and work of the societies, only one hundred and twenty millions have got Bibles. I want you to understand that not one person in one hundred in this world ever read the Bible, and no two ever understood it alike who did read it, and that no one person probably ever understood it aright. I want you to understand that where this Bible has been, man has hated his brother—there have been dungeons, racks, thumbscrews, and the sword. I want you to know that the cross has been in partnership with the sword, and that the religion of Jesus Christ was established by murderers, tyrants and hypocrites. I want you to know that the church carried the black flag. Then talk about the civilizing influence of this religion!

Now, I want to give an idea or two in regard to the Christian's heaven. Of all the selfish things in this world, it is one man wanting to get to heaven, caring nothing what becomes of the rest of mankind. "If I can only get my little soul in." I have always noticed that the people who have the smallest souls make the most fuss about getting them saved. Here is what we are taught by the church today. We are taught by it that fathers and mothers, brothers and sisters can all be happy in heaven, no matter who may be in hell; that the husband can be happy there with the wife that would have died for him at any moment of his life, in hell. But they say, "We don't believe in fire. What we believe in now is remorse." What will you have remorse for? For the mean things you have done when you are in hell? Will you have any remorse for the mean things you have done when you are in heaven? Or will you be so good then that you won't care how you used to be? Don't you see what an infinitely mean belief that is? I tell you today that, no matter in what heaven you may be, no matter in what star you are spending the summer, if you meet another man whom you have wronged you will drop a little behind in the tune. And, no matter in what part of hell you are, and you meet some one whom you have succored, whose nakedness you have clothed, and whose famine you have fed, the fire will cool up a little. According to this Christian doctrine, when you are in heaven you won't care how mean you were once. What must be the social condition of a gentleman in heaven who will admit that he never would have been there if he had not got scared? What must be the social position of an angel who will always admit that if another had not pitied him he ought to have been damned? Is it a compliment to an infinite God to say that every being He ever made deserved to be damned the minute He got him done, and that He will damn everybody He has not had a chance to make over. Is it possible that somebody else can be good for me, and that this doctrine of the atonement is the only anchor for the human soul?

For instance: here is a man seventy years of age, who has been a splendid fellow and lived according to the laws of nature. He has got about him splendid children whom he has loved and cared for with all his heart. But he did not happen to believe in this Bible; he did not believe in the Pentateuch. He did not believe that because some children made fun of a gentleman who was short of hair, God sent two bears and tore the little darlings to pieces. He had a tender heart, and he thought about the mothers who would take the pieces, the bloody fragments of the children, and press them to their bosom in a frenzy of grief; he thought about their wails and lamentations, and could not believe that God was such an infinite monster. That was all he thought, but he went to Hell. Then, there is another man who made a hell on earth for his wife, who had to be taken to the insane asylum, and his children were driven from home and were wanderers and vagrants in the world. But just between the last sin and the last breath, this fellow got religion, and he never did another thing except to take his medicine. He never did a solitary human being a favor, and he died and went to heaven. Don't you think he would be astonished to see that other man in hell, and say to himself, "Is it possible that such a splendid character should bear such fruit, and that all my rascality at last has brought me next to God?"

Or, let us put another case. You were once alone in the desert—no provisions, no water, no hope, just when your life was at its lowest ebb a man appeared, gave you water and food and brought you safely out. How you would bless that man. Time rolls on. You die and go to heaven; and one day you see through the black night of hell, the friend who saved your life, begging for a drop of water to cool his parched lips. He cries to you, "Remember what I did in the desert—give me to drink." How mean, how contemptible you would feel to see his suffering and be unable to relieve him. But this is the Christian heaven. We sit by the fireside and see the flames and the sparks fly up the chimney—everybody happy, and the cold wind and sleet are beating on the window, and out on the doorstep is a mother with a child on her breast freezing. How happy it makes a fireside, that beautiful contrast. And we say, "God is good," and there we sit, and she sits and moans, not one night but forever. Or we are sitting at the table with our wives and children, everybody eating, happy and delighted; and Famine comes and pushes out its shriveled palms, and, with hungry eyes, implores us for a crust. How that would increase the appetite! And yet that is the Christian heaven. Don't you see that these infamous doctrines petrify the human heart? And I would have everyone who hears me, swear that he will never contribute another dollar to build another church in which is taught such infamous lies. I want everyone of you to say, that you never will, directly or indirectly, give a dollar to any man to preach that falsehood. It has done harm enough. It has covered the world with blood. It has filled the asylums for the insane. It has cast a shadow in the heart, in the sunlight of every good and tender man and woman. I say let us rid the heavens of this monster, and write upon the dome "Liberty, love and law."

No matter what may come to me or what may come to you, let us do exactly what we believe to be right, and let us give the exact thought in our brains. Rather than have this Christianity true, I would rather all the gods would destroy themselves this morning. I would rather the whole universe would go to nothing, if such a thing were possible, this instant. Rather than have the glittering dome of pleasure reared on the eternal abyss of pain, I would see the utter and eternal destruction of this universe. I would rather see the shining fabric of our universe crumble to unmeaning chaos, and take itself where oblivion broods and memory forgets. I would rather the blind Samson of some imprisoned force, released by thoughtless chance, should so rack and strain this world that man in stress and strain, in astonishment and fear, should suddenly fall back to savagery and barbarity. I would rather that this thrilled and thrilling globe, shorn of all life, should in its cycles rub the wheel, the parent star, on which the light should fall as fruitlessly as falls the gaze of love on death, than to have this infamous doctrine of eternal punishment true; rather than have this infamous selfishness of a heaven for a few and a hell for the many established as the word of God.

One world at a time is my doctrine. Let us make some one happy here. Happiness is the interest that a decent action draws, and the more decent actions you do, the larger your income will be. Let every man try to make his wife happy, his children happy. Let every man try to make every day a joy, and God cannot afford to damn such a man. I cannot help God; I cannot injure God. I can help people; I can injure people. Consequently humanity is the only real religion.

I cannot better close this lecture than by quoting four lines from Robert Burns:

> "To make a happy fireside clime
> To weans and wife—
> That's the true pathos and sublime
> Of human life."

# INGERSOLL'S LECTURE ON SKULLS,—And His Replies To Prof. Swing, Dr. Collyer, And Other Critics—Reprinted from "The Chicago Times."

Ladies and Gentlemen: Man advances just in the proportion that he mingles his thoughts with his labor—just in the proportion that he takes advantage of the forces of nature; just in proportion as he loses superstition and gains confidence in himself. Man advances as he ceases to fear the gods and learns to love his fellow-men. It is all, in my judgment, a question of intellectual development. Tell me the religion of any man and I will tell you the degree he marks on the intellectual thermometer of the world. It is a simple question of brain. Those among us who are the nearest barbarism have a barbarian religion. Those who are nearest civilization have the least superstition. It is, I say, a simple question of brain, and I want, in the first place, to lay the foundation to prove that assertion.

A little while ago I saw models of nearly everything that man has made. I saw models of all the water craft, from the rude dug-out in which floated a naked savage—one of our ancestors—a naked savage, with teeth twice as long as his forehead was high, with a spoonful of brains in the back of his orthodox head—I saw models of all the water craft of the world, from that dug-out up to a man-of-war that carries a hundred guns and miles of canvas; from that dug-out to the steamship that turns its brave prow from the port of New York with a compass like a conscience, crossing three thousand miles of billows without missing a throb or beat of its mighty iron heart from shore to shore. And I saw at the same time the paintings of the world, from the rude daub of yellow mud to the landscapes that enrich palaces and adorn houses of what were once called the common people. I saw also their sculpture, from the rude god with four legs, a half dozen arms, several noses, and two or three rows of ears, and one little, contemptible, brainless head, up to the figures of today,—

to the marbles that genius has clad in such a personality that it seems almost impudent to touch them without an introduction. I saw their books—books written upon the skins of wild beasts—upon shoulder-blades of sheep—books written upon leaves, upon bark, up to the splendid volumes that enrich the libraries of our day. When I speak of libraries I think of the remark of Plato: "A house that has a library in it has a soul."

I saw at the same time the offensive weapons that man has made, from a club, such as was grasped by that same savage when he crawled from his den in the ground and hunted a snake for his dinner; from that club to the boomerang, to the sword, to the cross-bow, to the blunderbuss, to the flintlock, to the caplock, to the needle-gun, up to a cannon cast by Krupp, capable of hurling a ball weighing two thousand pounds through eighteen inches of solid steel. I saw too, the armor from the shell of a turtle that one of our brave ancestors lashed upon his breast when he went to fight for his country, the skin of a porcupine, dried with the quills on, which this same savage pulled over his orthodox head, up to the shirts of mail that were worn in the middle ages, that laughed at the edge of the sword and defied the point of the spear; up to a monitor clad in complete steel. And I say orthodox not only in the matter of religion, but in everything. Whoever has quit growing, he is orthodox, whether in art, politics, religion, philosophy—no matter what. Whoever thinks he has found it all out he is orthodox. Orthodoxy is that which rots, and heresy is that which grows forever. Orthodoxy is the night of the past, full of the darkness of superstition, and heresy is the eternal coming day, the light of which strikes the grand foreheads of the intellectual pioneers of the world. I saw their implements of agriculture, from the plow made of a crooked stick, attached to the horn of an ox by some twisted straw, with which our ancestors scraped the earth, and from that to the agricultural implements of this generation, that make it possible for a man to cultivate the soil without being an ignoramus.

In the old time there was but one crop; and when the rain did not come in answer to the prayer of hypocrites a famine came and people fell upon their knees. At that time they were full of superstition. They were frightened all the time for fear that some god would be enraged at his poor, hapless, feeble and starving children. But now, instead of depending upon one crop they have several, and if there is not rain enough for one there may be enough for another. And if the frosts kill all, we have railroads and steamship—enough to bring what we need from some other part of the world. Since man has found out something about agriculture, the gods have retired from the business of producing famines.

I saw at the same time their musical instruments, from the tomtom—that is, a hoop with a couple of strings of rawhide drawn across it—from that tomtom, up to the instruments we have today, that make the common air blossom with melody, and I said to myself there is a regular advancement. I saw at the same time a row of human skulls, from the lowest skull that has been found, the Neanderthal skull—skulls from Central Africa, skulls from the bushmen of Australia—skulls from the farthest isles of the Pacific Sea—up to the best skulls of the last generation—and I noticed that there was the same difference between those skulls that there was between the products of those skulls, and I said to myself: "After all, it is a simple question of intellectual development." There was the same difference between those skulls, the lowest and highest skulls, that there was between the dug-out and the man-of-war and the steamship, between the club and the Krupp gun, between the yellow daub and the landscape, between the tom-tom and an opera by Verdi. The first and lowest skull in this row was the den in which crawled the base and meaner instincts of mankind, and the last was a temple in which dwelt joy, liberty and love. And I said to myself, it is all a question of intellectual development.

Man has advanced just as he has mingled his thought with his labor. As he has grown he has taken advantage of the forces of nature; first of the moving wind, then of the falling water and finally of steam. From one step to another he has obtained better houses, better clothes, and better books, and he has done it by holding out every incentive to the ingenious to produce them. The world has said, give us better clubs and guns and cannons with which to kill our fellow Christians. And whoever will give us better weapons and better music, and better houses to live in, we will robe him in wealth crown him in honor, and render his name deathless. Every incentive was held out to every human being to improve these things, and that is the reason we have advanced in all mechanical arts. But that gentleman in the dugout not only had his ideas about politics, mechanics, and agriculture; he had his ideas also about religion. His idea about politics was "Might makes right." It will be thousands of years, may be, before mankind will believe in the saying that "right makes might." He had his religion. That low skull was a devil factory. He believed in Hell, and the belief was a consolation to him. He could see the waves of God's wrath dashing against the rocks of dark damnation. He could see tossing in the whitecaps the faces of women, and stretching above the crests the dimpled hands of children; and he regarded these things as the justice and mercy of

God. And all today who believe in this eternal punishment are the barbarians of the nineteenth century. That man believed in a devil, that had a long tail terminating with a fiery dart; that had wings like a bat—a devil that had a cheerful habit of breathing brimstone, that had a cloven foot, such as some orthodox clergymen seem to think I have. And there has not been a patentable improvement made upon that devil in all the years since. The moment you drive the devil out of theology, there is nothing left worth speaking of. The moment they drop the devil, away goes atonement. The moment they kill the devil, their whole scheme of salvation has lost all of its interest for mankind. You must keep the devil and, you must keep Hell. You must keep the devil, because with no devil no priest is necessary. Now, all I ask is this—the same privilege to improve upon his religion as upon his dug-out, and that is what I am going to do, the best I can. No matter what church you belong to, or what church belongs to us. Let us be honor bright and fair.

I want to ask you: Suppose the king, if there was one, and the priest if there was one at that time, had told these gentlemen in the dug-out: "That dug-out is the best boat that can be built by man; the pattern of that came from on high, from the great God of storm and flood, and any man who says he can improve it by putting a stick in the middle of it and a rag on the stick, is an infidel, and shall be burned at the stake;" what, in your judgment—honor bright—would have been the effect upon the circumnavigation of the globe? Suppose the king, if there was one, and the priest, if there was one—and I presume there was a priest, because it was a very ignorant age—suppose the king and priest had said: "The tomtom is the most beautiful instrument of music of which any man can conceive; that is the kind of music they have in Heaven; an angel sitting upon the edge of a glorified cloud, golden in the setting sun, playing upon that tom-tom, became so enraptured, so entranced with her own music, that in a kind of ecstasy she dropped it—that is how we obtained it; and any man who says it can be improved by putting a back and front to it, and four strings, and a bridge, and getting a bow of hair with rosin, is a blaspheming wretch, and shall die the death,"—I ask you, what effect would that have had upon music? If that course had been pursued, would the human ears, in your judgment, ever have been enriched with the divine symphonies of Beethoven? Suppose the king, if there was one, and the priest, had said "That crooked stick is the best plow that can be invented, the pattern of that plow was given to a pious farmer in an exceedingly holy dream, and that twisted straw is the ne plus ultra of all twisted things, and any man who says he can make an improvement upon that plow, is an atheist;" what, in your judgment, would have been the effect upon the science of agriculture?

Now, all I ask is the same privilege to improve upon his religion as upon his mechanical arts. Why don't we go back to that period to get the telegraph? Because they were barbarians. And shall we go to barbarians to get our religion? What is religion? Religion simply embraces the duty of man to man. Religion is simply the science of human duty and the duty of man to man—that is what it is. It is the highest science of all. And all other sciences are as nothing, except as they contribute to the happiness of man. The science of religion is the highest of all, embracing all others. And shall we go to the barbarians to learn the science of sciences? The nineteenth century knows more about religion than all the centuries dead. There is more real charity in the world today than ever before. There is more thought today than ever before. Woman is glorified today as she never was before in the history of the world. There are more happy families now than ever before—more children treated as though they were tender blossoms than as though they were brutes than in any other time or nation. Religion is simply the duty a man owes to man; and when you fall upon your knees and pray for something you know not of, you neither benefit the one you pray for nor yourself. One ounce of restitution is worth a million of repentances anywhere, and a man will get along faster by helping himself a minute than by praying ten years for somebody to help him. Suppose you were coming along the street, and found a party of men and women on their knees praying to a bank, and you asked them, "Have any of you borrowed any money of this bank?" "No, but our fathers, they, too, prayed to this bank." "Did they ever get any?" "No, not that we ever heard of." I would tell them to get up. It is easier to earn it, and it is far more manly.

Our fathers in the "good old times,"—and the best that I can say of the "good old times" is that they are gone, and the best I can say of the good old people that lived in them is that they are gone, too—believed that you made a man think your way by force. Well, you can't do it. There is a splendid something in man that says: "I won't; I won't be driven." But our fathers thought men could be driven. They tried it in the "good old times." I used to read about the manner in which the early Christians made converts—how they impressed upon the world the idea that God loved them. I have read it, but it didn't burn into my soul. I didn't think much about it—I heard so much about being fried forever in Hell that it didn't seem so bad to burn a few minutes. I love liberty and I hate all persecutions in the name of God. I never appreciated the infamies that have been committed in the name of religion until I saw the iron arguments that Christians used. I saw, for instance, the thumb-screw, two little innocent looking pieces of iron, armed with some little protuberances on the inner side to keep it from slipping down, and through each end a screw, and when some man had made some trifling remark, for instance, that he never believed that God made a fish swallow a man to keep him from drowning, or something like that, or, for instance, that he didn't believe in baptism. You know that is very wrong. You can see for yourself the justice of damning a man if his parents happened to baptize him in the wrong way—God cannot afford to break a rule or two to save all the men in the world. I happened to be in the company of some Baptist ministers once— you may wonder how I happened to be in such company as that—and one of them asked me what I thought about baptism. Well, I told them I hadn't thought much about it—that I had never sat up nights on that question. I said: "Baptism—with soap—is a good institution." Now, when some man had said some trifling thing like that, they put this thumb-screw on him, and in the name of universal benevolence and for the love of God—man has never persecuted man for the love of man; man has never persecuted another for the love of charity—it is always for the love of something he calls God, and every man's idea of God is his own idea. If there is an infinite God, and there may be—I don't know—there may be a million for all I know—I hope there is more than one—one seems so lonesome. They kept turning this down, and when this was done, most men would say: "I will recant." I think, I would. There is not much of the martyr about me. I would have told them: "Now you write it down, and I will sign it. You may have one God or a million, one Hell or a million. You stop that—I am tired."

Do you know, sometimes I have thought that all the hypocrites in the world are not worth one drop of honest blood. I am sorry that any good man ever died for religion. I would rather let them advance a little easier. It is too bad to see a good man sacrificed for a lot of wild beasts and cattle. But there is now and then a man who would not swerve the breadth of a hair. There was now and then a sublime heart willing to die for an intellectual conviction, and had it not been for these men we would have been wild beasts and savages today. There were some men who would not take it back, and had it not been for a few such brave, heroic souls in every age we would have been cannibals, with pictures of wild beasts tattooed upon our breasts, dancing around some dried-snake fetish. And so they turned it down to the last thread of agony, and threw the victim into some dungeon, where, in the throbbing silence and darkness, he might suffer the agonies of the fabled damned. This was done in the name of love, in the name of mercy, in the name of the compassionate Christ. And the men that did it are the men that made our Bible for us.

I saw, too, at the same time, the Collar of torture. Imagine a circle of iron, and on the inside a hundred points almost as sharp as needles. This argument was fastened about the throat of the sufferer. Then he could not walk nor sit down, nor stir without the neck being punctured by these points. In a little while the throat would begin to swell, and suffocation would end the agonies of that man. This man, it may be, had committed the crime of saying, with tears upon his cheeks, "I do not believe that God, the father of us all, will damn to eternal perdition any of the children of men." And that was done to convince the world that God so loved the world that He died for us. That was in order that people might hear the glad tidings of great joy to all people.

I saw another instrument, called the scavenger's daughter. Imagine a pair of shears with handles, not only where they now are, but at the points as well and just above the pivot that unites the blades a circle of iron. In the upper handles the hands would be placed; in the lower, the feet; and through the iron ring, at the centre, the head of the victim would be forced, and in that position the man would be thrown upon the earth, and the strain upon the muscle would produce such agony that insanity took pity. And this was done to keep people from going to Hell—to convince that man that he had made a mistake in his logic—and it was done, too, by Protestants—Protestants that persecuted to the extent of their power, and that is as much as Catholicism ever did. They would persecute now if they had the power. There is not a man in this vast audience who will say that the church should have temporal power. There is not one of you but what believes in the eternal divorce of church and state. Is it possible that the only people who are fit to go to heaven are the only people not fit to rule mankind?

I saw at the same time the rack. This was a box like the bed of a wagon, with a windlass at each end, and ratchets to prevent slipping. Over each windlass went chains, and when some man had, for instance, denied the doctrine of the trinity, a doctrine it is necessary to believe in order to get to Heaven—but, thank the Lord, you don't have to understand it. This man merely denied that three times one was one, or maybe he denied that there was ever any Son in the world exactly as old as his father, or that there ever was a boy eternally older than his mother—then they put that man on the rack. Nobody had ever been persecuted for calling God bad—it has always been for calling him good. When I stand here to say that, if there is a Hell, God is a fiend, they say that is very bad. They say I am trying to tear down the institutions of public virtue. But let me tell you one thing: there is no reformation in fear—you can scare a man so that he won't do it sometimes, but I will swear you can't scare him so bad that he won't want to do it. Then they put this man on the rack and priests began turning these levers, and kept turning until the ankles, the hips, the shoulders, the elbows, the wrists, and all the joints of the victim were dislocated, and he was wet with agony, and standing by was a physician to feel his pulse. What for? To save his life? Yes. In mercy? No. But in order that they might have the pleasure of racking him once more. And this was the Christian spirit. This was done in the name of civilization, in the name of religion, and all these wretches who did it died in peace. There is not an orthodox preacher in the city that has not a respect for every one of them. As, for instance, for John Calvin, who was a murderer and nothing but a murderer, who would have disgraced an ordinary gallows by being hanged upon it. These men when they came to die were not frightened. God did not send any devils into their death-rooms to make mouths at them. He reserved them for Voltaire, who brought religious liberty to France. He reserved them for Thomas Paine, who did more for liberty than all the churches. But all the inquisitors died with the white hands of peace folded over the breast of piety. And when they died, the room was filled with the rustle of the wings of angels, waiting to bear the wretches to Heaven.

When I read these frightful books it seems to me sometimes as though I had suffered all these things myself. It seems sometimes as though I had stood upon the shore of exile, and gazed with tearful eyes toward home and native land; it seems to me as though I had been staked out upon the sands of the sea, and drowned by the inexorable, advancing tide; as though my nails had been torn from my hands, and into the bleeding quick needles had been thrust; as though my feet had been crushed in iron boots; as though I had been chained in the cell of Inquisition, and listened with dying ears for the coming footsteps of release; as though I had stood upon the scaffold and saw the glittering axe fall upon me; as though I had been upon the rack and had seen, bending above me, the white faces of hypocrite priests; as though I had been taken from my fireside, from my wife and children, taken to the public square, chained; as though fagots had been piled about me; as though the flames had climbed around my limbs and scorched my eyes to blindness, and as though my ashes had been scattered to the four winds by all the countless hands of hate. And, while I so feel, I swear that while I live I will do what little I can to augment the liberties of man, woman and child. I denounce slavery and superstition everywhere. I believe in liberty, and happiness, and love, and joy in this world. I am amazed that any man ever had the impudence to try and do another man's thinking. I have just as good a right to talk theology as a minister. If they all agreed I might admit it was a science, but as all disagree, and the more they study the wider they get apart, I may be permitted to suggest, it is not a science. When no two will tell you the road to Heaven,—that is, giving you the same route—and if you would inquire of them all, you would just give up trying to go there, and say I may as well stay where I am, and let the Lord come to me.

Do you know that this world has not been fit for a lady and gentleman to live in for twenty-five years, just on account of slavery. It was not until the year 1808 that Great Britain abolished the slave trade, and up to that time her judges, her priests occupying her pulpits, the members of the royal family, owned stock in the slave ships, and luxuriated upon the profits of piracy and murder. It was not until the same year that the United States of America abolished the slave trade between this and other countries, but carefully preserved it as between the states. It was not until the 28th day of August, 1833, that Great Britain abolished human slavery in her colonies; and it was not until the 1st day of January, 1863, that Abraham Lincoln, sustained by the sublime and heroic North, rendered our flag pure as the sky in which it floats. Abraham Lincoln was, in my judgment, in many respects, the grandest man ever president of the United States. Upon his monument these words should be written: "Here sleeps the only man in the history of the world, who, having been clothed with almost absolute power, never abused it, except upon the side of mercy."

For two hundred years the Christians of the United States deliberately turned the cross of Christ into a whipping-post. Christians bred hounds to catch other Christians. Let me show you what the Bible has done for mankind: "Servants, be obedient to your masters." The only word coming from that sweet Heaven was, "Servants, obey your masters." Frederick Douglas told me that he had lectured upon the subject of freedom twenty years before he was permitted to set his foot in a church. I tell you the world has not been fit to live in for twenty-five years. Then all the people used to cringe and crawl to preachers. Mr. Buckle, in his history of civilization, shows that men were even struck dead for speaking impolitely to a priest. God would not stand it. See how they used to crawl before cardinals, bishops and popes. It is not so now. Before wealth they bowed to the very earth, and in the presence of titles they became abject. All this is slowly, but surely changing. We no longer bow to men simply because they are rich. Our fathers worshiped the golden calf. The worst you can say of an American now is, he worships the gold of the calf. Even the calf is beginning to see this distinction.

The time will come when no matter how much money a man has, he will not be respected unless he is using it for the benefit of his fellow-men. It will soon be here. It no longer satisfies the ambition of a great man to be king or emperor. The last Napoleon was not satisfied with being the emperor of the French. He was not satisfied with having a circlet of gold about his head. He wanted some evidence that he had something of value within his head. So he wrote the life of Julius Caesar, that he might become a member of the French academy. The emperors, the kings, the popes, no longer tower above their fellows. Compare, for instance, King William and Helmholtz. The king is one of the anointed by the Most High, as they claim—one upon whose head has been poured the divine petroleum of authority. Compare this king with Helmholtz, who towers an intellectual Colossus above the crowned mediocrity. Compare George Eliot with Queen Victoria. The queen is clothed in garments given her by blind fortune and unreasoning chance, while George Eliot wears robes of glory woven in the loom of her own genius. And so it is the world over. The time is coming when a man will be rated at his real worth, and that by his brain and heart. We care nothing now about an officer unless he fills his place. No matter if he is president, if he rattles in the place nobody cares anything about him. I might give you an instance in point, but I won't. The world is getting better and grander and nobler every day.

Now, if men have been slaves, if they have crawled in the dust before one another, what shall I say of women? They have been the slaves of men. It took thousands of ages to bring women from abject slavery up to the divine height of marriage. I believe in marriage. If there is any Heaven upon earth, it is in the family by the fireside and the family is a unit of government. Without the family relation that is tender, pure and true, civilization is impossible. Ladies, the ornaments you wear upon your persons tonight are but the souvenirs of your mother's bondage. The chains around your necks; and the bracelets clasped upon your white arms by the thrilled hand of love, have been changed by the wand of civilization from iron to shining, glittering gold. Nearly every civilization in this world accounts for the devilment in it by the crimes of woman. They say woman brought all the trouble into the world. I don't care if she did. I would rather live in a world full of trouble with the women I love, than to live in Heaven with nobody but men. I read in a book an account of the creation of the world. The book I have taken pains to say was not written by any God. And why do I say so? Because I can write a far better book myself. Because it is full of barbarism. Several ministers in this city have undertaken to answer me—notably those who don't believe the Bible themselves. I want to ask these men one thing. I want them to be fair.

Every minister in the City of Chicago that answers me, and those who have answered me had better answer me again—I want them to say, and without any sort of evasion—without resorting to any pious tricks—I want them to say whether they believe that the Eternal God of this universe ever upheld the crime of polygamy. Say it square and fair. Don't begin to talk about that being a peculiar time, and that God was easy on the prejudices of those old fellows. I want them to answer that question and to answer it squarely, which they haven't done. Did this God, which you pretend to worship, ever sanction the institution of human slavery? Now, answer fair. Don't slide around it. Don't begin and answer what a bad man I am, nor what a good man Moses was. Stick to the text. Do you believe in a God that allowed a man to be sold from his children? Do you worship such an infinite monster? And if you do, tell your congregation whether you are not ashamed to admit it. Let every minister who answers me again tell whether he believes God commanded his general to kill the little dimpled babe in the cradle. Let him answer it. Don't say that those were very bad times. Tell whether He did it or not, and then your people will know whether to hate that God or not. Be honest. Tell them whether that God in war captured young maidens and turned them over to the soldiers; and then ask the wives and sweet girls of your congregation to get down on their knees and worship the infinite fiend that did that thing. Answer! It is your God I am talking about, and if that is what God did, please tell your congregation what, under the same circumstances, the devil would have done. Don't tell your people that is a poem. Don't tell your people that is pictorial. That won't do. Tell your people whether it is true or false. That is what I want you to do.

In this book I read about God's making the world and one man. That is all He intended to make. The making of woman was a second thought, though I am willing to admit that as a rule second thoughts are best. This God made a man and put him in a public park. In a little while He noticed that the man got lonesome; then He found He had made a mistake, and that He would have to make somebody to keep him company. But having used up all the nothing He originally used in making the world and one man, He had to take a part of a man to start a woman with. So He causes sleep to fall on this man—now understand me, I do not say this story is true. After the sleep had fallen on this man the Supreme Being took a rib, or, as the French would call it, a cutlet, out of him, and from that He made a woman; and I am willing to swear, taking into account the amount and quality of the raw material used, this was the most magnificent job ever accomplished in this world. Well, after He got the woman done she was brought to the man, not to see how she liked him, but to see how he liked her. He liked her and they started housekeeping, and they were told of certain things they might do and of one thing they could not do—and of course they did it. I would have done it in fifteen minutes, I know it. There wouldn't have been an apple on that tree half an hour from date, and the limbs would have been full of clubs. And then they were turned out of the park and extra policemen were put on to keep them from getting back. And then trouble commenced and we have been at it ever since. Nearly all the religions of this world account for the existence of evil by such a story as that.

Well, I read in another book what appeared to be an account of the same transaction. It was written about four thousand years before the other. All commentators agree that the one that was written last was the original, and the one that was written first was copied from the one that was written last. But I would advise you all not to allow your creed to be disturbed by a little matter of four or five thousand years. It is a great deal better to be mistaken in dates than to go to the devil. In this other account the Supreme Brahma made up his mind to make the world and a man and woman. He made the world and he made the man and then the woman, and put them on the Island of Ceylon. According to the account it was the most beautiful island of which man can conceive. Such birds, such songs, such flowers, and such verdure! And the branches of the trees were so arranged that when the wind swept through them every tree was a thousand aeolian harps. Brahma, when he put them there, said: "Let them have a period of courtship, for it is my desire and will that true love should forever precede marriage." When I read that, it was so much more beautiful and lofty than the other, that I said to myself: "If either one of these stories ever turns out to be true, I hope it will be this one."

Then they had their courtship, with the nightingale singing and the stars shining and the flowers blooming, and they fell in love. Imagine that courtship! No prospective fathers or mothers-in-law; no prying and gossiping neighbors; nobody to say, "Young man, how do you expect to support her?" Nothing of that kind, nothing but the nightingale singing its song of joy and pain, as though the thorn already touched its heart. They were married by the Supreme Brahma, and he said to them, "Remain here; you must never leave this island." Well, after a little while the man—and his name was Adami, and the woman's name was Heva—said to Heva: "I believe I'll look about a little." He wanted to go West. He went to the western extremity of the island where there was a little narrow neck of land connecting it with the mainland, and the devil, who is always playing pranks with us, produced a mirage, and when he looked over to the mainland, such hills and vales, such dells and dales, such mountains crowned with snow, such cataracts clad in bows of glory did he see there, that he went back and told Heva: "The country over there is a thousand times better than this, let us migrate." She, like every other woman that ever lived, said: "Let well enough alone we have all we want; let us stay here." But he said: "No, let us go;" so she followed him, and when they came to this narrow neck of land, he took her on his back like a gentleman, and carried her over. But the moment they got over, they heard a crash, and, looking back, discovered that this narrow neck of land had fallen into the sea. The mirage had disappeared, and there was naught but rocks and sand, and the Supreme Brahma cursed them both to the lowest Hell.

Then it was that the man spoke—and I have liked him ever since for it—"Curse me, but curse not her; it was not her fault, it was mine." That's the kind of a man to start a world with. The Supreme Brahma said: "I will save her but not thee." And she spoke out of her fullness of love, out of a heart in which there was love enough to make all her daughters rich in holy affection, and said: "If thou wilt not spare him, spare neither me. I do not wish to live without him, I love him." Then the Supreme Brahma said—and I have liked him ever since I read it—"I will spare you both, and watch over you and your children forever." Honor bright, is that not the better and grander story?

And in that same book I find this "Man is strength, woman is beauty; man is courage, woman is love. When the one man loves the one woman, and the one woman loves the one man, the very angels leave Heaven, and come and sit in that house, and sing for joy." In the same book this: "Blessed is that man, and beloved of all the gods, who is afraid of no man, and of whom no man is afraid." Magnificent character! A missionary certainly ought to talk to that man. And I find this: "Never will I accept private, individual salvation, but rather will I stay and work, strive and suffer, until every soul from every star has been brought home to God." Compare that with the Christian that expects to go to Heaven while the world is rolling over Niagara to an eternal and unending Hell. So I say that religion lays all the crime and troubles of this world at the beautiful feet of woman. And then the church has the impudence to say that it has exalted women. I believe that marriage is a perfect partnership; that woman has every right that man has—and one more—the right to be protected. Above all men in the world I hate a stingy man—a man that will make his wife beg for money. "What did you do with the dollar I gave you last week? And what are you going to do with this?" It is vile. No gentleman will ever be satisfied with the love of a beggar and a slave—no gentleman will ever be satisfied except with the love of an equal. What kind of children does a man expect to have with a beggar for their mother? A man can not be so poor but that he can be generous, and if you only have one dollar in the word and you have got to spend it, spend it like a lord—spend it as though it were a dry leaf, and you the owner of unbounded forests—spend it as though you had a wilderness of your own. That's the way to spend it.

I had rather be a beggar and spend my last dollar like a king, than be a king and spend my money like a beggar. If it has got to go, let it go. And this is my advice to the poor. For you can never be so poor that whatever you do you can't do in a grand and manly way. I hate a cross man. What right has a man to assassinate the joy of life? When you go home you ought to go like a ray of light—so that it will, even in the night, burst out of the doors and windows and illuminate the darkness. Some men think their mighty brains have been in a turmoil; they have been thinking about who will be Alderman from the Fifth Ward; they have been thinking about politics, great and mighty questions have been engaging their minds, they have bought calico at five cents or six, and want to sell it for seven. Think of the intellectual strain that must have been upon that man, and when he gets home everybody else in the house must look out for his comfort. A woman who has only taken care of five or six children, and one or two of them sick, has been nursing them and singing to them, and trying to make one yard of cloth do the work of two, she, of course, is fresh and fine and ready to wait upon this gentleman—the head of the family—the boss. I was reading the other day of an apparatus invented for the ejecting of gentlemen who subsist upon free lunches. It is so arranged that when the fellow gets both hands into the victuals, a large hand descends upon him, jams his hat over his eyes—he is seized, turned toward the door, and just in the nick of time an immense boot comes from the other side, kicks him in italics, sends him out over the sidewalk and lands him rolling in the gutter. I never hear of such a man—a boss—that I don't feel as though that machine ought to be brought into requisition for his benefit.

Love is the only thing that will pay ten per cent of interest on the outlay. Love is the only thing in which the height of extravagance is the last degree of economy. It is the only thing, I tell you. Joy is wealth. Love is the legal tender of the soul—and you need not be rich to be happy. We have all been raised on success in this country. Always been talked with about being successful, and have never thought ourselves very rich unless we were the possessors of some magnificent mansion, and unless our names have been between the putrid lips of rumor we could not be happy. Every little boy is striving to be this and be that. I tell you the happy man is the successful man. The man that has won the love of one good woman is a successful man. The man that has been the emperor of one good heart, and that heart embraced all his, has been a success. If another has been the emperor of the round world and has never loved and been loved, his life is a failure. It won't do. Let us teach our children the other way, that the happy man is the successful man, and he who is a happy man is the one who always tries to make some one else happy.

The man who marries a woman to make her happy; that marries her as much for her own sake as for his own; not the man that thinks his wife is his property, who thinks that the title to her belongs to him—that the woman is the property of the man; wretches who get mad at their wives and then shoot them down in the street because they think the woman is their property. I tell you it is not necessary to be rich and great and powerful to be happy.

A little while ago I stood by the grave of the old Napoleon—a magnificent tomb of gilt and gold, fit almost for a dead deity—and gazed upon the sarcophagus of black Egyptian marble, where rest at last the ashes of the restless man. I leaned over the balustrade and thought about the career of the greatest soldier of the modern world. I saw him walk upon the banks of the Seine, contemplating suicide—I saw him at Toulon—I saw him putting down the mob in the streets of Paris—I saw him at the head of the army of Italy—I saw him crossing the bridge of Lodi with the tri-color in his hand—I saw him in Egypt in the shadows of the pyramids—I saw him conquer the Alps and mingle the eagles of France with the eagles of the crags. I saw him at Marengo—at Ulm and Austerlitz. I saw him in Russia, where the infantry of the snow and the cavalry of the wild blast scattered his legions like Winter's withered leaves. I saw him at Leipzig in defeat and disaster—driven by a million bayonets back upon Paris—clutched like a wild beast—banished to Elba. I saw him escape and retake an empire by the force of his genius. I saw him upon the frightful field of Waterloo, where chance and fate combined to wreck the fortunes of their former king. And I saw him at St. Helena, with his hands crossed behind him, gazing out upon the sad and solemn sea. I thought of the orphans and widows he had made—of the tears that had been shed for his glory, and of the only woman who ever loved him, pushed from his heart by the cold hand of ambition. And I said I would rather have been a French peasant and worn wooden shoes. I would rather have lived in a hut with a vine growing over the door, and the grapes growing purple in the kisses of the Autumn sun; I would rather have been that poor peasant with my loving wife by my side, knitting as the day died out of the sky, with my children upon my knees and their arms about me; I would rather have been that man and gone down to the tongueless silence of the dreamless dust than to have been that imperial impersonation of force and murder, known as Napoleon the Great. It is not necessary to be rich in order to be happy. It is only necessary to be in love. Thousands of men go to college and get a certificate that they have an education, and that certificate is in Latin and they stop studying, and in two years, to save their life, they couldn't read the certificate they got.

It is mostly so in marrying. They stop courting when they get married. They think, we have won her and that is enough. Ah! the difference before and after! How well they look! How bright their eyes! How light their steps, and how full they were of generosity and laughter! I tell you a man should consider himself in good luck if a woman loves him when he is doing his level best! Good luck! Good luck! And another thing that is the cause of much trouble is that people don't count fairly. They do what they call putting their best foot forward. That means lying a little. I say put your worst foot forward. If you have got any faults admit them. If you drink say so and quit it. If you chew and smoke and swear, say so. If some of your kindred are not very good people, say so. If you have had two or three that died on the gallows, or that ought to have died there, say so. Tell all your faults and if after she knows your faults she says she will have you, you have got the dead wood on that woman forever. I claim that there should be perfect equality in the home, and I can not think of anything nearer Heaven than a home where there is true republicanism and true democracy at the fireside. All are equal.

And then, do you know, I like to think that love is eternal; that if you really love the woman, for her sake, you will love her no matter what she may do; that if she really loves you, for your sake, the same; that love does not look at alterations, through the wrinkles of time, through the mask of years—if you really love her you will always see the face you loved and won. And I like to think of it. If a man loves a woman she does not ever grow old to him. And the woman who really loves a man does not see that he is growing older. He is not decrepit to her. He is not tremulous. He is not old. He is not bowed. She always sees the same gallant fellow that won her hand and heart. I like to think of it in that way, and as Shakespeare says: "Let Time reach with his sickle as far as ever he can; although he can reach ruddy cheeks and ripe lips, and flashing eyes, he can not quite reach love." I like to think of it. We will go down the hill of life together, and enter the shadow one with the other, and as we go down we may hear the ripple of the laughter of our grandchildren, and the birds, and spring, and youth, and love will sing once more upon the leafless branches of the tree of age. I love to think of it in that way—absolute equals, happy, happy, and free, all our own.

But some people say: "Would you allow a woman to vote?" Yes, if she wants to; that is her business, not mine. If a woman wants to vote, I am too much of a gentleman to say she shall not. But, they say, woman has not sense enough to vote. It don't take much. But it seems to me there are some questions, as for instance, the question of peace or war, that a woman should be allowed to vote upon. A woman that has sons to be offered on the altar of that Moloch, it seems to me that such a woman should have as much right to vote upon the question of peace and war as some thrice-besotted sot that reels to the ballot box and deposits his vote for war. But if women have been slaves, what shall we say of the little children, born in the sub-cellars, children of poverty, children of crime, children of wealth, children that are afraid when they hear their names pronounced by the lips of their mother, children that cower in fear when they hear the footsteps of their brutal father, the flotsam and jetsam upon the rude sea of life, my heart goes out to them one and all.

Children have all the rights that we have and one more, and that is to be protected. Treat your children in that way. Suppose your child tells a lie. Don't pretend that the whole world is going into bankruptcy. Don't pretend that that is the first lie ever told. Tell them, like an honest man, that you have told hundreds of lies yourself, and tell the dear little darling that it is not the best way; that it soils the soul. Think of the man that deals in stocks whipping his children for putting false rumors afloat! Think of an orthodox minister whipping his own flesh and blood, for not telling all it thinks! Think of that! Think of a lawyer for beating his child for avoiding the truth! when the old man makes about half his living that way. A lie is born of weakness on one side and tyranny on the other. That is what it is. Think of a great big man coming at a little bit of a child with a club in his hand! What is the little darling to do? Lie, of course. I think that mother Nature put that ingenuity into the mind of the child, when attacked by a parent, to throw up a little breastwork in the shape of a lie to defend itself. When a great general wins a battle by what they call strategy, we build monuments to him. What is strategy? Lies. Suppose a man as much larger than we are as we are larger than a child five years of age, should come at us with a liberty pole in his hand, and in tones of thunder want to know "who broke that plate," there isn't one of us, not excepting myself, that wouldn't swear that we never had seen that plate in our lives, or that it was cracked when we got it.

Another good way to make children tell the truth is to tell it yourself. Keep your word with your child the same as you would with your banker. If you tell a child you will do anything, either do it or give the child the reason why. Truth is born of confidence. It comes from the lips of love and liberty. I was over in Michigan the other day. There was a boy over there at Grand Rapids about five or six years old, a nice, smart boy, as you will see from the remark he made—what you might call a nineteenth century boy. His father and mother had promised to take him out riding. They had promised to take him out riding for about three weeks, and they would slip off and go without him. Well, after while that got kind of played out with the little boy, and the day before I was there they played the trick on him again. They went out and got the carriage, and went away, and as they rode away from the front of the house, he happened to be standing there with his nurse, and he saw them. The whole thing flashed on him in a moment. He took in the situation, and turned to his nurse and said, pointing to his father and mother, "There go the two d—t liars in the State of Michigan!" When you go home fill the house with joy, so that the light of it will stream out the windows and doors, and illuminate even the darkness. It is just as easy that way as any in the world.

I want to tell you tonight that you can not get the robe of hypocrisy on you so thick that the sharp eye of childhood will not see through every veil, and if you pretend to your children that you are the best man that ever lived—the bravest man that ever lived—they will find you out every time. They will not have the same opinion of father when they grow up that they used to have. They will have to be in mighty bad luck if they ever do meaner things than you have done. When your child confesses to you that it has committed a fault, take that child in your arms, and let it feel your heart beat against its heart, and raise your children in the sunlight of love, and they will be sunbeams to you along the pathway of life. Abolish the club and the whip from the house, because, if the civilized use a whip, the ignorant and the brutal will use a club, and they will use it because you use the whip.

Every little while some door is thrown open in some orphan asylum, and there we see the bleeding back of a child whipped beneath the roof that was raised by love. It is infamous, and a man that can't raise a child without the whip ought not to have a child. If there is one of you here that ever expect to whip your child again, let me ask you something. Have your photograph taken at the time and let it show your face red with vulgar anger, and the face of the little one with eyes swimming in tears, and the little chin dimpled with fear, looking like a piece of water struck by a sudden cold wind. If that little child should die, I can not think of a sweeter way to spend an Autumn afternoon than to take that photograph and go to the cemetery, when the maples are clad in tender gold, and when little scarlet runners are coming from the sad heart of the earth, and sit down upon that mound, and look upon that photograph, and think of the flesh, now dust, that you beat. Just think of it. I could not bear to die in the arms of a child that I had whipped. I could not bear to feel upon my lips, when they were withered beneath the touch of death, the kiss of one that I had struck. Some Christians act as though they really thought that when Christ said, "Suffer little children to come unto me," He had a rawhide under His coat. They act as though they really thought that He made that remark simply to get the children within striking distance.

I have known Christians to turn their children from their doors, especially a daughter, and then get down on their knees and pray to God to watch over them and help them. I will never ask God to help my children unless I am doing my level best in that same wretched line. I will tell you what I say to my girls: "Go where you will; do what crime you may; fall to what depth of degradation you may; in all the storms and winds and earthquakes of life, no matter what you do, you never can commit any crime that will shut my door, my arms or my heart to you. As long as I live you have one sincere friend." Call me an atheist; call me an infidel because I hate the God of the Jew—which I do. I intend so to live that when I die my children can come to my grave and truthfully say: "He who sleeps here never gave us one moment of pain."

When I was a boy there was one day in each week too good for a child to be happy in. In these good old times Sunday commenced when the sun went down on Saturday night and closed when the sun went down on Sunday night. We commenced Saturday to get a good ready. And when the sun went down Saturday night there was a gloom deeper than midnight that fell upon the house. You could not crack hickory nuts then. And if you were caught chewing gum, it was only another evidence of the total depravity of the human heart. Well, after a while we got to bed sadly and sorrowfully after having heard Heaven thanked that we were not all in Hell. And I sometimes used to wonder how the mercy of God lasted as long as it did, because I recollected that on several occasions I had not been at school, when I was supposed to be there. Why I was not burned to a crisp was a mystery to me. The next morning we got ready for church—all solemn, and when we got there the minister was up in the pulpit, about twenty feet high, and he commenced at Genesis about "The fall of man," and he went on to about twenty thirdly; then he struck the second application, and when he struck the application I knew he was about half way through. And then he went on to show the scheme how the Lord was satisfied by punishing the wrong man. Nobody but a God would have thought of that ingenious way. Well, when he got through that, then came the catechism—the chief end of man. Then my turn came, and we sat along on a little bench where our feet came within about fifteen inches of the floor, and the dear old minister used to ask us:

"Boys, do you know that you ought to be in Hell?"

And we answered up as cheerfully as could be expected under the circumstances.

"Yes, sir."

"Well, boys, do you know that you would go to Hell if you died in your sins?"

And we said: "Yes, sir."

And then came the great test:

"Boys"—I can't get the tone, you know. And do you know that is how the preachers get the bronchitis. You never heard of an auctioneer getting the bronchitis, nor the second mate on a steamboat—never. What gives it to the minister is talking solemnly when they don't feel that way, and it has the same influence upon the organs of speech that it would have upon the cords of the calves of your legs to walk on your tip-toes, and so I call bronchitis "parsonitis." And if the ministers would all tell exactly what they think they would all get well, but keeping back a part of the truth is what gives them bronchitis.

Well the old man—the dear old minister—used to try and show us how long we would be in Hell if we would only locate there. But to finish the other. The grand test question was:

"Boys, if it was God's will that you should go to Hell, would you be willing to go?"

And every little liar said:

"Yes, sir."

Then, in order to tell how long we would stay there, he used to say:

"Suppose once in a billion ages a bird should come from a far distant clime and carry off in its bill one little grain of sand, the time would finally come when the last grain of sand would be carried away. Do you understand?"

"Yes, sir."

"Boys, by that time it would not be sun-up in Hell."

Where did that doctrine of Hell come from? I will tell you; from that fellow in the dug-out. Where did he get it? It was a souvenir from the wild beasts. Yes, I tell you he got it from the wild beasts, from the glittering eye of the serpent, from the coiling, twisting snakes with their fangs mouths; and it came from the bark, growl and howl of wild beasts; it was born of a laugh of the hyena and got it from the depraved chatter of malicious apes. And I despise it with every drop of my blood and defy it. If there is any God in this universe who will damn his children for an expression of an honest thought I wish to go to Hell. I would rather go there than go to heaven and keep the company of a God that would thus damn his children. Oh it is an infamous doctrine to teach that to little children, to put a shadow in the heart of a child to fill the insane asylums with that miserable, infamous lie. I see now and then a little girl—a dear little darling, with a face like the light, and eyes of joy, a human blossom, and I think, "is it possible that little girl will ever grow up to be a Presbyterian?" Is it possible, my goodness, that that flower will finally believe in the five points of Calvinism or in the eternal damnation of man? Is it possible that that little fairy will finally believe that she could be happy in Heaven with her baby in Hell? Think of it! Think of it! And that is the Christian religion!

We cry out against the Indian mother that throws her child into the Ganges, to be devoured by the alligator or crocodile, but that is joy in comparison with the Christian mother's hope, that she may be in salvation while her brave boy is in Hell.

I tell you I want to kick the doctrine about Hell—I want to kick it out every time I go by it. I want to get Americans in this country placed so they will be ashamed to preach it. I want to get the congregations so that they won't listen to it. We cannot divide the world off into saints and sinners in that way. There is a little girl, fair as a flower, and she grows up until she is twelve, thirteen, or fourteen years old. Are you going to damn her in the fifteenth, sixteenth or seventeenth year, when the arrow from Cupid's bow touches her heart and she is glorified—are you going to damn her now? She marries and loves, and holds in her arms a beautiful child? Are you going to damn her now? When are you going to damn her? Because she has listened to some Methodist minister and after all that flood of light failed to believe? Are you going to damn her then? I tell you God can not afford to damn such a woman.

A woman in the State of Indiana forty or fifty years ago who carded the wool and made rolls and spun them, and made the cloth and cut out the clothes for the children, and nursed them, and sat up with them nights and—gave them medicine, and held them in her arms and wept over them—cried for joy and wept for fear, and finally raised ten or eleven good men and women with the ruddy glow of health upon their cheeks, and she would have died for any one of them any moment of her life, and finally she, bowed with age and bent with care and labor, dies, and at the moment the magical touch of death is upon her face, she looks as though she never had had a care, and her children burying her cover her face with tears. Do you tell me God can afford to damn that kind of a woman? One such act of injustice would turn Heaven itself into Hell. If there is any God, sitting above him in infinite serenity we have the figure of justice. Even a God must do justice; even a God must worship justice; and any form of superstition that destroys justice is infamous! Just think of teaching that doctrine to little children! A little child would go out into the garden, and there would be a little tree laden with blossoms, and the little fellow would lean against it, and there would be a bird on one of the boughs, singing and swinging, and thinking about four little speckled eggs, warmed by the breast of its mate—and singing and swinging, and the music in in happy waves rippling out of the tiny throat, and the flowers blossoming, the air filled with perfume, and the great white clouds floating in the sky, and the little boy would lean up against the tree and think about Hell and the worm that never dies. Oh! the idea there can be any day too good for a child to be happy in!

Well, after we got over the catechism, then came the sermon in the afternoon, and it was exactly like the one in the forenoon, except the other end to. Then we started for home—a solemn march—"not a soldier discharged his farewell shot"—and when we got home, if we had been really good boys, we used to be taken up to the cemetery to cheer us up, and it always did cheer me, those sunken graves, those leaning stones, those gloomy epitaphs covered with the moss of years always cheered me. When I looked at them I said: "Well, this kind of thing can't last always." Then we came back home, and we had books to read which were very eloquent and amusing. We had Josephus, and the "History of the Waldenses," and Fox's "Book of Martyrs," Baxter's "Saint's Rest," and "Jenkyn on the Atonement." I used to read Jenkyn with a good deal of pleasure, and I often thought that the atonement would have to be very broad in its provisions to cover the case of a man that would I write such a book for boys. Then I would look to see how the sun was getting on, and sometimes I thought it had stuck from pure cussedness. Then I would go back and try Jenkyn's again. Well, but it had to go down, and when the last rim of light sank below the horizon, off would go our hats and we would give three cheers for liberty once again.

I tell you, don't make slaves of your children on Sunday.

The idea that there is any God that hates to hear a child laugh! Let your children play games on Sunday. Here is a poor man that hasn't money enough to go to a big church and he has too much independence to go to a little church that the big church built for charity. He doesn't want to slide into Heaven that way. I tell you don't come to church, but go to the woods and take your family and a lunch with you, and sit down upon the old log and let the children gather flowers and hear the leaves whispering poems like memories of long ago, and when the sun is about going down, kissing the summits of far hills, go home with your hearts filled with throbs of joy. There is more recreation and joy in that than going to a dry goods box with a steeple on top of it and hearing a man tell you that your chances are about ninety-nine to one for being eternally damned. Let us make this Sunday a day of splendid pleasure, not to excess, but to everything that makes man purer and grander and nobler. I would like to see now something like this: Instead of so many churches, a vast cathedral that would hold twenty or thirty thousands of people, and I would like to see an opera produced in it that would make the souls of men have higher and grander and nobler aims. I would like to see the walls covered with pictures and the niches rich with statuary; I would like to see something put there that you could use in this world now, and I do not believe in sacrificing the present to the future; I do not believe in drinking skimmed milk here with the promise of butter beyond the clouds. Space or time can not be holy any more than a vacuum can be pious. Not a bit, not a bit; and no day can be so holy but what the laugh of a child will make it holier still.

Strike with hand of fire, on, weird musician, thy harp, strung with Apollo's golden hair! Fill the vast cathedral aisles with symphonies sweet and dim, deft toucher of the organ's keys; blow, bugler, blow until thy silver notes do touch and kiss the moonlit waves, and charm the lovers wandering 'mid the vine-clad hills. But know your sweetest strains are discords all compared with childhood's happy laugh—the laugh that fills the eyes with light and every heart with joy! O, rippling river of laughter, thou art the blessed boundary line between the beasts and men, and every wayward wave of thine doth drown some fretful fiend of care. O Laughter, rose lipped daughter of joy, there are dimples enough in thy cheeks to catch and hold and glorify all the tears of grief.

Don't plant your children in long, straight rows like posts. Let them have light and air and let them grow beautiful as palms. When I was a little boy children went to bed when they were not sleepy, and always got up when they were. I would like to see that changed, but they say we are too poor, some of us, to do it. Well, all right. It is as easy to wake a child with a kiss as with a blow; with kindness as with curse. And, another thing; let the children eat what they want to. Let them commence at whichever end of the dinner they desire. That is my doctrine. They know what they want much better than you do. Nature is a great deal smarter than you ever were.

All the advance that has been made in the science of medicine, has been made by the recklessness of patients. I can recollect when they wouldn't give a man water in a fever—not a drop. Now and then some fellow would get so thirsty he would say "Well, I'll die any way, so I'll drink it," and thereupon he would drink a gallon of water, and thereupon he would burst into a generous perspiration, and get well—and the next morning when the doctor would come to see him they would tell him about the man drinking the water, and he would say:

"How much?"

"Well, he swallowed two pitchers full."

"Is he alive?"

"Yes."

So they would go into the room and the doctor would feel his pulse and ask him:

"Did you drink two pitchers of water?"

"Yes."

"My God! what a constitution you have got."

I tell you there is something splendid in man that will not always mind. Why, if we had done as the kings told us five hundred years ago, we would all have been slaves. If we had done as the priests told us we would all have been idiots. If we had done as the doctors told us we would all have been dead. We have been saved by disobedience. We have been saved by that splendid thing called independence, and I want to see more of it, day after day, and I want to see children raised so they will have it. That is my doctrine. Give the children a chance. Be perfectly honor bright with them, and they will be your friends when you are old. Don't try to teach them something they can never learn. Don't insist upon their pursuing some calling they have no sort of faculty for. Don't make that poor girl play ten years on a piano when she has no ear for music, and when she has practiced until she can play "Bonaparte crossing the Alps," and you can't tell after she has played it whether Bonaparte ever got across or not. Men are oaks, women are vines, children are flowers, and if there is any Heaven in this world, it is in the family. It is where the wife loves the husband, and the husband loves the wife, and where the dimpled arms of children are about the necks of both. That is Heaven, if there is any—and I do not want any better Heaven in another world than that, and if in another world I can not live with the ones I loved here, then I would rather not be there. I would rather resign.

Well, my friends, I have some excuses to make for the race to which I belong. In the first place, this world is not very well adapted to raising good men and good women. It is three times better adapted to the cultivation of fish than of people. There is one little narrow belt running zigzag around the world, in which men and women of genius can be raised, and that is all. It is with man as it is with vegetation. In the valley you find the oak and elm tossing their branches defiantly to the storm, and as you advance up the mountain side the hemlock, the pine, the birch, the spruce, the fir, and finally you come to little dwarfed trees, that look like other trees seen through a telescope reversed— every limb twisted as through pain—getting a scanty subsistence from the miserly crevices of the rocks. You go on and on, until at last the highest crag is freckled with a kind of moss, and vegetation ends. You might as well try to raise oaks and elms where the mosses grow, as to raise great men and women where their surroundings are unfavorable. You must have the proper climate and soil. There never has been a man or woman of genius from the southern hemisphere, because the Lord didn't allow the right climate to fall upon the land. It falls upon the water. There never was much civilization except where there has been snow, and ordinarily decent Winter. You can't have civilization without it. Where man needs no bedclothes but clouds, revolution is the normal condition of such a people. It is the Winter that gives us the home; it is the Winter that gives us the fireside and the family relation and all the beautiful flowers of love that adorn that relation. Civilization, liberty, justice, charity and intellectual advancement are all flowers that bloom in the drifted snow. You can't have them anywhere else, and that is the reason we of the north are civilized, and that is the reason that civilization has always been with Winter. That is the reason that philosophy has been here, and, in spite of all our superstitions, we have advanced beyond some of the other races, because we have had this assistance of nature, that drove us into the family relation, that made us prudent; that made us lay up at one time for another season of the year. So there is one excuse I have for my race.

I have got another. I think we came from the lower animals. I am not dead sure of it, but think so. When I first read about it I didn't like it. My heart was filled with sympathy for those people who have nothing to be proud of except ancestors. I thought how terrible it will be upon the nobility of the old world. Think of their being forced to trace their ancestry back to the Duke Orang-Outang or to the Princess Chimpanzee. After thinking it all over I came to the conclusion that I liked that doctrine. I became convinced in spite of myself. I read about rudimentary bones and muscles. I was told that everybody had rudimentary muscles extending from the ear into the cheek. I asked: "What are they?" I was told: "They are the remains of muscles; that they became rudimentary from the lack of use." They went into bankruptcy. They are the muscles with which your ancestors used to flap their ears. Well, at first, I was greatly astonished, and afterward I was more astonished to find they had become rudimentary. How can you account for John Calvin unless we came up from the lower animals? How could you account for a man that would use the extremes of torture unless you admit that there is in man the elements of a snake, of a vulture, a hyena, and a jackal? How can you account for the religious creeds of today? How can you account for that infamous doctrine of Hell, except with an animal origin? How can you account for your conception of a God that would sell women and babes into slavery?

Well, I thought that thing over and I began to like it after a while, and I said: "It is not so much difference who my father was as who his son is." And I finally said I would rather belong to a race that commenced with the skull-less vertebrates in the dim Laurentian seas, that wriggled without knowing why they wriggled, swimming without knowing where they were going, that come along up by degrees through millions of ages, through all that crawls, and swims, and floats, and runs, and growls, and barks, and howls, until it struck this fellow in the dug-out. And then that fellow in the dugout getting a little grander, and each one below calling every one above him a heretic, calling every one who had made a little advance an infidel or an atheist, and finally the heads getting a little higher and looming up a little grander and more splendidly, and finally produced Shakespeare, who harvested all the field of dramatic thought and from whose day until now there have been none but gleaners of chaff and straw. Shakespeare was an intellectual ocean whose waves touched all the shores of human thought, within which were all the tides and currents and pulses upon which lay all the lights and shadows, and over which brooded all the calms, and swept all the storms and tempests of which the soul is capable. I would rather belong to that race that commenced with that skull-less vertebrate; that produced Shakespeare, a race that has before it an infinite future, with the angel of progress leaning from the far horizon, beckoning men forward and upward forever. I would rather belong to that race than to have descended from a perfect pair upon which the Lord has lost money every moment from that day to this.

Now, my crime has been this: I have insisted that the Bible is not the word of God. I have insisted that we should not whip our children. I have insisted that we should treat our wives as loving equals. I have denied that God—if there is any God—ever upheld polygamy and slavery. I have denied that that God ever told his generals to kill innocent babes and tear and rip open women with the sword of war. I have denied that and for that I have been assailed by the clergy of the United States. They tell me I have misquoted; and I owe it to you, and maybe I owe it to myself, to read one or two words to you upon this subject. In order to do that I shall have to put on my glasses; and that brings me back to where I started—that man has advanced just in proportion as his thought has mingled with his labor. If man's eyes hadn't failed he would never have made any spectacles, he would never have had the telescope, and he would never have been able to read the leaves of Heaven.

# COL. INGERSOLL'S REPLY TO DR. COLLYER.

Now, they tell me—and there are several gentlemen who have spoken on this subject—the Rev. Mr. Collyer, a gentleman standing as high as anybody, and I have nothing to say against him—because I denounced God who upheld murder, and slavery and polygamy, he said that what I said was slang. I would like to have it compared with any sermon that ever issued from the lips of that gentleman. And before he gets through he admits that the Old Testament is a rotten tree that will soon fall into the earth and act as a fertilizer for his doctrine.

Is it honest in that man to assail my motive? Let him answer my argument! Is it honest and fair in him to say I am doing a certain thing because it is popular? Has it got to this, that, in this Christian country, where they have preached every day hundreds and thousands of sermons—has it got to this that infidelity is so popular in the United States?

If it has, I take courage. And I not only see the dawn of a brighter day, but the day is here. Think of it! A minister tells me in this year of grace, 1879, that a man is an infidel simply that he may be popular. I am glad of it. Simply that he may make money. Is it possible that we can make more money tearing up churches than in building them up? Is it possible that we can make more money denouncing the God of slavery than we can praising the God that took liberty from man? If so, I am glad.

I call publicly upon Robert Collyer—a man for whom I have great respect—I call publicly upon Robert Collyer to state to the people of this city whether he believes the Old Testament was inspired. I call upon him to state whether he believes that God ever upheld these institutions; whether God was a polygamist; whether he believes that God commanded Moses or Joshua or any one else to slay little children in the cradle. Do you believe that Robert Collyer would obey such an order? Do you believe that he would rush to the cradle and drive the knife of theological hatred to the tender heart of a dimpled child? And yet when I denounce a God that will give such a hellish order, he says it is slang.

I want him to answer; and when he answers he will say he does not believe the Bible is inspired. That is what he will say, and he holds these old worthies in the same contempt that I do. Suppose he should act like Abraham. Suppose he should send some woman out into the wilderness with his child in her arms to starve, would he think that mankind ought to hold up his name forever, for reverence.

Robert Collyer says that we should read and scan every word of the Old Testament with reverence; that we should take this book up with reverential hands. I deny it. We should read it as we do every other book, and everything good in it, keep it and everything that shocks the brain and shocks the heart, throw it away. Let us be honest.

# INGERSOLL'S REPLY TO PROF. SWING

Prof. Swing has made a few remarks on this subject, and I say the spirit he has exhibited has been as gentle and as sweet as the perfume of a flower. He was too good a man to stay in the Presbyterian church. He was a rose among thistles. He was a dove among vultures and they hunted him out, and I am glad he came out. I tell all the churches to drive all such men out, and when he comes I want him to state just what he thinks. I want him to tell the people of Chicago whether he believes the Bible is inspired in any sense except that in which Shakespeare was inspired. Honor bright, I tell you that all the sweet and beautiful things in the Bible would not make one play of Shakespeare; all the philosophy in the world would not make one scene in Hamlet; all the beauties of the Bible would not make one scene in the Midsummer Night's Dream; all the beautiful things about woman in the Bible would not begin to create such a character as Perditu or Imogene or Miranda. Not one.

I want him to tell whether he believes the Bible was inspired in any other way than Shakespeare was inspired. I want him to pick out something as beautiful and tender as Burns' poem to Mary in Heaven. I want him to tell whether he believes the story about the bears eating up children; whether that is inspired. I want him to tell whether he considers that a poem or not. I want to know if the same God made those bears that devoured the children because they laughed at an old man out of hair. I want to know if the same God that did that is the same God who said, "Suffer little children to come unto me, for such is the kingdom of Heaven." I want him to answer it, and answer it fairly. That is all I ask. I want just the fair thing.

Now, sometimes Mr. Swing talks as though he believed the Bible, and then he talks to me as though he didn't believe the Bible. The day he made this sermon I think he did, just a little, believe it. He is like the man that passed a ten dollar counterfeit bill. He was arrested and his father went to see him and said, "John, how could you commit such a crime? How could you bring my gray hairs in sorrow to the grave?" "Well," he says, "father, I'll tell you. I got this bill and some days I thought it was bad and some days I thought it was good, and one day when I thought it was good I passed it."

I want it distinctly understood that I have the greatest respect for Prof. Swing, but I want him to tell whether the 109th psalm is inspired. I want him to tell whether the passages I shall afterward read in this book are inspired. That is what I want.

# INGERSOLL'S REPLY TO BROOKE HERFORD, D.D.

Then there is another gentleman here. His name is Herford. He says it is not fair to apply the test of truth to the Bible—I don't think it is myself. He says although Moses upheld slavery, that he improved it. They were not quite so bad as they were before, and Heaven justified slavery at that time. Do you believe that God ever turned the arms of children into chains of slavery? Do you believe that God ever said to a man: "You can't have your wife unless you will be a slave? You can not have your children unless you will lose your liberty; and unless you are willing to throw them from your heart forever, you can not be free?" I want Mr. Herford to state whether he loves such a God. Be honor bright about it. Don't begin to talk about civilization or what the church has done or will do. Just walk right up to the rack and say whether you love and worship a God that established slavery. Honest! And love and worship a God that would allow a little babe to be torn from the breast of its mother and sold into slavery. Now tell it fair, Mr. Herford, I want you to tell the ladies in your congregation that you believe in a God that allowed women to be given to the soldiers. Tell them that, and then if you say it was not the God of Moses, then don't praise Moses any more. Don't do it. Answer these questions.

# INGERSOLL GATLING GUN TURNED ON DR. RYDER

Then here is another gentleman, Mr. Ryder, the Rev. Mr. Ryder, and he says that Calvinism is rejected by a majority of Christendom. He is mistaken. There is what they call the Evangelical Alliance. They met in this country in 1875 or 1876, and there were present representatives of all the evangelical churches in the world, and they adopted a creed, and that creed is that man is totally depraved. That creed is that there is an eternal, universal Hell, and that every man that does not believe in a certain way is bound to be damned forever, and that there is only one way to be saved, and that is by faith, and by faith alone; and they would not allow anybody to be represented there that did not believe that, and they would not allow a Unitarian there, and would not have allowed Dr. Ryder there, because he takes away from the Christian world the consolation naturally arising from the belief in Hell.

Dr. Ryder is mistaken. All the orthodox religion of the day is Calvinism. It believes in the fall of man. It believes in the atonement. It believes in the eternity of Hell, and it believes in salvation by faith; that is to say, by credulity.

That is what they believe, and he is mistaken; and I want to tell Dr. Kyder today, if there is a God, and He wrote the Old Testament, there is a Hell. The God that wrote the Old Testament will have a Hell. And I want to tell Dr. Ryder another thing, that the Bible teaches an eternity of punishment. I want to tell him that the Bible upholds the doctrine of Hell. I want to tell Him that if there is no Hell, somebody ought to have said so, and Jesus Christ should not have said: "I will at the last day say: 'Depart from me, ye cursed, into everlasting fire prepared for the devil and his angels.'" If there was not such a place, Christ would not have said: "Depart from me, ye cursed, and these shall go hence into everlasting fire." And if you, Dr. Ryder, are depending for salvation on the God that wrote the Old Testament, you will inevitably be eternally damned.

There is no hope for you. It is just as bad to deny Hell as it is to deny Heaven. It is just as much blasphemy to deny the devil as to deny God, according to the orthodox creed. He admits that the Jews were polygamists, but, he says, how was it they finally quit it? I can tell you—the soil was so poor they couldn't afford it. Prof. Swing says the Bible is a poem, Dr. Ryder says it is a picture. The Garden of Eden is pictorial; a pictorial snake and a pictorial woman, I suppose, and a pictorial man, and maybe it was a pictorial sin. And only a pictorial atonement.

# INGERSOLL'S REPLY TO RABBI BIEN

Then there is another gentleman, and he a rabbi, a Rabbi Bien, or Bean, or whatever his name is, and he comes to the defense of the Great Law-giver. There was another rabbi who attacked me in Cincinnati, and I couldn't help but think of the old saying that a man got off when he said the tallest man he ever knew, his name was Short. And the fattest man he ever saw, his name was Lean. And it is only necessary for me to add that this rabbi in Cincinnati was Wise.

The rabbi here, I will not answer him, and I will tell you why. Because he has taken himself outside of all the limits of a gentleman; because he has taken it upon himself to traduce American women in language the beastliest I ever read; and any man who says that the American women are not just as good women as any God can make and pick his mud today, is an unappreciative barbarian.

I will let him alone because he denounced all the men in this country, all the members of Congress, all the members of the Senate, and all the judges upon the Bench; in his lecture he denounced them as thieves and robbers. That won't do. I want to remind him that in this country the Jews were first admitted to the privileges of citizens; that in this country they were first given all their rights, and I am as much in favor of their having their rights as I am in favor of having my own. But when a rabbi so far forgets himself as to traduce the women and men of this country, I pronounce him a vulgar falsifier, and let him alone.

Strange, that nearly every man that has answered me has answered me mostly on the same side. Strange, that nearly every man that thought himself called upon to defend the Bible was one who did not believe in it himself. Isn't it strange? They are like some suspected people, always anxious to show their marriage certificate. They want at least to convince the world that they are not as bad as I am.

Now, I want to read you just one or two things, and then I am going to let you go. I want to see if I have said such awful things, and whether I have got any scripture to stand by me. I will read only two or three verses. Does the Bible teach man to enslave his brother? If it does, it is not the word of God, unless God is a slaveholder.

"Moreover, all the children of the strangers that do sojourn among you, of them shall ye buy of their families which are with you, which they beget in your land, and they shall be your possession. Ye shall take them as an inheritance for your children after you to inherit them. They shall be your bondsmen forever."—(Old Testament.)

Upon the limbs of unborn babes this fiendish God put the chains of slavery. I hate him.

"Both thy bondmen and bondwomen shall be of the heathen round about thee and them shall ye buy, bondmen and bondwomen."

Now let us read what the New Testament has. I could read a great deal more, but that is enough.

"Servants, be obedient to them that are your masters, according to the flesh in fear and trembling, in singleness of your heart, as unto Christ."

This is putting the dirty thief that steals your labor on an equality with God.

"Servants, be subject to your masters with all fear; not only to the good and gentle but also to the froward."

"For this is thankworthy, if a man for conscience toward God endure grief, suffering wrongfully."

The idea of a man on account of conscience toward God stealing another man, or allowing him nothing but lashes on his back as legal-tender for labor performed.

"Let as many servants as are under the yoke count their own masters worthy of all honor, that the name of God and His doctrine be not blasphemed."

How can you blaspheme the name of God by asserting your independence? How can you blaspheme the name of a God by striking fetters from the limbs of men? I wish some of your ministers would tell you that. "And they that have believing masters let them not despise them." That is to say, a good Christian could own another believer in Jesus Christ; could own a woman and her children, and could sell the child away from its mother. That is a sweet belief. O, hypocrisy!

"Let them not despise them because they are brethren, but rather do them service because they are faithful and beloved, partakers of the benefit."

Oh, what slush! Here is what they will tell the poor slave, so that he will serve the man that stole his wife and children from him:

"For we brought nothing into this world, and it is certain we can carry nothing out. Having food and raiment let us be therewith content."

Don't you think that it would do just as well to preach that to the thieving man as to the suffering slave? I think so. Then this same Bible teaches witchcraft, that spirits go into the bodies of the man, and pigs, and that God himself made a trade with the devil, and the devil traded him off—a man for a certain number of swine, and the devil lost money because the hogs ran right down into the sea. He got a corner on that deal.

Now let us see how they believed in the rights of children:

"If a man have a stubborn and rebellious son which will not obey the voice of his father, or the voice of his mother, and that, when they have chastened him, will not harken unto them, then shall his father and his mother lay hold on him, and bring him out unto the elders of his city, and unto the gate of his place. And they shall say unto the elders of his city, 'This, our son, is stubborn and rebellious, he will not obey our voice, he is a glutton and a drunkard.' And all the men of this city shall stone him with stones, that he die, so shalt thou put evil away."

That is a very good way to raise children. Here is the story of Jephthah. He went off and he asked the Lord to let him whip some people, and he told the Lord if He would let him whip them, he would sacrifice to the Lord the first thing that met him on his return; and the first thing that met him was his own beautiful daughter, and he sacrificed her. Is there a sadder story in all history than that? What do you think of a man that would sacrifice his own daughter? What do you think of a God that would receive that sacrifice? Now, then, they come to women in this blessed gospel, and let us see what the gospel says about women. Then you ought all to go to church, girls, next Sunday and hear it. "Let the woman learn in silence with all subjection; but I suffer not a woman to teach nor to usurp authority over the man, but to be in silence for Adam was formed first, not Eve."

Don't you see?

"And Adam was not deceived, but the woman being deceived was in the transgression. Notwithstanding she shall be saved in child-bearing if they continue in faith and charity and holiness with sobriety." (That is Mr.

Timothy.) "But I would have you know that the head of every man is Christ, and the head of the woman is the man, and the head of Christ is God."

I suppose that every old maid is acephalous.

"For a man indeed ought not to cover his head, for as much as he is the image and glory of God; but the woman is the glory of the man. For the man is not of the woman, but woman of the man. Neither was the man created for the woman, but the woman for the man." "Wives, submit yourselves unto your own husband as unto the Lord, for the husband is the head of the wife even as Christ is the head of the Church."

Do you hear that? You didn't know how much we were above you. When you go back to the old testament, to the great law-giver, you find that the woman has to ask forgiveness for having borne a child. If it was a boy, thirty-three days she was unclean; if it was a girl, sixty-six. Nice laws! Good laws! If there is a pure thing in this world, if there is a picture of perfect purity, it is a mother with her child in her arms. Yes, I think more of a good woman and a child than I do of all the gods I have ever heard these people tell about. Just think of this:

"When thou goest forth to war against thine enemies, and the Lord thy God hath delivered them into thine hands, and thou hast taken them captive, and seest among the captives a beautiful woman and hast a desire unto her that thou wouldst have her to thy wife, then thou shalt bring her home to thine house, and she shall shave her head, and pare her nails."

Wherefore, ye must needs be subject not only for wrath but for conscience sake. "For this cause pay you tribute also, for they are God's ministers."

I despise this wretched doctrine. Wherever the sword of rebellion is drawn in favor of the right, I am a rebel. I suppose Alexander, czar of Russia, was put there by the order of God, was he? I am sorry he was not removed by the nihilist that shot at him the other day.

I tell you, in a country like that, where there are hundreds of girls not 16 years of age prisoners in Siberia, simply for giving their ideas about liberty, and we telegraphed to that country, congratulating that wretch that he was not killed, my heart goes into the prison, my heart goes with the poor girl working as a miner in the mines, crawling on her hands and knees getting the precious ore out of the mines, and my sympathies go with her, and my sympathies cluster around the point of the dagger.

Does the bible describe a god of mercy? Let me read you a verse or two:

"I will make mine arrows drunk with blood, and my sword shall devour flesh." "Thy foot may be dipped in the blood of thine enemies, and the tongue of thy dogs in the same."

"And the Lord thy God will put out those nations before thee by little and little; thou mayest not consume them at once, lest the beasts of the field increase upon thee."

"But the Lord thy God shall deliver them unto thee, and shall destroy them with a mighty destruction, until they be destroyed."

"And he shall deliver their kings into thine hand, and thou shalt destroy their name from under heaven; there shall no man be able to stand before thee, until thou have destroyed them."

I can see what he had her nails pared for. Does the bible teach polygamy? The Rev. Dr. Newman, consul general to all the world—had a discussion with Elder Heber of Kimball, or some such wretch in Utah—whether the bible sustains polygamy, and the Mormons have printed that discussion as a campaign document. Read the order of Moses in the 31st chapter of Numbers. A great many chapters I dare not read to you. They are too filthy. I leave all that to the clergy. Read the 31st chapter of Exodus, the 31st chapter of Deuteronomy, the life of Abraham, and the life of David, and the life of Solomon, and then tell me that the bible does not uphold polygamy and concubinage!

Let them answer. Then I said that the bible upheld tyranny. Let me read you a little: "Let every soul be subject unto the higher powers. For there is no power but of God. The powers that be are ordained of God."

George III was king by the grace of God, and when our fathers rose in rebellion, according to this doctrine, they rose against the power of God; and if they did they were successful.

And so it goes on, telling of all the cities that were destroyed, and of the great-hearted men, that they dashed their brains out, and all the little babes, and all the sweet women that they killed and plundered—all in the name of a most merciful God. Well, think of it! The Old Testament is filled with anathemas, and with curses, and with words of revenge, and jealousy, and hatred, and meanness, and brutality. Have I read enough to show that what I said is so? I think I have. I wish I had time to read to you further of what the dear old fathers of the church said about woman—wait a minute, and I will read you a little. We have got them running. St. Augustine in his 22d book says: "A woman ought to serve her husband as unto God, affirming that woman ought to be braced and bridled betimes, if she aspire to any dominion, alleging that dangerous and perilous it is to suffer her to precede, although it be in temporal and corporeal things. How can woman be in the image of God, seeing she is subject to man, and hath no authority to teach, neither to be a witness, neither to judge, much less to rule or bear the rod of empire."

Oh, he is a good one. These are the very words of Augustine. Let me read some more. "Woman shall be subject unto man as unto Christ." That is St. Augustine, and this sentence of Augustine ought to be noted of all women, for in it he plainly affirms that women are all the more subject to man. And now, St. Ambrose, he is a good boy. "Adam was deceived by Eve—called Heva—and not Heva by Adam, and therefore just it is that woman receive and acknowledge him for governor whom she called sin, lest that again she slip and fall with womanly facility. Don't you see that woman has sinned once, and man never? If you give woman an opportunity, she will sin again, whereas if you give it to man, who never, never betrayed his trust in the world, nothing bad can happen. Let women be subject to their own husbands as unto the Lord, for man is the head of woman, and Christ is the head of the congregation." They are all real good men, all of them. "It is not permitted to woman to speak; let her be in silence; as the law said: unto thy husband shalt thou ever be, and he shall bear dominion over thee."

So St. Chrysostom. He is another good man. "Woman," he says, "was put under the power of man, and man was pronounced lord over her; that she should obey man, that the head should not follow the feet. False priests do commonly deceive women, because they are easily persuaded to any opinion,—especially if it be again given, and because they lack prudence and right reason to judge the things that be spoken; which should not be the nature of those that are appointed to govern others. For they should be constant, stable, prudent, and doing everything with discretion and reason, which virtues woman can not have in equality with man."

I tell you women are more prudent than men. I tell you, as a rule, women are more truthful than men. I tell you that women are more faithful than men—ten times as faithful as man. I never saw a man pursue his wife into the very ditch and dust of degradation and take her in his arms. I never saw a man stand at the shore where she had been morally wrecked, waiting for the waves to bring back even her corpse to his arms but I have seen woman do it. I have seen woman with her white arms lift man from the mire of degradation, and hold him to her bosom as though he were an angel.

And these men thought woman not fit to be held as pure in the sight of God as man. I never saw a man that pretended that he didn't love a woman; that pretended that he loved God better than he did a woman, that he didn't look hateful to me, hateful and unclean. I could read you twenty others, but I haven't time to do it. They are all to the same effect exactly. They hate woman, and say man is as much above her as God is above man. I am a believer in absolute equality. I am a believer in absolute liberty between man and wife. I believe in liberty, and I say, "Oh, liberty, float not forever in the far horizon—remain not forever in the dream of the enthusiast, the philanthropist and poet; but come and make thy home among the children of men."

I know not what discoveries, what inventions, what thoughts may leap from the brain of the world. I know not what garments of glory may be woven by the years to come. I can not dream of the victories to be won. I do know that, coming upon the field of thought; but down the infinite sea of the future, there will never touch this "bank and shoal of time" a richer gift, a rarer blessing than liberty for man, woman and child.

I never addressed a more magnificent audience in my life, and I thank you, I thank you a thousand times over.

# INGERSOLL'S CATECHISM AND BIBLE-CLASS

Nothing is more gratifying than to see ideas that were received with scorn, flourishing in the sunshine of approval. Only a few weeks ago I stated that the Bible was not inspired; that Moses was mistaken, that the "flood" was a foolish myth; that the Tower of Babel existed only in credulity; that God did not create the universe from nothing, that He did not start the first woman with a rib; that He never upheld slavery; that He was not a polygamist; that He did not kill people for making hair-oil, that He did not order His Generals to kill the dimpled babes; that He did not allow the roses of love and the violets of modesty to be trodden under the brutal feet of lust; that the Hebrew language was written without vowels; that the Bible was composed of many books written by unknown men; that all translations differed from each other, and that this book had filled the world with agony and crime.

At that time I had not the remotest idea that the most learned clergymen in Chicago would substantially agree with me—in public. I have read the replies of the Rev. Robert Collyer, Dr. Thomas, Rabbi Kohler, Rev. Brooke Herford, Prof. Swing, and Dr. Ryder, and will now ask them a few questions, answering them in their own words.

First, REV. ROBERT COLLYER:

Question. What is your opinion of the Bible? Answer. "It is a splendid book. It makes the noblest type of Catholics and the meanest bigots. Through this book men give their hearts for good to God, or for evil to the Devil. The best argument for the intrinsic greatness of the book is that it can touch such wide extremes, and seem to maintain us in the most unparalleled cruelty, as well as the most tender mercy; that it can inspire purity like that of the great saints and afford arguments in favor of polygamy. The Bible is the text book of ironclad Calvinism and sunny Universalism. It makes the Quaker quiet and the Millerite crazy. It inspired the Union soldier to live and grandly die for the right, and Stonewall Jackson to live nobly and die grandly for the wrong."

Q. But, Mr. Collyer, do you really think that a book with as many passages in favor of wrong as right, is inspired? A. I look upon the Old Testament as a rotting tree. When it falls it will fertilize a bank of violets.

Q. Do you believe that God upheld slavery and polygamy? Do you believe that He ordered the killing of babes and the violation of maidens? A. "There is three-fold inspiration in the Bible, the first peerless and perfect, the Word of God to man;—the second simply and purely human, and then below this again, there is an inspiration born of an evil heart, ruthless and savage there and then as anything well can be. A three-fold inspiration, of Heaven first, then of the Earth, and then of Hell, all in the same book, all sometimes in the same chapter, and then, besides, a great many things that need no inspiration."

Q. Then, after all, you do not pretend that the Scriptures are really inspired? A. "The Scriptures make no such claim for themselves as the Church make's for them. They leave me free to say this is false, or this is true. The truth even within the Bible dies and lives, makes on this side and loses on that."

Q. What do you say to the last verse in the Bible, where a curse is threatened to any man who takes from or adds to the book? A. "I have but one answer to this question, and it is: Let who will have written this, I can not for an instant believe that it was written by a divine inspiration. Such dogmas and threats as these are not of God, but of man, and not of any man of a free spirit and heart eager for the truth, but a narrow man who would cripple and confine the human soul in its quest after the whole truth of God, and back those who have done the shameful things in the name of the Most High."

Q. Do you not regard such talk as slang?

(Supposed) Answer. If an infidel had said that the writer of Revelations was narrow and bigoted, I might have denounced his discourse as "slang," but I think that Unitarian ministers can do so with the greatest propriety.

Q. Do you believe in the stories of the Bible, about Jael, and the sun standing still, and the walls falling at the blowing of horns? A. "They may be legends, myths, poems, or what they will, but they are not the Word of God. So I say again, it was not the God and Father of us all who inspired the woman to drive that nail crashing through the king's temple after she had given him that bowl of milk and bid him sleep in safety, but a very mean Devil of hatred and revenge that I should hardly expect to find in a squaw on the plains. It was not the ram's horns and the shouting before which the walls fell flat. If they went down at all, it was through good solid pounding. And not for an instant did the steady sun stand still or let his planet stand still while barbarian fought barbarian. He kept just the time then he keeps now. They might believe it who made the record. I do not. And since the whole Christian world might believe it, still we do not who gather in this church. A free and reasonable mind stands right in our way. Newton might believe it as a Christian and disbelieve it as a philosopher. We stand then with the philosopher against the Christian, for we must believe what is true to us in the last test, and these things are not true."

SECOND, REV. DR. THOMAS.

Question. What is your opinion of the Old Testament? Answer. "My opinion is that it is not one book, but many—thirty-nine books bound up in one. The date and authorship of most of these books are wholly unknown. The Hebrews wrote without vowels and without dividing the letters into syllables, words or sentences. The books were gathered up by Ezra. At that time only two of the Jewish tribes remained. All progress had ceased. In gathering up the sacred book, copyists exercised great liberty in making changes and additions."

Q. Yes, we know all that, but is the Old Testament inspired? A. "There maybe the inspiration of art, of poetry, or oratory; of patriotism—and there are such inspirations. There are moments when great truths and principles come to men. They seek the man and not the man them."

Q. Yes, we will admit that, but is the Bible inspired? A. "But still I know of no way to convince any one of spirit and inspiration and God only as His reason may take hold of these things."

Q. Do you think the Old Testament true? A. "The story of Eden may be an allegory; the history of the children of Israel may have mistakes."

Q. Must inspiration claim infallibility? A. "It is a mistake to say that if you believe one part of the Bible you must believe all. Some of the thirty-nine books may be inspired, others not; or there may be degrees of inspiration."

Q. Do you believe that God commanded the soldiers to kill the children and the married women and save for themselves the maidens, as recorded in Numbers 31:2? Do you believe that God upheld slavery? Do you believe that God upheld polygamy? A. "The Bible may be wrong in some statements. God and right can not be wrong. We must not exalt the Bible above God. It may be that we have claimed too much for the Bible, and thereby given not a little occasion for such men as Mr. Ingersoll to appear at the other extreme, denying too much."

Q. What then shall be done? A. "We must take a middle ground. It is not necessary to believe that the bears devoured the forty-two children, nor that Jonah was swallowed by the whale."

THIRD, REV. DR. KOHLER.

Question. What is your opinion about the Old Testament? Answer. "I will not make futile attempts of artificially interpreting the letter of the Bible so as to make it reflect the philosophical, moral and scientific views of our time. The Bible is a sacred record of humanity's childhood."

Q. Are you an orthodox Christian? A. "No. Orthodoxy, with its face turned backward to a ruined temple or a dead Messiah, is fast becoming like Lot's wife, a pillar of salt."

Q. Do you really believe the Old Testament was inspired? A. "I greatly acknowledge our indebtedness to men like Voltaire and Thomas Paine, whose bold denial and cutting wit were so instrumental in bringing about this glorious era of freedom, so congenial and blissful, particularly to the long-abused Jewish race."

Q. Do you believe in the inspiration of the Bible? A. "Of course there is a destructive ax needed to strike down the old building in order to make room for the grander new. The divine origin claimed by the Hebrews for their national literature was claimed by all nations for their old records and laws as preserved by the priesthood. As Moses—the Hebrew law giver, is represented as having received the law from God on the holy mountains, so is Zoroaster, the Persian, Manu, the Hindoo, Minos, the Cretan, Lycurgus, the Spartan, and Numa, the Roman."

Q. Do you believe all the stories in the Bible? A. "All that can and must be said against them is that they have been too long retained around the arms and limbs of grown-up manhood to check the spiritual progress of religion; that by Jewish ritualism and Christian dogmatism they became fetters unto the soul, turning the light of heaven into a misty haze to blind the eye, and even into a Hell fire of fanaticism to consume souls."

Q. Is the Bible inspired? A. "True, the Bible is not free from errors, nor is any work of man and time. It abounds in childish views and offensive matters. I trust it will, in a time not far off, be presented for common use in families, schools, synagogues and churches, in a refined shape, cleansed from all dross and chaff, and stumbling-blocks on which the scoffer delights to dwell."

FOURTH, REV. MR. HERFORD.

Question. Is the Bible true? Answer. "Ingersoll is very fond of saying 'The question is not, is the Bible inspired, but is it true?' That sounds very plausible, but you know as applied to any ancient book it is simply nonsense."

Q. Do you think the stories in the Bible exaggerated? A. "I dare say the numbers are immensely exaggerated."

Q. Do you think that God upheld polygamy? A. "The truth of which simply is, that four thousand years ago polygamy existed among the Jews, as everywhere else on earth then, and even their prophets did not come to the idea of its being wrong. But what is there to be indignant about in that? And so you really wonder why any man should be indignant at the idea that God upheld and sanctioned that beastliness called polygamy? What is there to be indignant about in that?"

FIFTH, PROF. SWING.

Question. What is your idea of the Bible? Answer. "I think it a poem."

SIXTH, REV. DR. RYDER.

Question. And what is your idea of the sacred Scriptures? Answer. "Like other nations, the Hebrews had their patriotic, descriptive, didactic and lyrical poems in the same varieties as other nations; but with them, unlike other nations, whatever may be the form of their poetry, it always possesses the characteristic of religion."

Q. I suppose you fully appreciate the religious characteristics of the Song of Solomon? No answer.

Q. Does the Bible uphold polygamy? A. "The law of Moses did not forbid it, but contained many provisions against its worst abuses, and such as were intended to restrict it within narrow limits."

Q. So you think God corrected some of the worst abuses of polygamy, but preserved the institution itself?

I might question many others, but have concluded not to consider those as members of my Bible class who deal in calumnies and epithets. From the so-called "replies" of such ministers it appears that, while Christianity changes the heart, it does not improve the manners, and one can get into Heaven in the next world without having been a gentleman in this.

It is difficult for me to express the deep and thrilling satisfaction I have experienced in reading the admissions of the clergy of Chicago. Surely the battle of intellectual liberty is almost won when ministers admit that the Bible is filled with ignorant and cruel mistakes; that each man has the right to think for himself, and that it is not necessary to believe the Scriptures in order to be saved.

From the bottom of my heart, I congratulate my pupils on the advance they have made, and hope soon to meet them on the serene heights of perfect freedom.

# INGERSOLL'S NEW DEPARTURE—His Lecture Entitled "What Shall We do to be Saved?"—Delivered in McVicker's Theatre, Chicago, Sept. 19, 1880
[From the Chicago Times. Verbatim Report.]

Ladies and Gentlemen: Fear is the dungeon of the mind, and superstition is a dagger with which hypocrisy assassinates the soul. Courage is liberty. I am in favor of absolute freedom of thought. In the realm of the mind every one is monarch. Every one is robed, sceptered, and crowned, and every one wears the purple of authority. I belong to the republic of intellectual liberty, and only those are good citizens of that republic who depend upon reason and upon persuasion, and only those are traitors who resort to brute force.

Now, I beg of you all to forget just for a few moments that you are Methodists, or Baptists, or Catholics, or Presbyterians, and let us for an hour or two remember only that we are men and women. And allow me to say "man" and "woman" are the highest titles that can be bestowed upon humanity. "Man" and "woman." And let us if possible banish all fear from the mind. Do not imagine that there is some being in the infinite expanse who is not willing that every man and woman should think for himself and herself. Do not imagine that there is any being who would give to his children the holy torch of reason and then damn them for following where the holy light led. Let us have courage.

Priests have invented a crime called "blasphemy," and behind that crime hypocrisy has crouched for thousands of years. There is but one blasphemy, and that is injustice. There is but one worship, and that is justice.

You need not fear the anger of a God whom you cannot injure. Rather fear to injure your fellow-men. Do not be afraid of a crime you cannot commit. Rather be afraid of the one that you may commit.

There was a Jewish gentleman went into a restaurant to get his dinner, and the devil of temptation whispered in his ear: "Eat some bacon."

He knew if there was anything in the universe calculated to excite the wrath of the Infinite Being, who made every shining star, it was to see a gentleman eating bacon. He knew it, and He knew the Infinite Being was looking, and that he was the Infinite Eaves-dropper of the universe. But his appetite got the better of his conscience, as it often has with us all, and he ate that bacon. He knew it was wrong. When he went into that restaurant the weather was delightful, the sky was as blue as June, and when he came out the sky was covered with angry clouds, the lightning leaping from one to the other, and the earth shaking beneath the voice of the thunder. He went back into that restaurant with a face as white as milk, and he said to one of the keepers:

"My God, did you ever hear such a fuss about a little piece of bacon?"

As long as we harbor such opinions of Infinity; as long as we imagine the heavens to be filled with such tyranny, so long the sons of men will be cringing, intellectual cowards. Let us think, and let us honestly express our thought.

Do not imagine for a moment that I think people who disagree with me are bad people. I admit, and I cheerfully admit, that a very large proportion of mankind and a very large majority, a vast number, are reasonably honest. I believe that most Christians believe what they teach; that most ministers are endeavoring to make this world better. I do not pretend to be better than they are. It is an intellectual question. It is a question, first, of intellectual liberty, and after that, a question to be settled at the bar of human reason. I do not pretend to be better than the are. Probably I am a good deal worse than many of them, but that is not the question. The question is "Bad as I am, have I a right to think?" And I think I have, for two reasons.

First, I can't help it. And secondly, I like it. The whole question is right at a point. If I have not a right to express my thoughts, who has?

"Oh," they say, "we will allow you, we will not burn you."

"All right; why won't you burn me?"

"Because we think a decent man will allow others to think and express his thought."

"Then the reason you do not persecute me for my thought is that you believe it would be infamous in you!"

"Yes."

"And yet you worship a God who will, all you declare, punish me forever."

The next question then is: Can I commit a sin against God by thinking? If God did not intend I should think, why did He give me a "thinker." Now, then, we have got what they call the Christian system of religion, and thousands of people wonder how I can be wicked enough to attack that system.

There are many good things about it, and I shall never attack anything that I believe to be good! I shall never fear to attack anything I honestly believe to be wrong. We have, I say, what they call the Christian religion, and, I find, just in proportion that nations have been religious, just in the proportion they have gone back to barbarism. I find that Spain, Portugal, Italy are the three worst nations in Europe; I find that the nation nearest infidel is the most prosperous France. And so I say there can be no danger in the exercise of absolute intellectual freedom. I find among ourselves the men who think at least as good as those who do not. We have, I say, a Christian system, and that is founded upon what they are pleased to call system the "New Testament." Who wrote the New Testament? I don't know. Who does know? Nobody!

We have found some fifty-two manuscripts containing portions of the New Testament. Some of those manuscripts leave out five or six books—many of them. Others more others less. No two of these manuscripts agree. Nobody knows who wrote these manuscripts. They are all written in Greek; the disciples of Christ knew only Hebrew. Nobody ever saw, so far as we know, one of the original Hebrew manuscripts. Nobody ever saw anybody who had seen anybody who had heard of anybody that had seen anybody that had ever seen one of the original Hebrew manuscripts. No doubt the clergy of your city have told you these facts thousands of times, and they will be obliged to me for having repeated them once more. These manuscripts are written in what are called capital Greek letters. They are called Uncial characters; and the New Testament was not divided into chapters and verses, even, until the year of grace 1551. Recollect it.

In the original the manuscripts and gospels are signed by nobody. The epistles are addressed to nobody; and they are signed by the same person. All the addresses, all the pretended earmarks showing to whom they are written and by whom they are written are simply interpolations, and everybody who has studied the subject knows it.

It is further admitted that even these manuscripts have not been properly translated, and they have a syndicate now making a new translation; and I suppose that I cannot tell whether I really believe the Testament or not until I see that new translation.

You must remember, also, one other thing. Christ never wrote a solitary word of the New Testament—not one word. There is an account that He once stooped and wrote something in the sand, but that has not been preserved. He never told anybody to write a word. He never said: "Matthew, remember this. Mark, don't forget to put that down. Luke, be sure that in your gospel you have this. John, don't forget it." Not one word. And it has always seemed to me that a Being coming from another world, with a message of infinite importance to mankind, should at least have verified that message by his own signature.

Why was nothing written? I will tell you. In my judgment they expected the end of the world in a very few days. That generation was not to pass away until the heavens should be rolled up as a scroll, and until the earth should melt with fervent heat. That was their belief. They believed that the world was to be destroyed, and that there was to be another coming, and that the saints were then to govern the world. And they even went so far among the Apostles, as we frequently do now before election, as to divide out the offices in advance. This Testament was not written for hundreds of years after the Apostles were dust. These facts lived in the open mouth of credulity. They were in the wastebaskets of forgetfulness. They depended upon the inaccuracy of legend, and for centuries these doctrines and stories were blown about by the inconstant winds. And finally, when reduced to writing, some gentleman would write by the side of the passage his idea of it, and the next copyist would put that in as a part of the text. And, finally, when it was made, and the Church got in trouble, and wanted a passage to help it out, one was interpolated to order. So that now it is among the easiest things in the world to pick out at least one hundred interpolations in the Testament. And I will pick some of them out before I get through.

And let me say here, once for all, that for the man Christ I have infinite respect. Let me say, once for all, that the place where man has died for man is holy ground; and let me say, once for all, to that great and serene man I gladly pay the homage of my admiration and my tears. He was a reformer in His day. He was an infidel in His time. He was regarded as a blasphemer, and His life was destroyed by hypocrites, who have, in all ages, done what they could to trample freedom out of the human mind. Had I lived at that time I would have been His friend, and should He come again He would not find a better friend than I will be.

That is for the man. For the theological creation I have a different feeling. If He was, in fact, God, He knew that there was no such thing as death. He knew that what we call death was but the eternal opening of the golden gates of everlasting joy; and it took no heroism to face a death that was simply eternal life.

But when a man, when a poor boy sixteen years of age, goes upon the field of battle to keep his flag in heaven, not knowing but that death ends all—not knowing but that, when the shadows creep over him, the darkness will be eternal—there is heroism.

And so for the man who, in the darkness, said: "My God, why hast Thou forsaken Me?"—for that man I have nothing but respect, admiration, and love.

A while ago I made up my mind to find out what was necessary for me to do in order to be saved. If I have got a soul, I want it saved. I do not wish to lose anything that is of value. For thousands of years the world has been asking that question "What shall we do to be saved?"

Saved from poverty? No. Saved from crime? No. Tyranny? No. But "What shall we do to be saved from the eternal wrath of the God who made us all?"

If God made us, He will not destroy us. Infinite wisdom never made a poor investment. And upon all the works of an infinite God, a dividend must finally be declared. The pulpit has cast a shadow over even the cradle. The doctrine of endless punishment has covered the cheeks of this world with tears. I despise it, and I defy it.

I made up my mind, I say, to see what I had to do in order to save my soul according to the Testament, and thereupon I read it. I read the gospel, Matthew, Mark, Luke, and John. But I found that the Church had been deceiving me. I found that the clergy did not understand their own book. I found that they had been building upon passages that had been interpolated. I found that they had been building upon passages that were entirely untrue. And I will tell you why I think so.

The first of these gospels was written by St. Matthew, according to the claim. Of course he never wrote a word of it. Never saw it. Never heard of it. But, for the purpose of this lecture, I will admit that he wrote it. I will admit that he was with Christ for three years, that he heard much of His conversation during that time and that he became impregnated with the doctrines, or dogmas, and the ideas of Jesus Christ.

Now let us see what Matthew says we must do in order to be saved. And I take it that, if this be true, Matthew is as good an authority as any minister in the world.

The first thing I find upon the subject of salvation is in the fifth chapter of Matthew, and is embraced in what is commonly known as the sermon on the Mount. It is as follows:

"Blessed are the poor in spirit, for theirs is the kingdom of heaven." Good!

"Blessed are the merciful, for they shall obtain mercy." Good! Whether they belonged to any church or not; whether they believed the Bible or not.

"Blessed are the merciful, for they shall obtain mercy." Good!

"Blessed are the pure in heart, for they shall see God. Blessed are the peacemakers, for they shall be called the children of God. Blessed are they which are persecuted for righteousness' sake," (that's me, little) "for theirs is the Kingdom of Heaven."

In the same sermon he says: "Think not that I am come to destroy the law or the prophets. I am not come to destroy, but to fulfill." And then he makes use of this remarkable language, almost as applicable today as it was then: "For I say unto you that except your righteousness shall exceed the righteousness of the Scribes and Pharisees ye shall in no wise enter the kingdom of Heaven." Good!

In the sixth chapter I find the following, and it comes directly after the prayer known as the Lord's prayer: "For if you forgive men their trespasses your Heavenly Father will also forgive you; but if ye forgive not men their trespasses neither will your Father forgive your trespasses." I accept the conditions. There is an offer; I accept it. If you will forgive men that trespass against you, God will forgive your trespasses against Him. I accept, and I never will ask any God to treat me any better than I treat my fellowmen. There is a square promise. There is a contract. If you will forgive others, God will forgive you. And it does not say you must believe in the Old Testament, nor be baptized, nor join the Church, nor keep Sunday. It simply says, if you forgive others God will forgive you; and it must be true. No God could afford to damn a forgiving man. (A voice: "Will He forgive Democrats?") Oh, certainly. Let me say right here that I know lots of Democrats, great, broad, whole-souled, clever men, and I love them. And the only bad thing about them is that they vote the Democratic ticket. And I know lots of Republicans so mean and narrow that the only decent thing about them is that they vote the Republican ticket.

Now let me make myself plain upon that subject, perfectly plain. For instance, I hate Presbyterianism, but I know hundreds of splendid Presbyterians. Understand me. I hate Methodism, and yet I know hundreds of splendid Methodists. I dislike a certain set of principles called Democracy, and yet I know thousands of Democrats that I respect and like. I like a certain set of principles—that is, most of them,—called Republicanism, and yet I know lots of Republicans that are a disgrace to those principles.

I do not war against men. I do not war against persons. I war against certain doctrines that I believe to be wrong. And I give to every other human being every right that I claim for myself. Of course I did not intend today to tell what we must do in the election for the purpose of being saved.

The next thing that I find is in the seventh chapter and the second verse: "For with what judgment ye judge, ye shall be judged; and with what measure ye mete, it shall be measured to you again." Good! That suits me!

And in the twelfth chapter of Matthew: "For whosoever shall do the will of my Father that is in Heaven, the same is my brother and sister and mother. For the Son of Man shall come in the glory of His Father with His angels, and then He shall reward every man according—" To the church he belongs to? No. To the manner in which he was baptized? No. According to his creed? No. "Then he shall reward every man according to his works." Good! I subscribe to that doctrine.

And in the sixteenth chapter: "And Jesus called a little child to Him and stood him in the midst, and said: 'Verily, I say unto you, except ye become converted, and become as little children, ye shall not enter into the Kingdom of Heaven.'" I do not wonder that a reformer in His day that met the Scribes and Pharisees and hypocrites, I do not wonder that at last He turned to children and said: "Except ye become as little children," I do not wonder. And yet, see what children the children of God have been. What an interesting dimpled darling John Calvin was. Think of that prattling babe known as Jonathan Edwards! Think of the infants that founded the Inquisition, that invented instruments of torture to tear human flesh. They were the ones who had become as little children.

So I find in the nineteenth chapter: "And behold, one came and said unto Him: 'Good master, what good thing shall I do in order to inherit eternal life?' And He said unto him, 'why callest thou Me good? There is none good but one, and that is God, but if thou will enter into eternal life, keep the commandments,' and he said unto Him, 'Which?'"

Now, there is a pretty fair issue. Here is a child of God asking God what is necessary for him to do in order to inherit eternal life. And God says to him: Keep the commandments. And the child said to the Almighty: "Which?" Now if there ever had been an opportunity given to the Almighty to furnish a gentleman with an inquiring mind with the necessary information upon that subject, here was the opportunity. He said unto Him, 'which?' And Jesus said: "Thou shalt do no murder; thou shalt not commit adultery; thou shalt not steal; thou shalt not bear false witness; honor thy father and mother; and, thou shalt love thy neighbor as thyself." He did not say to him: "You must believe in Me—that I am the only begotten Son of the living God." He did not say: "You must be born again." He did not say: "You must believe the Bible." He did not say: "You must remember the Sabbath day, to keep it holy." He simply said: "Thou shalt do no murder. Thou shalt not commit adultery. Thou shalt not steal. Thou shalt not bear false witness. Honor thy father and thy mother; and, thou shalt love thy neighbor as thyself." And thereupon the young man, who I think was a little "fresh," and probably mistaken, said unto Him: "All these things have I kept from my youth up." I don't believe that.

Now comes in an interpolation. In the old times when the Church got a little scarce for money, they always put in a passage praising poverty. So they had this young man ask: "What lack I yet?" And Jesus said unto him: "If thou wilt be perfect, go and sell that thou hast and give it to the poor, and thou shalt have treasures in heaven." The Church has always been willing to swap off treasures in heaven for cash down.

And when the next verse was written the Church must have been nearly dead-broke. "And again I say unto you, it is easier for a camel to go through the eye of a needle than for a rich man to enter into the kingdom of God." Did you ever know a wealthy disciple to unload on account of that verse?

And then comes another verse, which I believe is an interpolation: "And every one that has forsaken houses, or brethren or sisters, or father or mother, or wife or children, or lands, for my name's sake, shall receive an hundredfold, and shall inherit everlasting life." Christ never said it. Never. "Whosoever shall forsake father and mother." Why He said to this man who asked him "What shall I do to inherit eternal life?" among other things, He said "Honor thy father and thy mother." And we turn over the page and He says: "If you will desert your father and your mother you shall have everlasting life." It won't do. If you desert your wife and your little children, or your lands—the idea of putting a house and lot on equality with wife and children. Think of that! I do not accept the terms. I will never desert the one I love for the promise of any God.

It is far more important that we shall love our wives than that we shall love God. And I will tell you why you cannot help Him. You can help her. You can fill her life with the perfume of perpetual joy. It is far more important that you love your children than that you love Jesus Christ.—And why? If He is God you cannot help Him, but you can plant a little flower of happiness in every footstep of the child, from the cradle until you die in that child's arms. Let me tell you to-day, it is far more important to build a home than to erect a church. The holiest temple beneath the stars is a home that love has built. And the holiest altar in all the wide world is the fireside around which gather father and mother and children.

There was a time when people believed that infamy. There was a time when they did desert fathers; and mothers, and wives and children. St. Augustine says to the devotee: "Fly to the desert, and though your wife put her arms around your neck, tear her hands away; she is a temptation of the devil. Though your father and mother throw their bodies athwart your threshold, step over them; and though your children pursue and with weeping eyes beseech you to return, listen not. It is the temptation of the evil one. Fly to the desert and save your soul." Think of such a soul being worth saving. While I live I propose to stand by the folks.

Here there is another condition of salvation. I find it in the 25th chapter: "Then shall the King say unto them on His right hand, 'Come, ye blessed of my father, inherit the kingdom prepared for you from the foundation of the world. For I was a hungered and ye gave Me meat; I was thirsty and ye gave Me drink; I was a stranger and ye took Me in; naked and ye clothed Me; and I was sick and ye visited Me; and I was in prison, and ye came unto me." Good! And I tell you tonight that God will not punish with eternal thirst the man who has put the cup of cold water to the lips of his neighbor. God will not allow to live in eternal nakedness of pain the man who has clothed others.

For instance, here is a shipwreck, and here is some brave sailor stands aside and allows a woman whom he never saw before to take his place in the boat, and he stands there, grand and serene as the wide sea, and he goes down. Do you tell me there is any God who will push the life-boat from the shore of eternal life, when that man wishes to step in? Do you tell me that God can be unpitying to the pitiful, that He can be unforgiving to the forgiving? I deny it; and from the aspersions of the pulpit I seek to rescue the reputation of the Deity.

Now, I have read you everything in Matthew on the subject of salvation. That is all there is. Not one word about believing anything. It is the gospel of deed, the gospel of charity, the gospel of self-denial; and if only that gospel had been preached, persecution never would have shed one drop of blood. Not one. Now, according to the testimony, Matthew was well acquainted with Christ. According to the testimony, he had been with Him, and His companion for years, and if it was necessary to believe anything in order to get to heaven, Matthew should have told us. But he forgot it. Or he didn't believe it. Or he never heard of it. You can take your choice.

The next is Mark. Now let us see what he says. And for the purpose of this lecture it is sufficient for me to say that Mark agrees, substantially, with Matthew, that God will be merciful to the merciful; that He will be kind to the kind that He will pity the pitying. And it is precisely, or substantially, the same as Matthew until I come to the 16th verse of the 16th chapter, and then I strike an interpolation, put in by hypocrisy, put in by priests, who longed to grasp with bloody hands the sceptre of universal authority.

Let me read it to you. And it is the most infamous passage in the Bible. Christ never said it. No sensible man ever said it. "And He said unto them"—that is, unto His disciples—"Go ye into all the world and preach the gospel to every creature. He that believeth and is baptized shall be saved, and he that believeth not shall be damned."

Now, I propose to prove to you that that is an interpolation. Now how will I do it? In the first place, not one word is said about belief in Matthew. In the next place, not one word is said about belief in Mark, until I come to that verse. And when is that said to have been spoken? According to Mark, it is a part of the last conversation of Jesus Christ—just before, according to the account, He ascended bodily before their eyes. If there ever was any important thing happened in this world, that is one of them. If there was any conversation that people would be apt to recollect, it would be the last conversation with God before He rose through the air and seated Himself upon the throne of the Infinite. We have in this Testament five accounts of the last conversation happening between Jesus Christ and His apostles. Matthew gives it. And yet Matthew does not state that in that conversation He said: "Whoso believeth and is baptized shall be saved, and whoso believeth not shall be damned." And if He did say those words, they were the most important that ever fell from His lips. Matthew did not hear it, or did not believe it, or forgot it.

Then I turn to Luke, and he gives an account of this same last conversation, and not one word does he say upon that subject. Now it is the most important thing, if Christ said it, that He ever said.

Then I turn to John, and he gives an account of the last conversation, but not one solitary word on the subject of belief or unbelief. Not one solitary word on the subject of damnation. Not one.

Then I turn to the first chapter of the Acts, and there I find an account of the last conversation; and in that conversation there is not one word upon this subject. Now, I say, that demonstrates that the passage in Mark is an interpolation.

What other reason have I got? That there is not one particle of sense in it. Why? No man can control his belief. You hear evidence for and against, and the integrity of the soul stands at the scales and tells which side rises and which side falls. You cannot believe as you wish. You must believe as you must. And He might as well have said: "Go into all the world and preach the gospel, and whosoever has red hair shall be saved, and whosoever hath not shall be damned."

I have another reason. I am much obliged to the gentleman who interpolated these passages. I am much obliged to him that he put in some more—two, more. Now hear:

"And these signs shall follow them that believe." Good.

"In My name shall they cast out devils. They shall speak with new tongues, and they shall take up serpents and if they drink any deadly thing it shall not hurt them. They shall lay hands on the sick, and they shall recover."

Bring on your believer! Let him cast out a devil. I do not claim a large one, "just a little one for a cent." Let him take up serpents. "And if he drink any deadly thing it shall not hurt him." Let me mix up a dose for the theological believer, and if it does not hurt him I'll join a church. O, but, "they say those things only lasted through that apostolic age." Let us see. "Go ye into all the world and preach the gospel to every creature. He that believeth and is baptized shall be saved, but he that believeth not shall be damned. And these signs shall follow them that believe."

How long? I think at least until they had gone into all the world. Certainly these signs should follow until all the world had been visited. And yet if that declaration was in the mouth of Christ, he then knew that one-half of the world was unknown and that he would be dead 1,492 years before his disciples would know that there was another world. And yet he said, "Go into all the world and preach the gospel," and he knew then that it would be 1,492 years before anybody went. Well, if it was worth while to have signs follow believers in the old world, surely it was worth while to have signs follow believers in the new world. And the very reason that signs should follow would be to convince the unbeliever, and there are as many unbelievers now as ever, and the signs are as necessary today as they ever were. I would like a few myself.

This frightful declaration, "He that believeth and is baptized shall be saved, but he that believeth not shall be damned," has filled the world with agony and crime.

Every letter of this passage has been sword and fagot; every word has been dungeon and chain.

That passage made the sword of persecution drip with innocent blood for ten centuries. That passage made the horizon of a thousand years lurid with the flames of fagots. That passage contradicts the sermon on the mount. That passage travesties the Lord's prayer. That passage turns the splendid religion of deed and duty into the superstition of creed and cruelty. I deny it. It is infamous. Christ never said it! Now I come to Luke, and it is sufficient to say that Luke substantially agrees with Matthew and with Mark. Substantially agrees, as the evidence is read. I like it.

"Be ye therefore merciful, as your Father also is merciful." Good!

"Judge not, and ye shall not be judged. Condemn not, and ye shall not be condemned; forgive and ye shall be forgiven." Good!

"Give, and it shall be given unto you, good measure, pressed down, and shaken together, and running over." Good! I like it.

"For with the same measure that ye mete withal, it shall be measured to you again."

He agrees substantially with Mark; he agrees substantially with Matthew; and I come at last to the nineteenth chapter.

"And Zaccheus stood and said unto the Lord, 'Behold, Lord, the half of my goods I give to the poor, and if I have taken anything from any man by false accusation, I restore him four-fold.' And Jesus said unto him, 'This day is salvation come to this house.'"

That is good doctrine. He didn't ask Zaccheus what he believed. He didn't ask him, Do you believe in the Bible? Do you believe in the five points? Have you ever been baptized-sprinkled? Oh! immersed. "Half of my goods I give to the poor, and if I have taken anything from any man by false accusation, I restore him four-fold." "And Christ said, 'This day is salvation come to this house.'" Good!

I read also in Luke that Christ when upon the cross forgave His murderers, and that is considered the shining gem in the crown of His mercy—that He forgave His murderers. That He forgave the men who drove the nails in His hands, in His feet, that plunged a spear in His side; the soldier that in the hour of death offered Him in mockery the bitterness to drink; that He forgave them all freely, and that yet, although He would forgive them, He will in the nineteenth century damn to eternal fire an honest man for the expression of his honest thoughts. That won't do. I find too, in Luke, an account of two thieves that were crucified at the same time. The other gospels speak of them. One says they both railed upon Him. Another says nothing about it. In Luke we are told that one did, but one of the thieves looked and pitied Christ, and Christ said to that thief:

"This day shalt thou meet me in Paradise."

Why did He say that? Because the thief pitied Him. And God cannot afford to trample beneath the feet of His infinite wrath the smallest blossom of pity that ever shed its perfume in the human heart!

Who was this thief? To what church did he belong? I don't know. The fact that he was a thief throws no light on that question. Who was he? What did he believe? I don't know. Did he believe in the Old Testament? In the miracles? I don't know. Did he believe that Christ was God? I don't know. Why, then, was the promise made to him that he should meet Christ in Paradise. Simply because he pitied innocence suffering on the cross.

God cannot afford to damn any man that is capable of pitying anybody.

And now we come to John, and that is where the trouble commences. The other gospels teach that God will be merciful to the merciful, forgiving to the forgiving, kind to the kind, loving to the loving, just to the just, merciful to the good.

Now we come to John, and here is another doctrine. And allow me to say that John was not written until centuries after the others. This, the Church got up:

"And Jesus answered and said unto him: 'Furthermore I say unto thee that except a man be born again he cannot see the "Kingdom of God."'"

Why didn't He tell Matthew that? Why didn't He tell Luke that? Why didn't He tell Mark that? They never heard of it, or forgot it, or they didn't believe it.

"Except a man be born of water and of the Spirit he cannot enter into the Kingdom of God." Why?

"That which is born of the flesh is flesh, and that which is born of the spirit is spirit. Marvel not that I said unto thee, 'ye must be born again.' That which is born of the flesh is flesh, and that which is born of the spirit is spirit,"—and He might have added that which is born of water is water.

"Marvel not that I say unto thee, 'ye must be born again.'" And then the reason is given, and I admit I did not understand it myself until I read the reason, and will understand it as well as I do; and here it is: "The wind bloweth where it listeth, and thou hearest the sound thereof, and canst not tell whence it cometh and whither it goeth." So I find in the book of John the idea of the real presence.

So I find in the book of John, that in order to be saved we must eat of the flesh and we must drink of the blood of Jesus Christ, and if that gospel is true, the Catholic Church is right. But it is not true. I cannot believe it, and yet for all that it may be true. But I don't believe it. Neither do I believe there is any God in the universe who will damn a man simply for expressing his belief.

"Why," they say to me, "suppose all this should turn out to be true, and you should come to the day of judgment and find all these things to be true. What would you do then?" I would walk up like a man, and say, "I was mistaken."

"And suppose God was about to pass judgment on you, what would you say?" I would say to Him, "Do unto others as you would that others should do unto you." Why not?

I am told that I must render good for evil. I am told that if smitten on one cheek I must turn the other. I am told that I must overcome evil with good. I am told that I must love my enemies; and will it do for this God who tells me, "Love my enemies," to say, "I will damn mine." No, it will not do; it will not do.

In the book of John all this doctrine of regeneration; all this doctrine that it is necessary to believe on the Lord Jesus Christ; all the doctrine that salvation depends upon belief—in this book of John all these doctrines find their warrant; nowhere else.

Read these three gospels and then read John, and you will agree with me that the gospels that teach "We must be kind, we must be merciful, we must be forgiving, and thereupon that God will forgive us," is true, and then say whether or no that doctrine is not better than the doctrine that somebody else can be good for you, that somebody else can be bad for you, and that the only way to get to heaven is to believe something that you do not understand.

Now upon these gospels that I have read the churches rest; and out of those things that I have read they have made their creeds. And the first Church to make a creed, so far as I know, was the Catholic. I take it that is the first Church that had any power. That is the Church that has preserved all these miracles for us. That is the Church that preserved the manuscripts for us. That is the Church whose word we have to take. That Church is the first witness that Protestantism brought to the bar of history to prove miracles that took place eighteen hundred years ago; and while the witness is there Protestantism takes pains to say: "You can't believe one word that witness says, now."

That Church is the only one that keeps up a constant communication with heaven through the instrumentality of a large number of decayed saints. That Church is an agent of God on earth. That Church has a person who stands in the place of Deity; and that Church, according to their doctrine, is infallible. That Church has persecuted to the exact extent of her power—and always will. In Spain that Church stands erect, and that Church is arrogant. In the United States that Church crawls. But the object in both countries is the same, and that is the destruction of intellectual liberty. That Church teaches us that we can make God happy by being miserable ourselves. That Church teaches you that a nun is holier in the sight of God than a loving mother with a child in her thrilled and thrilling arms. That Church teaches you that a priest is better than a father. That Church teaches you that celibacy is better than that passion of love that has made everything of beauty in this world. That Church tells the girl of 16 or 18 years of age, with eyes like dew and light—that girl with the red of health in the white of her beautiful checks—tells that girl, "Put on the veil woven of death and night, kneel upon stones, and you will please God."

I tell you that, by law, no girl should be allowed to take the veil, and renounce the beauties of the world, until she was at least 25 years of age. Wait until she knows what she wants.

I am opposed to allowing these spider-like priests weaving webs to catch the flies of youth; and there ought to be a law appointing commissioners to visit such places twice a year, and release every person who expresses a desire to be released. I don't believe in keeping penitentiaries for God. No doubt they are honest about it. That is not the question.

Now this Church, after a few centuries of thought, made a creed, and that creed is the foundation of orthodox religion. Let me read it to you:

"Whosoever will be saved, before all things it is necessary that he hold the Catholic faith; which faith, except every one do keep entire and inviolate, without doubt, he shall everlastingly perish." Now the faith is this: "That we worship one God in trinity, and trinity in unity."

Of course you understand how that's done, and there's no need of my explaining it. Neither confounding the persons nor dividing the substance. You see what a predicament that would leave the Deity in if you divided, the substance.

"For one is the person of the Father, another of the Son, and another of the Holy Ghost; but the Godhead of the Father, and of the Son, and of the Holy Ghost is all one "—you know what I mean by Godhead. In glory equal, and in majesty co-eternal. Such as the Father is, such is the Son, such is the Holy Ghost. The Father is uncreated, the Son uncreated, the Holy Ghost uncreated. The Father incomprehensible, the Son incomprehensible, the Holy Ghost incomprehensible.

And that is the reason we know so much about the thing. "The Father is eternal, the Son eternal, the Holy Ghost eternal," and yet there are not three eternals, only one eternal, as also there are not three uncreated, nor three incomprehensibles, only one uncreated, one incomprehensible.

"In like manner, the Father is almighty, the Son almighty, the Holy Ghost almighty." Yet there are not three almighties, only one Almighty. So the Father is God, the Son God, the Holy Ghost God, and yet not three Gods; and so likewise, the Father is Lord, the Son is Lord, the Holy Ghost is Lord, yet there are not three Lords, for as we are compelled by the Christian truth to acknowledge every person by himself to be God and Lord, so we are all forbidden by the Catholic religion to say there are three Gods, or three Lords. "The Father is made of no one, not created or begotten. The Son is from the Father alone, not made, nor created, or begotten. The Holy Ghost is from the Father and the Son, not made nor begotten, but proceeded—" You know what proceeding is.

"So there is one Father, not three Fathers." Why should there be three Fathers, and only one Son?

"One Son, and not three Sons; one Holy Ghost, not three Holy Ghosts; and in this Trinity there is nothing before or afterward, nothing greater or less, but the whole three persons are coeternal with one another, and coequal, so that in all things the unity is to be worshiped in Trinity, and the Trinity is to be worshiped in unity, and therefore we will believe." Those who will be saved must thus think of the Trinity. Furthermore, it is necessary to everlasting salvation that he also believe rightly the incarnation of our Lord Jesus Christ.

Now the right of this thing is this: That we believe and confess that our Lord Jesus Christ, the Son of God, is both God and man. He is God of the substance of His Father begotten before the world was. That was a good while before His mother lived.

"And He is man of the substance of His mother, born in this world, perfect God and perfect man, and the rational soul in human flesh subsisting equal to the Father according to His Godhead, but less than the Father, according to His manhood, who being both God and man is not two but one—one not by conversion of God into flesh but by the taking of the manhood into God."

You see that it is a great deal easier than the other. "One altogether, not by a confusion of substance, but by unity of person, for as the rational soul and flesh is one man, so God the man, is one Christ, who suffered for our salvation, descended into hell, rose again the third day from the dead, ascended into heaven, and He sitteth at the right hand of God, the Father Almighty, and He shall come to judge the living and the dead."

In order to be saved it is necessary to believe this. What a blessing, that we do not have to understand it. And in order to compel the human intellect to get upon its knees, before that infinite absurdity, thousands and millions have suffered agonies; thousands and millions have perished in dungeons and in fire; and if all the bones of all the victims of the Catholic Church could be gathered together, a monument higher than all the pyramids would rise in our presence, and the eyes even of priests would be suffused with tears.

That Church covered Europe with cathedrals and dungeons. That Church robbed men of the jewel of the soul. That Church had ignorance upon its knees. That Church went into partnership with the tyrants of the throne, and between these two vultures, the altar and the throne, the heart of man was devoured. Of course I have met, and cheerfully admit that there is thousands of good Catholics; but Catholicism is contrary to human liberty. Catholicism bases salvation upon belief. Catholicism teaches man to trample his reason under foot. And for that reason, it is wrong.

Now, the next Church that comes along in the way that I wish to speak of is the Episcopalian. That was founded by Henry VIII., now in heaven. He cast off Queen Catherine and Catholicism together. And he accepted Episcopalianism and Annie Boleyn at the same time. That Church, if it had a few more ceremonies, would be Catholic. If it had a few less, nothing. We have an Episcopalian Church in this country, and it has all the imperfection of a poor relation. It is always boasting of a rich relative. In England the creed is made by law, the same as we pass statutes here. And when a gentleman dies in England, in order to determine whether he shall be saved or not, it is necessary for the power of heaven to read the acts of Parliament. It becomes a question of law, and sometimes a man is damned on a very nice point. Lost on demurrer.

A few years ago, a gentleman by the name of Seabury, Samuel Seabury, was sent over to England to get some apostolic succession. We hadn't a drop in the house. It was necessary for the bishops of the English church to put their hands upon his head. They refused; there was no act of Parliament justifying—it. He had then to go to the Scotch Bishops; and, had the Scotch Bishops refused, we never would have had any apostolic succession in the new world. And God would have been driven out of half the world; and the true church never could have been founded. But the Scotch Bishops put their hands on his head, and now we have an unbroken succession of heads and hands from St. Paul to the last bishop.

In this country the Episcopal Church has done some good, and I want to thank that Church. Having, on an average, less religion than the others, on an average you have done more good to mankind. You preserved some of the humanities. You did not hate music, you did not absolutely despise painting, and you did not altogether abhor architecture, and you finally admitted that it was no worse to keep time with your feet than with your hands. And some went so far as to say that people could play cards, and God would overlook it, or would look the other way. For all these things accept my thanks.

When I was a boy, the other Churches looked upon dancing as probably the mysterious sin against the Holy Ghost; and they used to teach that when four boys got in a hay-mow, playing seven-up, that the Eternal God stood whetting the sword of His eternal wrath waiting to strike them down to the lowest hell. And so that Church has done some good.

After a while, in England, a couple of gentlemen, or a couple of men by the name of Wesley and Whitfield, said: "If everybody is going to hell, nearly, somebody ought to mention it." The Episcopal clergy said: "Keep still; don't tear your gown." Wesley and Whitfield said: "This frightful truth ought to be proclaimed from the housetops at every opportunity, from the highway of every occasion." They were good, honest men. They believed their doctrine. And they said: "If there is a hell, and a Niagara of souls pouring over an eternal precipice of ignorance, somebody ought to say something." They were right; somebody ought, if such thing was true. Wesley was a believer in the Bible. He believed in the actual presence of the Almighty. God used to do miracles for him; used to put off a rain several days to give his meeting a chance; used to cure his horse of lameness; used to cure Mr. Wesley's headaches.

And Mr. Wesley also believed in the actual existence of the devil. He believed that devils had possession of people. He talked to the devil when he was in folks, and the devil told him that he was going to leave; and that he was going into another person; that he would be there at a certain time; and Wesley went to that other person, and there the devil was, prompt to the minute. He regarded every conversion as an absolute warfare between God and this devil for the possession of that human soul. Honest, no doubt. Mr. Wesley did not believe in human liberty. Honest, no doubt. Was opposed to the liberty of the colonies. Honestly so. Mr. Wesley preached a sermon entitled, "The Cause and Cure of Earthquakes," in which he took the ground that earthquakes were caused by sin and the only way to stop them was to believe in the Lord Jesus Christ. No doubt an honest man.

Wesley and Whitfield fell out on the question of predestination. Wesley insisted that God invited everybody to the feast. Whitfield said He did not invite those He knew would not come. Wesley said He did. Whitfield said: "Well, He didn't put plates for them, anyway." Wesley said He did. So that, when they were in hell, he could show them that there was a seat left for them. And that Church that they founded is still active. And probably no Church in the world has done so much preaching for as little money as the Methodists. Whitfield believed in slavery and advocated the slave trade. And it was of Whitfield that Whittier made the two lines:

He bade the slave ships speed from coast to coast, Fanned by the wings of the Holy Ghost.

We have lately had a meeting of the Methodists, and I find, by their statistics, that they believe they have converted 130,000 folks in a year. That in order to do this, they have 26,000 preachers, 226,000 Sunday-school scholars, and about $1,000,000,000 invested in church property. I find, in looking over the history of the world, that there are 40,000,000 or 50,000,000,000 of people born a year, and if they are saved at the rate of 30,000 a year, about how long will it take that doctrine to save this world? Good, honest people; they are mistaken.

In old times they were very simple. Churches used to be like barns. They used to have them divided—men on that side, and women on this. A little barbarous. We have advanced since then, and we now find as a fact, demonstrated by experience, that a man sitting by the woman he loves can thank God as heartily as though sitting between two men that he has never been introduced to.

There is another thing these Methodists should remember, and that is, that the Episcopalians were the greatest enemies they ever had. And they should remember that the Free-Thinkers have always treated them kindly and well.

There is one thing about the Methodist Church in the North that I like. But I find that it is not Methodism that does that. I find that the Methodist Church in the South is as much opposed to liberty as the Methodist Church North is in favor of liberty. So it is not Methodism that is in favor of liberty or slavery. They differ a little in their creed from the rest. They do not believe that God does everything. They believe that He does His part, and that you must do the rest, and that getting to heaven is a partnership business.

The next church is the Presbyterians—in my judgment the worst of all, as far as creed is concerned. This Church was founded by John Calvin, a murderer! John Calvin, having power in Geneva, inaugurated human torture. Voltaire abolished torture in France. The man who abolished torture, if the Christian religion be true, God is now torturing in hell; and the man who inaugurated torture, is now a glorified angel in heaven. It won't do.

John Knox started this doctrine in Scotland, and there is this peculiarity about Presbyterianism, it grows best where the soil is poorest. I read the other day an account of a meeting between John Knox and John Calvin. Imagine a dialogue between a pestilence and a famine! Imagine a conversation between a block and an ax! As I read their conversation it seemed to me as though John Knox and John Calvin were made for each other; that they fitted each other like the upper and lower jaws of a wild beast. They believed happiness was a crime; they looked upon laughter as blasphemy, and they did all they could to destroy every human feeling, and to fill the mind with the infinite gloom of predestination and eternal damnation. They taught the doctrine that God had a right to damn us because He made us. That is just the reason that He has not a right to damn us. There is some dust. Unconscious dust! What right has God to change that unconscious dust into a human being, when He knows that human being will sin; and He knows that human being will suffer eternal agony? Why not leave him in the unconscious dust? What right has an infinite God to add to the sum of human agony? Suppose I knew that I could change that piece of furniture into a living, sentient human being, and I knew that that being would suffer untold agony forever. If I did it, I would be a fiend. I would leave that being in the unconscious dust. And yet we are told that we must believe such a doctrine, or we are to be eternally damned! It won't do.

In 1839 there was a division in this Church, and they had a lawsuit to see which was the Church of God. And they tried it by a judge and jury, and the jury decided that the new school was the Church of God, and then they got a new trial, and the next jury decided that the old school was the Church of God, and that settled it. That Church teaches that infinite innocence was sacrificed for me! I don't want it! I don't wish to go to heaven unless I can settle by the books, and go there because I ought to go there. I have said, and I say again, I don't want to be a charity angel. I have no ambition to become a winged pauper of the skies.

The other day a young gentleman, a Presbyterian, who had just been converted, came to me and gave me a tract and he told me he was perfectly happy. Ugh! Says I: "Do you think a great many people are going to hell?" "Oh, yes." "And you are perfectly happy?" "Well, he didn't know as he was quite." "Wouldn't you be happier if they were all going to heaven?" "O, yes." "Well, then you are not perfectly happy?" "No, he didn't think he was." Says I: "When you get to heaven, then you would be perfectly happy?" "Oh, yes." "Now, when we are only going to hell, you are not quite happy; but when we are in hell, and you in heaven, then you will be perfectly happy?" You won't be as decent when you get to be an angel as you are now, will you? "Well," he said, "that was not exactly it." Said I: "Suppose your mother were in hell, would you be happy in heaven then?" "Well," he says, "I suppose God would know the best place for mother." And I thought to myself, then, if I was a woman, I would like to have five or six boys like that.

It will not do. Heaven is where are those we love, and those who love us. And I wish to go to no world unless I can be accompanied by those who love me here. Talk about the consolations of this infamous doctrine. The consolations of a doctrine that makes a father say, "I can be happy with my daughter in hell"; that makes a mother say, "I can be happy with my generous, brave boy in hell"; that makes a boy say, "I can enjoy the glory of heaven with the woman who bore me, the woman who would have died for me, in eternal agony." And they call that tidings of great joy.

I have not time to speak of the Baptists,—that Jeremy Taylor said were as much to be rooted out as anything that is the greatest pest and nuisance on the earth. Nor of the Quakers, the best of all, and abused by all. I can not forget that George Fox, in the year of grace 1640, was put in the pillory and whipped from town to town, scarred, put in a dungeon, beaten, trampled upon, and what for? Simply because he preached the doctrine: "Thou shalt not resist evil with evil. Thou shalt love thy enemies." Think what the Church must have been that day to scar the flesh of that loving man! Just think of it! I say I have not time to speak of all these sects. And of the varieties of Presbyterians and Campbellites. The people who think they must dive in order to go up. There are hundreds and hundreds of these sects, all founded upon this creed that I read, differing simply in degree. Ah but they say to me: "You are fighting something that is dead. Nobody believes this, now." The preachers do not believe what they preach in the pulpit. The people in the pews do not believe what they hear preached. And they say to me: "You are fighting something that is dead. This is all a form, we do not believe a solitary creed in it. We sign it and swear that we believe it, but we don't. And none of us do. And all the ministers they say in private, admit that they do not believe it, not quite." I don't know whether this is so or not. I take it that they believe what they preach. I take it that when they meet and solemnly agree to a creed, I take it they are honest and solemnly believe in that creed.

The Evangelical Alliance, made up of all orthodox denominations of the world, met only a few years ago, and here is their creed: They believe in the divine inspiration, authority, and sufficiency of the Holy Scriptures; the right and duty of private judgment in the interpretation of Holy Scriptures, but if you interpret wrong you are damned. They believe in the unity of the Godhead and the trinity of the persons therein. They believe in the utter depravity of human nature. There can be no more infamous doctrine than that. They look upon a little child as a lump of depravity. I look upon it as a bud of humanity, that will, under proper circumstances, blossom into rich and glorious life.

Total depravity of human nature! Here is a woman whose husband has been lost at sea; the news comes that he has been drowned by the ever-hungry waves, and she waits. There is something in her heart that tells her he is alive. And she waits. And years afterwards as she looks down toward the little gate, she sees him; he has been given back by the sea, and she rushes to his arms and covers his face with kisses, and with tears. And if that infamous doctrine is true, every tear is a crime, and every kiss a blasphemy. It won't do. According to that doctrine, if a man steals and repents, and takes back the property, the repentance and the taking back of the property are two other crimes if he is totally depraved: It is an infamy. What else do they believe? "The justification of a sinner by faith alone," without works, just faith. Believing something that you don't understand. Of course God cannot afford to reward a man for believing anything that is reasonable. God rewards only for believing something that is unreasonable, if you believe something that you know is not so. What else? They believe in the eternal blessedness of the righteous, and in the eternal punishment of the wicked. Tidings of great joy! They are so good that they will not associate with Universalists. They will not associate with Unitarians. They will not associate with scientists. They will only associate with those who believed that God so loved the world that He made up his mind to damn the most of us. Then they say to me: "What do you propose? You have torn this down; what do you propose to give in the place of it?" I have not torn the good down. I have only endeavored to trample out the ignorant, cruel fires of hell. I do not tear away the passage, "God will be merciful to the merciful." I do not destroy the promise, "If you will forgive others, God will forgive you." I would not for anything blot out the faintest stars that shine in the horizon of human despair, nor in the horizon of human hope; but I will do what I can to get that infinite shadow out of the heart of man.

"What do you propose to put in place of this?"

Well, in the first place, I propose good fellowship—good friends all around. No matter what we believe, shake hands and let it go. That is your opinion. This is mine: "Let us be friends." Science makes friends, religion—superstition—makes enemies. They say, "Belief is important." I say no, good actions are important. Judge by deed, not by creed, good fellowship. We have had too many of these solemn people. Whenever I see an exceedingly solemn man, I know he is an exceedingly stupid man. No man of any humor ever founded any religion—never. Humor sees both sides, while reason is the holy light; humor carries the lantern and the man with a keen sense of humor is preserved from the solemn stupidities of superstition. I like a man who has got good feeling for everybody—good fellowship. One man said to another:

"Will you take a glass of wine?"

"I don't drink."

"Will you smoke a cigar?"

"I don't smoke."

"Maybe you will chew something?"

"I don't chew."

"Let us eat some hay."

"I tell you I don't eat hay."

"Well, then, good-bye; for you are no company for man or beast."

I believe in the gospel of cheerfulness, the gospel of good nature, the gospel of good health. Let us pray to our bodies. Take care of our bodies, and our souls will take care of themselves. Good health! And I believe that the time will come when the public thought will be so great and grand that it will be looked upon as infamous to perpetuate disease. I believe the time will come when man will not fill the future with consumption and insanity. I believe the time will come when we study ourselves, and understand the laws of health, that we will say, "We are under obligation to put the flags of health in the cheeks of our children." Even if I got to heaven, and had a harp, I would hate to look back upon my children and grandchildren, and see them diseased, deformed, crazed, all suffering the penalties of crimes I had committed.

I, then, believe in the gospel of good health, and I believe in a gospel of good living. You can not make any God happy by fasting. Let us have good food, and let us have it well cooked—and it is a thousand times better to know how to cook it than it is to understand any theology in the world. I believe in the gospel of good clothes. I believe in the gospel of good houses, in the gospel of water and soap. I believe in the gospel of intelligence, in the gospel of education. The school-house is my cathedral. The universe is my Bible. I believe in that gospel of justice that we must reap what we sow.

I do not believe in forgiveness. If I rob Mr. Smith and God forgives me, how does that help Smith? If I, by slander, cover some poor girl with the leprosy of some imputed crime, and she withers away like a blighted flower, and afterward I get forgiveness, how does that help her? If there is another world we have got to settle. No bankrupt court there. Pay down. The Christians say, that among the ancient Jews, if you committed a crime you had to kill a sheep, now they say,—"Charge it." "Put it upon the slate." It won't do, for every crime you commit you must answer to yourself and to the one you injure. And if you have ever clothed another with unhappiness, as with a garment of pain, you will never be quite as happy as though you hadn't done that thing. No forgiveness. Eternal, inexorable, everlasting justice. That is what I believe in. And if it goes hard with me, I will stand it, and I will stick to in logic and I will bear it like a man.

And I believe, too, in the gospel of liberty, in giving to others what we claim for ourselves. I believe there is room everywhere for thought, and the more liberty you give away the more you will have. In liberty, extravagance is economy. Let us be just. Let us be generous to each other.

I believe in the gospel of intelligence. That is the only lever capable of raising mankind. Intelligence must be the savior of this world. Humanity is the grand religion, and no God can put another in hell in another world who has made a little heaven in this. God cannot make a man miserable if that man has made somebody else happy. God cannot hate anybody who is capable of loving anybody.

So I believe in this great gospel of generosity.

"Ah! but," they say, "it won't do. You must believe. I say no. My gospel of health will bring life. My gospel of intelligence, my gospel of good living, my gospel of good-fellowship will cover the world with happy homes. My doctrine will put carpets upon your floors, pictures upon your walls. My doctrine will put books upon your shelves, ideas in your minds. My doctrine will rid the world of the abnormal monsters born of the ignorance of superstition. My doctrine will give us health, wealth, and happiness. That is what I want. That is what I believe in. Give us intelligence. In a little while a man may find that he cannot steal without robbing himself. He will find that he cannot murder without assassinating his own joy. He will find that every crime is a mistake. He will find that only that man carries the cross who does wrong, and that the man who does right the cross turns to wings upon his shoulders that will bear him upwards forever. He will find that intelligent self-love embraces within its mighty arms all the human race.

"Oh," but they say to me, "you take away immortality." I do not. If we are immortal it is a fact in nature, and we are not indebted to priests for it, nor to Bibles for it, and it cannot be destroyed by unbelief.

As long as we love we will hope to live, and when the one dies that we love, we will say: "Oh, that we could meet again!" And whether we do or not, it will not be the work of theology. It will be a fact in nature. I would not for my life destroy one star of human hope; but I want it so that when a poor woman rocks the cradle, and sings a lullaby to the dimpled darling, that she will not be compelled to believe that, ninety-nine chances in a hundred, she is raising kindling-wood for hell. One world at a time—that is my doctrine.

It is said in the Testament, "Sufficient unto the day is the evil thereof" and I say, sufficient unto each world is the evil thereof. And suppose, after all, that death does end all, next to eternal joy, next to being forever with those we love and those who have loved us, next to that is to be wrapt in the dreamless drapery of eternal peace.

Next to external life is eternal death. Upon the shadowy shore of death the sea of trouble casts no wave. Eyes that have been curtained by the everlasting dark will never know again the touch of tears. Lips that have been touched by eternal silence will never utter another word of grief. Hearts of dust do not break; the dead do not weep. And I had rather think of those I have loved, and those I have lost, as having returned, as having become a part of the elemental wealth of the world—I would rather think of them as unconscious dust—I would rather think of them as gurgling in the stream, floating in the clouds, bursting in the foam of light upon the shores of worlds—I would rather think of them as the inanimate and eternally unconscious, that to have even a suspicion that their naked souls had been clutched by an orthodox God.

But for me, I will leave the dead where nature leaves them. And whatever flower of hope springs up in my heart I will cherish; but I can not believe that there is any being in this universe who has created a human soul for eternal pain. And I would rather that every God would destroy himself; I would rather that we all should go to eternal chaos, to black and starless night, that that just one soul should suffer eternal agony. I have made up my mind that if there is a God, he will be merciful to the merciful. Upon that rock I stand. That he will forgive the forgiving. Upon that rock I stand. That every man should be true to himself, and that there is no world, no star, in which honesty is a crime. And upon that rock I stand. The honest man, the good, kind, sweet woman, the happy child, has nothing to fear, neither in this world, nor the world to come. And upon that rock I stand.

# INGERSOLL'S ANSWER TO PROF. SWING, DR. THOMAS, AND OTHERS

After looking over the replies made to his new lecture, Col. Ingersoll was asked by a Tribune reporter what he thought of them. He replied as follows:

I think they dodge the point. The real point is this: If salvation by faith is the real doctrine of Christianity, I asked on Sunday before last, and I still ask, why didn't Matthew tell it? I still insist that Mark should have remembered it, and I shall always believe that Luke ought, at least, to have noticed it. I was endeavoring to show that modern Christianity has for its basis an interpolation. I think I showed it. The only gospel on the orthodox side is that of John, and that was certainly not written, or did not appear in its present form, until long after the others were written. I know very well that the Catholic Church claimed during the Dark Ages, and still claims, that references had been made to the gospels by persons living in the first, second and third centuries; but I believe such manuscripts were manufactured by the Catholic Church. For many years in Europe there was not one person in 20,000 who could read and write. During that time the Church had in its keeping the literature of our world. They interpolated as they pleased. They created. They destroyed. In other words, they did whatever in their opinion was necessary to substantiate the faith. The gentlemen who saw fit to reply did not answer the question, and I again call upon the clergy to explain to the people why, if salvation depended upon belief in the Lord Jesus Christ, Matthew did not mention it. Some one has said that Christ didn't make known this doctrine of salvation by belief or faith until after His resurrection. Certainly none of the gospels were written until after His resurrection; and if He made that doctrine known after His resurrection, and before His ascension, it should have been in Matthew, Mark, and Luke, as well as John.

The replies of the clergy show that they have not investigated the subject; that they are not well acquainted with the New Testament. In other words, they have not read it except with the regulation theological bias. There is one thing

I wish to correct here. In an editorial in the Tribune it was stated that I had admitted that Christ was beyond and above Buddha, Zoroaster, Confucius, and others. I didn't say so. Another point was made against me, and those who made it seemed to think it was a good one. In my lecture I asked why it was that the Disciples of Christ wrote in Greek, whereas, in fact, they understood only Hebrew. It is now claimed that Greek was the language of Jerusalem at that time; that Hebrew had fallen into disuse; that no one understood it except the literati and the highly educated. If I fell into an error upon this point it was because I relied upon the New Testament. I find in the twenty-first chapter of the Acts an account of Paul having been mobbed in the city of Jerusalem; that he was protected by a Chief Captain and some soldiers; that, when upon the stairs of the castle to which he was being taken for protection, he obtained leave from the Captain to speak unto the people. In the fortieth verse of that chapter I find the following:

"And when he had given him license, Paul stood on the stairs and beckoned with the hand unto the people; and when there was made a great silence he spake unto them in the Hebrew tongue, saying—"

And then follows the speech of Paul, wherein he gives an account of his conversion. It seems a little curious to me that Paul for the purpose of quieting the mob, would speak to that mob in an unknown language. If I were mobbed in the city of Chicago, and wished to defend myself with an explanation, I certainly would not make that explanation in Chocktaw, even if I understood that tongue. My present opinion is that I would speak in English; and the reason I would speak in English is, because that language is generally understood in this city. And so I conclude from the account in the twenty-first chapter of the Acts that "Hebrew was the language of Jerusalem at that time, or that Paul would not have addressed the mob in that tongue."

"Did you read Mr. Courtney's answer?"

"I read what Mr. Courtney read from others, and think some of his quotations very good; and have no doubt that the authors will feel complimented by being quoted."

"But what about there being belief in Matthew?"

"Mr. Courtney says that certain people were cured of diseases on account of faith. Admitting that mumps, measles, and whooping-cough could be cured in that way, there is not even a suggestion that salvation depended upon a like faith. I think he can hardly afford to rely upon the miracles of the New Testament to prove his doctrine. There is one instance in which a miracle was performed by Christ without His knowledge. And I hardly think that even Mr. Courtney would insist that any faith could have been great enough for that. The fact is, I believe that all these miracles were ascribed to Christ long after His death, and that Christ never, at any time or place, pretended to have any supernatural power whatever. Neither do I believe that He claimed any supernatural origin. He claimed simply to be a man—no less, no more. I don't believe Mr. Courtney is satisfied with his own reply."

"And now as to Prof. Swing?"

"Mr. Swing has been out of the orthodox church so long that he seems to have forgotten the reasons for which he left it. I don't believe there is an orthodox minister in the city of Chicago who will agree with Mr. Swing that salvation by faith is no longer preached. Prof. Swing seems to think it of no importance who wrote the Gospel of St. Matthew. In this I agree with him. Judging from what he said, there is hardly difference enough of opinion between us to justify a reply on his part. He, however, makes one mistake. I did not in the lecture say one word about tearing churches down. I have no objection to people building all the churches they wish. While I admit that it is a pretty sight to see children on a morning in June going through the fields to the country church, I still insist that the beauty of that sight doesn't answer the question how it is that Matthew forgot to say anything about salvation through Christ. Prof. Swing is a man of poetic temperament; but this is not a poetic question."

"How did the card of Dr. Thomas strike you?"

"I think the reply of Dr. Thomas in the best possible spirit. I regard him to day as the best intellect in the Methodist denomination. He seems to have what is generally understood as a Christian spirit. He has always treated me with perfect fairness, and I should have said long ago many grateful things, had I not feared I might hurt with his own people. He seems to be by nature a perfectly fair man; and I know of no man in the United States for whom I have a profounder respect. Of course I don't agree with Mr. Thomas. I think in many things he is mistaken. But I believe him to be perfectly sincere. There is one trouble about him,—he is growing; and this fact will no doubt give great trouble to many of his brethren. Certain Methodist hazelbrush feel a little uneasy in the shadow of his oak."

"Are you going to make a formal reply to their sermons."

"Not unless something better is done than has been. Of course I don't know what another Sabbath may bring forth. I am waiting. But of one thing

I feel perfectly assured; that no man in the United States, or in the world, can account for the fact, if we are to be saved only by faith in Christ, that Matthew forgot it, that Luke said nothing about it, and that Mark never mentioned it except in two passages written by another person. Until that is answered, as one grave-digger says to the other in "Hamlet," I shall say: 'Ay, tell me that and unyoke.' In the meantime, I wish to keep on the best terms with all parties concerned. I cannot see why my forgiving spirit fails to gain their sincere praise."